# Pssst, hey!

*Wanna see something fun?*

*Flip quickly through the pages*

*to watch Baby Back run!*

# All-American COWBOY

## DYLANN CRUSH

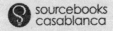

sourcebooks
casablanca

Published by Sourcebooks Casablanca, an imprint of Sourcebooks, Inc.
P.O. Box 4410, Naperville, Illinois 60567-4410
(630) 961-3900
Fax: (630) 961-2168
sourcebooks.com

Printed and bound in the United States of America.
OPM 10 9 8 7 6 5 4 3 2

# ONE

NO THREE-HUNDRED-POUND PIECE OF PRIME PORK WAS going to get the best of her. Charlie Walker adjusted the tilt of her cowboy hat against the glare of the Texas sun and leaned down, putting herself eye to eye with the enormous pig. "Someone's not feeling very photogenic today, huh?"

Baby Back grunted in response and made a break for the right. Charlie dove after her, trying to grab the pig's blinged-out collar. She missed by a country mile and went down, sending a cloud of dust flying as her hip hit the gravel with a crunch.

"You've got to be kidding me." Charlie scrambled to her feet with a scowl. If that's the way the hellacious hog wanted to handle things, then so be it. But she was going to play this *smart*. Her mama always said the best way to get someone to cooperate was to kill them with kindness. Forcing something close to a smile, Charlie took the giant marshmallow she'd been saving as a special treat out of her back pocket. Baby Back obviously wasn't going to earn the reward with good behavior. Might as well use it as a bribe. "*Sooey!* Here piggy, piggy."

Baby Back's ears perked.

"You want an ooey, gooey marshmallow?" Charlie tore off a tiny bit and tossed it in Baby Back's direction.

The pig snuffled it out of the dirt, squealing in appreciation.

"Come on, piggy. Want some more?" Charlie lobbed another chunk, waiting until Baby Back was snout-deep in her search before taking a tentative step forward. If she could just grab the collar... She leaned in, her fingers almost grasping the hot-pink band of leather.

Before she could so much as blink, Baby Back rushed her, snagging the marshmallow out of her hand, knocking her flat on her rear, and dashing toward the damaged stretch of fence. With a thud and a crack, the rail split. Baby Back bolted through the break in the fence and disappeared.

Again.

Add another exclamation point to the day from hell.

"Almost had her that time," Darby, Charlie's best friend since birth, called from her safe perch. "I swear, if you'd just lunged a little bit farther..." She raised a bottle of Coke in Charlie's direction and took a swig.

Charlie took her time getting to her feet. "*Almost* doesn't count—"

"Except in horseshoes and hand grenades, right?" Darby served up a wink alongside the smart-ass comment.

"Yeah. That's what Sully used to say anyway." Sully, her boss, her mentor, and the last living Holiday in Holiday, Texas. Well, the last living Holiday until he'd passed away, leaving Charlie struggling to keep everything together.

Darby's amusement faded, her eyes crinkling with concern. "How you holdin' up, sweetie?"

"Okay, I guess. I just wish I knew what was going to happen to the Rambling Rose."

Sully's lawyer had surprised everyone by keeping his mouth shut for a change. The only tidbit of gossip anyone had been able to extract from Buddy Hill, Esquire, was that he'd been trying to contact Sully's grandson—some hoity-toity real estate tycoon from New York City—about the will. The Rambling Rose was the oldest honky-tonk in Texas and had been in the Holiday family for more than 125 years. Charlie couldn't imagine working anywhere else.

Hopefully she wouldn't have to.

"I know Buddy's trying to figure that out," Darby said. "Hard to believe this will be the first time in history we don't have a Holiday on the Rose's float for the Founder's Day parade."

A deep ache pulsed in Charlie's chest. She rubbed the spot over her heart with her palm. Sully had always loved being the grand master of the annual parade. But she couldn't think about that now—she had bigger issues. Like the fact that her maintenance man had walked out on her this morning, her bartender forgot to put in an order for the favorite local brew, and she hadn't crossed off a single item on her to-do list for the biggest concert of the year.

Or—she huffed out a sigh—the fact that a tour bus full of senior citizens had pulled up not ten minutes ago, wanting some of the Rambling Rose's famous ribs and a picture with the most celebrated pig in Conroe County.

*One problem at a time.*

"Damn pig. I'd better get the truck and chase her down. Last time she got out, she plowed through Mrs. Martinez's garden and ate all of her green peppers." Charlie secured the gate behind her—not that it would do much good unless she found someone to fix the fence. "I'm still getting blamed for her salsa coming in second place at the county fair."

"Remind me why y'all insist on having a pet pig as a mascot?" Darby climbed off the rail and fell into step with Charlie.

"Tradition. You know Sully. The Rambling Rose has had a pig on staff ever since it opened. They sure as heck aren't going to lose one on my watch." Not even if her watch might be coming to an abrupt end. She ducked through the back door of the honky-tonk and grabbed her keys off a hook. "You coming?"

Darby shook her head, sending her dark curls bouncing. "I'll leave the pig wrangling to you. I gotta get home and get dinner going. Waylon will skin me alive if he finds out I spent all afternoon hanging out with his baby sister."

"Now I know that's a lie." Charlie yanked open the door of the late-model dually pickup. "He's got you on such a high pedestal I'm surprised you don't get a nosebleed from the lack of oxygen."

"He does love me, doesn't he?" Darby slung her arm around Charlie's neck and pulled her in for a hug. "We'll try to stop by later, if your mama's up for watching the kids."

Darby and Waylon had been married for nine years, but it could still get weird, thinking about her BFF swapping spit with her brother. So Charlie tried not to think about it at all. As in, ever. "Has she ever not been up for watching them?"

"True. Be sure to save us some seats up front tonight, okay? That band is supposed to be real good." With a squeeze and a quick kiss on the cheek, Darby stepped away. "And don't worry about Sully's grandson. He'll probably fly down, take a look at the place, tell you what a great job you're doing, and be on a plane back to New York City before you even have a chance to pour him a draft of Lone Star."

Charlie snorted. "Oh yeah? With my luck, he'll realize he's always wanted to manage the oldest honky-tonk in Texas, and he'll toss me out on my backside."

"He might just like your backside." Darby waggled her perfectly plucked eyebrows.

"My backside isn't up for review. Besides, if he ever does have the nerve to show up around here, he'll be the one getting tossed on his ass. Would it have killed him to pick up the phone and give Sully a call sometime? Maybe even come down for a visit?"

"Honey, I know you loved Sully like family. But not everyone loves as fierce as you. Give the guy a chance."

A chance? In the eight years she'd worked for Sully, there'd been no word from either his son or his grandson. It had broken her heart to watch the cancer eat away at him, knowing she was just about the only family he had left.

But Darby was right about one thing—Charlie did love fierce. Fierce enough to know that the most important thing to Sully was keeping the Rambling Rose in the family. So even if it killed her, she'd do whatever she could to ensure his dying wish came true. She'd try to give his grandson a chance, assuming he had the decency to show up sometime in the near future.

"Hey, will you let Angelo know I'm hog hunting? Maybe he can stall lunch so I have a chance to bring back the prodigal pig to pose for pictures."

"You bet. Good luck."

With a final nod to Darby, Charlie climbed onto the bench seat and cranked over the engine. How many times had Baby Back broken out over the past month? Two? Three? She'd lost count of how many mascots they'd had over the years, but none of them had ever been as ornery as Baby Back. That pig had a devilish streak as long and wide as the Rio Grande.

She shifted the truck into drive and wondered if anyone would believe her if she said Baby Back got taken out by a combine. Sully was the only one beyond the tourists who gave a hot damn about the pig. She gripped the steering wheel tightly, fighting back a fresh surge of emotion.

*For Sully.*

Then she put the pedal to the metal and fishtailed out onto the main two-lane road that would take her through the center of Holiday in pursuit of the runaway porker.

*H*

Beckett Sullivan Holiday III scrolled through the slides of his presentation one final time. He'd been working his butt off for the past four months, and he was determined that this would be the project his father would finally trust him to handle on his own from concept to completion.

He'd done the legwork. He'd done the research. He'd done the whole damn thing short of signing the papers. There was no reason he shouldn't be allowed to take the lead. No reason except his dad's uncompromising need to maintain a viselike grip on all things under the Holiday Enterprises umbrella. Which, fortunately or unfortunately, depending on how he looked at it, also included Beck.

The way Beck saw it, the project up in Morris Park should be a slam dunk. Holiday Enterprises would garner some positive press for a change, and he'd be able to come through on a long-overdue promise to an old friend. He was ready.

His phone beeped, and he silenced the alarm. *Showtime.*

Beck tucked his laptop under one arm and headed toward the conference room. No matter how much time he spent in the room his dad considered his pride and joy, the view managed to steal his breath every time he entered. Two walls of glass provided a 180-degree view. In this room, in a corner of the fifty-fifth floor, standing up against the windows always made him feel like he was floating above Midtown Manhattan.

"Ready, Son?" The elder Holiday stood at the head of the table.

Beck nodded and took the seat next to him as the rest of the management team filtered in. As head of one of the most successful real estate development firms in Manhattan, his father—or just Holiday as he preferred to be called, even by his son—usually had his pick of opportunities. It was up to his team to come up with the ideas, do the grunt work, and make recommendations at their weekly management meetings.

This time, Beck would get the go-ahead. He could feel it.

Beck sat through the six presentations ahead of his. He listened, took notes, and tried to swallow the lump of apprehension that had taken up residence in his throat. He'd been through the drill hundreds of times over the years. But he'd never pitched a project like this before.

He wiped a clammy palm over his suit pants. No need to be nervous. He'd worked with these people his entire career. Besides, how could his dad refuse the chance to spread some goodwill when the neighborhood—and their company—so obviously needed it?

Holiday shot down the executive golf course one of his minions had spent the past nine months putting together, then turned an appraising eye on his son. Beck swallowed and stood.

"Most of you know about the upscale condos we're building in the Bronx. What you probably don't know is that by building on those Morris Park lots, we're displacing the kids who have been using that property as a safe place to play." Beck scanned the faces of his coworkers. No one offered a smile of encouragement. No one gave him a sly thumbs-up. No one knew what to make of this departure from the *money makes more money* mentality. But they'd catch on.

He continued, pulling at their heartstrings. "There's another lot two blocks over with a condemned apartment building sitting on it. The city is willing to sell it well below market value. I'm going to show you why it makes sense for Holiday Enterprises to use that space to build its first community park."

By the time he wrapped up with a detailed analysis of the tangible and intangible benefits of the park, the smile on his dad's face pretty much guaranteed approval.

But then Holiday steepled his fingers under his chin and shook his head.

"So you want me to buy a crumbling building and knock it down so a handful of kids have a safe place to hang out and sell drugs."

Beck almost didn't know what to say to that. "No, sir. I want us to buy a property for pennies on the dollar and create goodwill by donating it back to the community as a place where the residents can gather." Beck pointed to the screen where the last slide still appeared. "Imagine the ribbon cutting. The press would go nuts. This kind of project is unprecedented."

"It's unprecedented because it's not a good idea. I appreciate all the work you put into this, Beck. But I've decided to have you manage the details on the boutique hotel in the Village instead."

Beck's heart went into a free fall. "The Village?" He cleared his throat, trying to prevent his voice from cracking. "But the P&L shows we won't break even on that project for at least ten years." Not to mention the last thing downtown needed was another trendy hotel. The park would actually *mean* something to those kids.

"What can I say?" Holiday shrugged. "I like the Village."

"But you're wrong. We need the good publicity, and the Bronx needs—" *Shit.* He'd violated Rule Number One: never criticize the boss. Especially in front of the entire management team.

"Sorry, Son. It's a pass. Try again next time." The smile spread over his father's lips but didn't reach his eyes. Beck felt like he was looking into the face of a great white shark. Predatory. Cunning. Lethal.

He'd already shot himself in the foot. Might as well bury himself while he was at it. But before he could finish the job and tell his dad exactly what he thought of his new plan, the intercom buzzed.

"What is it, Joyce?" Holiday asked.

"Sir, I'm sorry to interrupt. You have an urgent call on line two."

"We're in a meeting." His tone was clipped, flat, unemotional.

Joyce's voice faltered. "I know, sir. But it's, well, it's your father."

Holiday's chest puffed up, and he leaned over the speakerphone. "You tell that son of a bitch that I don't care what kind of emergency he has down there. He needs something from me, he can go through my lawyer."

An awkward silence fell over everyone present. Eyes sought out interesting patterns in the marble floor, fingers toyed with expensive fountain pens, and legs shifted under the table.

"Um, sir. He's not actually on the phone. It seems he's passed. His attorney would like to speak to you."

His dad hissed out a breath, and an unreadable flicker of emotion flashed across his face so fast that Beck thought maybe he'd just imagined it. He'd never seen his dad react that way to anything and wasn't sure how to respond. Holiday had made it clear on numerous occasions that the family he'd left behind in Texas was not up for discussion.

"Sir?" the voice came through the speaker.

"Dad?" Beck murmured. "You okay?" He put his hand on his father's shoulder.

With a quick shake of the head, Holiday swatted Beck's hand away and regained his bearings. "Meeting's over. Can I have a few minutes?" The team stood and filed out of the conference room. "Beck, stay."

Once the room cleared, his dad shifted the speaker to the end of the table. "Go ahead and patch him through."

The phone line clicked. Beck cleared his throat while he studied his old man. How would he feel if his father died? A fleeting twinge passed through his gut. They saw each other every day. They worked together, wined and dined connections as a team, and both appreciated a day spent on the golf course.

But they'd never been close. Emotional distance ran deep in his family, at least based on how Holiday seemed to be handling the news of his own father's death.

"Beckett Holiday here. To whom am I speaking?"

"Hi there, Mr. Holiday. This is Buddy Hill calling from Holiday, Texas. Your father, well, he passed. I'm so sorry for your loss."

Based on his father's reaction, they could have been discussing the weather. No flicker of pain, no momentary hint of grief, no sign of emotion crossed his face.

"What can I do for you, Mr. Hill?"

"He asked me to, well…upon his death, he wanted me to contact you. We need to know what kind of arrangements y'all would like to make. And then there's the matter of the will."

Holiday reached for a pile of papers and tapped them into a uniform stack. "I trust you to make any necessary arrangements."

"Certainly, sir."

"And you can send a copy of the will to my attorney. I'll have Joyce get the contact information for you. Now if that's all—"

"Wait." Mr. Hill must have sensed the conversation was coming to an abrupt end. "About the will. One of the stipulations is that it must be read in person."

"Figures that old bastard would find a way to pull me back there one way or another. Couldn't do it while he was alive, so—"

"It's not for you, sir. Your son, Beckett Sullivan Holiday the Third, is the only beneficiary named in the will. We'll need to know how to reach him."

Beck shifted in his seat as his dad's blank gaze settled on him. He'd never met his grandfather. Never even had a conversation with the old man. What could he possibly have left him in Texas?

"Sir?" Mr. Hill's voice floated through the phone.

"Beck's right here, Mr. Hill. Just give us a moment." His dad pressed the mute button, then pushed back from the table and stood. "Good timing, Son. Since you won't be wasting your efforts on that park anymore, you'll have time to scoot on down south and find out what kind of lame inheritance the old geezer left for you before you get started on that new hotel."

Beck grappled for a response. He didn't have time to take off for Texas. Not with everything else going on. But the lawyer with the Southern twang had piqued his curiosity. Why would his grandfather, a virtual stranger, name him in his will? There was only one way to find out.

He unmuted the phone. "Hi, Mr. Hill. What can I do for you?"

"Beckett Sullivan Holiday the Third?"

"Yes, sir. But please call me Beck. How long do you need me down there?" he asked.

"Well, ideally a few days. At least on this initial trip."

"What do you mean 'initial trip'?" Visiting his dad's hometown might be fun for a day or two. Maybe he'd get a chance to learn about the mysterious family Holiday had left behind. But more than one trip? He didn't like the sound of that.

"I can explain everything when I see you in person. How soon can you be here?"

Beck swiped through the calendar on his phone. His schedule was jam-packed for the next week and a half. But it would be best if he got down there and took care of things as quickly as possible. He wanted to ask about his grandfather—how did he die, did he suffer at all, was he alone at the end—but a quick glance at his dad's frigid profile made him bite down before he uttered a word.

"Are you there, Beck?" Mr. Hill asked.

"Yes. The earliest I can make it would be next week. I can fly down on Friday morning and spend the weekend."

"Per your grandfather's instructions, we'll have to have the service before that."

Beck glanced up as the door clicked shut behind his dad. "That's fine. I understand."

"I'll have my secretary contact you with the details."

Beck gave the man his cell number and ended the call. He stood, taking a deep breath while he replayed the past few minutes in his head. What would he find in Texas? He stepped to the window to study the controlled chaos of the city streets far below. His father rarely mentioned the small town where he was born and raised. Beck knew his grandmother had died before he was born and that his grandfather once owned some tiny little hole-in-the-wall bar. But he'd never heard from the man, and his dad had always been a stone-cold wall of silence on the subject.

His gut twinged with a pang of regret. He should have pushed harder. Now he'd never have the chance to learn more about his roots. Maybe there would be someone in Holiday he could ask about his family. There had to be records, photos, something left over from his dad's younger days.

He glanced at the larger-than-life picture of his dad that decorated the conference room wall and felt that flicker of regret fade. Holiday had come a long way from that tiny Texas town. If he'd wanted Beck to know about his childhood, he would have shared. His dad was right. The old man probably left him a hound dog or a pickup truck. Beck would get in and out of there as fast as possible. It would be a pain to rearrange his schedule to make the trip, but he'd be back before the Manhattan society page even knew he'd been gone.

He blew out a breath, then turned his attention back to his laptop to pore over the details of his rejected proposal. He was many things but not a quitter. There must have been an angle he hadn't explored.

With the sun beginning its descent over the Manhattan skyline, he settled in for another long night of work, his mind already back on business and his thoughts thousands of miles away from whatever waited for him in the Lone Star State.

## chapter
# TWO

Beck wrapped one hand around the steering wheel and used the thumb of his other hand to jab at the buttons on his phone. His cell service had drifted in and out since he'd turned off the main highway. *Damn technology.* Rocks pinged against the underside of the giant SUV he'd rented in Austin, and a cloud of dust floated up behind him as he navigated down the deserted dirt road.

No attorney would have an office out here in the middle of nowhere. He must have made a wrong turn. The map flashed across his phone, and he focused all his attention on the tiny screen, trying to figure out where he was before the image disappeared again.

No luck.

He glanced up just in time to see something charge across the road. Squinting behind his dark shades, he tried to see where it went. Was it a cow? Were cows that agile? He'd only ever seen them on TV, and even then, they just stood around chewing.

He'd been sweating since he'd landed in Austin. Even with the air-conditioning blowing on high, the heat and humidity made him feel like he'd stepped into a steam room. His sunglasses slipped down his nose. As he reached up to push them back in place, whatever he'd seen before darted into the road again, this time so close it nearly clipped the bumper.

*What the hell?* He slammed his foot on the brake. The SUV fishtailed. "No, no, no." His hands turned the wheel, trying to straighten out the back end, but it was too late. The tires couldn't catch on the gravel. He ended up doing a one-eighty before sliding down the embankment and coming to a stop in the drainage ditch. The vehicle sat at about a thirty-degree angle with the passenger door on the low side next to a field of tall grass.

"Dammit!" He slapped both palms against the steering wheel, his heart battering against the walls of his chest like a pissed-off bird shoved in a cage. He closed his eyes for a moment and took a deep breath. No pain. Nothing broken. Everything was okay.

The driver's side door groaned in protest as he pushed it open. With a grunt, he extricated himself from the seat belt and scrambled up the embankment to the side of the road. Hands on his hips, he assessed the situation. There was absolutely no way he'd be able to get the SUV out of the ditch on his own. When would he catch a freaking break?

A glance at his phone confirmed he still had no service. The attorney had probably given up on him by now. It was pushing four o'clock, and their appointment had been scheduled for three. How was he supposed to know his flight would be delayed and it would take him an hour to get the rental car from the Austin airport? With no cell service, he didn't have a way to call. He should have just printed the directions Hill's secretary had emailed him.

He didn't even know which way to walk. Hadn't seen another car on the road for more than a half hour. And what the hell had run across the road? Hopefully whatever it was had fared better than his SUV.

He put his hand to his forehead to block the unforgiving sun and tried to determine which direction offered the better option—an endless dirt road to the right or…oh yeah, an endless dirt road to the left.

Screw it. He reached into his pocket for a quarter, ready to let fate choose for him, when he noticed a cloud of dust in the distance. As he baked in the hundred-degree heat, without even a stirring of a breeze, the dust ball moved closer. With his luck, it was probably a stampede of runaway longhorns coming to crush him into the dirt.

He knew he should never have left New York.

—⧓—

Charlie sang along to the radio, performing an impromptu duet with her country crush, Blake Shelton, as she made her way over to the stretch of dirt cutting through the Martinez's acreage. Where could that ornery pig be? Baby Back couldn't have gone too far. The patch job Dwight assured her would hold "even against Houdini" had barely kept the pig contained for the past week since her last wild escape.

With Sully gone and the honky-tonk temporarily her responsibility, Charlie didn't have time to chase the stupid sow halfway across Conroe County *again*. The truck bounced down the dirt road; she squinted ahead. What in the world was that? Who would be out for a walk in this heat in the middle of nowhere?

She slowed the truck, taking in the sight of the tall, sandy-blond, seriously cut stranger. It wouldn't be the first time she'd hallucinated on a deserted back road. The combination of humidity and heat could do that to a lonely gal.

But as she got closer, she noticed the brand-new SUV tilted in the ditch. This was no mirage. She studied the man again. A starched button-down shirt with the sleeves rolled up exposed strong forearms. Flat-front khakis stretched tightly across muscular thighs. Spiffy shades, fancy leather shoes... This had to be Beckett Sullivan Holiday III, Sully's long-lost grandson. Tongues were wagging all over Holiday about him coming to town this weekend.

Her appreciation of his physique morphed into something between indifference and disgust. Served him right for driving his fancy car off the road. Tempted to pass right by, she was compelled to bring the truck to a stop only by her affection for Sully.

The man approached the driver's side, his mouth curled into a sheepish smile.

She forced a tight grin and leaned out the window. "What seems to be the trouble?"

"Thank God. I was starting to think I might die right here on the side of the road." He rested one of those sinewy forearms on her door. A hint of expensive cologne wafted off his skin. "I seem to have lodged my rental in the ditch."

Charlie ignored an uptick in her pulse and peered past him. "You did a nice job wedging yourself in there."

He glanced toward his SUV, then back at her. "Yeah, I don't really do things half-assed. Lucky for me you came along." He offered another apologetic grin.

She didn't reciprocate. Might be lucky for him, but her luck had apparently run dry. Who the hell had she pissed off recently to deserve a day like today? First she had to deal with Baby Back and now this city boy.

He waited a beat for a response that didn't come, then tapped his hand against the doorframe. "So, yeah, something ran across the road, and I had to slam on the brakes. I've got Triple A. Does your cell phone work? I've got no service out here, but if yours works, I can call for a tow truck. I'm sure they'll have me out of here in no time."

The Yankee continued to spout off about cell towers and roadside assistance while she slid out of the truck. She turned her back to him and walked to the edge of the road. "There's only one tow truck in town," Charlie finally interrupted. "You're welcome to give him a call. But I heard he went fishing. Depending on how the fish are biting, might take him a while to tear himself away."

Beckett wiped away the sweat beading at his brow and shook his head. "Damn."

He probably deserved to get stuck here all day waiting on a tow. She almost climbed back into her truck. But something about the way he cocked his hip and funneled a hand through his hair reminded her of Sully. Dammit.

With her hands clamped on her hips, she nodded toward the bed of her truck. "Why don't you hand me a rope and I'll see if I can pull you out?"

"You sure?"

"Unless you want to sit in the ditch all day."

"No, ma'am." The dimple on his left cheek practically winked at her as he climbed onto the bumper and stepped into the bed.

She ran her gaze over his classy khakis, catching a glimpse of bare ankle at the hem. Loafers with no socks? Seriously? The local boys were going to chew this guy up like a wad of Skoal and spit him out before he even had a chance to settle that fine-looking ass onto a barstool.

"Will this work?" He held up a coil of rope.

"That'll be fine. If you toss one end down here, I'll tie it up."

The whole truck rocked as he climbed over the edge and hopped out. "I can do that for you."

She smirked at the chivalrous offer. "Just toss me the rope. I wouldn't want you to get your fancy shoes dirty."

Beckett glanced down at his feet before shrugging and tossing her the rope. "I guess nobody told me loafers weren't fit for Texas." He was so easygoing about it, she almost felt bad for poking fun. But then she thought of all the years Sully had waited for some word from his family out east, and it made her want to shake him up even more.

"Boots aren't a requirement. But they do come in handy when you find yourself wading through the tall grass to rescue a city boy in distress." The end of the rope sailed her way and she snagged it out of the air, then scrambled down the embankment to secure it underneath the front bumper.

"I'll try to avoid any further trouble." He offered her a hand as she climbed out of the ditch. "I sure do appreciate your help."

Charlie opted to take it. Warm, firm grip, smooth… Not like the hands of the men who worked on her family's ranch. Those were calloused and rough.

"Plus, they help keep the ticks away." She reached the road and reclaimed her hand, not wanting to admit to herself how nice it felt to be touched by a man. Even if it was *this* man.

He paused. "Ticks?"

"Yep. Ticks like to hang out in the weeds." Charlie brushed her hands against her thighs, trying to wipe away the tingles of contact before she bent down to secure the other end of the rope to her trailer hitch.

"Then I'd better keep my car on the road from now on. So what do we do next?" Beckett shifted his weight, gesturing to the SUV. "Do you think this will work?"

Standing, she squinted up at him. "Now you put it in drive and aim for the road, and I pull you out of the ditch." She directed a pointed look to the SUV.

"That easy, huh?"

Charlie angled her hip. "Helps if you get in the car."

He let out a deep laugh, and she had to bite back her grin. She didn't want to admit to herself how much she was enjoying their little exchange. It had been a long time since she'd made a man laugh.

He half stepped, half slid down the embankment and climbed into the driver's seat while she clambered up into the cab of her truck.

The truck engine roared to life, and she yelled out the window. "On three, okay?"

She caught his nod in her rearview mirror…along with her own reflection. *Nice, Charlie.* A smudge of dirt decorated her cheek, and her hair had escaped her ponytail to stick out from under her hat like she'd been electrocuted. She reached up to smooth down her hair but stopped herself. Whatever. Not like she needed to impress anyone.

Turning her attention back to the steering wheel, she held her hand out the window and lifted a finger. "One."

She shifted into drive and held up another finger. "Two."

With her boot on the gas pedal, she held up a final finger and floored it. "Three!"

The truck surged forward and stopped, straining, trying to gain purchase on the dusty dirt road. Then, slowly, inch by inch, the SUV rolled up and out of the ditch. She drove a few feet, just to make sure they cleared the edge of the road, and put the truck into park before climbing out.

He met her halfway between their vehicles. "Wow, I really didn't think that was going to work. Thanks so much for your help."

"Too bad I didn't have the winch on the back. You'd have been in for a real treat." She rocked back on the heels of her boots, not sure how to bring the somewhat awkward, somewhat pleasant interaction to a close.

"A winch? I take it you make a habit out of rescuing strangers from the dangerous back roads around here?"

"Ha. Only the ones who can't fend for themselves."

"Hey, no fair," he said with a laugh. "I can fend for myself."

A flirtatious smile sneaked past her lips. "You *fended* yourself right into the ditch, didn't you?"

His voice dropped a notch as he flirted right back. "I talked you into helping me, didn't I?" He winked, sending a jolt of electricity straight to her gut. "I'm just a little out of my element here, that's all."

A little out of his element? That was an understatement. Charlie shook her head, trying to keep her voice calm, even though her heart still played hopscotch in her chest. "You didn't talk me into anything. I wouldn't be able to live with myself if I drove on by and found out later something bad happened to you."

He lifted his arm to wipe the sweat off his brow again. "You mean besides melting on the side of the road?"

"Or worse." *Get your head out of your butt, Charlie.* Nothing good would come out of flirting with Sully's grandson, no matter how much she enjoyed it.

He reached for his wallet. "Can I pay you something for your time?"

She backed away, offended. "No. People around here help each other out because it's the right thing to do. We don't expect to get paid for it."

His smile faded. "Oh, right. I'm sorry. It's a little different where I'm from."

"I can imagine." And thank God for that. She leaned down to untie the rope connecting their vehicles.

"Let me get that." His fingers connected with hers on the knot.

She backed away like she'd been struck by a rattle-snake. Sully had never mentioned that his grandson looked like a cross between Thor and that good-looking actor who starred in the chick flicks she'd watched all by herself last weekend. Although, in his defense, Sully hadn't met the man, and his idea of attractive probably didn't coincide with hers.

Beckett cleared his throat and handed her the coil of rope. "Sorry for being a smart-ass. It's my superpower."

"Yeah," she said, still off-balance. "Just like your granddad."

"You knew my grandfather?" He leaned closer, like he wanted to hear more but didn't want to appear *too* eager. The effect was almost charming.

"You're the grandson, aren't you?" At the blank look he gave her, she clarified. "Beckett Sullivan Holiday?"

His brow furrowed. It was probably hard for someone who lived on an overcrowded island with several million strangers to realize what life in a true small town would be like. He'd learn soon enough that people around Holiday would often know his business before he did.

"Just call me Beck. But I didn't catch your name, Miss, um?"

"Charlotte."

He slid his shades off his nose. She wasn't prepared for the hint of humor in his kind, blue eyes. Could they really be the exact same shade as the bluebonnets dotting the hillside of her family's ranch? She cringed at the cheesy thought. Wouldn't do her any good to go soft all of a sudden. The combination of heat, dust, and an attractive relative stranger's attention must have made her a little woozy.

"I'll be around for the weekend, staying at the bed-and-breakfast on Valentine."

Yeah, she knew that too. Darby's parents owned the historic B and B just off the main road and had been telling everyone in town that Sully's grandson had booked two nights there.

"I'd love to hear more about my grandfather, but I'm running late for an appointment. Can I buy you a drink later?"

She wanted to dislike Sully's heir on sight. But he reminded her so much of her old friend it was hard to give him the cold shoulder. Plus, he had such a charming smile, and those hands…

"Or even just a coffee sometime?" he pressed.

What was that saying? Keep your friends close and your

enemies closer? Something like that. Maybe it would be in her best interest to be on speaking terms with Sully's heir. At least until she figured out what his plans were for the Rose. "Sure. Coffee would be great."

"Then it's a date." One side of his mouth quirked up into a lopsided grin as he realized what he'd said. "I didn't mean a *date* date."

Her face flushed. "Yeah, I know what you meant." When was the last time she'd had a *date* date? She didn't even want to try to think about it, especially not now, when she could still feel the weight of his gaze on her, even through the shades he'd slid back over his eyes.

"So how does tomorrow sound? Ten o'clock? Is there a Starbucks in town?"

Oh, he was so out of place he was like a turkey at a tea party. It was almost painfully cute…if he hadn't been the self-proclaimed smart-ass grandson of her favorite person in the whole wide world.

"Not unless you want to have coffee in San Marcos. I'm sure we'll run into each other sometime this weekend." Probably a lot sooner than he realized, since he'd most likely be stopping by the Rose later on. She climbed into the cab and leaned out the window, a thought occurring to her. "Can I ask you something?"

"Of course."

"You said you saw something run across the road. Was it a pig?"

He pinched the bridge of his nose and let out a self-deprecating laugh before turning that dazzling grin on her again. "I thought it was a cow but then assumed maybe I was just seeing things. Do you have wild pigs around here?"

She bit the inside of her cheek, ignoring the faint flutter in her chest. Wild pigs ought to be the least of his worries. "Something like that. Which way did it go?"

"Over there." He pointed to the right, in the direction of Mrs. Martinez's garden.

*Not again.* It might be time for Baby Back to retire. "Thanks." She shifted into gear, then hesitated. Maybe this youngest Holiday wasn't as bad as she'd feared. She'd toss him a bone, just this once. For Sully. "Can I offer you a piece of advice?"

"Sure."

She pointed to his loafers. "If you want to fit in, you might want to pick yourself up a pair of ropers along with some boot-cut Levi's. And don't even think about tucking your jeans into your boots, cowboy."

He glanced at his shoes, then smiled. "Thanks, I appreciate the advice."

"Oh, and one more thing." Beck met her gaze. "Don't forget to check yourself for ticks before you bunk down tonight. I hear they especially like that rich Yankee blood."

He swiped at the legs of his pants, but before he had a chance to respond, she eased away. The reflection in the rearview mirror showed him standing in the middle of the road, in the center of the cloud of dust her tires kicked up. He looked so out of place in his fancy shoes and wrinkle-free dress pants, she almost turned the truck around. She could have done more. Like offered to let him follow her into town. Or warned him about what a busy Friday night at the oldest honky-tonk in Texas might entail.

But until she got a read on what his plans were, she

might as well let him flounder. If he was half the man his granddad thought he was, he'd figure things out on his own.

*Oh, Sully.* Maybe it was better that the old cowboy wasn't around to see what a hopeless city boy his grandson had turned out to be.

# THREE

BECK CURSED UNDER HIS BREATH AS HIS RESCUER drove off in her giant truck. He should have asked her for directions. Too late now. Why did his first run-in with a local have to be with such a saucy blond? He hadn't wanted to show it, but she'd rattled him a little. The way she jerked on that rope and knew just what to do to get his truck out of the ditch…she was tough. Pretty damn cute, too.

Oh well. No use getting too intrigued. He was only sticking around long enough to hear the will and make arrangements for his grandfather's belongings.

He managed to make his way back to a paved road and onto what appeared to be the main street running through town. If it could be called a town. Took him about ninety seconds to drive from one side to the other, and that included waiting for an old woman with a cane to hobble across the crosswalk. She actually stopped right in the middle of the road and gave him a friendly wave. Wouldn't see something like that in New York.

Finally, he stopped in front of a building marked *Law Office*. With any luck, Mr. Hill would still be waiting for him and he'd get everything cleared up.

A bell on the handle of the door jangled as he entered. An empty desk sat in what might be considered the reception area. He checked his watch. Five o'clock. If he'd missed the man and had to wait around until Monday morning to catch a different flight home, he'd be mad as hell.

Thankfully, that didn't appear to be the case. A short, balding man with a bad comb-over walked into the room. "Mr. Holiday, I presume?"

Beck took the man's hand; he had a surprisingly firm handshake. "Yes. Mr. Hill, thanks so much for waiting for me. I ran into some trouble finding you. Please, call me Beck."

Mr. Hill led him into the office. "Sorry, my receptionist only works part-time. Things around here aren't nearly as busy as what you're probably used to in New York. Have a seat, son. My condolences on your grandfather's passing. He was a good man."

"Thank you. I know I'm late and don't want to cut into your Friday night, so I'll get right to the point. You mentioned something on the phone about his will?"

"Indeed." He stepped to a sideboard cabinet and poured two tumblers of amber liquid, handing one to Beck as he gestured toward a chair. "A little local whiskey for you?"

"Thanks." Beck sat down, tipped the glass back, and let the liquid slide down his throat. This kind of hospitality he could handle.

Mr. Hill drained his drink and took a seat behind the desk. "Now, about Sully's will—"

"Sully?" His eyebrows rose in surprise.

"Oh, that's what everyone called him. We're not much for formalities around here. Your grandfather was a pillar of the community."

Beck scoffed and set his empty tumbler on the edge of the desk. "Really?"

Mr. Hill sat up straighter, thick eyebrows crumpling into a wiggly line. "You doubt your grandfather's contribution to the town?"

*Great.* Now he'd gone and offended the attorney. "It's just that my dad never mentioned anything about my grandfather being such an important man." Quite the opposite. On the rare occasions Beckett Sullivan Holiday Jr. spoke about his father at all, he shared nothing but negativity for his hometown and the family he'd left behind. Beck tried to recall his father's exact words when he'd left the office before heading to the airport. Something about how he'd be better off burning down that hole-in-the-wall bar and collecting on the insurance.

Mr. Hill shuffled a stack of papers on his desk. "Well, folks around here sure thought so."

"And about the will?" Beck pressed.

"Yes, yes. Your grandfather left everything to you. That includes his residence, about a thousand acres he currently rents out for pasture, and, of course, the Rambling Rose."

"The Rambling Rose?" That must be the bar.

"Surely you've heard about your family's connection to the Rambling Rose?"

Beck ran his palms over his thighs. "Look, Mr. Hill, let's just say my dad and grandfather didn't exactly get along. The only thing I've heard about my dad's time spent in Texas was how my grandfather tossed him out on his ass and how happy he was to leave."

"I remember your father." Hill took his reading glasses off. The chair creaked as he leaned back and laced his fingers across his bulging beer belly. His voice took on a wistful tone. "Things in Holiday never seemed to be enough for him."

"From what I've seen so far, I can't imagine my dad spending any time here at all."

"Well, he did. We went to school together. He was a year ahead of me, but we played on the same football team. That was the year we made it to State."

"Huh." Beck leaned forward in his seat. "He never mentioned that."

"I don't suppose he would have. We were up by three points when your father decided to ignore the coach's call to take a knee. He wanted the glory of throwing another touchdown, especially during the final game of his senior year, but he fumbled the snap. With fourteen seconds left on the clock, he shoulda taken the damn knee."

Beck's stomach twinged, already anticipating the answer to his next question. "What happened?"

"The other team threw a Hail Mary pass and won the game. Your dad couldn't handle it. He was always pulling stunts like that."

Mr. Hill's words hung heavily between them. Beck had never known his father to fail at anything. No wonder he wasn't eager to come back to Holiday. It would be a slap-in-the-face reminder of the one time he hadn't managed to pull off a win. But Mr. Hill had said *stunts*. "What other kind of stunts did he pull?"

"I'm not sure I'm the right person to talk to about this." Mr. Hill ran his finger along the neck of his shirt like it had suddenly grown too tight.

"I'd just like to get a bit more information about

my family's history. You said you knew my dad. Can't you tell me any more?"

Mr. Hill sighed. "All I can tell you is that Sully always wanted your dad to take over the Rambling Rose, to keep it in the family, but your dad hated the place."

"Why?"

"Son, you'll have to talk to your dad about that. They had a pretty big falling-out. Your dad left after graduation, and as far as I know, he's never been back."

A falling-out? The way his dad described it, Sully had tossed him out without a dime to his name. No wonder Holiday had never looked back.

Mr. Hill opened the desk drawer with a squeak and handed Beck a crowded ring of keys. "Here are keys to the residence and a set to the Rambling Rose. Any other keys to the outbuildings and gates are at the house."

"You keep mentioning this Rambling Rose. *Is* that the bar my grandfather owned?"

Mr. Hill's paunchy cheeks scrunched into a frown like a squirrel that'd just taken a bite of a rotten acorn. "Son, the Rambling Rose isn't a *bar*."

An uneasy knot formed between his shoulder blades. "Then what is it?"

The lawyer's voice rose as he lifted his body out of the chair and placed his hands flat on the desk. "It's the oldest honky-tonk in the great state of Texas, probably the whole United States."

Beck couldn't see the difference between a honky-tonk and a bar, but there was obviously no sense in arguing with the man. "Okay, got it. So now what am I supposed to do? It's not like I'm going to move down here and take over a bar—" Mr. Hill's eyebrows rose.

"Excuse me, I mean a *honky-tonk*. Any idea what the value might be?"

"You can't be considering selling?"

Leaning forward with his forearms on his thighs, Beck shook his head. "Mr. Hill, my life is in New York. I have a business, my family. There's no way I'm staying in Texas, especially in a town my dad couldn't wait to leave."

Mr. Hill held up a piece of paper, slid his glasses back in place, and lowered himself into his seat. "Yes, well, there is of course a stipulation to the will."

"Of course there is." Beck slumped against the back of the chair. "Please, go ahead. What is it?" This day was turning into a giant clusterfuck. He could use another pour of that smooth whiskey to settle his rattled nerves.

"Before the title or any other assets can be transferred into your name, your grandfather's will requires you to spend time in Holiday and oversee the day-to-day operations of the Rambling Rose until the next Founder's Day parade."

Beck shook his head again. "That's ridiculous. Why would he care about that?"

"In the 125-year history of Holiday, there's never been a Founder's Day parade without a member of the founding family of the town on the float."

"And I'm supposed to represent the founding family?"

Mr. Hill nodded.

"When's this parade happening?"

"Lucky for you, it's only three months away—the Saturday of Labor Day weekend. The whole town comes out to celebrate."

"September? That's crazy." Beck got to his feet and towered over the attorney. "This has been a waste of my time."

"Mr. Holiday—"

"*Beck*."

"Beck, you might want to think twice before walking away. If you don't meet the requirements of the will, then all of your grandfather's assets will revert to a third party."

"Which is?"

Mr. Hill removed his glasses again and stood, putting him a good six inches shy of Beck's eye level. "Regrettably, I'm unable to divulge that information at this point, but I suggest you consider your options carefully. Even without the Rambling Rose, your grandfather amassed quite a net worth over the years. Between the value of his land, the residence, and the cash bonds in his safety deposit box, we're talking over five million dollars."

That number caught Beck off guard. "What did you say?"

"Sully had some of the best pasture acres in the county. And he'd been buying savings bonds since he was old enough to ride his pony to the bank."

"And if I stay here for three months, I can sell the Rambling Rose and everything else becomes mine?"

Mr. Hill's shoulders lifted and sagged in a defeated shrug. "Well, he hoped that you'd stay. The Rambling Rose has been in the Holiday family for more than 125 years. I'm sure your grandfather wanted it to continue—"

"Like I said, my home is in New York. I can't put my life on pause to fulfill an old man's dream. Sully was a stranger to me. I'd love to learn more about my family and my past, but staying in Holiday for good is definitely not in my future." Beck took a breath. "So, if I stay until this Founder's Day deal, I can sell if I want, right?"

"That's right. According to the will, you have to ride on the Rambling Rose's float in the Founder's Day parade. After that, everything is yours."

With that much cash, he'd be able to invest in some projects of his own. The possibilities began to spin infinite webs in his head. But could he do it? Three months in Podunk? What would happen to the lot in Morris Park? And the town…why would he want to willingly stay in a place that had given his dad such painful memories?

"Why don't you take the weekend to think about it?" Mr. Hill walked around the desk and held out his hand.

Beck grasped it in a firm shake. "I will. Where do I find this Rambling Rose? I want to swing by and check it out."

"Head south out of town and take a right. You can't miss it. Charlie Walker is in charge for now. They've actually got a big concert there tonight to celebrate Rocky Mountain Oyster Days. It'll give you a chance to see the place hopping and the whole team in action."

"Rocky Mountain oysters?"

"They're a local delicacy. One thing you'll find out about Holiday is that we don't need much of an excuse for a celebration." The man laced his fingers over his stomach and rocked back on his heels. "Folks around here will celebrate just about anything."

"I appreciate your help. Thanks, Mr. Hill."

"Good luck to you, Beck. I'll expect to hear something from you by the beginning of next week."

Beck nodded and showed himself out. Standing on the front porch of the law office, he slid his sunglasses back over his eyes and looked up and down the street. A mini-mart occupied the building across the road. Next to that, an antique store took up the first floor of an old stone building. A diner, a western wear shop, and a gas station lined the road. His side held a post office, a couple of gift shops, and a barbecue joint. Not much else going on. How could anyone consider spending more than an afternoon here?

He turned toward the western shop, the advice of the very competent blond playing on repeat in his ears. The least he could do was turn in his loafers for a pair of boots. Then he could get settled into the bed-and-breakfast and think about dropping in on the honky-tonk.

His rubber-soled boat shoes padded across the wood-plank walkway. A loud *moo* sounded over his head as he entered the front doorway of Whitey's Western Wear. Cowboy hats in various colors were stacked to the ceiling. Suede chaps, jeans studded with sparkly rhinestones, and belt buckles the size of his head plastered the walls. Maybe he wasn't up for this. Surrounded by a sea of denim and plaid, he located the single employee.

"Well, hi there, stranger. What can I do you for?"

"I guess I need some new jeans and boots."

"Hmm"—the string bean of a man tapped his finger against his lip—"we've got some new ropers. Or were you thinking more like a dress boot?"

What the hell was a dress boot? "I'll put my faith in your capable hands."

"Come on over. I think I've got just the thing."

Beck followed the salesman through racks of plaid and floral-print shirts. Three months. He could do anything for three months once he set his mind to it. And for five million dollars in assets, he'd figure out a way to make this work. As he passed yet another rack of shirts, he fingered a purple paisley long-sleeved oxford with pearlized buttons and at least five pounds of sequins stuck to each sleeve.

Well, maybe not *anything*.

Charlie scanned the main room of the honky-tonk. Her only full-time waitress, Dixie, had strung giant foam seashells from the overhead beams and draped fisherman's netting over the tables. If that's how she wanted to decorate for the annual Rocky Mountain Oyster Days, Charlie was more than happy to let her take the lead. Once less thing for Charlie to take care of.

Sully would have been proud.

Everyone had rallied after his death and done their part to keep things going. The place would never be the same without him, but Charlie would do her best to make sure the Rambling Rose retained the down-home, Texas hospitality it had been known for over the years.

And to think, all of this could be hers.

A lightness filled her chest as she considered what that would mean. She'd met with Mr. Hill that morning, and he'd gone over Sully's will. She'd known how important it was to Sully that the Rambling Rose stay in the family. Toward the end, he'd sent multiple letters to his son and grandson. They'd all gone unanswered.

Charlie always felt like the granddaughter he'd

never had, but to hear him express the same sentiment right before he died made her more determined than ever to find his family and convey how important it was to keep the place going. Yet as close as they'd been, she'd never expected Sully to see her as a potential *heir*.

So when Mr. Hill told her the will stipulated that Sully's grandson had until the Founder's Day parade to prove himself or the Rambling Rose would be hers, Charlie had almost fallen out of her chair. Now she had a decision to make—either help the floundering fish out of water, or make sure he didn't succeed. Based on what she'd seen so far, it wouldn't take much to run him out of town.

She sighed and stepped behind the long bar. Playing dirty wasn't her style. Unless she was knee-deep in mud, wrestling with Baby Back. She'd do what she needed to do to make good on her promise to Sully and try to keep the Rambling Rose in the Holiday family. Although, spending three months with the wise-cracking, good-looking New Yorker might feel like an eternity.

"Hey, Boss." Shep, one of the regular bartenders, shot her a smile as he unloaded a rack of beer mugs onto a shelf. "Looks like we'll be packin' 'em in tonight."

Charlie nodded while she ran a rag over a spill on the counter. "You need any help behind the bar tonight, just holler, okay? I'm still looking for a backup for you."

"Oh, I'll be able to keep up. And if I get into a jam, I'll grab Cash or Waylon or someone to help."

"Sounds good." Her brothers had really come through for her over the past couple of months. Family came first. That was one of the values her parents had instilled in all of the Walker kids.

It was still early, but most of the long wood tables had already been claimed. Folks lined the hard-plank benches, enjoying the warm-up band. They were here for the headliner—a kid from San Marcos who had taken Nashville by storm. Playing the Rambling Rose was a rite of passage, especially for a relative local, and though she'd been in charge of managing the nightly shows for the past eight years, even Charlie didn't know who might show up and take the stage for an impromptu set.

Shep set the empty rack on the ground, then stepped around her to pull on the tap and fill a mug. Charlie moved down to an empty section of the bar. She leaned on her elbows, resting her chin in her hands. Dixie bobbed through the tables, delivering mugs and bottles of beer. Music blared from the speakers while the crowd clapped along to the beat. The neon signs cast a warm glow around the edges of the room, and the scent of just-smoked ribs drifted out of the kitchen.

Looked like another successful Friday night was on tap at the Rose. Before things got rocking, she'd better make sure Baby Back got her dinner.

"Hey, I'm gonna go feed Baby Back," she called out to Shep as she hung the dishrag on a hook.

"That crazy-ass pig's given you more trouble than the last two or three combined," Shep said.

"I know, I know. But it's a tradition, right?"

"If you ask me, they got some pretty strange traditions around here." Shep held the empty dish rack to his side and passed her on his way to the kitchen.

He was right about that. He'd only been there for

about four months. Just wait until he saw what kind of "traditions" they had coming over the summer.

Charlie followed him down the hall and grabbed the bucket of kitchen scraps the cook always saved for Baby Back. The pig was spoiled rotten. Maybe that was part of the reason she took off all the time. She was probably bored to within an inch or her life and looking for adventure. Baby Back had gotten used to being coddled with kitchen scraps and behind-the-ear scratches. If she had to do more than pose for pictures and sniff out marshmallows, she might not have the energy to take off every chance she got.

With thoughts of how to unspoil Conroe County's most precious pig running through her head, Charlie pushed the screen door open right into the late-afternoon humidity.

And right into the rock-solid body of Beck.

Apple shavings, corncobs, and juicy slop splattered between them, covering them both in a mixture of solids and liquid. The slippery mess splattered onto the stairs, and as she took a step forward, her feet slid out from under her.

Charlie's arms flailed. She tried to grab onto the rail, the door, anything before she hit the ground. Her fingers briefly hooked on something, slowing her fall.

*Rippppppppppppppppppppppppp.*

The noise dragged on, her fist now closed around a swatch of denim. Beck caught her around the waist seconds before her butt bounced on the top step, and she took him down with her. He flung one hand out to his side in an attempt to brace himself. He must have slipped because his body collided with hers.

"Oooooof." Her breath rushed out as she caught his chin in the center of her breastbone.

The bucket clattered down the steps, banging and clanging until it hit the grass. Finally, the movement ceased.

Charlie was afraid to move. She couldn't take in a deep breath. Not with the hit to her chest and the head of sandy-blondish hair nestled in between her belly button and her—oh my God—her pubic bone.

The hair moved. Beck lifted his head, his mouth hovering just inches above the apex of her thighs. She battled the overwhelming urge to jerk her knee to his groin.

"What was that?" He lifted himself up with one arm and swiped at his eyes with the other. A slow smile spread across his face as recognition took root.

Charlie scrambled backward like a crab. She couldn't get out from under him fast enough. "What are you doing? Nobody's supposed to come through this door. Didn't you see the sign? *Employees only.*"

He rose onto his knees while he wiped the slop off his cheeks with his sleeve. "I know you from earlier. You're the angel with the truck who pulled me out of the ditch."

"Guilty as charged." Although she was feeling anything but angelic at the moment. She got to her feet, not sure what part of her had suffered the bigger bruise: her backside or her pride.

"And you work here?" He stood, towering over her, making her feel small and all of a sudden unsure of herself.

Smart as a whip, this one. "You figure that out all by yourself there, Einstein?" She didn't mean to lash out, but he set her off balance, and firing back with words had always been her go-to move.

"Whoa. Are you always this friendly, Miss Charlotte?"

She blew out a breath, embarrassed. Her mama had raised her with better manners than this. "Sorry. It's been a long day."

"You're telling me." Beck looked over the slop covering his sleeves. "What is this? Smells like someone's leftovers."

"That's one thing you're right about. I was on my way to feed the pig her freaking dinner." She held the swatch of denim out to him. "I think this belongs to you."

He squinted at the offering. "What's that?"

Flushed, she lowered her gaze to the tips of his boots. "I believe it's...sorry, *was* your pocket."

Beck patted his ass with his hand, then twisted around, trying to see where the pocket had been. "You stole my pocket?"

Charlie bit her lip and cast her eyes toward the sky, wishing, hoping, maybe even saying a little prayer that this was all a dream. A bad one. A nightmare of epic proportions.

The clouds didn't part. Looked like she was on her own. "Hey, I'm sorry about ripping your jeans."

"My new jeans." He finally took the piece of fabric.

"Your *new* jeans. I'd be happy to replace them." She scooted past Beck to retrieve the bucket from the grass. He put out a hand to catch her, but the slop had lubed up her forearm and it slid from his grip.

He called after her. "Before you stomp off into the sunset, can you direct me to the man in charge? Mr. Hill said I needed to ask for Charlie."

She whirled around to face him. "Are all of you Yankees so obtuse?"

"Excuse me?"

"Charlotte Walker. I go by Charlie."

"Oh crap." Beck lifted a hand to his head like he wanted to run it through his hair but thought better of it and let it fall to his side. "You're the one who's been taking care of the place since my grandfather passed?"

"Since he passed and for about eight years prior." *So much for making nice.* She bit her tongue to keep from unleashing everything she wanted to say to Sully's sorry-ass grandson. How could he let Sully's letters go unanswered? Why didn't he ever call or write or visit? How much effort would it have taken for him to give the poor old man a tiny bit of joy in his final months?

"And you're a woman."

She couldn't have prevented her eyes from rolling even if she had wanted to. "Last time I checked."

"I'm sorry. I assumed…Ms. Walker…Charlotte… can I call you Charlie?"

"Suit yourself."

"I think we're getting off on the wrong foot. Can we start over?" A smile she was sure had prevented many women from getting a good night's sleep graced his face. Even covered in splatters of slop, undeniable charm rolled off this man in waves. He offered her his hand. "Charlie. It's nice to officially meet you."

Her gaze lingered on his fingers, which were still covered in potato peelings and a thin layer of slop. What the heck—hers were just as bad. She gripped his hand, feeling the warmth, even through the slime. His smile hit her with a slow burn, low in the gut.

She squeezed her eyes shut into a long blink and

gave a jerky shake of the head. *Don't even go there, Charlie.* She slid her hand from his. If he thought he could barge in here, flip on the charm, and instantly earn her support, well, he had another think coming.

This day had gone from bad to worse. Of all the men in New York City, why had she been saddled with this one?

Because he was Sully's grandson, that's why. At the thought of her old boss, her anger petered out. *For Sully,* she reminded herself. At the rate she was going, she'd have to chant the reminder for the next three months.

"Do you have a towel or something I can use to clean up?" Beck asked.

"Sure." Charlie wheeled around and led him inside a few steps, to the storeroom. She handed him a clean bar towel and pointed toward the sink. "You can clean up over there, although you'll probably want to run over to the B and B to shower and maybe change your jeans. When you get back, I'll show you around and introduce you to the rest of *your* staff."

His head cocked at the emphasis. "Thanks." He turned toward the sink, wiping his face free of Baby Back's dinner.

She lingered, letting her gaze run up the long, denim-clad legs, over his perfect ass, snugly encased in a new pair of Levi's. Minus the pocket, of course. Her gaze darted to his feet. The sockless loafers were gone, replaced by a pair of working man's ropers. Whitey had probably had a heyday giving Beck a proper Hill Country makeover. If he was willing to take her advice, maybe he wasn't completely hopeless.

A drop of slop slid down her forehead, onto her nose, reminding her she probably looked like a modern-day Swamp Thing. She figured she had just enough time to find something to feed Baby Back, then run home and get cleaned up herself.

"So, I'll be back in a bit, okay?"

"Sounds good." Beck lifted his hand in an awkward wave.

She headed toward the door, dipping her finger into her front pocket and brushing over the lucky Texas Centennial half-dollar Sully had given her right before he died. Even in death, that man knew how to keep her tripping around on her toes.

*For Sully*, she chanted in her head. And if Beck ruined his chances on his own, she'd be happy to pick up the pieces.

# chapter

# FOUR

BECK TAPPED HIS FEET ALONG WITH THE BEAT OF THE catchy bluegrass tune. He'd never been one for country music, but even he could appreciate someone who could wrangle kitchen spoons into some kind of song. *Spoons,* for crying out loud.

The performer sat on an old wood barrel on the stage. A row of spotlights dropped down from a bar hanging from the ceiling. The inside of the Rose looked like a barn with all the giant beams and coarse-wood walls. Not that he would know exactly what the inside of a barn looked like, since he'd never been in one himself. But he could imagine it would look a lot like this.

Probably felt a lot like this, too. The combination of heat from the lights and the press of denim-clad, boot-wearing patrons who twirled and spun around the dance floor made him pull his shirt away from his body in an attempt to catch some air. Either the space didn't have any air-conditioning or the locals preferred the scent of fresh-cut grass and musty earth that floated in through the giant open windows on the barely there breeze.

His dad had filled his head with visions of a two-barstool hole-in-the-wall, but this place was so much more than he'd pictured—it really pulled people in. Between the packed dance hall where the waitresses ran trays full of longnecks back and forth to the rough-hewn bar where the bartender filled orders for people two or three deep, the Rambling Rose was hopping.

And Charlie Walker orchestrated it all.

She'd cleaned up pretty well, and he couldn't help but appreciate the way her tight jeans clung to every curve. They sat so low on her hips that, every once in a while, he could catch a sliver of skin between her waistband and where she'd knotted a pink-plaid shirt. She might be just over five feet tall, but she kept a tight rein on the employees and the patrons. Hell, he'd already seen her break up a fight between two cowboys who must have outweighed her by two hundred pounds. She bussed tables, filled mugs from the tap, and took to the stage to make introductions between acts. His grandfather had obviously known what he was doing when he'd put his faith in Charlie. It was becoming as clear as the starlit sky that if he wanted to give it a shot for the next three months, he'd have to get her on his side.

The band wrapped up their set, and he took advantage of the break to check in at the bar.

"What can I get you, Boss?" The bartender rubbed at an invisible spot on the bar with a rag. "Have you tried a Lone Star yet? If you're hungry, we've got specials for Rocky Mountain Oyster Days."

Before Beck had a chance to ask about the seafood special, a guy in a dirty baseball cap on the stool next to him swiveled around. "So you're Sully's grandson, huh?"

"Yeah. Beck Holiday. And you are?" Beck asked.

"No one of consequence," Charlie said, setting a tray of empty bottles down on the edge of the bar.

"Now is that any way to treat your sweetheart?" the guy crooned.

Charlie rolled her eyes. "Dwight here owns the gas station."

"Oh yeah? Which one?" Beck asked.

They both gave him blank looks. "*The* gas station. There's only one. It's got the old Texaco sign and the ancient pumps." Charlie unloaded the empty bottles behind the bar and picked up a new load of drinks before hoisting the tray onto her shoulder.

"Need some help with that?" Beck reached for an edge of the tray.

Charlie backed up before he could touch it. "And have you tip this over and cover me in a couple gallons of wasted beer? I got this." She whisked the tray away, heading back into the fray.

"Is she always that ornery?" Beck wrapped his hand around the glass the bartender set in front of him and took a swig of the foamy brew.

"Nah, usually she's ornery *and* mean." Dwight thrust his hand at Beck. "Damn glad to meet ya. You need any advice about how to fit in around here, you just check in with me, ya hear?"

Beck shook Dwight's hand, noticing the grease-stained fingers and the smell of sweat and oil that drifted off his coveralls. "Thanks, man."

"You bet. Me and Charlie are kind of an item. You think she's feisty now, you should get a load of her under the sheets."

Beck raised a brow. He'd just met the woman earlier today, but Dwight definitely didn't seem like her type.

"Not that I'm suggesting you try that or anything."

Dwight popped a toothpick in the corner of his mouth. "Like I said, we're kind of a thing."

"Yeah, I hear you. So you're local?" May as well pump the guy for any information he could.

"Born and raised. I did spend some time in the army after high school. But my bum knee got me kicked out, and I came back here to take over the family business."

Beck moved out of the way as a waitress navigated through the crowded bar with a tray full of beer and food held high over her head. The scent of barbecue lingered as she brushed past, on a hurry to somewhere. "Is this place always this busy?"

"Heck yeah. Weeknights you might only have a handful of folks depending on whether there's music. But Charlie here's been gettin' the word out, and we got city folk comin' all the way from San Antonio and Austin. Those college kids from San Marcos can whoop it up a bit too much from time to time. But Charlie, she don't take crap from anyone. She's got an iron boot." Dwight smiled then gulped down half his bottle of beer.

*Huh.* Beck couldn't wait to get his hands on the financials. Based on the action he'd seen so far, they were probably pulling in a nice profit. If he could build on that, max out the selling price…he could head back to New York with enough cash in his account to do the Morris Park project on his own.

"So what's Charlie's story?"

Dwight's eyes narrowed, like he was suspicious of the question. "Whadda ya mean?"

"It's just, my grandfather never mentioned her.

Were they close?" Dwight didn't need to know his grand-father had never mentioned *anything* to him, much less the attractive and competent blond.

"Tighter than two coats of paint. Why, Charlie's been workin' for Sully since the day her fiancé—"

"Hey now." The bartender had stepped back in front of them to fill another pint from the tap. "Don't need to go spillin' everyone else's beans now, do you?"

"Just bein' neighborly." Dwight nabbed his beer and vacated the stool. "If you'll excuse me. I could piss over a ten-foot fence right now." He ambled away, weaving his way through the crush of people like he'd been doing it all his life.

"By the way, I'm Shep." The bartender gestured toward Dwight's departing backside. "Don't pay any attention to him. He thinks the sun comes up just to hear him crow."

Beck nodded. "Beck Holiday. Nice to meet you. About Charlie...does she live around here?"

"Yep. The Walker ranch is over off County Road H. But I wouldn't get any ideas about making a play for her."

"I wasn't. Besides, Dwight seems pretty possessive?"

Shep let out a snort. "He wishes."

*Hmm.* Dwight was all talk. That made more sense. Charlie was obviously way out of the guy's league. "Not that I'm interested, but what do you mean about not making a play?"

"Dude, she has brothers. Big brothers. And by big, I mean as tall as Trace Adkins and as ready for a brawl as George Foreman himself. Did you know he was born in Texas? Anyhow, all of 'em live around here except for Strait, and all of 'em know how to mess a guy up, if you know what I mean."

Beck digested that piece of information. As the only child of two people who'd barely stayed together long enough for the ink on their marriage license to dry, he couldn't imagine what it would be like to be surrounded by family. He might work with his dad, but that didn't mean they were close. Quite the opposite. He often suspected the only reason Holiday pulled him into the business was so he would have another vote to control if he needed it.

"Can I get you another beer?" Shep asked.

"No thanks. I think I'll just hang out a bit and see how things go." Beck pulled a twenty out of his wallet and set it on the bar. "If I don't see her, can you tell Charlie I'll be back in the morning? What time does she normally get here?"

"I don't know that she ever leaves unless she's chasing after that crazy pig." Shep slid the twenty off the bar and handed it back. "Pretty sure your money's no good around here. Now that you own the place and all."

Beck shook his head. "Then consider it a tip."

Shep pocketed it. "Thanks. Can I give you a tip, too?"

"Sure." At this point, he'd take any advice, unsolicited or not.

"Charlie looks mighty tough, but she ain't. She might seem like she's got a shell as thick and hard as an armadillo, but inside, she's like a marshmallow. She's been tied up in this place forever, and it's gonna be damn near impossible for her to let it go if it comes to that."

"Got it." He'd never seen an armadillo. Weren't

they those ugly, rat-looking rodents with scales? He'd have to look it up. But he'd caught the general gist of Shep's warning. As far as Beck was concerned, Shep didn't have anything to worry about. Making sure Charlie was on his team was the only way he'd survive the next three months.

Well, her help and maybe a miracle or two.

~*HH*~

The band launched into a tune everyone could line dance to, and a mass of boot-scootin', heel-stompin', beer-buzzin' customers took to the dance floor. Charlie leaned against the edge of the bar, smiling to herself as a busty brunette tried to pull Beck out for a dance. Soon some of her girlfriends joined in the effort, and they got him close to the edge of the fray.

After a few missteps, he caught on to the moves and almost looked like he was having fun. Until he bumped into the girl on his left when everyone else shifted right. Instead of tucking his tail and retreating to his seat, he laughed it off and tried again. The carefree attitude suited him. His new fan club must have thought so, too. They didn't seem to have any issue with taking him by the arm or shoulder and helping him get back into his groove.

The shirt Whitey had sold him stretched tight across his chest, and he'd pushed up the sleeves, exposing those strong forearms. Charlie could practically feel the hard ridge of muscle under her fingers as his shoulders rolled. *Get a grip, girl.* She sighed, not wanting to admit that getting a grip was exactly what she'd been thinking about. Turning a cold shoulder to the dance floor, she nabbed a few dirty glasses from the bar and stacked them on a tray underneath the counter. Last call would be in about a half hour. She just needed to survive a little while longer.

The band switched tunes, and she looked up to see Beck heading her way, the trio of coeds hot on his heels.

"Come on, Beck. Just one more dance?" The gal who'd dragged him onto the dance floor tugged on his hand and whined.

"Sorry, girls, but I'm still in training. I've got a lot of work left to do tonight—right, Boss?" His eyes begged her to let him off the hook. Charlie almost felt sorry for him.

No harm throwing him a lifeline. "That's right. I've still got to show you how to, uh, take a tap apart and clean it out."

"Yep. See? All work and no play. Another time, okay, ladies?" He recovered his hand and mouthed "thanks" to Charlie. The trio turned back toward the dance floor, probably scoping out another victim.

"You card at the door, right?" Beck asked. "Those girls don't look like they could be more than nineteen or twenty."

"You must be getting old. They look younger and younger every year."

He rubbed the pad of his thumb over his lips. "What are you, like twenty-two? You say that like you're knocking on the door of middle age."

She had to give the guy points for being so smooth. "Twenty-two, huh? I'll give you a hint. I've been working for Sully for the past eight years. Twenty-two isn't even close."

"So my grandfather was a cradle robber? I can't

imagine he'd hire you until you could legally serve a beer. No way you're in your thirties though. No freakin' way."

"My first job was working the register up front. I'd run the guest checks through and sell T-shirts and stuff. Don't worry. He didn't let me pull on a tap until I was twenty-one."

"Rumor has it you're the grease that keeps this big wheel turning."

"Now that doesn't sound like something you came up with on your own." Charlie kept her hands busy with mundane tasks behind the bar. Stocking the cocktail napkins, adding a few more toothpicks to the dispenser— things that would distract her from the mass of muscle sitting across from her.

"You're right about that. I've been polling the locals. Everyone around here loves you. Says you're the only reason Sully was able to keep the doors open. I suppose I ought to thank you for that." He put his elbows on the bar and leaned closer.

"I've enjoyed it." That was the understatement of the millennium. Sully had saved her, in more ways than one. When he'd offered her a job all those years ago, he'd had no idea how he'd pulled her away from the edge. She'd found something to look forward to again, and she'd be forever grateful to the Holiday family, past, present, and future, for the role they'd played, whether they knew it or not.

She supposed, if she was feeling generous, that might mean Beck, too.

"So what do you call what they're doing now?" Beck jerked his chin toward the dance floor where couples spun around the perimeter.

"Just a two-step."

"A whatta?" His eyes crinkled at the edges with the force of his smile.

She focused her attention on a particularly stubborn spot on the glass she'd been drying, ignoring the flutter low in her belly. "Texas two-step. It's not hard. I'm sure one of your new fans would be happy to teach you."

"How about you?" He held out a hand.

She shook her head. "Oh, I don't know. There's a lot to do—"

"Come on, two minutes of two-stepping? I promise not to crush your toes."

"I haven't two-stepped in a long time."

"Good. Then you won't make me look so bad. What do you say?"

No. She had to say no. She didn't have time to trip around the dance floor. Not when there were customers to serve, tables to wipe, and an annoying attraction she wouldn't acknowledge. The "no thanks" hovered on the tip of her tongue. Just sat there, refusing to vocalize into a polite refusal.

He smiled. The dimple winked at her. Her toes curled. She'd always been a sucker for dimples. She swallowed the "no" she'd intended to give him.

"Fine." She wiped her palms on the back pockets of her jeans and slid her hand into his. The kickback to the center of her nervous system rivaled the jolt she'd gotten the last time she'd shot her cousin's 7mm rifle.

Shaking it off, she led him to a corner of the dance floor and spun to face him. "So you put your hand here." She slid his hand right under her arm, to rest on her back, then put her hand on his shoulder. "And then you hold my other hand with yours, like so."

The moment Beck cradled her in his embrace, her breath hitched in her chest, the air detouring away from her windpipe. Her lungs protested in a cough, and she had to pull her arms away from him to cover her flaming cheeks until her little fit subsided.

"You okay?" Beck asked, his face showing a mix of concern and amusement.

"Yeah, my breath just went down the wrong pipe. Song's almost over—here, let's try again." She slid her arm up to clamp onto his shoulder. His body heat seeped through the thin cotton of his shirt, and something deep within her flickered. She became acutely aware of the way his thumb grazed her ribs right under the cup of her bra. *Sweet Jesus.* Maybe she should've listened to Darby when she'd said Charlie needed to get out more.

"Like this?" His hand clamped onto hers, and his fingers pressed into her back.

She nodded. Now for the footwork. "So the two-step is just a series of, well, two steps. First you take a step and bring your feet together. Then you take two steps like you're walking from one point to another. The tempo kind of goes… Step together, slow, slow." She demonstrated by taking a quick step backward, bringing her feet together, then taking two more slow steps.

The other dancers whirled around them as Beck tried again and again to execute the basic move.

"This is harder than it looks." He stopped for a moment, letting his arms drop. "I think I'd do better at a dance club—or, even better, a slow song."

As if on demand, the fast-paced twangy tune came to an end, and the band started in on a slow, bluesy ballad. Beck held out his arms, challenging her with a lift of the eyebrows. "This is more my speed. One more dance?"

She backed away, shaking her head. "I've got to start going through the closing routine. We've got a big day tomorrow."

"Come on, humor me. This might be the one time I don't look like a complete fool on the dance floor."

She tried to say no. Really, she did. But then the dimple reappeared, and she found herself melting into his open embrace. She put a hand on his shoulder and let him take the other in his.

As his arm wrapped around her waist, pulling her tight against him, she inhaled. No doubt about the shirt being brand new. That fresh-off-the-rack scent hung over the lapel, but something else simmered underneath. A mix of expensive cologne, maybe some shower gel, and the unmistakable earthy scent of a male in his prime. She relaxed into his arms, enjoying the feel of being held by a man.

And not just any man.

A man who didn't know her history, who hadn't formed opinions about who she was or what kind of a guy she needed or what she could handle.

An unfamiliar sense of safety and security overwhelmed her. But instead of her usual reaction of wanting to get as far away as quickly as possible, she somehow ached for more. More of his nearness. More of his strength. More of his touch.

His thumb caressed the small of her back, and

his hand dipped lower, pulling her in closer so their hips grazed. Unprepared for the way her body responded to his, Charlie became acutely aware of each one of his movements. Her skin pebbled as a buried need raced through her. She swayed out of time to the slow beat of the song.

"You okay there?" Beck adjusted his step to match hers.

"I'm tired, that's all. It's been crazy around here since Sully died. So much to do, and there never seems to be enough time to get it all done."

His hand splayed over her back. "I know how that goes. Sometimes I wish there were an extra three or four hours in a day. I'd probably still spend them all at my desk."

Charlie tilted her head to get a good, close look at him. Word around Holiday was that he worked for his dad's company. But she had no idea what he actually did for a living. "What exactly do you do for work?"

"Build things. Tear things down. Rip them apart and try to put them back together again so they're stronger, more streamlined."

His hands were way too smooth to have seen the working end of a hammer. "When you say you 'build things,' you don't actually mean you're in the field, right?"

He shuffled them to the right to avoid a couple standing dead still in the middle of the dance floor. "Nah. All the building I get to do is on paper. But I do get to wear a hard hat every once in a while if I visit a job site."

Beck in a hard hat. The thought made her grin.

"What are you all smiles about?"

"Just picturing you with a yellow hard hat on your head. I bet you'd look like a tall minion."

"A minion?" He wrinkled his brow. "Whose minion?"

"You know, the little yellow guys. *Despicable Me*? Gru and Dr. Nefario?"

Beck shook his head. "No. Not ringing a bell."

"Really? I can't remember their actual names. Oh wait. Dave. The one you'd probably look the most like is Dave."

"Why Dave?"

"Well, he has two eyes."

"Hey, if that's all we have in common…" He shrugged.

"It's a kids' movie." Charlie landed a playful swat on his pec. No give there. "My nieces and nephews love it. You must not spend a lot of time around kids."

"Um, no. No minions or two-eyed Daves for me." He tugged her closer.

Charlie let him pull her in. She rested her cheek against the granite of his chest, relaxing against him, relishing the feel of something—no, someone—warm and solid.

"So how about you, Miss Charlotte? What do you do for fun around here when all the work is done?" His voice reverberated through his upper body, a low, rich baritone that tugged at places deep within her.

"Ha. That's just it. All the work is never done." He'd find out soon enough what she meant by that if he stuck around.

"Well, now that I'm here, that will be my top priority."

"What? Making sure the work gets done? Because we don't have the staff as it is to—"

"No." He pulled back to meet her gaze. "Making sure you have more fun."

His eyes held either a hint of a promise or a full-fledged challenge. Maybe a bit of both. But Charlie was too far out of her element to decipher it.

She tucked her head back against his chest. "Fun's overrated."

"We'll see about that."

She smiled into his neck. Where had this guy come from? He wasn't anything like she'd imagined. She'd pictured Sully's grandson to be some uptight, pencil-pushing yes-man who slicked his hair back and wouldn't be caught dead in a pair of ropers. Thank goodness she'd been wrong.

The band continued to play while she and Beck slowly circled the dance floor. It had been so long since she hadn't had to be in charge. It was nice to let him take the lead, if only for a song.

A song she didn't want to end.

Beck turned as another couple bumped into them, shielding her from the impact. As he did, his foot slid between her boots. Their hips pressed together for the briefest of moments before his leg brushed against the apex of her thighs.

They both moved forward at the same time, and the friction—the sweet, undeniable friction of his thigh on her—oh dear Lord—made her freeze. Her chest heaved. Her face ignited. Her whole body shuddered.

"You okay, Charlie?" His expression changed from concern to surprise as he must have realized the terrible awkwardness of the moment. Mortified, she jerked away and made some flimsy excuse about having to check something in the back room.

Beck released his grasp, and she forced her way across

the crowded dance floor to seek refuge in her office. Finally, slumped in her chair, in the privacy of her own space, her breathing slowed. She tried to convince herself he hadn't noticed. He'd been busy steering her around the dance floor. And they'd been bumped and jostled from every angle. He probably just thought she'd been pushed from behind. It would be her little secret.

No one ever needed to know that she'd almost had her first orgasm in more than eight years on the thigh of a stranger in the middle of the Rambling Rose's crowded dance floor.

⎯Ht⎯

By the time Charlie gathered her wits about her and ventured out of the office to start the closing routine, the band had wrapped up its set. While she cleared tables and swept peanut shells off the floor, the last few customers finished their beers, searched for their car keys, and said their goodbyes. Those horny enough to find a hookup ushered their one-night stands out the door. Charlie took a break to rest her feet and check in with her favorite, and only, sister-in-law.

"You looked pretty darn cozy cuttin' a rug out there tonight. How long did you say your New Yorker was staying in town?" Darby nudged Charlie with her hip, sending her sailing a few inches down the bench.

"First off, he's not *my* New Yorker. Second, he's staying with your parents. You know better than I do. Just through the weekend, right?" Aside from their unfortunate slow dance, the aftermath of which she was still trying to squeeze out of her system, Charlie had tried to pay as little attention to Beck as humanly possible. But even when only allowing herself to shoot an occasional glance his direction, she'd still felt his presence in the bar. He repelled and pulled her in, like a magnet that kept flipping polarity, and it had thrown her off all night. She hadn't wanted to face him after their dance. Thank God he must have left while she hid out in her office.

"He and Dwight sure seemed to hit it off." Darby took a long draw on the striped straw sticking out of her tall lemonade.

"Dwight could talk the ears off a chicken."

Darby giggled. "True. But I saw you checking Beck out."

"Hard not to. He's at least half a head taller than anyone else in the bar. Almost had to duck under the doorway into the dance hall. Maybe we should lower it so he knocks himself out." Maybe then he'd run back to New York, and she wouldn't have to spend the next three months dousing herself in ice water.

"Come on. Don't you want him to keep the Rambling Rose in the family? You told me that's what Sully asked."

Charlie cursed herself for confiding in Darby. She never should have told her about Sully's dying wish. At least she hadn't broken the stipulation of the will. Mr. Hill had made it clear that if she revealed the fact she'd inherit the Rambling Rose if Beck couldn't hack it, she'd forfeit her claim as well.

"I just don't know if he'll be able to pull it off. You should have seen the shoes he had on earlier today."

"He sure looked fine in those Levi's." Darby wiggled her eyebrows.

Charlie's cheeks heated at the thought of exactly how

fine those jeans had been to her. "You aren't supposed to be looking at anyone's Levi's, my friend. Don't make me tell my big brother you were checking out Mr. Manhattan."

"Your big brother likes it when I come home from the bar all hot and bothered."

Charlie covered her ears with her hands. "La la la. I'm not listening. TMI, Darbs, TMI."

Darby slung her arm around Charlie's shoulder and planted a smacking smooch on her cheek. "Love ya, babe."

"Love you, too, sweets. Now get on outta here before Waylon reads me the riot act for keeping you out past curfew."

"Big wimp. He didn't even make it to ten o'clock. He'll be sound asleep by the time I get home. Probably snoring like a freight train. At least until I wake him up for a little *you know what*."

"No more. My ears can't take any more."

"Don't work too hard." Darby stood, keys in hand. "You're still coming by tomorrow to help with Baby Back's costume, right?"

"I can't believe you're going to keep that contest going."

"Are you kidding me? It's a tradition. Besides, Baby Back has to defend her title. I think we're a shoo-in."

"Does your New Yorker know he's in charge of a pig beauty pageant?"

Charlie smirked, imagining the look on Beck's face when she broke the news. "Not yet, but he will." Then the rest of what Darby had said sank in. Her smile morphed into a scowl. "And stop calling him *my* New Yorker. I don't want to have anything to do with him. What kind of guy ignores his dying grandfather's calls for help?" She wasn't ready to address the love/hate thing she had going for the man with the magic jeans. As far as she was concerned, tonight had proven one thing: he had turned into her personal kryptonite.

Darby linked her arm with Charlie's, and together they made their way to the back door. "Maybe the kind who didn't know his grandfather was dying? I don't know. He seems like a nice guy. I'm having a hard time believing he's as coldhearted as you think."

Charlie screwed her lips into a puckered frown and pondered that thought for a moment, not wanting to admit that Darby's assessment might match her own. At least so far. "Whatever. You don't think he'll actually move here, do you? Leave his family and friends in New York and settle in for the next few months?"

"I guess we'll have to wait and see. But I figure a lot of that will depend on you."

"Me?"

"Yeah. Are you going to help him?"

Charlie let out a long sigh. "I don't think I have a choice."

"You've always got a choice, hon. It's just that you're so used to doing the right thing you don't know how to say no to someone in need."

"It's not that. I promised Sully."

"Don't get me started. You and your promises. I love you for them, but you make me crazy sometimes. Always putting everyone else first."

Charlie gave her best friend a gentle nudge. "Get on outta here."

"I'm going. Good night."

Darby unlocked her four-by-four truck with the key fob, and Charlie stood in the doorway, caught between the eerie quiet of the deserted honky-tonk and the almost musical barrage of thousands of cicadas, to make sure Darby got to the truck safely. It had been a long day. Just like the ones before it and the ones that would come after.

She turned back into the Rambling Rose, picking up where she'd left off clearing the tables. That's how she liked it—routine, predictable, safe. And no out-of-town city boy was going to sweep in and mess up her mojo.

Not if she had anything to say about it.

## FIVE

BECK PULLED INTO THE GAS STATION AND TOSSED THE to-go cup of coffee into the tall metal trash can. The coffee they served at the bed-and-breakfast wasn't bad. It just wasn't his usual triple-dark espresso. And when he didn't get his regular caffeine fix, his whole day was thrown off. Maybe the gas station had a commercial coffee machine—something that might be a tad bit closer to his preferred brew.

He picked up the end of the hose, fiddling with the pump as Dwight came out of the small convenience store and ambled over to the SUV. "Mornin'."

"Good morning." Beck held the handle in one hand and his credit card in the other. "Where's the slot to pay at the pump?"

Dwight took the handle from him, then shoved it into the opening of the gas tank. "We do things the old-fashioned way around here. You gotta come inside to pay."

"Oh, sure." Beck swept his gaze around the small gas station. He should have been able to figure that out—it was just that he hadn't actually filled a car with gas in quite a while. Unless he was traveling outside of Manhattan, he usually kept his two-door sports car garaged and used his dad's driver or a town car service. He decided not to share that information with Dwight. No sense in letting him think Beck was even more out of place than he already felt.

"Ya have fun last night?" Dwight tucked his thumbs through his belt loops, studying Beck from under the brim of his ball cap.

"Yeah. I didn't realize how busy the bar would be. Seems to do a good business."

"The Rambling Rose is about the only big draw we got. Well, that and all the freakin' festivals. People around here want to have a party for the damndest stuff. Charlie's been doing a good job keeping things going." He popped a toothpick in his mouth and moved it to the corner of his lips.

Beck nodded and glanced up the street. Few people were out and about this morning. Was it the threat of rain or just a typical Saturday morning in June in a place like Holiday? If he'd been at home, he would have already hit the gym and the shower and either be heading into the office or reading the paper at the coffee bar on the ground floor of his building.

"So have you got any coffee shops around here?" Dwight would probably know.

"What, like a place that just sells coffee?" Dwight shook his head and fingered the toothpick. "Nah. But I can make you a pot of Folgers if you want."

The pump ground to a stop and clicked off, the crabby machinery mimicking the groan Beck stuffed down inside. "No, that's okay. I can probably get something at the bar."

The ball cap bobbed in agreement. "Yeah, Charlie makes a mean cup of coffee. A good breakfast, too. Course, she likes to eat early in the morning. Sometimes even before the darn roosters start crowing. She's an early riser." Dwight's eyes narrowed as if checking to see if Beck was buying into what that implied.

"Great." He screwed the gas cap back in place, ignoring Dwight's claim. If there was anything going on, Beck had no doubt it was strictly one-sided. "So should I come in so you can run my card?"

"Yeah." Dwight turned toward the store, and Beck followed. "So, man to man, can I ask you a question?"

"Sure. What's up?"

"I started to ask you last night. What are you gonna do with the Rambling Rose? Everybody in town knows about Sully's will."

"They do?"

Dwight snorted. "Before you'd even left Hill's office, word was on the street that you don't get a darn thing until you spend three months here."

"Word travels fast, I guess." So much for attorney–client confidentiality.

"Might be the only thing that moves fast around here."

Beck made it a point to file that piece of information away to ponder later—one more thing to take into consideration. If he moved to Holiday, he'd be giving up the cloak of anonymity that living in a huge metropolis like New York provided. He'd never been overly concerned about his privacy; spending half his life as the sidekick of his outspoken father had cured him of that. But what would it be like to have his business spread from stranger to stranger before he even knew about it himself? That wasn't something he necessarily wanted to experience firsthand.

"I haven't figured out what I'm going to do yet. The news hasn't quite sunk in, but I'll be sure to let you know when I make up my mind."

Dwight handed him his credit card along with a receipt for his signature. "Hill tell you what happens if you don't stick around?"

"You mean what happens to Sully's inheritance?"

"Yeah, the old blowhard fill you in on that?"

"No, I'm afraid he said he wasn't at liberty to share that information."

"I bet. He ain't very good at keeping secrets though. I'll see what I can find out."

"Uh, thanks."

The drawer of the cash register dinged when Dwight opened it to slide the credit card slip inside. "You take care now, ya hear?"

"See you around." Beck passed through the door, causing the bells above to jangle. Maybe Dwight wasn't so bad. Beck could benefit from having someone looking out for him around town. He'd have to comp Dwight a few rounds next time he came to the bar. He seemed like the kind of guy who would appreciate a few free beers. And if it kept Beck in his good graces, all the better.

*Ht*

A few minutes later, Beck cringed as his SUV approached the Rambling Rose. Last night, set against a red-and-orange sky, the building had taken on an almost romantic, glowing tone. Now, under the unforgiving bright light of day, the rosy-pink-clapboard building showed its age. A hundred-plus years of sitting in the dusty, blistering-hot Texas heat had caused the paint job to fade in spots. What crazy-ass ancestor had insisted on painting the whole building Pepto-Bismol pink?

"More like Pepto Dismal," he muttered under his breath. The heat must have been getting to him. Had he actually said that out loud? But the building stuck out like a giant eyesore among the other old-fashioned storefronts with their small-town-Americana vibe. Why hadn't someone updated it over the years?

The marketing team in New York would have a blast reworking the honky-tonk concept, bringing the bar into the current century. He took a turn around the building, cringing as his gaze ran over the peeling paint, rusty hinges, and sparse landscaping efforts. Even he could take a stab at sprucing the place up. He'd been involved in a nightclub project a couple of years before. When he got back to New York, he'd make sure to pull the files and see if any of those concepts would transfer from the Meatpacking District of Manhattan to the backwater town of Holiday. Not likely, but he might get lucky and come up with a few ideas.

He walked under a banner promoting the oyster festival. Since he'd opted for his slip-on loafers that morning, his footsteps landed on the wood-plank entrance ramp with a soft thunk. Much better than the loud clatter when he'd been wearing those new boots. The guy at the western wear place had assured him they'd loosen up once he'd worn them for a bit, but the blisters on his heel and pinky toe had made him hesitate to slide them back on this morning. It wasn't like he was required to wear boots…was he?

The screen door squeaked as he yanked it open. Didn't anyone know how to use a can of WD-40? Charlie and another woman looked up as he entered the nearly empty dance hall. A giant pile of pink fabric and a sewing machine sat in front of them.

"Oh, hey, didn't expect you until later on today." Charlie turned her attention back to the machine.

"What's going on?" Shiny ribbon, beads, and silvery sparkly stuff covered half of the long table.

"I don't think we've met." The other woman swung her legs over the bench and stood. "I'm Darby, Charlie's sister-in-law. So nice to meet you, Beckett."

"Please, call me Beck." Something about the friendly brunette put him at ease. Could have been the warm brown eyes. Or maybe it was the fact that she actually smiled at him as opposed to Charlie's distinct disinterest this morning. "Sister-in-law, you said?"

"Yep. I'm married to one of her brothers."

"The ugly one." A man entered the ballroom with a stack of papers in his hand. "Charlie, I need you to take a look at these numbers." He stopped in front of Beck. "Hey, I'm Statler, the good-looking one."

"How many brothers do you have again?" Beck asked, taking Statler's hand in a firm grip.

"Five. Waylon is Darby's husband. Then there's Cash, Statler here, Presley, and Strait." Charlie rattled off their names without looking up. "I'm the youngest of six with five older brothers. Can't you just imagine all the guys who were willing to risk the wrath of the Walker brothers and take me out to scoop the loop?"

Beck digested that information. Five older brothers? If the other four looked anything like Statler, he could imagine Charlie's dating prospects had been limited. The guy was built like a Mack truck.

A Mack truck that had swallowed a tank.

"So you're Sully's grandson?" Statler tipped up the brim of his cowboy hat and gave Beck the once-over.

"That's me. You said you had numbers for Charlie to look at?" Beck asked. "Do you do the books?"

Charlie let out a sigh and stood up, abandoning the mess of sparkly pink fabric. "Darby, we'll have to finish this later." She turned to Beck. "Statler's a CPA in San Marcos, but he's been helping Sully with the books on the side. Come on, let's head back to the office."

Beck followed as Charlie and Statler led the way, their boots clomping on the wood floors. He hadn't been able to get a good look at the inside of the bar last night since there'd been so many people. As he passed through the cavernous space, his gaze ran over the decor. Photographs lined the walls—mostly black and white and all of them autographed. Hundreds of pictures of what he assumed were country-western stars. A few neon signs clustered over the long bar. Every inch of space held either a framed photograph or a piece of memorabilia: street signs, guitars, even an old washboard. Eclectic and odd—a strange combination and a far cry from the places he typically frequented.

Charlie entered the office first, rounded the desk, and plopped into a tall chair. "What's up, Statler?" She gestured to a folding chair across from the desk, and Beck sat down.

She sure had herself worked up over something this morning. He'd had a good time last night, and she'd seemed to be enjoying herself, too. But now she'd erected some sort of frosty facade between them. That was too bad. He actually wouldn't have minded taking another turn around the dance floor with her nestled in his arms. He'd spent most of his life trying to figure out the complicated layers of the fairer sex, with limited success.

But business he could handle. He pushed thoughts of the soft, warm, compliant Charlie from the night before out of his head and focused on the information in front of him.

"Good news and some bad." Statler dropped the stack of papers onto the corner of the huge, old desk. Beck and Charlie both leaned in to take a look at the top sheet. "Event business is up, but day-to-day numbers are down."

"Event business like what?" Beck asked.

"We rent out for private events." Charlie crossed her arms over her chest, and the chair creaked as she leaned back again. "Weddings, corporate stuff, private concerts, you know."

Weddings? Beck shook his head, trying to dislodge a vision of a bride and groom saying their vows in front of the tacky, twinkling arbor he'd spotted tucked back toward the rear of the stage. To each their own.

"We've got the pageant coming up. That always draws in a big crowd and should make up some of the numbers. And the tourists ought to pick up over the summer months, especially with the Father's Day Fiesta and the Founder's Day Festival. We've still got money set aside for a new coat of paint, right?"

Statler nodded.

"Good. I wouldn't worry about it too much yet." Charlie tapped her fingers on the edge of the desk. "I'll see if I can add a few more performers to the calendar for July or come up with something to generate more hype. Maybe have Angelo mix up the menu or bring in some special seasonal brew like last year."

"Uh, shouldn't you ask him what he wants to do?" Statler pointed the end of his mechanical pencil at

Beck. "Being the new owner and from the big city and all, I'm sure he's got some great ideas."

The weight of both their stares landed squarely on Beck. "Yeah, I'd like to get involved. See what you've got planned. I've managed a few projects where we revamped a nightclub and started up a micro gastropub. I'll see if any of those ideas will transfer over."

"What, like a dance club?" Charlie asked. Her face puckered and wrinkled, making her look like a raisin with serious doubts.

"Yeah." Beck automatically shifted into defensive mode. "Same kind of business concept."

Charlie snorted, passing a he-don't-know-nothin' look to her brother.

Beck's gut bristled. "You think that's funny?"

"Funny? No." Charlie leveled him with her glacier-blue gaze, freezing him in place. "It's asinine that you think you can come in and start changing the way we've done things around here for decades based on how you've been doing them in New York. In case you haven't noticed, you're not in New York anymore, Mr. Manhattan."

Beck leaned forward. "That's for sure. If I were in the city, I wouldn't have fifty blisters on my feet from those damn boots. Now, all that aside, I believe we have a common goal."

The spot between Charlie's eyebrows wrinkled. "Oh yeah?"

"Yes. Do what's best for the Rose. I'm not saying I have all the answers, but I do know a thing or two about business."

"Oh, that's right. You've got that piece of paper with the initials on it. What are they again? MBA."

How did she know he even had an MBA? He hadn't mentioned that to her. She must have noticed his confusion.

"Buddy wanted to make sure everyone knew about your Ivy League education. Four years at Columbia, MBA from Harvard... What do I know, huh? I don't even have a four-year degree. Just eight years of breaking my back, trying to keep this place going."

Statler stood. "Hey now. No need to get your britches in a wad. Beck, you don't want to piss off my baby sister. And, Charlie, give the man a chance before you automatically think the worst, okay?"

The silence stretched between them, charged with all that was left unsaid. Beck lifted his chin in her direction. "I'm going to need your help. From what I've heard, you know this place better than anyone, probably even better than my grandfather—"

Charlie's hands went to her hips. "Sully. For God's sake, can you call the man Sully?"

*That's* what she wanted to argue about? "Fine. Sully."

"And who exactly have you been talking to? You just got here last night."

"Everyone says so. The bartender—"

"Shep," Charlie interjected.

"The gal who served me my beer last—"

"Dixie," Charlie said.

"I'll learn everyone's name eventually. Hey, Dwight said so, too. He was very complimentary when I stopped in for—"

"You can ignore everything that comes out of Dwight's mouth." Charlie sagged back into the chair.

Statler chuckled, and Beck's head jerked toward the sound. He'd almost forgotten the man was even in the office.

"Yeah, if you haven't noticed, poor Dwight is somewhat taken with my baby sis." Statler rubbed a hand over the scruff on his chin, hiding his smirk.

"Dwight's harmless. Are we going to talk about business, or should I go finish my project?" Charlie swiveled toward Statler. "Got any other news to share?"

"Nope. I'll just leave these with you." He tapped the pile of papers. "I'm gonna take off now. Me and some of the guys are going tubing today."

Charlie's eyes sparkled. "Oh, you should take Beck. Introduce him to some of your friends and show him what life's like on the Guadalupe. I bet they don't tube down the Hudson, am I right?"

"Tubing?" Beck asked.

"Yeah"—Statler clapped him on the shoulder—"in an inner tube. You know, floating on a tube down the river. You're welcome to join us."

"Uh, I think I better use my time to learn more about the Rose. Maybe next time?" Beck asked.

"Sure thing. Don't work too hard." Statler walked to the doorway, then stopped and turned. "Oh, and Charlie?"

She looked up from the paperwork.

"Be nice to the poor guy, okay?" With a final wink, Statler left, and for the first time since that awkward moment last night, Beck was all alone with Charlie.

⟋⟋⟍

*Be nice?* Who was her brother kidding? Charlie clucked her tongue as she swept the papers Statler had left behind into an orderly stack. She could be nice. Heck, she was the epitome of nice.

Summoning all the sugary sweetness she carried inside, she pasted a smile on her lips and gestured to the papers in front of her. "Do you want to go over the calendar for the next few months, or do you have something else in mind?"

"Sorry, I'm still trying to absorb everything. I had no idea my grandfather"—he glanced at Charlie with what might pass as an apology in his baby blues—"I mean Sully, had so much going on down here. From what my dad told me, it seemed like there was a crappy bar and a two-room shack."

"Have you been by the house yet?" Charlie asked. Obviously he hadn't or he'd know how close to the mark a "two-room shack" might be in describing Sully's place. She'd been after Sully for years to update the hundred-year-old ranch house, but he'd preferred to invest his time and energy in the Rambling Rose instead.

"No, not yet. I was planning on heading over this afternoon."

"What are your other plans?" Had he decided whether to make a go of things in Holiday? The pot of coffee she'd downed earlier that morning slid around in her gut, and she pressed a palm to her stomach to stifle the gurgles. She couldn't believe her entire future hung in the balance, based on the whims of a guy who might find it fun to play cowboy for a few months.

He lifted a hand to rub the back of his neck and rolled his head from side to side. "You mean am I moving to Texas?"

Charlie shrugged. "People are curious. The folks around here don't like change."

"You're telling me." Beck blew out a breath. "No offense to you, but it looks like the bar could use a little updating."

Updating, great. What did the renegade outsider have in mind? She and Sully had made updates over the years. Sure, they needed a new coat of paint. Hadn't she just said that was in the budget? And the front might benefit from some new bushes, but those were minor things. Charlie stiffened, the hairs on her arms actually standing on end like a pissed-off porcupine, but she bit back a sharp retort. *Calm down, cowgirl. No use in getting all riled up.*

She took a deep breath and let her silent mantra play through her head. *For Sully. For Sully.* "Tell ya what. Why don't we grab a bite from the kitchen for lunch, and then I'll run you out to Sully's place? If you're up for it, we can cover the Rose together tonight, and you can get a real sense of what 'normal' looks like before you start makin' big plans to change it all up."

Beck stood, and she mimicked his posture, shoving her hands in the front pockets of her jeans and copying the shrug of his shoulders.

"That would be great. If it's not too much trouble?"

"No trouble at all." She moved around to the front of the desk and rested her butt against it. Aiming for a friendly, non-riled tone, she smiled. "Now, what sounds good for lunch? Chicken-fried steak, homemade mashed potatoes and gravy? Barbecue? We might have some homemade tamales left over."

"What kind of barbecue? Have you ever tried Korean barbecue? There's a fantastic place about a block from my condo."

"Seriously? You're in Texas. Home of the best barbecue in the world. Come on, you're having brisket." She almost linked her arm through his, remembered the last time they'd gotten too close, and ended up sidestepping to lead him down the hall. Korean barbecue? Her kitchen crew would have a coronary.

Beck took one long step to every two of hers as they passed through the back and into the dance hall. Darby must have gotten tired of waiting for her to come back. At least she'd picked up their sewing mess. The lunch crowd had shown up in force. Most of the locals avoided the place on the weekends because of the tourist crowd, but she recognized several neighbors and friends at the tables around the room. They probably just wanted to check out Sully's grandson. Well, let 'em get their fill.

She nudged Beck toward an empty table that just happened to be in the center of the room. "Why don't you get comfortable, and I'll put our order in right quick?"

Beck stepped over the bench and settled in.

Charlie almost patted him on the shoulder but reconsidered. Kryptonite. It would be best if she avoided contact. "Make yourself at home. I'll be back in a sec." How long would it take for someone to sidle up and introduce themselves? She scanned the room as she walked toward the kitchen. Her gaze landed on her cousin, a former competitor in the Junior Miss Texas competition. Yep, Brittany would be the one. As Charlie pushed through the swinging doors of the kitchen, Brittany had already scrambled over her seat on the bench across the room and headed in Beck's direction.

"Hey, Angelo," Charlie called out the back door of the kitchen, toward the barbecue pit where Angelo manned the spit.

His dark head of hair bobbed up and down—he probably had his earbuds in again. His love for blaring, head-banging heavy metal while he worked over the barbecue pit had forced her to require him to wear headphones. Otherwise the whole building shook with the bass boost from his boom box. She stepped down onto the dusty gravel drive and moved toward her favorite employee.

He nearly jumped into the nearby mesquite tree when she tapped him on the shoulder. Whipping around, he ripped the headphone wire out of the jack. A wailing guitar solo screamed from the speakers.

"Sorry, Boss." He dove for the volume dial while Charlie closed her eyes and drew in a deep breath.

Baby Back snorted through the fence. Angelo swore the pig loved it when he played his tunes. Charlie couldn't believe she was a fan of Angelo's favorite band, Porking Fetti, but the swine rubbed against the fence and grunted when the music ended as if she wanted more.

The threat of rain hung in the air. Charlie could smell it underneath the mouthwatering aroma of mesquite and slow-cooked brisket. She glanced toward the darkening clouds rolling in from the west. The crops could use a nice long drink, but the parking lot would turn into a mud pit if they got much rain. Nothing she could do about that.

"Hey, Angelo, Sully's grandson is having lunch with us today. Do you have any special cuts you can add to his brisket platter?"

"I heard he was in town. What did he say? Is he going to close us down? Has he made any decisions?" Like the rest of the staff, Angelo depended on his job at the Rambling Rose. Charlie wouldn't allow herself to think about what would happen to the employees if Beck decided to make a bunch of big changes. They were like a giant extended family, and she'd sworn to herself she'd protect them and their jobs as best she could.

"The only thing he's decided so far is that he'd like brisket for lunch. Can you make sure the guys fix up a good plate?"

"Oh, sure. I'm done out here for now anyway." Even though Angelo ran the kitchen, he preferred to handle the pits himself. The technique had been handed down from generation to generation, but some of their systems were top secret. Until Angelo had one hundred percent complete faith in the kitchen cooks, he wouldn't let them touch his sacred barbecue pit.

Charlie waited until the screen door slammed behind him, then took in a comforting breath. She'd never get tired of the ever-present smell of manure and the sweet aroma of freshly cut grass. Home sweet home.

"How you doing, girl?" She stepped to the edge of the pigpen and held out a couple slices of dried apricot she'd grabbed on her way out the door.

Baby Back snorted, gingerly snatching the treats from her hand. Since Sully had passed, Charlie had found herself talking to the crazy pig more and more. Baby Back was a good listener, too. As long as the treats and the scratches behind the ears kept coming.

"I can do this, right?" She reached through the fence to run her hand down the pig's coarse back. She'd cart Beck around and get a sense of what his plans were, if he'd even made any yet. Until then, she'd keep a good, tight rein on her temper—and her attraction—and trust that it would all work out.

Baby Back stuck her snout through the fence, trying to seek out another treat. It almost looked like she nodded in agreement. Charlie would take that as a yes. She turned over her last apricot, then brushed her palms over her thighs. Sully wouldn't have handed over his friends' futures to someone who would put them at risk. He must have had some sense of what kind of person his grandson had become, even if they'd never actually met.

Convinced she was doing the right thing, at least for the time being, she turned toward the bar. She might have to work with the man for now, but that didn't mean she wouldn't have a good time introducing him to some of their local traditions and specialties. With a smile on her lips and a swagger in her hips, she entered the honky-tonk and headed toward the kitchen.

They'd start with lunch.

# chapter
# SIX

"WHAT DID YOU SAY THIS WAS?" BECK CHEWED ANOTHER bite of his lunch. The meat had so much flavor, he'd stuffed himself past the point of full. If he didn't lay off, he'd have to unbutton his jeans.

"Just brisket. House specialty. You like it?" Charlie slid a bite into her mouth and chewed.

"Mmm." Beck nodded. "Delicious. And what are these? You said they were oysters?" He lifted one of the deep-fried nuggets from the paper-lined basket and turned it over in his fingers.

"I said they were Rocky Mountain oysters. They're a local specialty, and this weekend we're celebrating Rocky Mountain Oyster Days. You don't have to try them if you don't want to. Some folks don't like the thought of eating—"

"How do you like it, Boss? All's good?" A guy in a white apron stopped by the table.

Charlie dabbed at the corner of her mouth with a napkin. "Beck, this is our head cook, Angelo. He's the master of the barbecue."

"Nice to meet you, man." Angelo wiped his palm on his apron and offered it to Beck.

Beck popped the oyster into his mouth and grasped Angelo's hand for a quick shake.

"Oh." Charlie's eyes went wide.

He swallowed the rubbery bite, wondering what had ruffled her feathers this time. "Nice to meet you, too. This barbecue is fantastic. I've never had anything like it before."

The younger man looked at his feet and played off the compliment. "Aw, you know how it is. Just slap some seasonings on and cook it real slow in the pit."

Beck nodded like he had a clue about what Angelo meant. "And these little oysters are interesting, although I've got to say, they taste more like calamari."

Angelo put his hands up, palms out, in a gesture of self-defense. "Charlie thought you might like 'em. They're a real cowboy delicacy."

Charlie took a sip of her lemonade and coughed.

"What am I missing?" Beck asked.

"I tried to warn you, but you didn't give me a chance." Charlie's lips quirked into a lopsided smile.

"They're good. I just can't figure out where you get fresh seafood around here. Do you have it shipped in from the Gulf?"

"Seafood?" Angelo's forehead wrinkled. "Who told you they were seafood?"

"Oysters. Bottom of the ocean, live in a shell, right?" What was the big deal? Everyone knew where oysters came from.

"Oh, man." Angelo's hand went up to his mouth and covered a smile. "Those ain't real oysters, dude."

Beck tossed another one in his mouth, chewed, and swallowed. "Then what are they?"

Angelo glanced at Charlie, who appeared to be stifling a giggle, then leveled his gaze at Beck. "Bull testicles."

Beck's stomach rolled over, and the contents spun around like a Tilt-A-Whirl. "Wait. You're feeding me bull testicles? Like, cow balls?" He grabbed his napkin and wiped at his lips.

Charlie hunched over the table, her shoulders shaking in silent laughter.

"Yo, sorry, man. Charlie thought you might want to try them." Angelo backed away toward the kitchen door.

Charlie lifted her head. Her eyes watered. She'd laughed so hard she'd cried. And all at his expense. She wiped at her cheeks with her napkin. "I'm sorry. I really did try to warn you. But the expression on your face…"

Her mouth split into a wide, sunny smile. *Beautiful,* Beck thought before pushing it away.

"All right," he said, beginning to grin back, "you got me. What's with the fishnets though? You've got seashells hanging from the ceiling."

"Dixie gets a kick out of playing up the oyster part. It's kind of a joke." She bit her lip again in what appeared to be an attempt to keep from smiling. "I really am sorry. Think of it as kind of an initiation." The plates clanged together as she stacked their dirty dishes. "And you passed."

"Yay me," Beck said with a laugh. "Hey, at least you don't serve Zungenwurst here."

"What's that?"

"A type of blood sausage. My nanny used to make it. Pig tongues, bacon, a little bit of blood, and onions." He stood.

Charlie wrinkled her nose. "That sounds disgusting."

"No worse than cow balls."

"Aw, come on. Just having a little bit of fun." Her hip nudged his when she passed him on the way to the kitchen.

Easy for her to say. He didn't see Charlie tossing back any bull balls. He followed her out of the dance hall, shooting a glance back to the fishnets and plastic seashells. The hot brunette who'd stopped by to introduce herself earlier lifted her fingers and wiggled them in his direction.

Charlie must have noticed the exchange. "I'd steer clear of her."

"Oh yeah? What makes you say that?" Beck asked. She seemed friendly enough. A heck of a lot friendlier than the hot-and-cold vibes he kept getting from the jokester next to him.

"That's my cousin Brittany. She's working on her MRS degree."

MRS... Was that some kind of nursing program? "I don't get it. Is that a local thing?"

Charlie snorted. "Oh, you could say that. She's on the hunt for a husband. MRS...get it? Missus? She thought she had a guy from Austin hooked a few months ago, but it fell through."

"She seems nice enough."

"Yeah, as long as your credit card has a big limit, you'll be fine." Charlie dropped the dishes off in a bin in the kitchen and washed her hands at the sink. "Ready to go check out Sully's place? I have to be back here by four. We've got live music tonight, and it's going to be pretty busy."

"Sure. Let's go."

Charlie said her goodbyes to the staff and led him through the maze of hallways to a back door. "You want to drive so you know how to get there?"

"Yeah, okay." He walked past a fenced-in enclosure, doing a double take when a giant pig rubbed against the wood planks and snorted. *What the hell?*

"Hold up." Charlie walked over and scratched behind the pig's ears through the fence. "I don't think you've officially met Baby Back. She's the Rose's formal mascot and the reason you ran off the road yesterday."

Beck grabbed the top plank and leaned over the fence. The pig squealed and snorted, apparently enjoying Charlie's attention. "Why—"

"Why what? Why a pig?"

He nodded. "Yeah, unless you're planning on serving a lot of bacon. Is it sanitary to keep a pet pig so close to where people eat their dinner?"

Charlie's jaw dropped. "Don't insult the reigning Rambling Rose's Sweetest Swine."

"Excuse me? The Rambling Rose what?"

Baby Back continued to rub against the fence as Charlie dug into the flesh behind her ears. "She was crowned the Rose's Sweetest Swine in last year's pageant. She'll defend her title in a couple of weeks. That's what I was working on when you got here— her costume."

"Wait a minute. You put this pig in a costume? For some sort of *pageant*?" Jeez, this place was weirder than he'd originally thought. Bull balls and costuming ginormous pigs. What other whacked-out traditions would he be subjected to before he got back to civilization?

Charlie stood and crossed her arms over her chest. She seemed to take that stance with him a lot, and they hadn't even known each other twenty-four hours yet. "I'll have you know that folks come from hundreds of miles around for our annual competition. It's a huge draw, and we pull in buckets of money that weekend."

"And all these people come to see your pig in a costume? Sounds like a porker of a good time."

"Not just my pig. We usually get upward of fifty entries. Just wait and see. Baby Back will win again, won't you?" She leaned over the top rail to run her hand along the pig's back.

"Fifty pigs in costumes?" Beck laughed. "Definitely won't want to miss that."

"Go ahead, make fun. But when you see the profits, you'll be squealing too."

"And anyone can enter?" Who were these crazy people who toted dressed-up pigs hundreds of miles? He'd for sure plan to be in town that weekend to check it out. That is, if he decided to try to make a go of it.

"Yeah, you should enter."

He caught the challenge in her voice even before he saw it in her eyes. She didn't think he could do it.

"Maybe I will." He reached a tentative hand through the fence to swipe a palm over the pig's back.

"Here, give her an apricot and she'll love you forever." Charlie dug into her pocket and pulled out a handful of dried apricot slices.

"I've got to say, I've never been on the receiving end of a pig's affection." He held an apricot through the fence, and the pig snuffled it out of his fingers, leaving a little slobber on his hand. It tickled. What was a little pig drool anyway?

"She likes you." Charlie gave him an authentic smile, not the forced, icy ones she'd been tossing him all day.

"Maybe I've got an undeveloped talent for working with pigs. All this time and I never realized."

"Maybe you do. Enter the contest, and we'll find out. Baby Back needs some stiff competition this year."

Beck held out another apricot. "All right. I will." At that moment, he vowed not only to find a freaking pig and enter the contest, but also to win.

"Good. We probably ought to head out. Looks like it's going to rain, and you'd probably rather have a chance to walk around the property without getting soaked."

The sky had darkened even more in the few moments since they'd stepped outside. "Okay, let's go."

Charlie gave the pig one last pat, then caught up to Beck on the way to his SUV. "I can't wait for you to see the place."

Beck beeped the key fob to unlock the car. He and Charlie were taking off for unchartered territory...it would be just the two of them this afternoon. Alone. Hopefully they'd be able to avoid any additional uncomfortable interactions. It wasn't his fault they'd shared an awkward moment last night. After the frosty reception she'd given him earlier, she'd seemed to put it behind her, pretended like nothing had happened, and moved on.

Hopefully he'd be able to do the same.

◆

Charlie pointed out the property lines as they drove onto Sully's land. "He's got a thousand acres. Most of it rents out for grazing to my folks. I think the house sits on about three acres or so. At least that's how much we kept mowed for him."

"So your family lives next door?"

"Kind of." For Beck, "next door" probably meant sharing a wall. Would he be able to grasp the idea of having neighbors he couldn't actually see? "My family's ranch butts up against Sully's land on two sides. We've got about a hundred thousand acres."

"Is that a lot?"

Charlie wiggled her shoulders into a half-hearted shrug. She didn't want to brag, but the land had been in her family for more than a hundred years, and her dad managed one of the oldest family-owned ranches in Texas. "I suppose it's a lot. There are others that are a lot bigger." And even more that had been swallowed up or sold off bit by bit over the years. Hopefully her family ranch would never see the same fate, at least not with Waylon taking over.

Beck stopped the SUV in front of the single-car garage as the first juicy raindrop plopped onto the windshield. "Should we make a run for it?" he asked.

"You have the keys, right?"

He held up his key ring and opened his door. A crack of lightning split across the sky, and Charlie flung the door open and raced to the stoop of Sully's tiny rambler.

Beck fumbled with the keys, trying to find the one that fit the lock.

The front of Sully's place didn't have an overhang or any protection from the weather. Fat drops of rain splashed down from an angry sky, soaking through their shirts and pasting their clothes to their skin.

"Forget it." Charlie grabbed Beck's arm and dragged him toward a door on the side of the garage. "Let me see if the garage is unlocked." She turned the knob, wiggled it a bit, and turned it the other way. The door swung wide open into the pitch-black garage.

A flash of lightning raced across the sky, sending a burst of light through the windows. Charlie wondered what Beck would make of the tarp-covered monstrosity taking up every square inch of the space. He moved past it toward the interior door, not seeming to notice. The door creaked open as he turned the knob, and the walls of Charlie's chest squeezed together, causing her heart to falter for a beat.

Sully.

The familiar smell of saddle soap and boot cream smacked into her as she entered the spotless kitchen. She hadn't been in his house since the night he'd died, and she was unprepared for the way her grief bubbled up and overflowed. Hadn't she said her goodbyes? If only he'd been at peace when he'd passed. Up until the end, he'd asked about Beck... if he'd responded to his letters or the messages the hospice nurse had left.

Suddenly, she felt an urgent need to understand exactly why Beck hadn't come. It was too late for Sully to hear it for himself, but Charlie was sure his spirit lingered nearby. Beck owed him an explanation, and she would be the one to wrangle it from him.

"So, what do you think?" She flipped the kitchen light on—an ancient brass fixture meant to look like an old-style lantern that hung over the small two-seater table.

"It's, uh, quaint?" Beck's observation sounded more like a question.

"Sully didn't believe in living high on the hog. He was very conservative when it came to spending his money—and kind. He was truly one of the most caring people I've ever met."

Beck shifted his weight from foot to foot. "That's

not exactly how my dad described him. I wish I'd had the chance to meet your version of my grandfather."

Charlie reached into a drawer by the freestanding range and passed Beck a dish towel, then took one for herself. "But you did have the chance to meet him. How come you never came? He sent dozens of letters. They all came back."

"I don't know what you're talking about. I never received—or expected—any letters. My dad said there was bad blood between the two of them. As far as I know, when my grandfather kicked my dad out, he never heard another word from him. He started up his business in New York, he met my mom, they had me, they got divorced, he met my stepmom, and then he met the second stepmom. You know how the story goes, right?"

Charlie narrowed her eyes. "So you had no idea Sully was trying to reach you?"

Beck placed his palms flat on the retro white Formica counter with its golden starbursts. "No. Like I said, I barely heard about him. My dad said they weren't close. He never wanted to talk about it, and I suppose I just let it go."

"Let it go?" She couldn't imagine not being surrounded by family. She'd spent her whole life in Texas and had never wanted to be anywhere else. "You never wondered about your own flesh and blood?"

"Sure I did. It's…" Beck blew out a long breath and met her gaze. "It's complicated. Can we just leave it at that for now?"

His eyes begged for a break. A hint of grief mixed with resignation and defeat. She'd seen a similar look on her dad's face before. It was the look of regret, of wishing things might have been different. She'd let it go. For now.

"So you want to see the rest of the place?" she asked.

"Sure, lead the way." Beck ran his hands over his face, then shoved them in his back pockets and followed her through the doorway into the living room.

A large picture window stretched across the front wall. Sully's beat-up recliner angled toward the ancient television set, and a woodburning stove perched in the corner of the room. If she closed her eyes, she could picture Sully rocking back and forth, a static-filled baseball game on the screen and his lucky coin flipping between his fingers.

What she wouldn't give for a chance to ask him for guidance. Did he really think his grandson could handle the Rose? Did he want this complete stranger who didn't know anything about family and the importance of tradition to take over instead of her? She waited, wishing and hoping for some kind of sign.

Nothing.

Beck moved to a wall of picture frames. Newspaper clippings, some faded and yellow, some more recent, hung on the fake wood paneling. Charlie had studied them during visits in the past. Beck's dad's career could be traced from his first big sale to some of his most recent projects in the frames on the wall. Photos clipped from magazines and newspapers pressed against the glass. There was even a picture of Beck when he was little from an article about his dad and his second wife, some supermodel.

Charlie would have given a Buffalo nickel to know what Beck was thinking as his gaze passed over each frame. Did he wonder about the kind of man his grandfather had been? Was he sorry he'd never had the chance to know him? She paused while he studied the images and headlines in the murky light. Her finger hovered on the light switch, but she didn't want to disturb the moment.

Beck reached the end of the pictures and poked his head through one of the three doorways in the hall. "What's in here?"

"That's the guest room. I think your grandmother used it for a sewing room a long time ago. Probably was your dad's room when he lived here, but that was way before my time."

Beck flipped the light on, and Charlie stepped behind him as he surveyed the tiny room. A sewing machine cabinet sat along one wall, and a single bed had been tucked into the corner. The air felt denser here, like no one had disturbed the space for a long, long time.

"Sully's room is over here, and then there's a bathroom. That's it. It's not much, but he sure loved it."

Beck glanced in the bathroom, then walked the length of the hall and entered Sully's room. Charlie didn't follow. The last time she'd been in that room, she'd held Sully's hand as he took his last breath. She wasn't ready to confront the emptiness yet.

"So that's it?" Beck asked, reentering the hall.

"Yep, that's it. Like I said, it's not much." Why did she feel the need to apologize? It wasn't like she cared what Beck thought of the place or even what he thought of Holiday for that matter. "I'd offer to show you around the yard, but I'm not sure you'd be able to see anything in this rain."

While they'd been inside, the skies had opened up, and a full-blown summer thunderstorm now raged outside the windows.

"That's okay. Another time. Which way did you say your family lives?"

"Um, I didn't." She walked back into the kitchen and stood against the back window. "Can you see that fence over there?"

Beck came up next to her, and goose bumps popped up on her skin as his arm brushed hers. "Over there?"

"Yeah." As she moved her arm away, she caught sight of their reflection in the window. He stood slightly behind her, his eyes wide, probably trying to take in the vast openness of Sully's land. Beck looked completely out of his element, but something about his stance reminded her of Sully. His breath tickled her ear, making her hyperaware of how close he was. She wanted to step back from the window, but her feet wouldn't budge. Instead, she cleared her throat, dismissing the dizzying sensation of his body next to hers. "Beyond that fence is our land. We kind of have a large L, and Sully's—well, your property now—sits in the crook of it."

Beck half turned to her, a crease wrinkling his forehead. "So I'm surrounded by you on two sides."

"Well, fortunately for you, my place is on the opposite side. So you're really butting up against the pasture land we use for grazing."

"Who are my other neighbors?"

"A couple of hobby farms and a tract of land that belongs to somebody up in Dallas. It's pretty quiet around here." She turned back toward the living room. "One more thing. Sully asked me to make sure you got his letters."

He followed her to a built-in cabinet by the TV.

"There are a bunch of them. I think he saved every single one." She pulled open the door and had to use both hands to grab the old leather case. "He wanted to make sure you got them."

Beck nodded toward the case. "These are all to me?"

"You and your dad." She unzipped the case and picked a yellowed envelope out of the stack. "Return to sender" had been scrawled in angry red ink across the front. "I haven't read them. He just asked me to make sure you got them if you ever came around."

Beck held the envelope she handed him for a drawn-out moment, like he didn't know what to do with it. The far-off look in his eyes told her he was a world away, lost in his own thoughts. Finally, he set it back in the case.

"You don't want to take them with you?" She didn't mean to pry. But if she knew Sully, he'd probably filled the letters with his hopes and dreams for the Rose. If Beck read the letters, surely he'd realize how important the honky-tonk was to the town. And how important the town was to Sully.

"I'll get them later. I've only got a carry-on with me, so I don't have a way to get them home."

Eyes narrowed into slits, she battled between begging him to read the letters and telling him to shove the suitcase up his pasty-white Yankee ass. Before she could arrange her words into the perfect insult, the scent of saddle soap tickled her nose.

*For Sully.*

Dammit, the old man better not be wrong. It wasn't just her job he'd gambled on; it was the future of the Rose—the future of Holiday itself. The town wouldn't be anything without the honky-tonk. And if Sully thought his grandson would be able to rise to the task, well, she'd promised him she'd do what she could to help.

Fine. She bit back the bitter words she wanted to hurl and made her way to the door to the garage. "Let's head back. It's a big night at the Rose, and with this weather, we won't be able to seat anyone outside."

Beck didn't follow, just stood in the middle of the small living room, dwarfing it with his presence. He didn't belong here. She could make all the suggestions she wanted, dress him up like a cowboy Ken doll and teach him how to two-step like a western Fred Astaire, and he still wouldn't fit in. But she owed Sully the effort.

She took a few steps back and placed her hand on his arm. The same spark she'd felt last night ignited in her core.

"Look. I don't mean to press about Sully. It's just that…he was like a second dad to me." Her eyes welled. *Do not let him see you cry, not here, not now.* She let her hand fall from his arm and wiped away the unshed tears.

Beck turned to her, the grief she'd suspected before now etched across his face. "I wasn't expecting…" He turned in a slow circle. "This. I wasn't expecting anything like this."

Charlie struggled to tamp down her raw emotion. Before she could second-guess herself, she wrapped her arms around his midsection and hugged him tight. His arms went around her back, clamping her against him. She wanted to lean in, unleash the enormous bundle of heartache she'd been shouldering on her own.

With her nose pressed against his chest, she inhaled his scent, so foreign yet so comforting. She closed her eyes, drawing from his strength. The moment turned into minutes, and still they stood, locked together in the fading light of Sully's living room. Her breath slowed, matching his, and she became aware of the *thump thump thump* of his heartbeat under her cheek.

"You okay?" His voice came out gruff, like he was trying to stuff down any and all emotion.

She sighed. "Yeah."

His fingers brushed her hair back, tucking it behind her ear. She leaned into his touch, letting herself take comfort from his gentle caress. Almost imperceptibly, his breath quickened, but she could feel it in his chest. She pulled back, trying to read his face. What was he thinking?

His hands went to her shoulders. She lifted her chin to meet his gaze. There was regret in his eyes but something else too. Something that reached across their differences. Something that bound them together in this moment. She recognized the pain in his eyes because it was the pain she carried with her, too. Her chest expanded with the knowledge that someone else finally understood.

His gaze moved to her mouth, and her heart sparked. Oh dear God, he was going to kiss her. She wanted that kiss, could practically taste his lips on hers. With memories of Sully swirling around them, cloaking them in their shared grief, for the first time in a very long time, she felt a tiny spark of hope for the future.

But this was wrong. Not here. Not now. Not like this.

His lips met hers. Her nerve endings crackled to life, lighting up one at a time like a long-dormant circuit board.

The sparks traveled down the length of her body, then back up again. Her head tried to stomp on the brakes. But her mouth…her mouth wanted to devour him.

His hands went to her hair, cradling her head as his lips parted. She couldn't wait any longer. Before he had a chance, she deepened the kiss, clinging to his shoulders, holding on for dear life as sensations she hadn't allowed herself to think about in years raced through her limbs.

She hadn't let a man touch her like this since, well…since Jackson.

A war raged within her. It would be so easy to give in. Part of her wanted to. But she couldn't. Not here. Not now. Not with him. She pulled back, already missing the exquisite feel of his lips on hers before she broke contact completely.

"I can't. I'm sorry. This didn't happen." She turned and covered the short distance to the safety of the garage in a few short strides.

"Charlie, wait!"

Charlie burst through the door, out into the storm, not even noticing the pelting rain that soaked through her shirt and caused her makeup to run down her face. Her hand rubbed up and down her arm, trying to erase the trail of tingles Beck had incited. She'd do what she needed to do to give him every chance possible to meet the stipulations of Sully's will. But if he couldn't cut it or wanted to give up, she wouldn't stop him.

One thing Holiday didn't need was another outsider coming in and trying to change things. Especially an outsider with a sexy-as-hell smile who'd already breached her weak defenses and left her feeling raw, unprotected, and vulnerable.

She could still hear him calling for her from inside. If he wanted to make a go of it, he'd better get used to trying to keep up because she sure wasn't going to slow down for anyone.

## SEVEN

BECK CLAMBERED INTO THE QUIET SUV AND FOUND his way back to the Rambling Rose, a silent Charlie beside him. She didn't say a word for almost the entire fifteen-minute drive. What the hell had happened back there? He hadn't meant to kiss her. Especially not with all the talk of family and his dead grandfather and the thoughts of all the could-have-beens running through his head.

They'd gotten lost in a moment. An ill-timed, emotional, spur-of-the-moment moment. And as much as he hated to admit it to himself, it was a moment he wouldn't mind finding again.

But she'd been right to insist they pretend it had never happened. It would be a bad idea to try to start something with Charlie, no matter how awesome her ass looked in those low-slung jeans she always seemed to favor. No matter how fantastic her lips had felt on his. No matter how much she tugged on his heartstrings, trying to make him face his unknown past.

Best to keep things professional. And he'd start by making a peace offering. "Thanks for showing me around Sully's place."

Charlie stared straight ahead. "No problem. Like I said, it's not much, but he was happy there."

"I'll need to go through his things. Is that something you might be willing to help me with?"

They'd reached the bar, and she flung the door open before the SUV came to a complete stop. "We'll see. Right now we've got bigger things to worry about."

Beck peered out through the rain-spattered windshield to where two groups of guys shouted at each other on the covered porch of the Rambling Rose. Shep stood between them, hands out to his sides in an effort to preserve the peace. But then the yells turned to pushes and shoves. One man took a swing at the other right as Charlie dove into the fray. Before he had a chance to think about it, Beck launched himself from the front seat and hurled himself in the path of the bigger guy. Beck threw a block, frantically searching to make sure Charlie was okay, but he couldn't find her among what had quickly devolved into an all-out, old-fashioned barroom brawl.

Fists flew, bodies thumped against the wall of the building, and the frenzied energy of too much testosterone hung over the crowd. Dodging an uppercut to the chin, Beck thought he caught a glimpse of golden hair before someone plowed into him, sending him crashing into the railing of the porch.

A shriek whistled through the air, and fists and elbows fell. Charlie stood in the middle of it all, her fingers shoved between her lips, and whistled again.

"Enough. What's going on here? Where's Shep?" Even though she stood at least a head shorter than any of the guys, there was no mistaking who was in charge.

"Right here." Shep spoke up, holding his palm to his temple, a line of blood trickling down his arm.

"Double-booking snafu, Charlie. The fellas figured they'd settle it themselves out here in the parking lot."

"How did that happen? And why are you bleeding? I can't leave this place for an hour without someone doing something stupid." She stomped up the steps toward the front door. "Billy Ray, Presley, y'all come with me. Shep, go clean yourself up and make sure the bar's ready to go. It's gonna be a wild night tonight—I can feel it already."

The two heavyweights followed Charlie into the bar, and Beck stood by, wondering if he was supposed to trail after them.

"Beck, you might want to get in here, too." Her voice carried through the screen door, and he scrambled up the steps. By the time he found them in the office, she'd slumped into the chair behind the desk with a large calendar spread out in front of her. "I see what happened. Looks like Sully had Billy Ray on the books, but then it got erased. Did you cancel?"

"Naw." The guy with the bigger beer belly and lamb-chop sideburns looked down at his boots. "Not exactly, Miss Charlie. For half a second, I thought I might have to work tonight. But I called back and let Shep know I'd be here."

Charlie glanced at Beck. "Billy Ray works as an ER nurse and plays here on the weekends when he can."

Beck's eyes widened. Lamb Chops was a nurse? He wouldn't want that guy anywhere near him with a needle, much less a bedpan.

"But Waylon told me y'all needed someone to play tonight. I talked my whole band into coming down here. Now you're gonna send us home?" The other opponent crossed his arms over his chest. Something about the gesture reminded Beck of Charlie.

"Presley, don't whine. Mama says it's not attractive, plus it's not going to get you anywhere with me. You oughtta know that by now." She rolled her eyes and tilted her chin up toward Beck. "Presley, meet Beck. He's Sully's grandson and might be taking over the Rose."

Beck offered his hand for a quick shake. "Presley?"

"Yeah, all my siblings got named after country-music superstars, and I got saddled with *Presley*. Talk to me about life being fair." The blank look on Beck's face must have conveyed how completely at a loss he was because Presley continued. "You don't look like you know much about country music. Lemme fill you in. Waylon's the oldest. Named after Waylon Jennings, right? Cash lucked out being named after the Man in Black."

Waylon Jennings? The Man in Black? Beck scratched his head. They were all staring at him like he'd grown an extra arm or two.

"Johnny Cash? 'I Walk the Line'? 'Folsom Prison Blues'?" Presley shot a wide-eyed look to Charlie. "Where'd you find this guy?"

She crossed her arms over her chest, unconsciously mimicking Presley's pose from moments before. "New York City."

Presley clucked his tongue. "That explains it. So Statler's after the Statler Brothers, Strait because my mama got knocked up with him the night she saw George Strait play here. Then there's baby Charlotte. Dad finally settled on that when Mama convinced him he couldn't name her just Charlie after the Charlie Daniels Band." He shook his head. "And then there's freakin' Elvis Presley. Mama still remembers seeing him play the Rose all those years ago. Lucky me, huh?"

Beck almost laughed at the dejected look on his face. "Now Elvis is one I've heard of. Didn't know he was into country music though."

Billy Ray made the sign of the cross, let his eyes drift shut, and shook his head. "Don't let anyone else around here hear you say that. You see that shrine with the spotlight set up for him in the front room?"

How would he know if he had or not? The whole place was filled to the ceiling with crap. For now, he'd play along. "Sure. What about it?"

"That napkin belonged to the King himself. Rumor has it he wiped his mouth with it after trying a deep-fried peanut-butter-and-banana sandwich. He signed it, too. It was the one and only time he played the Rose," Billy Ray said.

"So about tonight." Charlie stood and shoved her hand in her front pocket. "We'll split the pay, and y'all can alternate sets. Billy Ray, call it—heads or tails." She withdrew a coin from her pocket and flipped it in the air.

"Heads," Billy Ray yelled.

It landed with a clatter and spun around before finally settling on the desk. "Heads it is," Charlie said, reaching for the coin.

"What kind of quarter is that?" Beck squinted at the shiny silver coin. On a second look, it appeared to be larger in size and shape than a regular quarter.

"It's a Texas Centennial half-dollar. Something Sully left me." Charlie handed it to him, and he rubbed his finger over the star and eagle on the front before passing it back.

"You want to go first or second, Billy Ray?" she asked.

"I'll let Pres go first. He can warm everybody up and get 'em ready for some *real* honky-tonk music." Billy Ray pursed his mouth into a smug smirk.

"If that's the way you want it…they won't want to stick around for your hog-calling after hearing me play," Presley spit out.

Charlie slid the half-dollar back into her pocket. "If y'all can't work it out, I'm sure I can get half a dozen other folks who'd be more than happy to come play tonight."

"That won't be necessary, Miss Charlie." Billy Ray threw an arm around the leaner man's shoulder. "Pres and me are happier than two hogs in a shit bath to get to share a stage. Ain't that right, hoss?"

Presley nodded. "You bet."

Charlie slapped a hand against her forehead. "Baby Back! I forgot to feed her this morning."

"Can I ask a question?" Three pairs of eyes landed on Beck. "What is it with the pig? I know you said tradition and all, but it seems to be a ton of trouble."

"A tradition's a tradition. Now come on, and I'll show you how it's done. Billy Ray, Pres, go get your stuff set up before I change my mind and kick all of y'all out of here."

The two men scuffled down the hall, and Beck had no choice but to follow Charlie through the kitchen and out the back door. "About the pig," he said, "I still don't get it. I can't believe the health department doesn't have a problem with that. Hell, in New York that kind of thing wouldn't fly."

Charlie rounded on him, hands on her hips. "There are a

lot of things you 'don't get' around here. And you *won't* get them unless you try pulling your head out of your butt and give this place a shot. We keep a pig because it's a tradition. This whole town *runs* on tradition." She pointed a finger at him like she wanted to poke him in the chest. "Stick around, and you'll see how much money this tradition makes during the pig beauty pageant. Things work just fine around here, and we don't need you coming in and shaking everything up."

Beck backed away, palms up. "Hey, I'm not trying to change things. I've barely been here twenty-four hours. Just trying to figure out why you keep a swine on staff."

The rain had slowed to a sprinkle but left the dirt parking lot a mess of mud. Charlie stomped over to a shed and came out with a bucket of grain. She climbed onto the fence and dumped it into a feed trough. "Not that it makes any difference to you, but people like her. She's got her own fan club on Facebook. I bet you don't have a mascot at your gastrointestinal nightclub."

"It was a nightclub and a gastropub. Separate businesses." Why he felt the need to explain himself, he wasn't sure. Neither one of those places even slightly resembled the kind of unique community Charlie and Sully had created in the Rose.

"The kids like her, too." Charlie towered over him, her feet still on the bottom rail of the fence as a dark shape moved toward the food, snorting and squealing along the way.

"And you serve a lot of kids here?" Beck asked. From what he could tell, the clientele consisted mainly of cowboy-boot-wearin', attitude-totin' adults.

"More than you might think." Charlie reached over the fence and snagged an empty bucket then walked over to a hose and filled it with water. "We've got a kids' open mic once a month, and we serve a family-style brunch on Saturday mornings."

Come to think of it, he had seen quite a few kids when he first arrived that morning. This place was turning out to be so much more than just the two-seater bar his dad had led him to expect.

Charlie heaved the bucket of water up to the fence.

"Let me help you with that." Beck took a step toward her and made a grab for the bucket.

"No, I got it." She struggled, not wanting to let the handle go.

"It's heavy. Let me help you."

"I said I got it." She jerked on the handle as he relented.

The edge tilted toward her as if in slow motion. Beck tried to make a grab for it, but the water splashed over, drenching the front of her shirt.

She dropped the bucket to the ground and glared up at him. The fire in her eyes burned hotter than a bonfire. A bonfire with gasoline poured over it.

He winced. "Charlie, I'm sorry. I was just trying to help."

"That's what I've been trying to tell you. I don't need your help. You want to be in charge? Go ahead. I'm going home to get out of these wet clothes and take a Saturday night off for the first time in five years. Have fun tonight, Beck."

*Oh no.* "Wait." He followed her retreating backside across the mud pit that had been a parking lot a couple of hours before.

She waved a hand over her head without turning around. "Enjoy being in charge."

Beck raced to catch up with her, sinking his foot into a giant puddle of mud as he dashed across the parking lot. He took two steps forward then stopped when he realized he'd lost his shoe a step back.

"Dammit." He whipped around, hoping to see his loafer sitting behind him. No luck. He half hopped with one shoe, one sock, slipping and sliding through the puddles. "Wait, Charlie. Let's talk about this."

She climbed into her truck and backed out of her parking spot. He almost caught her bumper, but then the tires spun, flinging mud and water and God only knew what else. By the time he wiped the muck out of his eyes, she was gone.

He turned back to face the honky-tonk. The hot-pink building loomed over the rapidly filling parking lot. A line of customers snaked along the front porch, working their way through the doorman... What was his name again? Didn't matter. He was sure the guy was another relative of Charlie's. She seemed to be related to the whole town. With a groan, he glanced down at the mud covering another one of his brand-new outfits. Did he have time to run back to the B and B to change? Probably not.

Dammit. She knew he wasn't ready to handle a night on his own. Probably couldn't wait for him to fail so she could laugh about him with the whole town. Maybe she'd even planned this as a setup.

Beck groaned. No, not Charlie. She wasn't the get-even type. Didn't have it in her.

She was probably flat-out exhausted from trying to keep things going on her own. Beck hobbled toward the back door. He'd check in with the staff, make sure everything was on track, and then step out to clean up. How hard could it be to keep the place going for one night? From what he'd seen, the Rambling Rose practically ran itself.

He could do this—with or without Charlie Walker's help.

*H*

Charlie fishtailed out of the parking lot, putting as much distance between herself and the know-it-all jerk as quickly as possible. She hadn't cried when Sully died, hadn't shed a tear while she watched them lower his coffin into the ground. And now, twice within twenty-four hours, she'd lost control of her emotions and had to fight back a breakdown.

It was Beck.

How dare he strut right in and start questioning the way she did things? Sully had trusted her for the past eight years to single-handedly run the place. Once she'd taken over and he'd been satisfied she knew enough to get the job done, he'd stepped back and let her take charge. What had he been thinking, leaving the fate of the Rambling Rose to a grandson he'd never even met?

And that kiss. She didn't want to admit it, but that kiss had rocked her world, lifted her off her feet, twisted her around, and set her down again, feeling like she'd been left upside down and inside out.

She'd been a fool to leave him alone on a Saturday night, but she'd had to get away from him. Still, what if things got out of control? What if Billy Ray and Presley didn't make good on their truce and resorted to another fistfight between sets? No, they wouldn't dare. But something else could go wrong. There were always little things she had to take care of.

She almost turned around, even slowed down at the turnoff to the back pasture. But she stopped herself before she pulled off the road. Shep was there. Between him and Angelo, Beck wouldn't be able to mess things up too much. And while he was learning the ropes the hard way, she could take the chance to put a little distance between them. She needed to be able to clear her head if she wanted to help him succeed.

Because no matter what her conflicted feelings about Beck were, Sully's dying wish came first. She'd never be able to live with herself if she didn't give it her all and try to keep the Rose in the Holiday family. She'd start fresh tomorrow. Tonight she needed a break. The past few days had been too much. Too much pressure, too much waffling, too much Beck.

She wiped her arm across her nose, smearing mud and snot over her cheek. Dang it. Why did she have to be such an ugly crier? She couldn't go home like this—her folks would see her headlights when she drove past the main house, and they'd know something had happened. Before she reached the turnoff to her family ranch, she swerved into Waylon and Darby's long drive. If anyone could make her feel better right now, her best friend could.

Five minutes later, she'd been ushered into the house, wrapped in a hug, and handed a tall glass of sweet tea. Thank God for family and friends. Although Charlie would shrivel up like a roly-poly bug if Waylon found out why she was here. Thankfully, Darby had sent him up to the main house for dinner with the kids.

"Now, get out of those wet clothes and tell me what's going on." Darby handed her a pair of jean shorts and a T-shirt.

Charlie stepped into the half bath and left the door open a crack while she changed. "It's Sully's grandson. He's absolutely unbearable."

"Mm-hmm." Darby stood just outside the doorway. "What happened?"

"He's questioning everything. From how many kids we serve to why we keep Baby Back around."

"It's a tradition."

"That's what I told him!" Thankful for the dry clothes, Charlie rolled her wet things into a ball and tucked them into a plastic bag she found under the bathroom sink before rejoining Darby.

"Come on, let's spike that tea—then you can sit a spell and tell me what's really going on." Darby linked her arm through Charlie's and tugged her to the kitchen, where she added a liberal pour of vodka to each of their glasses. "Let's sit out on the porch, and you can fill me in on how much you hate poor Beck Holiday."

Charlie grabbed her drink from the counter. "The third."

"The third what?" Darby asked.

"He's a third. Beck Holiday the Third. Didn't you pick up on that?"

Darby shook her head. "Guess not."

"Doesn't that sound so pretentious? Who wants to be the third of something?"

"Honey, sit down." They'd reached the front porch, and Darby patted the cushion next to her on the big swing.

Charlie sighed, then slumped onto the seat and began to move the swing back and forth.

Darby pulled Charlie's head down onto her shoulder. "You know I love you more than anything, right?"

"Sure."

"Then listen close when I tell you to get your head out of your butt and don't let that man intimidate you."

Charlie straightened, her jaw dropping like someone had just oiled the hinges. "Wha... Just wait a sec... I don't—"

Darby shook her head back and forth. "You're scared, Char. This man can take everything away from you."

"I don't—"

"You've poured your heart and soul into the Rose. For the past eight years...weekends, holidays, twelve- to fourteen-hour days. I know. I was there. And if Beck decides to keep it, there's a chance he might not want your help."

The jaw snapped shut, and Charlie clenched her teeth together. Sometimes it downright sucked having someone who knew her so well always around. She took a deep breath. "I just don't want Sully's memory, well, for lack of a better word...sullied."

Darby smiled, the kind of smile that did a piss-poor job of covering up the pity she must have felt. "Sweetie, ever since Jackson—"

"I don't want to talk about it, D."

"It's been eight years. Sully was a saint to give you that job back then. But maybe it's time for a backup plan—"

"I said I don't want to talk about it." Charlie sprang from the swing and paced the porch, her bare feet slapping on the smooth floorboards.

"Honey, you never want to talk about it. But think about it. Beck is threatening the safety net you built for yourself. If he decides he doesn't need you, what are you going to do?"

Charlie spun around, her heart skittering and trying to find its groove like an old 45 record with a deep, long scratch. "I came here thinking you'd make me feel better, not worse."

Darby stood and made a move toward her, but Charlie rocketed off the porch and toward the truck. "Charlie, come back. Let's talk about this."

She climbed in the truck and hightailed it out of there while Darby stood on the porch shaking her head. They'd be fine. It would take more than an uncomfortable conversation to put any strain on the ties that bound them together.

It hurt to admit it, but Darby was right. Charlie's whole life was wrapped up in the Rose. It had saved her, and she couldn't let it go without a fight. Not unless she knew it would be in good hands. As far as she could tell, the only thing Beck's hands were good for didn't have anything to do with managing a rough-and-tumble honky-tonk.

Sully may have wanted to keep things in the family, but she was more of a family to him than his own grandson had ever been. She'd do her best to help the guy out of love for his grandfather, but she'd be darned if she'd let him take the whole town down with him.

And that had nothing to do with the way he made her feel inside. She hadn't unlocked that part of her heart since fate had taken a hacksaw to it. Eight years might seem like a long time to her friends and family, and she'd been told on more than a few occasions that she was wasting her life and needed to get on with things. She knew Jackson wouldn't want her to spend the rest of her life mourning him. If roles had been reversed and she'd been the one who'd had to leave this good earth too soon, she'd want him to go on. To find someone who could make him smile, who could do all the things they talked about when they spent long afternoons down by the creek.

But roles weren't reversed. He was gone, and she was stuck navigating a life she never wanted all on her own. Instead of getting married and traveling the world with the man she loved, she'd made sure she built another kind of life. A life that would never require her to leave the safe confines of her small hometown. There was no way she'd let Beck threaten that now. What had happened between them was the result of hormones. Purely a physical release. She vowed to spend more time with her battery-operated boyfriend so she could avoid something similar in the future. Maybe even starting tonight.

She promised herself that she'd enjoy her night off. Take a long bubble bath, pop in a chick flick, and get a good night's sleep. The Rose wasn't open on Sunday, so she'd be able to avoid seeing Beck again before he left town.

After spending one night on his own with the locals, he'd get a taste of what it took to run the place. Maybe then he'd be a little more willing to take the advice she offered. She could secure her place at the Rose, and her life could stay the same. That would be smart. That would be best. That would be safe.

## chapter
# EIGHT

BACK IN MIDDLE SCHOOL, BECK'S DAD HAD TAKEN him on one of his business trips to Vegas. They spent an entire evening meeting with a potential client at a country-themed bar and restaurant. Holiday had tossed back shots and harassed the pretty cowgirls. Beck had sat quietly on a barstool at the end of the bar, soaking in the ten-gallon cowboy hats and the way the dance floor shook when the majority of the diners took to the tiny parquet square during a well-known tune.

That memory came up in black and white compared to the living color of his first night on his own at the Rambling Rose.

Presley and Billy Ray alternated sets. The crowd didn't seem to care who was onstage as long as the music kept playing. The walls vibrated, the floor pulsed, and the thunderous echo of hundreds of pairs of boots slamming into the dance floor ricocheted through his head. He sat back and watched for a while. The whole place operated like a well-oiled machine. So when he stepped behind the bar and tried to help Shep handle the mass of bill-waving customers waiting to order a beer, he wasn't sure if he was being helpful or getting in the way.

"I can't serve this—look at the head on this pour." The

mug he'd just filled reappeared in front of him, the foamy top cascading over the edge of the glass.

"Sorry, I'm still learning the ropes."

At the sound of Beck's voice, the redheaded waitress spun around. "You're not Shep."

"No." Beck smiled, already refilling another mug.

"Oh my gosh, you're Sully's grandson, aren't you?" Her eyes went wide, and a flush spread over her cheeks.

"That's me. Beck Holiday. Nice to meet you… uh…" He slid the mug across the bar, waiting for her to introduce herself.

She didn't move. One hand balanced the full tray. The other splayed across her chest like she'd just had the shock of her life.

"You are?" He ignored the guy leaning over the bar who was trying to get his attention by waving a twenty-dollar bill in his face.

"Dixie!" She sprang back to life, snagging the beer and finding a spot to set it down on the overcrowded tray. "I'm so sorry. Like I said, I thought you were Shep."

"Don't worry about it." He waved his hand, trying to downplay the exchange as she disappeared into the crowd.

"Well, that's gotta be a first." Dwight slid onto a stool in front of him.

"What?" Beck moved to grab two longnecks out of the cooler and fumbled with the bottle opener attached to the bar.

"I ain't never seen Dixie rendered speechless. That gal's always got somethin' to say, even if it ain't worth hearing about." Dwight pointed at the tap. "How about a beer on the house tonight, seein' as how we're friends and all?"

"Sure. First one's on me. As long as you do me a favor?" Beck slid another foamy beer across the bar.

Dwight squinted at his mug. "Tilt the glass while you fill it. You'll get less head that way."

"Thanks." It had been a long time since Beck had been on the serving side of anything, much less an ancient walnut bar in a honky-tonk in the middle of freaking nowhere. "Can you tell me how many employees they have here?"

Dwight took a swig of his beer and wiped the foam away on the sleeve of his checkered shirt. He must have traded in his coveralls for a big Saturday night out. "You met Shep, right?"

Beck nodded and listened while he tried to keep up with the demanding drink orders on the other side of the bar.

"So he's the main bartender. Angelo runs the kitchen. Dixie and Charlie work the floor. They've got some part-time gals who help with the weekends. Like Brittany— she's Charlie's cousin, y'know, and was up for Junior Miss Texas a while back. Watch out for her. Oh, and watch out for Dixie, too."

"Oh yeah, why?"

"Her daddy's the preacher." Dwight cupped his hand to his mouth like he was about to divulge a classified secret. "Rumor has it she's saving herself, if ya know what I mean." He waggled his eyebrows, apparently thinking Beck needed the extra emphasis to decipher what that implied.

Beck cut his eyes toward the redhead across the room. Yep. Everyone's business was everyone's business around here, that was for sure.

"Oh, and lemme tell ya about Billy Ray. Back in high

school he got wasted one night and they found him with Mrs. Martinez's goat—"

Beck thrust a palm toward Dwight, the universal sign to shut up. "I don't need to know any more."

Dwight snickered. "But it's funny. He was so trashed—"

"Really." Beck turned his attention to a group of giggly coeds and took their drink orders. They wanted three fuzzy navels, a sex on the beach, and buttery nipple shots all around. "Uh, Shep? Can you take this one?"

When Shep stepped over to mix the drinks, Beck bailed from behind the bar. Should have known better than to try to engage Dwight in conversation. There was something missing upstairs with that one. He'd have to ask Charlie about it when and if she ever decided to start speaking to him again. He worked his way around the room, shaking hands with locals who wanted to introduce themselves, clearing empty bottles and mugs from the tables, and sidestepping an older woman who reached out and claimed a handful of his ass.

He finally made it back to the kitchen to drop off the empties, where Angelo passed him a trayful of food and asked him to deliver it to the Ellisons. How was he supposed to know who the Ellisons were? He couldn't very well pass through the crowd asking people to give him their names.

A flash of red hair caught his eye. "Hey, Dixie?"

She whirled around, the same wide-eyed look of surprise on her face. "Yeah?"

"Can you take this to the Ellisons for me?"

"Sure thing." She snagged the tray along with another load of beverages and took off toward the stage.

Beck stumbled down the hallway in the direction of the office. A few minutes later, he collapsed into Charlie's chair and attempted to pull the boots off his swollen feet.

Before he had the chance to examine the burning blisters covering his heels, someone knocked on the door. "Hey, Boss?"

"Come in." He sat up straight in the chair. Never let 'em see you sweat. That was his dad's motto. Or maybe some slogan he'd heard on a TV commercial at some point. His head swam with drink orders, names of the people he'd met, and the food orders he'd turned in to the kitchen.

Angelo stuck his head through the doorway. "We got a situation. One of the college kids is trying to throw a saddle on Baby Back."

Huh? The name sounded familiar, but Beck couldn't remember. Was that one of the neighbors he'd met a few hours ago? No, it was…damn, Charlie's pig!

He thrust his feet back into his boots and cringed as the raw skin rubbed against his sock, next to the stiff leather. "Be right there."

Angelo ducked out, and Dwight strolled in.

"Couple of city boys are about to throw down in the parking lot out front. Thought you might want to know." Dwight shrugged, like fights happened all the time. For all Beck knew, they probably did.

"Where's the bouncer?" He staggered to a standing position, his heels silently screaming in protest.

"He's out there. But he might need some backup. It's kind of like one frat house takin' on another."

"Dammit." Beck ran his hand through his hair. "What would Charlie do?" Well crap, he hadn't meant to utter that out loud. The last thing he wanted was for word to get back to her that he couldn't handle a lousy Saturday night alone.

"She'd probably turn the hose on 'em and send 'em back to Austin with their tails tucked." Dwight snickered. "She's good at that kind of stuff."

"Yeah. That's a good idea. Can you take care of the hose while I head out back to save the pig?"

"You bet." Dwight strolled toward the door. "I'm assuming there's gonna be a mini-keg with my name on it for helpin' you out of this hot spot, hey, hoss?"

"Yeah, sure, whatever. Just get out there, okay?" He waited until Dwight cleared the corner then limped toward the back door.

Someone had pulled a truck up in front of the pigpen, letting the headlights illuminate the action taking place in the mud. A buzzed hotshot stood on the perimeter of the pen, a saddle of some sort in both hands. Based on the way he swayed back and forth, he must have been more than a little inebriated. A crowd of onlookers shouted encouragement. Beck scanned the pigpen. Where was the pig?

He walked around to the gate and stepped into the pen, making sure it latched behind him. "You're not supposed to be in here. Go home. Party's over."

The kid sneered at him. "Who the hell are you? Party's not over until me and my buddies get a picture riding the pig."

"Yeah, that's not going to happen." Beck crossed his arms and took a deep breath, extending to his full height, which had to be at least a few inches taller than the beanpole in front of him. "Come on out of here, and we'll pretend this never happened."

"No way. I ain't even ever seen you around before. I'm not leavin' until I sit on the pig."

Finally, Beck's gaze landed on Baby Back. She had backed herself into a corner opposite the guy like she wanted to get a running start to charge him. Beck took a few slow steps her way. Why did he think climbing into the pen was a good idea? The porker had to outweigh him by a hundred pounds. She could probably fend for herself without his help.

"You're not touching the pig. You'll have to go through me to get to her, and I'm warning you, it's not worth the headache you'd wake up with tomorrow to even try."

The guy looked unsure of himself, but his buddies kept at him. Finally, he lunged toward the pig. Beck grabbed him by the back of his jeans and the collar of his shirt to set him on his feet. But Beck's hand slipped, so instead he sent him flying into the mud. The kid landed with a splat. His friends' cheers turned to snickers.

"Get out of here," the hopeful pig wrangler yelled to the crowd. Sensing the excitement had come to an abrupt end, they began to head back inside. The kid turned toward Beck. "You can't throw me around like that." Dripping in mud, he scrambled to his feet.

Beck dodged him the first time, but the kid charged again, catching him by surprise with a shoulder to the gut and sending both of them crashing into the bottom rail of the pigpen. The board split, cracking in two.

Beck looked up just in time to see Baby Back sail past him, through the fence and out into the parking lot.

"Dammit." He got to his feet, half limping, half staggering

after the pig. The kid grabbed on to his ankle, holding on with both hands. Beck dragged him halfway across the pigpen before Baby Back rounded the building toward the front parking lot and disappeared.

Beck struggled against the death grip preventing him from chasing after the pig. Teeth sank into his calf and he went down, dropping an elbow into the center of the kid's back. The grip loosened. Finally free from his determined opponent, Beck tried to catch up to the pig before she hit the open field.

He rounded the corner. Even Baby Back paused at the scene unfolding before them. A mass of denim, hats, and western shirts scuffled under a torrential spray of water. Dwight and Shep stood on the porch, wrestling a giant fire hose between them. *That* was the hose? If Beck thought the mud was a problem before, it was a catastrophe now. Tires spun, splattering mud and water all over the other parked cars. The guys who were still throwing punches were quickly being covered in a thick layer of muck.

Baby Back dove into the fray, splashing through the mud. She paused every once in a while to roll around in a particularly attractive puddle or two. Anytime Beck got near, she'd take off again, barreling through the crowd, knocking cowboys over like bowling pins.

Beck chased after her, hopping over the fallen men Baby Back left groaning and moaning in her wake. "Catch the pig! Can someone please catch the damn pig?"

A few guys tried to slow her down. One stood in front of her, waving his hands in an attempt to get her to break her stride. She paused long enough for Beck to wrap his hand around the strap of leather Charlie had secured around her neck. Was this supposed to be a collar? Before he could brace himself to jerk her back toward the pigpen, she took off again. Only now instead of chasing her, he was being dragged next to her, his hand still clasping the hot-pink band around her neck.

As his ass bounced over the combination of dirt, mud, and gravel, he tried to get his feet underneath him. She was fast. Faster than he ever imagined a pig could be. But then again, he'd never ridden sidecar to a runaway sow before.

The roar of water continued to rain down, drenching everyone and everything. Hands grabbed for Baby Back's collar, but she prevailed, shaking off any potential capture attempts. Beck had almost had it. He was ready to let go and let the pig be on her way. If she wanted her freedom this badly, maybe she deserved it.

The crack of a shotgun rang out. The water went from a blast to a spray to a dribble. Even the pig stopped—at least long enough for Beck to get to his feet and secure her collar in both hands. A sheriff's SUV blocked the exit to the parking lot. Lights flashed, bouncing red and blue off anything that hadn't been covered in mud.

"Where's Charlie?" The brawny deputy lowered the gun and shouted into the crowd.

Beck cleared his throat. "Charlie's not here tonight."

Brown eyes, pissed-off brown eyes, turned his way. "Then who's in charge?"

He swallowed. "That would be me. Hi, I'm Beck. Beck Holiday." He made a move to offer his hand but realized he was still holding on to the pig. Afraid to let go, he shrugged. "Charlie took a night off."

The deputy let out a gruff laugh. "Some night off. Somebody's going to have hell to pay tomorrow."

Shep rushed over with a rope and secured it around Baby Back's neck. "Hey, Cash. Some Saturday night, huh?"

Cash nodded toward Beck. "Beck Holiday, nice to meet you. I'm Cash Walker."

Walker, dammit. Another one of Charlie's brothers.

By the time they'd patched the pigpen and secured Baby Back, the party had mostly wound down. While the rest of them had been outside, Presley and Lamb Chops had taken it upon themselves to do an impromptu battle of the bands and blown a fuse. Half the building sat in darkness, including the kitchen and the bar, which meant no more food, no more music, and no more beer.

Beck learned that was the fastest way to shut down a honky-tonk in Texas—telling the crowd they couldn't serve any more beer.

Before tonight, he'd thought he was tough. He'd thought he could hold his own in any situation. He'd thought wrong.

At this rate, three months would feel like three hundred years. He needed to suck it up and make up with the hardest-working, hardest-headed, hardest-hearted gal he'd ever met.

But first he needed to salvage what remained of his pride and limp back to his temporary home to shower away the mud, the poop, and all the memories of what had happened tonight. Especially the bit with the pig.

Priorities were a bitch.

## chapter

# NINE

BECK TUCKED IN THE FRONT OF HIS SHIRT WITH ONE hand while grasping the mini-mart bouquet of red, white, and blue carnations in the other. He licked his lips and knocked on the massive wood door of the Walker family compound. Cash had said it would just be a family dinner, but from the number of pickup trucks parked in the tree-lined drive, it looked like half the town was there. The humidity had to be at least ninety percent, and the air clung to him like he was being wrapped in plastic wrap. How could everyone around here strut around in jeans all year long?

This was a bad idea. He should have just returned the rental car and caught the flight out of Austin this after-noon, not forced his way into a Sunday family supper. But the night before, Cash had pretty much ordered him to come. Said he owed it to Charlie to apologize in person for the way he'd handled things at the Rose. Plus, if he wanted to make a go of it at the bar, he needed to meet the family. Cash had said his parents could tell Beck more about his grandfather in an hour than Mr. Hill could in the next six weeks.

So he'd changed his flight to Monday and booked another night at the B and B. And here he was, spend-ing his third day in a row in a pair of new jeans and the blistering boots. He hadn't found his loafer in the mud pit, so he'd earn a few more blisters before he could hobble back to NYC.

A herd of footsteps clambered on the other side of the door before someone cracked it open.

"Who are you?" The voice came from hip level, and he lowered his gaze to a curly-haired little girl in hot-pink cowgirl boots, surrounded by mini versions of the Walker brothers.

"I'm, uh—"

"That's Mr. Holiday, Allie." Presley came up behind the small crowd of kids. "He's the new owner of the Rose, and that makes him our new neighbor, too."

"Does that mean Aunt Charlie doesn't work there anymore?" Her brow furrowed, and she chewed on her bottom lip. With her two front teeth missing, it gave her the look of a tiny vampire cowgirl.

"Not exactly. Why don't you go tell Grandma that Mr. Holiday's here? And y'all go play out back." Presley ruffled the hair of the nearest kid, a towheaded boy wearing a button-down oxford and boots that came up to his knees. "Come on in. Everyone's in the kitchen."

Beck followed Presley into the blessedly cool house. No mistaking a serious cowboy lived here. A stone fireplace stretched from the floor to the ceiling, a giant cow head with three-foot-long horns hung above the mantel, and a wall of windows framed both sides. The house sat on a bit of a hill, and acres of pasture stretched as far as he could see.

"Is that Sully's grandson?" A woman rounded the corner, her face lit up in a warm, welcoming smile.

"Yes, ma'am. Beck, this is my mother, Ann Walker," Presley said.

Ann shook his hand with one hand and slid the other around his back to give him a half hug. "It's so nice to meet you, Beck."

"Nice to meet you, too, Mrs. Walker."

"Oh, call me Ann. Now come on in. I want to introduce you to everyone." She led him into a huge kitchen where a group of what he assumed were Charlie's brothers and other relations stood around an island filled with snacks.

"These are for you." Beck handed Ann flowers that seemed to have wilted even more in the ten minutes since he'd bought them.

"How thoughtful. Thank you. Charlotte, honey, grab a vase, will you?"

Beck's gaze lit on Charlie, who shoved a tortilla chip in her mouth and climbed off her stool. She didn't even bother to look at him. The way she slammed the crystal vase down on the counter in front of him told him she was already well aware of his failure to keep things under control the night before. Looked like he had some major sucking up to do if he wanted to make sure the Rose would still be standing when he came back.

Ann put a hand on his shoulder, propelling him closer to the island. A couple dozen eyeballs focused on him, their curiosity pressing down on him, causing his stomach to tighten and a tic to pulse in his temple. Why was he so nervous? He'd made presentations in front of some of the most influential men on Wall Street and spoken before thousands of real estate investors at conferences. Somehow the small crowd of Walkers set him more on edge.

"Y'all, say hi to Beck, Sully's grandson and hopefully

our new neighbor." Ann arranged the flowers in the vase and nodded toward her children. "You know Charlie and Presley. Have you had a chance to meet the rest of my offspring?"

"Hey, I'm Waylon." A grizzly-sized bear of a man grasped his hand in a tight shake. "You've met my wife, Darby." Charlie's best friend lifted her hand in a tiny wave, bounced a wide-eyed baby on her hip, and winked at him. "The welcoming committee belongs to us, too, at least most of them. Ryder's eight, Luke is seven, Allie's five, and June here just turned thirteen months."

"We had the pleasure of meeting last night." Cash reached across the island and shook his hand. "My daughter, Kenzie, is running around here somewhere. Probably getting her cousins in all kinds of trouble."

Beck's head spun already with the new influx of names. He'd never be able to keep them all straight. He nodded at Cash and turned to the next body. Thank goodness, a familiar face.

"Statler. We met at the bar yesterday."

"That's right. Good to see you again." Before he had a chance to try to commit any names to memory, Ann pressed a small plate into his hands.

"Help yourself. Supper will be ready in just a bit. Charlotte, where's your father? I want him to meet Beck."

Charlie rested a hip against the island, her arms crossed over her chest. She had on a long, flowy skirt and a tank top that bared her sun-kissed shoulders. With her hair swept up in a knot of some sort, he could better appreciate the graceful curve where her collarbone and neck met. She was soft in all the right places; he knew that from experience. But she was also hard. Hard like steel, or what was it Shep had said? Hard like the armor of an armadillo—that's right.

What was it about the woman that sent inappropriate thoughts crashing through his brain? He was standing in her mom's kitchen...*with* her mom, for Christ's sake.

"Dad's out back messing with the four-wheeler. The kids want to go riding." She leaned over the counter onto her elbows. He couldn't help but toss a glance her way—and accidentally got an eyeful right down the front of her shirt. She frowned and stood as he quickly looked away.

"I told him not today. It's too hot out, and we're going to have supper in just a bit. Honey, will you go tell him Beck is here?"

"I'll go with you." Darby handed the baby over to her husband, and she and Charlie disappeared down a hallway, their boots clacking on the tile floor.

"How about a beer, Beck?" Presley clapped him on the shoulder. "Dad keeps a stash out on the porch. Let's get a cold one."

Now there was an idea he could get behind. Beck set the plate on the counter and let Presley lead him out onto an enclosed four-season porch that looked more like a game room. A full-size refrigerator sat in a corner, and a pool table took up a good portion of the floor space. A huge flat-screen TV blared a fast-moving cartoon. Presley snagged the remote and hit the power button.

"Kids pretty much have the run of the place. Wasn't like that when I grew up here, that's for sure." He opened the fridge and gestured to the shelves of longneck bottles and cans. "What's your pleasure? Dad's a Lone Star fan, but he's got a few local brews and the regular Coors, Bud, Miller, and Michelob."

Beck moved closer to the refrigerator. "I'd love to try something local."

"Here, try this one." Presley handed him an oversized can.

"Cactus Juice Brewing?" Beck studied the label.

"Good stuff." Presley popped the cap off his own bottle and took a seat on a stool. "So what are your plans for the Rose?"

Beck rubbed a hand over the scruff on his chin. He usually couldn't stand to go a day without shaving, but somehow keeping a day or two of growth on his chin made him feel more like one of the rugged cowboys he served at the bar. "Not sure yet. I've got a lot to think about, that's for sure."

"Yeah, and a lot of asses to kiss if you want to stick around."

He winced. "I know. Your sister didn't look like she was up to hearing an apology yet."

"Oh, it ain't just her I meant. That kid you tossed out of the pigpen last night is some senator's son from Austin. I hear his dad's not too happy this morning. He ripped Charlie a new one over the phone."

Beck closed his eyes for a long blink and took in a deep breath, trying to ease the tightness in his chest. "Got any advice on how to suck up to your sister? Flowers? Chocolates? Champagne?"

"You're on your own with that one." Presley nodded toward the pool table. "You play?"

He'd have to ask Emily to send something down

when he got back to his office tomorrow. She'd know what to do. "I'm not very good."

"Great. Then it'll be easy to take you for say, twenty bucks?"

"Sure, why not?" At least a game of pool would keep his mind off of Charlie and give him an excuse to stay out of the kitchen. He stepped to the rack of cue sticks and hefted one, trying to get a feel for the weight and balance while Presley gathered up the balls.

"Hell, Pres, can you at least let the man break bread with us before you swindle him out of his hard-earned paycheck?" A short, balding man entered the room and thrust his hand at Beck. "Tom Walker. Glad to meet you, son."

"Mr. Walker, it's my pleasure. Thanks so much for having me over for dinner."

"The missus woulda skinned me alive if she found out you were in town and we didn't invite you over. It's a damn shame about your grandfather. He was a good man."

Why did everyone have to keep telling him that? According to his dad, his grandfather was a hermit who kicked him out for no good reason and couldn't hold a conversation with a cow. Where was the major disconnect? Instead of asking for clarification, Beck just nodded. No need to argue or give the Walker family any additional reason to want to run him out of town.

Tom went to the fridge and pulled out a Lone Star. "A beer sure tastes good on a day like today. What's the weather like in New York City? I bet you're not used to dripping with sweat the second you climb out of the shower."

Beck smiled. Yeah, that's pretty much what had happened, even with the window unit blasting cool air into his room at the historic B and B.

"Folks up north want radiant heat on their floors," Tom continued. "I'd give my left nut for a radiant floor cooler."

"No one wants your left nut, Mr. Walker." Ann entered the room and pressed a kiss to her husband's temple. "Supper's ready. Come on before it gets cold, y'all."

Beck followed Presley to the kitchen where a line of Walkers snaked through the kitchen and the smell of a perfectly cooked steak greeted his nose. His mouth watered as he identified the source—a platter of rib eyes took up a corner of the island. Side dishes of every color covered the rest of the counter space. Ann rattled off the options…fried okra; homemade bourbon-and-brown-sugar baked beans; creamy, whipped coleslaw. He could get used to this.

Everyone stepped back when Tom came in. He took a plate and made his way through the line first. Waylon gestured for Beck to go next, so he picked up his plate and started looking over the choices. When he'd piled his plate as high as he could without anything falling off the edge, he took a spot where Tom directed him at the long dining room table.

As if by some unspoken plan, Charlie was the last to the table and had to take the one empty seat… which just happened to be on Beck's right. From the way she stared straight ahead as she slumped into the chair, she didn't seem too happy about it.

"What's wrong, Baby Sis? You want to trade spots?" Presley teased from the other end of the table.

"Oh, shut up." She stuck her tongue out at him like they were still in elementary school.

"Or maybe you'd be more comfortable at the kids' table," he joked.

"Presley, kiss my ass and go to hell."

Darby snorted. Tom clenched his jaw. Statler laughed.

"Aunt Charlie owes the curse word jar," one of the girls called out from where the kids were eating in the kitchen.

"Cash, why'd you have to go start that with her? You trying to get us all to finance her college education?" Charlie glared at her brother across the table.

"At the rate you're going, you just might do that all by yourself," Cash said with a wink.

"Are y'all done yet?" Tom glanced around the table, silencing his offspring with just a look. Charlie and Presley dropped their gazes into their laps, apparently chastised by their father.

Beck would have to make peace, and fast. But not until after he got to sink his teeth into that steak.

Tom waited until silence descended before they all joined hands. Charlie put her hand out, and Beck had no choice but to clasp it for the blessing. The men had removed their hats, and Beck glanced around the table when everyone bowed their heads.

Family dinners for him had consisted of a reservation at one of his dad's favorite four-star restaurants and a stuffy three-course meal. And that was if they even happened. Usually his dad and whichever wife or girlfriend he had at the time would leave Beck with the nanny and go out on their own. When he finally got old enough not to need a babysitter, he preferred to stay home by himself. Sitting around an enormous table with two dozen relative strangers both intimidated him and piqued his curiosity. Was this how all big families did things?

Tom wrapped up the blessing with a thank-you for having Beck join them for dinner and ended with a group chorus of "Amen." Forks clinked on plates, the salad dressing was passed, and the kids' table erupted in giggles and snorts. Beck felt like a welcome guest and an intruder at the same time. Charlie passed him the basket of flaky buttered biscuits, and their fingers brushed. He didn't acknowledge the spark that passed between them.

"Thanks." He set a biscuit on his plate and passed the basket on to Tom. "I take it you didn't know I would be here today?" Beck muttered under his breath.

She turned her head. Their gazes met for a moment before she focused her attention on slicing into her steak. "We always end up with a few extras at Sunday supper."

"Can we talk after dinner, in private?"

"No need. Statler, can you pass the salt?"

Beck sighed, then took a gulp of iced tea. Her family may have been as warm as the bright rays of sun filtering through the huge picture windows, but Charlie seemed to have erected an icy wall between them. Good thing he was used to the cold. He had no doubt he'd be able to find a way to get through to her. All he needed was a plan. And he'd start thinking about it…right after he enjoyed his first home-cooked meal in as long as he could remember.

Charlie's stomach had turned itself inside out the moment she sat down next to Beck. Her skin felt like it had been charged with static electricity, just like when she used to try to shock her siblings on purpose by rubbing her socks on the carpet. But instead of expelling the static on her brothers, this time, she didn't have an outlet. What was it about the man sitting next to her that kept her revved up? Hopefully he wouldn't stick around long enough for her to find out.

Conversation flowed around them, leaving her and Beck a silent island in the middle of her talkative relatives. She pushed a bite of homemade macaroni and cheese—her favorite side dish—around on her plate, waiting for the uncomfortable meal to come to an end.

"Beck, what are your plans? Have you decided what to do with the Rambling Rose?" Ann asked the question everyone at the table had been wondering. Leave it to her mom to go there. Charlie frowned at the wide-eyed, feigned innocent interest reflected in her mother's face. Her mother was anything but innocent. She always had an agenda.

Beck cleared his throat, and his leg brushed against hers as he shifted in his seat. She jerked away, and his knee bumped the underside of the table, causing his plate to clatter as it settled in front of him.

"Everything okay over there?" Statler arched a brow. "Nothing kinky going on under the table, is there, Char?"

Her face flamed, and a rash of heat crept across her chest and up her neck, flooding her cheeks with angry pinpricks. She gave her brother her best eat-shit-and-die look, then took a savage bite of roll.

"Sorry about that—you just caught me off guard." Beck met her mother's gaze. "To be honest, I haven't had a chance to give it a ton of thought yet. I didn't know anything about my grandfather or the bar until last week."

Ann nodded. "I'm sure it came as quite a shock. Your dad didn't mention it at all?"

"Not really. I knew he was from some town in Texas, but he never wanted to talk about it."

Tom snorted, earning him a disapproving glance from Ann before she turned her full attention back to Beck. "Your dad was quite a character."

"You know him?" Beck's voice held an underlying edge of hope.

"Well, I knew of him. He was two years ahead of me in high school. Same class as Tom. They used to hang out and get in all kinds of trouble together, didn't you?"

Charlie hadn't heard about her dad being close friends with Sully's son. Why didn't people around here like to talk about him much?

Her dad wiped his mouth with a blue bandana that her mom liked to set out for napkins and leaned back from the table. "Yeah, Beckett and me used to raise a ruckus every now and again. Those were good times. Before the…well, before he left."

"What happened? If you don't mind me asking—Mr. Hill said my dad and Sully had some sort of falling-out, but Dad never talked about it." Beck's hand hovered, a bite of steak on his fork, frozen in midair.

"I think you'd best ask your dad about that. It's his story to share, son. Now, who's ready for dessert and coffee?" Her dad pushed back from the table, picked up his plate, and headed to the kitchen. Her mom followed, leaving the kids and grandkids to fend for themselves.

"Another biscuit, Beck?" Darby held the basket out.

"No, thanks. I can't eat another bite." He clasped his hands together over his stomach.

"Nothing like a Sunday supper at the ranch. I'll take another biscuit." Presley held out his hand, and Darby passed him the basket. "Char, you going to finish your steak? No sense in wasting a good cut of beef."

"Have at it." She stood and handed her plate across the table. How was it her brothers could put away three huge meals a day and never seem to gain a pound?

"What's for dessert?" Cash asked.

"Peach cobbler. Want me to bring you a plate?" Charlie paused on her way into the kitchen.

"Sure. Cup of coffee, too?" Cash winked. "You're a doll."

"Anyone else?" She may have been in charge at the honky-tonk, but her family home still subscribed to an outdated view that womenfolk belonged in the kitchen. It would take more than a few generations to turn that tide on the Walker homestead.

"I'll help." Beck pushed back and cleared his place, then picked up Waylon's and Darby's plates as well.

Charlie tried not to do a double take at the offer. Maybe Beck being different wasn't all bad. "If you just set them on the counter, I'll load up the dishwasher."

He followed her into the kitchen, where her mother pulled a piping-hot peach cobbler out of the lower oven. "I can do it. I'm not much good at cooking, but dishes I can handle." Beck unbuttoned the cuffs of what appeared to be another recent purchase from Whitey's and rolled up his sleeves.

The sight of his forearms shouldn't have made her want to fan herself, but it did. She blinked hard, attempting to erase the vision of how his muscles rippled while he worked to push the sleeves up. It didn't work. The action had been imprinted on the back of her eyelids and played on repeat.

She jammed the stopper in the bottom of the giant farmhouse sink and flipped the faucet on. "Dish soap is under the counter. I'll clear the rest of the table."

He leaned down to crack the cabinet, and she ducked into the dining room, putting some much-needed distance between them. What the heck was her problem? She was surrounded by men of every age, shape, and size practically 24/7 at the bar. Quite a few of them even hit on her. At least the ones from out of town. The local guys knew better than to waste their breath. Well, except for Dwight. But he was harmless.

Something about Beck got under her skin, like a chigger bite. She needed to figure out how to dislodge whatever was going on before any feelings had a chance to set in and fester.

Charlie took another load of dishes from the dining room to the kitchen, passing her mom, who had already started delivering cobbler and coffee to the men in the other room. Beck had filled the sink with soapy water and stood scrubbing the dirty plates with a hot-pink nylon scrub pad, the kind her mom crocheted for holiday gifts. With a dish towel slung over his shoulder, he appeared to be quite at home in front of the sink. Did he host big dinner parties at his place in New York? She knew he wasn't married thanks to the gossip grapevine that wound its way throughout Holiday, but maybe he had someone special at home, someone he'd bring back with him if and when he returned. That thought made her even sorrier that she'd responded to his kiss.

Darby set a few more plates on the counter. "Where did you learn how to scrub a dirty dish, Beck? Girlfriend back home got you trained?" Her mouth quirked up at the corner, and she shot a smug smile in Charlie's direction.

Leave it to Darby to read her freaking mind. Torn between wanting to fake disinterest and moving closer so she didn't miss his response, Charlie fished for the roll of foil in a drawer.

A rumble of laughter rolled from Beck's chest. "No girlfriend at home. My nanny was German. She made sure I learned how to clean up after myself. You should see the hospital corners on my sheets."

Darby waggled her ring finger at him. "Tempting, but I'm a married woman. Charlie here might take you up on that offer though."

Who needed friends when she had a traitorous BFF like Darby? Charlie smacked the snitch's denim-covered ass with the roll of foil, twisted her face into a scowl, then stormed through the doorway to the porch.

"Ouch. What was that for?" Darby followed her to the other room and ripped the foil out of her hands. "It's true, Char. It's about time someone invited you to check out his sheets."

Charlie wrapped her hand around her friend's upper arm and growled, "Would you be quiet? I don't need you trying to fix me up. Especially in front of my whole family—"

Darby wrenched her arm away. "Nobody heard me."

"Especially not with him." Charlie put her palms flat on the pool table and looked out the huge window. Her parents stood at the edge of the giant driveway with her brothers, watching the kids climb over the four-wheelers. Thank God they were outside. Except for Beck. Her stomach rolled around, twisting and turning like Baby Back when let loose in a puddle of mud.

"I'm sorry. What's wrong with the gorgeous man scrubbing dishes in your mama's kitchen? Do you know how many times Waylon has helped me clean up?" When Charlie didn't answer, she held up a hand and counted off her fingers. "Once, before we got married, he helped with Thanksgiving dishes. And then when I was pregnant, he actually loaded the dishwasher when we had everyone over for Easter. That's it."

"There's more to being attracted to someone than how well he knows how to make soapy water."

"Agreed. That's why I up and married your brother anyway."

Charlie cleared her throat. "Uh, you married him because he got you knocked up with my adorable nephew."

"Well, there was that," Darby said. "But I've seen the way that man looks at you, and it's not like he wants to run his soapy hands all over your mama's everyday Corelle."

"You're impossible."

"And you're going on eight years without a fling."

"That's not true. I almost slept with that guy from Austin six years ago."

The sound of something clunking to the kitchen floor made her look at the doorway inside where Beck leaned over to pick up a container of margarine he must have dropped while putting it away in the fridge. Darby covered her giggle with a hand and turned her back to Charlie. Great, just great. With her cheeks burning like she'd just seared them on the grill, she stepped past Beck and headed for the front door, grabbing her purse on the way.

"Charlie, wait."

She turned to watch Beck hobble across the foyer. New boots could have that effect on a guy when not broken in properly. "What?"

"We need to talk. Can we go somewhere?"

"What do we need to talk about?"

"Well, the Rose for one. I'm going to need your help. Last night was, well, it was an eye-opener. I've got to go back to New York tomorrow to take care of a few things and clear my schedule. I know Sully counted on you to pretty much run the place. Is that something you'd be willing to do for me?"

What would she be willing to do for him? Based on the way her nervous system jacked into overdrive every time he got near her, she'd be willing to do a whole lot more than run the Rose for a few days. As much as she hated to admit it to herself, Beck did seem like he was trying to do the right thing, even though he had a piss-poor way of going about it so far.

True, he was kind of like a square peg trying to fit into a Lone Star–shaped hole, but something inside her wanted to help him. And not just because of Sully's last wish—or because he turned her steel core to mush. That right there was the number one reason she *shouldn't* help him. When and if she decided she was ready to go hunting for love again, it would be with someone close, not someone who couldn't wait to get out of town, who'd leave her behind.

Beck must have sensed reluctance on her part because he sweetened the deal. "I don't know what Sully was paying you, but I'll up it by twenty-five percent. What do you say?"

With her future as clear as the algae-covered pond in the back pasture, she didn't have a choice but to agree. She needed to hold on to her job as long as she could. Besides her love for the Rambling Rose and all it stood for, other employment options in Holiday were in short supply—as in nonexistent. The thought of having to drive into Austin or San Marcos for some stuffy job every day gave her the creepy-crawlies.

For now, she'd have to take whatever offer Beck tossed her way.

"Fine. First, let's fix your boots. Then we can go somewhere to talk, okay?"

Beck let out a breath he'd appeared to be holding. Did he really think she had a choice? "What do you mean fix my boots? What's wrong with them?"

"Sit down, and I'll tell you all about it."

He slumped into a cowhide chair. Charlie lifted one of his legs and propped it on the matching ottoman. She flung one leg over his, straddling his shin, struggling to pull the boot from his foot.

"Give me the other one."

Beck obliged, sliding his bootless foot out from under her and trading it for the other. She wrestled that boot off as well, then picked them both up and took them to the kitchen. If she was going to be working for the guy, the least she could do was make sure he'd be able to walk.

## chapter
# TEN

BECK SWIVELED ON HIS STOOL AND FACED CHARLIE just as she took a sip of her beer. The neon lights behind the bar played over her skin, making it glow in shades of pink and purple. His gaze followed the path of her swallow as it passed down her slender neck. That little white tank top had been driving him crazy since he first saw her in it. With so much skin exposed, he could see the smattering of freckles across her shoulders. He'd give about anything to be able to reach out and brush the few strands of hair away from her face.

The way she dressed, the way she moved, so natural, contrasted so much with the women in power suits he'd been dealing with for the better portion of his adult life. For the most part, he gravitated toward smart women who had a killer business sense. Charlie didn't look the type, but she definitely had the inner makings of a tough, savvy entrepreneur.

It hurt to admit how he'd completely botched things at the Rose the night before and ask for forgiveness. She took it better than he thought she would, especially the ass-chewing from the senator.

"So you're going to listen to me from now on, right?" Charlie asked, turning the full force of her icy-blue eyes on him.

"Absolutely."

"And not do anything else to try to sabotage your own business?"

"You got it."

The lights flashed off and on. Everyone raised their glasses, gave a shout, and took a drink.

"What in the hell was that?" Beck asked.

"Somebody must have gotten a strike on the bowling lanes." She wiped a bit of moisture from the side of her mouth. "So we have a truce." She thrust her hand out in front of him. "Let's shake on it."

He wrapped his hand around hers, tamping down that same damn spark. The one that seemed to ignite in his gut every time they touched. He needed to rein in whatever attraction he had for the woman. At least the frosty wall she'd erected between them had begun to melt. Having a truce would be a welcome change. He'd worked with gorgeous women before and never mixed business with pleasure. It would have to be the same here. He'd make sure.

"Good. Now, I don't want to talk business anymore. I need to dance." She slid off the stool and swayed to the rockabilly tune squawking from the antiquated jukebox in the corner. With the low ceilings and yellow-tinged overhead lights, he felt like they were in some western-themed speakeasy.

They'd been at the bar/bowling alley/bingo hall for the past hour and a half. She'd filled his head with all kinds of info about the Rose, and he'd been making mental checklists of all the things he'd have to do to bring it into the twenty-first century and maximize the selling price.

She tugged on his arm. "You coming?"

"Nah, I'll sit this one out." And give his feet a chance to heal. Thanks to Charlie, his boots had gone from excruciatingly painful to almost comfortable. She'd held them over a pot of water for twenty minutes, and the leather had softened up enough to mold to his feet. No telling why he hadn't thought to give his new boots a steam treatment. Maybe because in his world, footwear belonged on his feet, not suspended over a vat of boiling water.

"Okay, but you're missing out." She waggled a finger at him and backed toward the dance floor.

He twisted around so he could keep an eye on her. Charlie had told him this was the only other watering hole within thirty miles. With dark-wood paneling and a dance floor that shared space with the bingo board, it didn't appear to be much competition. Especially since the cheers coming from the next room where a handful of bowlers manned the four lanes drowned out the music from time to time.

Charlie wiggled her hips and kicked up her heels as she kept time with the other dancers. Slightly buzzed Charlie was fun. The couple of beers had softened those razor-sharp edges and brought out her smile more. Made him wonder what she'd be like after a shot. Right on cue, the bartender leaned over the counter and asked if he needed a refill on his club soda. Why not? Beck ordered two shots of tequila and shifted on his seat as the music came to an end.

She climbed back onto the stool just as the bartender set the shots down in front of them. "For me?" she asked, her fingers already wrapping around the cowboy boot–shaped shaker of salt.

"Yeah, I thought we should celebrate."

"Celebrate what?"

Beck licked his hand and nodded toward the salt. Charlie shook it over the wet spot, then ran her tongue over the back of her own hand and did the same.

"To you—for helping me out with the Rose." Beck clinked his glass against hers.

"All right. And to you—for not making me look for another job."

The lights flickered on and off again. In unison, they licked the salt off their hands, downed their shots, and sucked on one of the lemon slices the bartender had set out on a plate. The jukebox started playing another tune, and a handful of couples took to the dance floor in a two-step.

"Come on, I know you know how to do this one." Charlie laced her fingers with his and pulled him toward the small dance floor.

Why not? They did deserve to celebrate. He could give the woman a dance. That wouldn't violate his "don't get involved" rule. He wrapped his arm around her back, and after a few awkward starts, they began to move. It felt natural holding her in his arms. But his resolve to keep things professional began to slip as his hand slid to her lower back.

"Have you been practicing?" She leaned closer, mumbling into his neck.

Her chest pushed against his, and he tightened his grip on the thin cotton tank. He could feel the vertebrae of her spine through her shirt, and he pulled her closer against him. She didn't need to know he'd been watching YouTube videos. He had a history of being successful in pretty much any endeavor he'd undertaken. Fitting in around Holiday was not going to be an exception.

He spun her out and under his arm, then clasped her around the back and pressed her close again. "You *have* been practicing." She gazed up at him through heavy-lidded eyes while a slight smile played across her lips.

"Just trying to make you look good, Ms. Walker." Not that she needed any help in that area. There was something about her that drew a man's attention. Beyond her good looks, she had a spark, a sizzle, some crackling force that surrounded her and demanded to be noticed.

"You're doing a fine job of that." She nodded to herself and leaned her head against his chest.

He liked the way it felt, the heat from her cheek pressing against his heart. Hell, he liked the way all of her felt, nestled into his arms.

"About earlier...can I ask you a question?" His chin rested on her hair, and he let himself breathe her in. The scent of sunshine and peach cobbler layered over something else. Something that was just Charlie.

"Sure."

"Are you seeing anyone?"

A wrinkle appeared between her brows. "You're asking because of what Darby said, aren't you?"

He shifted to the left, spinning them out of the way of a couple in full square-dance gear who spiraled around the small dance floor.

"Just curious. If you don't want to talk about it, we don't have to."

"Good." She nodded. "I don't want to talk about it."

Fine. For now. He wasn't lying—he *was* curious. Why wouldn't a woman like Charlie be involved with someone?

She was smart and sassy as hell, had a great sense of humor and curves that wouldn't quit.

She wrapped her arms tighter around him, making him lose track of the simple steps he'd been counting in his head.

He tried to recover but ended up stepping on her foot instead. "Sorry. I guess I'm still learning."

"Have you always been such a slow learner?" she teased.

He'd play along. "You sure it doesn't have something to do with the talent of my teacher?"

Charlie's eyes sparkled, then narrowed. "What are you trying to imply? I'll have you know your teacher is a two-time two-stepping Texas teen champ."

Beck chuckled. "I bet you can't say that ten times fast."

"Two-time two-stepping Texas teen champ. Two-time two-stepping Texas—"

He laughed and covered her mouth with his hand. Her lips moved against his palm, soft and fluttery like a butterfly's kiss. He leaned close to her ear, nestling his nose in her hair. "I was just joking."

She nipped at his palm, sending a charge rocketing through him. "Don't make bets you don't intend to pay."

A dangerous burn flared low in his gut. "Hey, watch it there, champ."

"Or what?" Rolling her eyes, Charlie added a little extra twist in her step.

He exhaled his next words, trying to squelch the fire she'd sparked inside. "Or else."

She spun out and around, then resettled herself

against his chest. "I'm shaking in my boots. Or else? That's all you've got? I'm utterly terrified."

"Are you mocking me?" Damn if she didn't get under his skin. The sass, the smiles, the way her cute Texas twang taunted and teased him.

"What if I am?" She drew her head back and met his gaze, her mouth curved up in a grin. Their feet stopped moving, and they stood frozen, in the middle of the dance floor, the other couples swirling around them. Her arms went around his neck, and he tightened the circle of his arms around her waist. Their hips snapped together, drawn with a magnetic force. His skin crawled with anticipation, every nerve ending crackling, waiting. His eyes searched hers for encouragement. Yes? No? Did she want him to kiss her? Would it be another mistake?

"A part of me wants to kiss you right now, Charlie."

Her fingers toyed with the hair at the nape of his neck. "Just a part of you?"

"A big part," he admitted.

"I'm not familiar with all of your parts yet, Manhattan. What kind of part are we talking about here?" She glanced up at him through lowered lashes.

He knew he was about to cross a line. Ironically enough, it was a line he'd put into play. The line that was supposed to keep things on a professional level. He lowered his head, his mouth inches from hers. "Do you want me to?"

She drew in a sharp breath. "What do you think?"

He was close enough to feel the slow exhale on his chin. "I don't know what to think when I'm around you. You rattle my brain, make my head hurt."

"Then don't."

"You're right." He pulled back. "We shouldn't."

The confusion in her eyes didn't match the way her hands gripped him tighter. "I didn't mean don't kiss me. I meant don't think about it so hard." Then she tilted her head up and met his lips with hers.

Their mouths barely touching, the force of the impact rocked through him, and he fought like hell to suppress the need surging inside him.

Her hands worked under the edge of his shirt and branded the tender skin at his waistband. His tongue swept the inside of her mouth, where the taste of tequila and salt and lemon lingered. With their bodies pressed together from hip to hair, they swayed out of time to the beat of their own internal tune.

She made him ache with a hunger so deep it bordered on painful. Lost in the whirlwind of Charlie, he didn't come up for air until the music shifted to a fast-paced rock tune and the vibration of dozens of boots stomping on the raised floor shook him out of the stupor he'd nose-dived into.

"You want to get out of here?" He leaned close to her ear so she could hear him.

Her breath tickled his ear. "I don't know. A part of me might—"

He shook his head. "Just a part, huh?"

She hesitated. Now she was in the hot seat. He waited, ready for a long, drawn-out explanation of why this would be a bad idea. Instead, he felt her agreement in the nod of her head. Any words were lost to the racket around them. As they passed the bar, he tossed a few bills in the direction of the bartender and pushed the door open for Charlie. They didn't make it two feet out the front door before she grabbed him by the front of his shirt and yanked him her way. Caught off balance, he stumbled toward her and bounced off the bumper of a jacked-up pickup truck. Lips locked, they ricocheted between parked cars and trucks like two balls in a pinball machine as they stumbled toward where she'd parked.

This was crazy. His whole body hummed. It was like she was possessed with some sort of urgency. Maybe she felt the need to move fast, before she changed her mind. Her hands ran under his shirt, blazing a trail beneath her touch, leaving a longing afterburn in their wake.

This could make things awkward. He should stop. She'd regret this when she sobered up, and he'd feel like shit for not ending it.

"Charlie, I—"

Her hand slid inside the waistband of his jeans. "Yes, Beck?"

He hissed in a breath and tried to speak between kisses. "I don't think this is such a good idea."

"You're right." She nibbled on his bottom lip. "I absolutely agree."

"You've had a lot to drink, and I—"

"Are you serious?" She broke the kiss, her hand still wedged into his waistband. "I've had two beers and one shot over the past two hours. I'm perfectly capable of consent, cowboy." Her eyes flared as she pulled her hand out of his pants. "If you're looking for an excuse, just say so."

He already missed the heat of her touch. "I'm not looking for an excuse." He reached up to brush her hair back and tuck it behind her ear. The heat, the need, the want in her gaze pulled at him.

"Then what are you waiting for?" She crooked a finger

and took a few steps backward. He followed, taking one long stride to every two of hers.

They'd reached the truck. He opened the door and lifted her into the back seat, then climbed in after her. She scooted across the bench seat, her skirt splayed around her legs.

The rational part of his brain shut down like someone had pulled the power plug. Raw physical need took over.

Charlie leaned against the opposite door, the glow from the parking lot floodlight framing her in a silvery light. Her hair had escaped the knot she'd tied, and strands stuck out from her head in all directions. A fine sheen of sweat covered the skin exposed by her spaghetti-strap tank. So much skin. Beck wanted to run his hands, his lips, his tongue over every square inch.

She reached out to palm the front of his jeans. A growl started in the back of his throat and rumbled through his chest, unleashing a primal desire.

"Are we doing this?" he asked. The thought of shutting things down sent a shock wave of protest through his system. He'd gone too far for a cold shower to cool him off. If Charlie didn't want to see this through, he'd be spending some time getting reacquainted with his right hand.

She didn't respond—just stared up at him in the semidarkness. Her chest rose and fell in hypnotizing breaths. Since he'd first seen her in that tank, his mind had been crammed with thoughts of yanking her shirt over her head and running his hands all over her bronzed skin.

Hovering over her on hands and knees, he cleared

his throat and lifted his head to survey the sea of parked cars. "Yeah, I figured it was—"

A flash of white pulled his gaze back to Charlie as she whipped the tank top over her head and tossed it into the front seat. Her practical, no-nonsense, white bra pushed her breasts up like an offering, one he was all too happy to accept. He reached for her, cupping her cheek with a hand and running his finger down her jaw and along her neck, and pausing at the sweet hollow at the base of her throat.

Her even breath turned ragged when he lowered his mouth to run his lips along her collarbone. What was he doing? His heart crashed against the walls of his chest like an out-of-control junker in a demolition derby. She fumbled with the buttons on his shirt, finally giving up and tugging in an attempt to pull it over his shoulders. It bunched around his chest, and her hands began working his undershirt up, allowing the skin on their torsos to connect. He felt a sizzle like when bacon hits a hot skillet, the heat of skin-to-skin contact making him desperate to feel her, all of her, under him.

Lips mashed together, tongues swirled, his hands fumbled, trying to find a way under the long, flowy skirt. Someone could come along at any moment. He needed to stop. At least take her back to her place, if not abandon this crazy hookup altogether. That would be smart.

But then her fingers skimmed his abs, paused to unbutton his jeans, and eased down the zipper fly. He hissed as she wrapped her hand around his shaft and worked her thumb over his tip. He could have let himself go right here and now if he'd wanted to. Instead, he gathered every scrap of willpower he had and pulled her over on top of him.

"Charlie, we should go. Let me drive us back to your place."

She raised up over him, peeled her bra off, and finished the job she'd started on his buttons.

"It's too far." She flung one leg over his, grinding into his thigh as the air whooshed out of him.

Screw it. He wasn't ready to deal with the emotional stuff yet. It was too new, too raw. But the physical—he couldn't wait to start dealing with that.

Finally free of his shirt and her bra, their chests aligned, her breasts pressing down on his pecs. Heat radiated out from his core, smoldering through his limbs, flaring at each and every place their bare skin touched.

She felt so good. No, not just good. She felt fucking fantastic. Her lips pressed kisses along his jaw, then she nipped at his earlobe and ran her tongue along the shell of his ear. Her mouth was everywhere at once, licking, sucking, kissing, searing his skin. He was putty in her capable hands.

His fingers finally found a way through the yards of material bunched up around her waist, and he cupped her incredible ass with both hands, kneading the soft skin and pressing her hips harder into his thigh.

Charlie moaned into his mouth. He wanted to slow it down, savor every sensation and let them take their time getting to know each other's bodies. He wanted to see every uncovered inch of her. But she wouldn't let up. Next time. Damn, he hoped there would be a next time.

Did he have a condom? He worked his wallet out of the back pocket of his jeans, and it fell on the floor. His fingers felt for the familiar foil packet. A sigh escaped his chest as his fingers closed around the crackling package. Thank God for small favors.

*HH*

"You sure about this?" Beck's voice cut through the fog of lust that had crowded all rational thoughts from her brain. What was she doing? She hadn't had sex in more than eight years, and she was willing to hook up with a one-night stand in a parking lot where anyone could see them? No. This wasn't right. She couldn't be a notch on the cover of his leather portfolio.

But it felt so good. Underneath the ridiculous shirt Whitey must have sold him off the clearance rack, hard pecs, a six-pack—no, make that a twelve-pack—of abs felt like an escape route to some sort of nirvana. Not to mention the promise of salvation she still palmed in his pants. Her little battery-operated ticket to the land of O's had nothing on what Beck could offer.

This was wrong. Wrong on so many counts. First, the employer–employee thing. Second, they were in a parking lot. A freaking parking lot. How had she managed to lose every shred of control? Third, she hadn't had sex since Jackson. Her heart squeezed as a mental image of the last time they'd been together fuzzed at the edges of her mind.

Beck's finger slid along the waistband of her panties, and she shuddered, a long shiver that hit every nerve ending she had. She bit her lip to keep from crying out. Jackson would have wanted her to go on. Why couldn't her brain seem to follow instructions?

As Beck pushed her underwear down over her hips, a tear worked its way out of her clenched eyelids and rolled down her cheek. Dammit. She should be enjoying this. She *was* enjoying this. His hand drifted between them, edging its way toward the epicenter of her need. *Just do it, get it over with.*

"You okay?" Beck stilled underneath her. "Charlie?"

She sniffled, wiping at her cheek. Great. Now he'd know what an emotional hot mess she was.

"Hey"—his hand brushed her cheek—"we don't have to do this."

But she did. She wanted to. God, how she wanted to. "It's just been a long time."

"Okay." His fingers brushed along her arms, grazing her back. "You're in charge. We can take it as slow as you want."

How could she explain? She didn't want to go slow. She wanted him to erase all the hurt in her heart. Wanted him to wipe her memory clean of any pain. Wanted him to satisfy the deep, aching need she'd been carrying around with her for the past eight years.

She pulled his hand to her mouth, kissed his palm. It was time to move on from Jackson. And she wanted to go there with a man like Beck. No, not just *a man like Beck*. The realization hit her like a two-by-four to the heart. She wanted to go there with Beck.

Committed to opening herself up to this man, unlocking the chains and padlocks she'd wrapped around her heart, she slipped her panties off her legs. He slid the condom into place. She hovered over him, his hands on her hips, ready to guide her, to take her where she needed to go. Every nerve ending she had concentrated in that one spot, desperate for him to put an end to her need.

A loud knock sounded on the driver's side window. Beck banged his head on the roof of the cab as he shot to a seated position. She straddled him, her skirt still bunched up around her waist, bare breasts pressed against his chest.

"Charlie?" A beam of bright light sliced through the darkness, illuminating Beck's face. He ran a hand over the delicious scruff that had been scraping along her skin just moments before.

"Oh my God. I don't believe it." She climbed halfway over the front seat to locate her shirt and bra. Coming up empty-handed, she made a grab for Beck's instead and shoved her arms through the sleeves as the front door creaked open.

"Who is it?" Beck asked.

"Charlie? You okay?" The light bounced around the inside of the cab, finally stopping on her face.

Blinded, she put her hand out to shield her eyes. "Tippy, get the damn light out of my eyes."

"Oh shit. Shit. Shit. Shit." The light disappeared, and the whole truck shifted as Cash's best friend and coworker stepped off of the running board and onto the ground.

Charlie yanked the shirt over her shoulders and squelched the panic rising in her chest. Just her luck. She ran her hands over her hair in an attempt to wrangle it back into place.

"What the hell?" Beck rebuttoned his jeans before clambering out of the truck. She held her breath as the two men faced each other. A few folks had gathered around in the parking lot. Everyone for fifty miles around would recognize her truck. No sense pretending she wasn't here. She cracked the door, drawing Tippy's and Beck's attention.

"Damn, Charlie. What are you doing out here? I got a call from Dwight saying he thought something awful was going down in your truck, seeing as the windows were all steamed up." Tippy had his hands on the hips of his polyester uniform. With his sheriff's deputy hat covering the receding hairline and an official sidearm in the holster on his waist, he looked like he meant business.

"Can we just get out of here? Obviously the only thing going down out here is my reputation." To hell in a handbasket.

Tippy chuckled. "Yeah, but I logged it. Need to follow up with a report. What do you want me to say I found when I arrived on the scene?"

Charlie glared at the man who'd spent more time at her parents' place than his own home. "Tippy, I swear to you—"

"Get out of here. I will have to report it though, you know that." He tipped his hat to her, then turned and crunched across the gravel parking lot to where he'd left his squad car.

Her hand shook as she lifted it to climb back into the cab.

"You okay?" Beck asked. "And who is Tippy?"

Beck looked ridiculous standing in the dimly lit parking lot with no shirt on. She'd messed up his hair when she'd run her hands through it. She wanted to reach up and smooth down the adorable cowlick but pressed her arm against her side instead.

"No, I'm not okay. And Tippy works with Cash. Family friend and all that. What time does your flight take off tomorrow?"

"Ten. Figured I'd leave for the airport around seven."

"Leave at five."

A crease appeared across his forehead. "Why?"

"Because that way you might just avoid the gossipmongers." He still didn't get it. "Right now, Tippy is radioing in that he found us half-naked in the parking lot of the Suds Club. Whitey keeps a scanner and will pick up on the news. Within five minutes, half of Conroe County will know that you and I were doing a horizontal two-step in the back seat of my truck."

Beck blinked. "You've got to be exaggerating. Don't people around here have better things to do on a Sunday night?"

Her phone buzzed with an incoming text. She glanced at the screen, then held it out for Beck. Darby's "WTF" had a slew of exclamation points and question marks after it.

"Still don't believe me?" She climbed over the center console to the passenger seat. "Keys are above the visor."

Beck settled into the driver's seat. "I don't get it."

"Of course you don't. You probably grew up in a place where your neighbors didn't keep tabs on your comings and goings for their own entertainment. People around here know my business before I do sometimes."

"Sorry. I didn't know this would cause all kinds of trouble for you." He navigated out of the parking lot and onto the dark, two-lane county road.

She turned to look out the window. "It's my fault. I should have known better."

"Should have known better about what?"

"Nothing." How would she be able to explain it to him? He didn't grow up around here—he'd never get it.

"Don't shut me out here, Charlie. Tell me what you mean. I want to understand."

She pulled his shirt tighter around her. "Not tonight. It's late. You have to leave early. Can we talk about it when you get back?"

"Fine." He reached over and squeezed her hand. "But we will talk about this. I mean it."

She'd made a mistake. But with the bluish glow of the dashboard bouncing off his still-naked chest, her unsatisfied traitorous body argued with her.

She couldn't deny the attraction. She couldn't deny he'd awakened a part of her she'd stuffed away years ago. She couldn't deny the fact that if she had to do it all again, she'd have done the same damn thing.

# chapter

# ELEVEN

BECK EXITED THE TERMINAL AT LA GUARDIA AND inhaled the muggy heat of a New York City summer. He'd missed the city. As his dad's regular driver navigated the bumper-to-bumper traffic, the sight of concrete and high-rises calmed his nerves. The blare of horns and the unmistakable sounds of midday Manhattan were like a lullaby to his ears. It was too quiet in Holiday. Set him on edge and made him jittery. He cracked the window, letting the competing smells from hot dog stands, garbage, and exhaust heal him from the inside out. Damn, it was good to be home.

Forty-five minutes later, he stepped off the elevator in a high-rise bearing his last name. His boots clacked on the Italian marble floors as he strode past the reception area. The perfectly poised blond who worked the front desk turned in his direction and raised an eyebrow at his attire. He winked and barreled toward his office at the end of the hall. Eager to get back to work, he hadn't wanted to waste time stopping at his apartment. Not when he had an extra change of clothes here.

His assistant, Emily, rounded her desk when she saw him heading her way. "Welcome back, Mr. Holiday. I take it you, uh, enjoyed your time in Texas?"

She ran her gaze up and down, probably not sure what

to think about the jeans, cowboy boots, and few days of scruff on his usually clean-shaven chin.

"It was interesting, that's for sure." He took the pile of paperwork she handed him and continued to his corner office. Pausing to appreciate the view, he took in a deep breath and stood by the window. That's how he enjoyed nature—bathed in air-conditioning and from behind tinted glass.

Emily entered the office, clipboard in hand. "I wasn't sure what time you'd be back today. Your dad is having drinks with the mayor at five, and he wants you to go to that fund-raiser at the Plaza tonight at seven. Oh, and that lawyer called."

"Which one?" He turned to face her. He'd never noticed how pale her skin looked next to her crisp white button-down. Did the woman ever get out in the sun?

"The one with the accent—Mr. Hill."

"Thanks, Emily. Please tell my dad I'll meet him for drinks and gladly represent at the Plaza."

"He RSVP'd for two. Will you be taking someone with you?"

The only person he'd want to take anywhere was a thousand miles away. "No, I'll just stop in by myself. Oh, and can you send something to Charlotte Walker at the Rambling Rose? I owe her an apology."

"Flowers okay? The usual spend?"

"That would be great. Thanks, Em."

Emily nodded and left the office, closing the door behind her.

Beck ducked into the bathroom attached to his office to get cleaned up. While he showered and shaved, he let his mind drift to thoughts of Charlie and what she might be doing on a Monday afternoon in Holiday. She'd probably wrestled with the crazy pig and put in a full day's work at the Rose already. What would she look like in a floor-length ball gown like the women at the fund-raiser were sure to be wearing tonight? Red. She'd have to wear red. She'd stand out like a wildflower against the fifty shades of black couture. He nicked himself with the razor. *Damn.* No more thinking about Charlie.

Once he'd returned to his standard Monday-through-Friday uniform of a tailor-made suit and tie, he began to feel more like himself. He'd just eased into his padded desk chair when Emily poked her head through his office doorway.

"Your father wants to see you in the conference room."

"Can it wait? I need to get the financials done on that boutique hotel in the Village. He said he wanted them ASAP."

Emily held her ground just inside the door. "He's mad. He told me to tell you"—she consulted the notepad in her hand—"if you don't get your ass down here right now, the sanitation department will be scraping it off the sidewalk." She gave an apologetic shrug. "His words, not mine."

Beck paused. "He does sound mad."

The poor girl looked like she'd burst into tears any moment. "I'm sorry, Mr. Holiday. It's all my fault."

"What? What are you talking about? Em, whatever it is, I'm sure it's fine."

"I'll understand if you want to let me go. But he told me if I didn't tell him, I'd get fired anyway, so—"

Not sure whether he should touch her, he shifted from foot to foot. But she looked so lost, he wrapped his hands around her upper arms in an effort to provide some comfort. "I don't know what you're talking about. Want to fill me in here so I can help?"

She sniffled and lifted her glasses to wipe a tear from under her eye. "It's that Morris Park project. He knows you made contact with the broker before you left town. I'm so sorry."

"Everything will be fine." He should have known better than to try to make a move of his own. All he'd done was make a phone call. His dad couldn't get too upset over that. He moved past her, hoping he was right, and entered the giant conference room.

Beckett Sullivan Holiday Jr. sat at the head of the table, his most trusted adviser, Stu, on his right and Beck's coworker and confidante, J.T., on his left.

"What's this?" Beck asked. He twisted his wrist to check his watch. "I've got a ton of work to catch up on. Can't this wait?"

"You tell me, Son, since you seem to want to call the shots now."

"What are you talking about?" Beck fired a look at J.T., who lifted his shoulders and let them sag into a defeated shrug.

His dad stood. "Going behind my back? You think you're ready to make big decisions on your own?"

It was just a phone call. Beck put his hands out, palms up, in an attempt to pacify his old man. "No one's talking about making any kind of decisions."

Holiday crossed the plush carpet to the built-in bar and lifted the crystal topper off the decanter of single malt he kept on hand. "I'm hearing a different story from your partner in crime here. So one of you must be lying."

J.T. examined his cuticles, engrossed in his left thumb. Beck wouldn't be getting any backup from him.

The elder Holiday poured a glass of scotch. "You know I don't tolerate liars. So which one of you is it? Which one of you is going to leave this conference room without a job?"

J.T.'s head snapped up. "Mr. Holiday, sir, no one was trying to go behind your back. We—"

The shattering of an empty crystal tumbler on the granite counter silenced poor J.T. But Beck had seen his father bully associates like this before. If he could play along, string out the conversation until the old man calmed down, he could defuse the bomb ticking away in his dad's chest. But he didn't have the time or energy to play this game. Which left him with one choice. Suck up. Hard.

He cleared his throat. "No one's lying. Yes, I consulted J.T. about alternatives for financing the park project when you passed on it. But that's all it was. A conversation."

J.T.'s head bobbed up and down in agreement.

Now he needed to layer it on. But not too thick. "How stupid do you think we are? We'd be idiots to go behind your back. I just think we're passing up an opportunity to create a hell of a lot of goodwill for minimal investment. That's all." Not to mention the personal stakes he had at play. But that would only make his dad push back harder. Beck slumped into the chair, the jackhammer of his heartbeat a complete one-eighty from the forced I-don't-give-a-crap facade.

J.T. jumped in. "That's right, Mr. Holiday, just a conversation. Not even a long one. I think—"

"I'll be the one to tell you what to think around here." The glare Holiday trained on J.T. shut the poor sap down for good. "Now, I don't want to hear any more talk about deals under the table, is that clear?"

"Yes, sir." Beck stood. J.T. just nodded.

"I'm leaving next month to take Marion on that cruise she's been harping about for years, and I don't want to have to worry about you two dumbasses trying to orchestrate a coup while I'm gone. If either of you want out, you'd better speak up now. I'll have Stu here toss you out so fast your ass hits the pavement before your brain knows you've even moved." He traveled down the long length of the room as he spoke, stopping when he reached Beck. Then he leaned over, close enough that only Beck could hear. "You try to screw me over, and you'll be dead to me, Son. You understand?"

Beck nodded, sealing his fate.

"I ever hear talk about you doing something behind my back, and I'll make sure every door in this town is closed to you." He slung an arm around Beck's shoulders and clapped him on the chest with the other. "Glad we got that worked out, boys. J.T., can you give us a few minutes?"

"Sure." J.T. swung out from the table and made a beeline for the door.

Once it clicked shut behind him, Holiday took a seat.

"So here's what we're going to do. You get the title to the Rambling Rose yet?"

Beck slumped into the chair next to him. "Well, actually, Sully's—"

The mention of his grandfather's name caused a twitch at the corner of his dad's eye. "I haven't heard my old man called that in decades. Did he leave you everything or not?"

"The will stipulates I need to run the bar for three

months in order to inherit the Rambling Rose and his other property."

"Damn bastard. He knew he'd get his hooks into us one way or another. Even from the grave." The chair swiveled around, and his dad stood to stare out the wall of windows.

"Why do you hate him so much? I don't get it. People around there thought he was a good man. They—"

"They don't know shit in Holiday, Texas. You want to waste your time in that hellhole, you go right on ahead. Stick around for three months and try to find a buyer." He turned around and leveled his gaze at a point just past Beck's head. "Or you can get a start on that park project after all."

"What are you talking about?"

"For some reason, you've got a bleeding heart for Morris Park. You want to take on that project. I want to get what's due to me...the Rose. The way I see it, it's a win-win. Once you get the title, you transfer it over to me, and in return, we finance your little community cause."

"You're serious?"

Holiday clapped a hand on Beck's shoulder. "It's about time you started taking on more responsibility around here, and building goodwill is a fine place to start."

Beck tensed. It seemed an innocent enough exchange. He'd get a chance to make good on his promise, and his dad would get what probably ought to have been his anyway, as Sully's rightful heir. He'd probably been trying to prove himself to his hometown his entire life. Maybe this would give him a chance to make amends with the town and heal the emotional scars that had him running away from Holiday in the first place.

"You've got a deal." Beck thrust his hand toward his dad to seal the agreement with a handshake. "But promise me you'll keep the staff. They're a hardworking group of people." Especially Charlie. He wouldn't be able to live with himself if he thought he'd be putting her job in jeopardy.

"I swear I won't make any changes to the staff. Now you promise me you'll keep this to yourself. The good folks of Holiday might not be so eager for me to take over, so I'd like to be the one to tell them when the time comes. You spill the beans to anyone"—his eyes narrowed to slits—"and our deal is off."

"You got it." Who would he tell anyway? It's not like he was making lifelong friends down there.

"I'm glad to see you taking a real role in this company. It'll be yours someday, Son."

Beck waited for some sort of euphoria to fill his chest at his father's pseudo-compliment, the first he could remember. A gurgle bubbled in his gut—not quite the explosion of happiness he expected at hearing he was on his way to partner.

"I took the liberty of having Stu here draw up some paperwork. Just an agreement like we talked about." Holiday winked. "No harm in making things official."

Beck skimmed over the one-page document. "You mind if I take a look at this later and get it back to you? I really need to get started on the financials for that hotel in the Village."

"Take all the time you need." Holiday clapped his hands together. "In fact, why don't you clear your schedule now? The projects you're working on here can wait. The most important thing is for you to do whatever you need to do to take care of the Rambling Rose."

"Sure." Beck shuffled back to his office. His good mood at returning to New York had seeped out like helium from a balloon, leaving him deflated and empty.

"Everything okay?" Emily twisted her hands together. "Was he mad?"

"It's fine. Everything's going to be just fine."

"Oh good. Mr. Hill called again. Said it was urgent." Emily handed him the phone number scrawled across a piece of paper with Holiday Enterprises stamped on the top.

"Hold my calls, okay? Oh, and cancel the drinks and fund-raiser tonight." He'd get a few things settled at home, then head back to Holiday in a couple of days and take advantage of the break from his busy schedule. Without the massive decision of what to do about the Rose hanging over his head, it would be like a little vacation. He might even enjoy himself a bit.

"You sure everything's okay, Mr. Holiday?"

He hoped his smile conveyed the level of confidence he felt. "Not yet. But it will be."

Charlie slammed another mug of beer on the bar in front of Presley.

"And then she hopped back in the truck, and they fishtailed out of the parking lot." He held a few of the regulars captive with his rendition of what happened between her and Beck on Sunday night.

"You weren't even there, so don't go spreading rumors about things you don't know anything about." She turned her back on him, Dwight, and the others, searching for a friendly face on the other side of the room.

"Did you give him his shirt back? I'll let you have mine if you want to go hang out in my truck for a few minutes." Dwight's voice held a hint of jealousy under the humor.

Presley muttered something too low for her to hear, and the guys whooped and laughed. Screw it. Shep could handle things this late on a slow Wednesday night. She grabbed her keys from the office, intentionally ignoring the massive wreath of flowers Beck had sent over the day before. The poor kid who delivered them felt the need to explain that they didn't have anything in the shop that fit the budget Beck had supplied except a giant premade funeral wreath. Poppy had at least strung a pink ribbon across the middle with stick-on letters reading "Sorry." Charlie was surprised Presley hadn't set the tacky display up on the bar—something else he could mock her about.

She ducked out the back door and headed toward the hammock Cash had strung between two trees at the edge of the grass. The Sweetest Swine pageant was coming up on Saturday, and she still had a million things to do if she wanted to have everything ready.

Her phone pinged, and she glanced at the screen. Darby. She'd been giving Charlie crap for the past few days about the hookup, and Charlie was tired of hearing about it. It wasn't anybody's business what she did or with whom she did it. She was a grown woman. But that's not the way things worked around Holiday. With a groan, she tapped on the screen and read over the text.

**Darby:**     Guess who's back in town...
**Charlie:**   ???
**Darby:**     Come on, guess.
**Charlie:**   Just tell me already.
**Darby:**     You're no fun. Beck booked another extra-
               long weekend at the B and B. Just checked in.

Charlie didn't respond right away. What was he doing
back in town so soon? She thought she'd scared the
man off the last time she'd seen him. He'd left her place
without a shirt, taking all of her pride with him. There was
only one reason he'd come back. The Rose. He must have
decided to make a go of it.

As much as she wanted to honor her promise to Sully,
the Rose was the one thing that had kept her going for
the past several years. She couldn't stand to lose it. And
as much as she liked Beck, he didn't belong around here.
He'd never understand the importance of tradition. A
guy like him wouldn't be content to spend the rest of his
life sweeping the floor of a place like the Rambling Rose.
What would that mean for the folks who counted on the
Rose for their jobs, their social lives? It was the anchor that
held the whole town of Holiday in place.

**Darby:**     Charlie? You there? I bet he's headed your
               way. Mom says he just left.

She wasn't ready to see him. And if he showed up here
tonight, well, that would just give Presley more fuel for
the fire he was stirring up. She tucked her phone into her
pocket and made her way back into the bar.

"Hey, Shep?"

"Yeah, Boss?"

"Can you close up tonight? I'm not feeling so hot and think I'm going to head home."

"You got it. See you tomorrow?"

"Yeah. I'll be in first thing. I have to finish sewing the sequins on Baby Back's costume."

Shep shook his head. "Crazy Texans."

"You'll love the pageant."

"I didn't say I wouldn't love it. But I still think y'all are crazy. Dressing up a bunch of pigs."

"Hey, Baby Back's a ringer this year. We've got to defend her crown."

"You're right about that. Hey, feel better."

"Thanks." She'd be lost without Shep. But what would Beck do about the employees and staff? Most of them would probably stay. It's not like they had a slew of folks sitting around twiddling their thumbs, just waiting for a position to open up at the Rose. They could always use another bartender, especially on the weekends. But Beck would have to keep everyone else. At least for the time being. She'd make sure. Of course, that would require a conversation, which probably meant she'd have to see him face-to-face.

Her cheeks burned as she remembered the time spent in the back of the truck. After they'd steamed up the windows but before they'd been busted by Tippy. She'd been about to throw her reservations out one of the fogged-up windows and let Beck have his way with her. Her heart raced and a warm tingle started in the lowest part of her belly as she recalled the feel of his fingers on her skin. The way his mouth slid down her neck and the fluttery little kisses he'd left along her jaw.

*Stop it, Charlie.*

Her phone rang, a blessed distraction. "What?"

Darby squealed. "Did you get my text? Have you seen him yet?"

"Don't you have kids to put to bed or something?"

"Is he there yet?"

"I don't know, and I don't care. Shep is closing up tonight. I'm headed home to a glass of wine and a long, hot bath." Her boots crunched on the gravel as she crossed the parking lot to her truck.

"What's wrong with you? Can't you see this is your chance? Turn around."

Charlie kept her eyes trained on the ground. "Mind your own business. What happened on Sunday was a mistake, one I'm not willing to repeat, no matter how hot he is."

"A mistake?" The voice came from her right, and her head jerked in that direction.

Darby chatted on, her voice muffled as Charlie lowered the phone from her ear and pressed it against her leg.

"Is that what happened? A mistake? Whew. And here I was thinking I'd have to figure out how to handle things now that I'm back." Beck shrugged his shoulders and gave her a tight-lipped smile. The kind that tossed the ball back into her court and required a response.

She lifted the phone back to her ear. "Darby, I gotta go." Then she clicked the End button without any other kind of explanation and turned toward Beck. "So you're back."

"Looks that way, seeing as how I'm standing right here."

"Hey, when I said it was a mistake, I meant my part, not yours."

"Takes two to two-step, right? At least that's what my talented instructor taught me. I'm as much to blame for letting things get out of control as you are." He had on a Yankees T-shirt that stretched tight across broad shoulders, highlighting the contours of the chest she'd run her hands over not even seventy-two hours before. "And I can promise I'll never let it happen again."

Her heart flip-flopped in her chest like a fish that suddenly found itself flapping around on a dock. She bit her lower lip before she let herself say something she'd regret. He'd said never. Never was a very long time. Never was exactly what she needed. Never was the last thing her body wanted from Beck.

"So you're back to stay?"

"At least for three months. And I'm going to need your help. You know the ins and outs of this place better than anyone. You're going to stay on as manager, right? We can keep things professional. No more mistakes."

He kept his tone light, but she'd hurt him. She could tell by the way he wouldn't make eye contact. The tension practically snapped and crackled between them with everything left unsaid.

"Beck, I'm sorry. About the mistake comment. It really is me, not you. There are just things you don't understand."

His eyes met hers for a moment. "You're right, and I won't. Not unless you decide you're ready to share."

She looked away first. Could it really be that easy? Could she share about Jackson? Pry him out of her heart and pretend he didn't matter anymore? No, not yet. Maybe not ever. So she chose the easier path... the path where she'd pretend everything was fine between them. She worked with men and had grown up with five brothers. She'd just treat Beck like one of the crew. "What are your plans? I mean after the three months are over?"

"I have to survive them first, right?"

She studied his face. "You expect me to believe you're going to stay in Holiday after you get the title?"

He made eye contact, then focused on some invisible spot on the ground. "I haven't made it that far yet. But I promise you I'm not making any changes to the staff."

"There are a lot of people who depend on this place. Not just the folks who work here but the whole dang town. I don't know that you realize how important the Rose is or how much it meant to your grandfather. If you sell it or—"

"I didn't say anything about selling it." Beck thrust a hand at her. "So are we on?"

Feeling like her back was pressed against a wall, even though nothing stood behind her except acres of rolling pasture land, Charlie slid her hand into Beck's. The shock of feeling his skin on hers, even in something as innocent as a handshake, rolled through her nervous system, flickering along the way.

If he felt it too, he didn't show any outward sign. "Good. Looks like you're heading out for the night. What time should we get started tomorrow?"

Charlie pulled her hand away and jammed it into her back pocket. "I'll be here by eight. I need to finish Baby Back's costume for the pageant this weekend."

"Great. I'll see you tomorrow. You can start teaching me everything I need to know."

She nodded, anxious to reach the sanctity of her truck, where she could process their interaction in private.

"Good night, Charlie."

"Good night." She whirled around and took steady, measured steps to the edge of the lot, where she'd parked early that morning. She didn't want him to think he'd gotten under her skin. But he had. And now she'd committed herself to working with the man for the next few months under the watchful eye of the entire town. Should be a piece of cake. Or more like a cow patty with some frosting slapped on it…only time would tell.

# chapter
# TWELVE

BECK SLID INTO HIS BOOTS, THEN PULLED A FRESH button-down shirt over his shoulders. He'd pretty much cleaned out Whitey's store the other day. At least the decent options. As long as he was in Holiday and had to play the part of the long-lost prodigal grandson returning to make good on the family business, he'd look the part, too. The blisters on his heels had healed, and the boots had molded into a custom fit. He wouldn't admit it to anyone back home, but they actually felt pretty good. The shirt was a different matter though. No matter how much he tried to appreciate the wild patterns and colors on the western shirts, he didn't think he'd ever feel comfortable in purple paisley or turquoise plaid.

At least he had access to real caffeine. His espresso machine had arrived yesterday via overnight delivery. Should have been there the day before, but he'd found out overnight didn't actually mean overnight when the delivery address wasn't on a regular route. Still, no more weak coffee for him. He waited for the sputtering and steam to stop and then poured the dark liquid into a thermal to-go cup. He'd need to move everything over to Sully's place soon and take up a more permanent residence. But first to get through the pig pageant today.

What better way to show his commitment to the

Rambling Rose and Holiday than by taking part in what he'd been told was one of their longest-standing traditions? With Dwight's help, he planned on stealing the title right out from under Charlie and her obnoxious hog.

Dwight had promised to take care of the pig, and Beck had pulled a few strings to get a last-minute costume from one of the stylists his current stepmom used. Now to go meet his prize-winning contestant.

Forty-five minutes later, he stood in the center of the dance hall listening to Charlie bark out orders to the staff. They'd hired extra help for the event, and she ran through a list of jobs and expectations. Angelo had been working the barbecue pits nonstop for the past three days, and the smell of smoked brisket and—ironically—baby back ribs smothered everything. Didn't matter where he was—inside, outside, even a couple miles away—he couldn't avoid the mouthwatering scent of homemade sauce.

Charlie wrapped up the meeting, and everyone got to work in the hot-pink T-shirts she'd special-ordered for the event. The front read "The Rambling Rose Has Gone Hog Wild" with a set of pig footprints underneath. On the back, she had the date and "125th Annual Pig Pageant" with a pig-snout-and-tiara graphic. She hadn't pressed Beck to wear the shirt. Trying to fit in only made him stand out more anyway.

"Hey." Charlie met him at the corner of the bar. "You ready for this?"

"Oink. Oink."

She rolled her eyes. "Very funny. You won't be making fun when you're counting up the till later."

"So you've been telling me. What do I need to do today? Anything special? I want to pitch in." Charlie had been doing a good job getting him up to speed on the happenings at the Rose. But she'd stay in charge, and he was fine with that.

"Hopefully we've got everything under control. If you want to stick by me, we can tackle anything that comes up together."

"Tackle together? Sign me up."

"Not that kind of tackling." Her cheeks flushed a shade slightly lighter than her shirt.

He needed to knock it off. They'd made a grown-up decision not to act on the sizzling tension that crackled just under the surface of their workplace interactions. But something about designating her as off-limits made her that much more attractive. Like telling himself he would quit drinking but leaving one more beer in the back of the fridge. He'd never be stupid enough to try that. Having Charlie at his fingertips all day long was like looking at that beer, knowing how it would taste on his lips, and having to shut the fridge door anyway. And it had only been three days. He'd have to find another distraction for all that pent-up energy.

"Hey, y'all." Charlie's cousin Brittany sashayed across the ballroom and sidled up to the bar. "Ready for me to steal that sash back?"

"You'll have to steal it because you'll never win it fair and square." Charlie nodded toward her cousin. "Brittany here thinks her Sweet Caro-Swine is going to win this year."

Beck's gaze drifted over to Brittany. Her hair hung down her back in a brown sheet from underneath the brim of a straw cowboy hat. A sliver of tanned skin peeked out from the gap between her hot-pink halter top and the waistband of a pair of Daisy Duke jean shorts.

She winked a heavily made-up eye at him, and her bubble-gum-pink lips swirled into a slanted smile. "That's right. Sweet Caro-Swine has been practicing, and she's going to sweep the pageant this year. If you're a betting man, you'd best put your money on my pig."

Beck smiled back. "Don't tell me someone actually takes bets on the outcome of this ridiculous thing?"

"Ridiculous? Sugar, you just watch and see. I'm gonna make a killing by putting my money where my mouth is." As if there were any doubt in his mind where her mouth was, she blew him an air-kiss to be sure.

When he'd wished for a distraction, he hadn't mean to summon it in the form of Brittany Walker. To drive her overly overt point home, she leaned close and whispered in a voice dripping with the sticky sweetness of honey, "My mouth is good at other things, too."

Beck jerked away so fast that his knee banged on the stool next to him, and it toppled over onto the floor.

Brittany smirked and fluttered long, mascaraed lashes. "I've gotta go get Sweet Caro-Swine ready. My makeup artist is probably already at the trailer. See y'all later." She squeezed Beck's bicep and scooted out the side door.

Charlie set the stool upright and narrowed her eyes at him. "I warned you about Brittany once. You're a big boy though, so if you want to fan those flames, go right on ahead."

Beck cleared the awkward bubble from his throat.

"I've got no plans to fan anything. If you don't need my help right away, I'm going to head out back and see if my pig's here yet."

"Your pig?" She set the clipboard down on the bar and looked at him in a mixture of disbelief and amusement. "Where in the world would you get a pig?"

"I've made connections around here, and I think I've got a real contender."

Her hands went to her hips, and she appeared to stifle a laugh. "Well, okay then. You'd better go check on your pig. What's her name? I want to make sure I don't miss her in the lineup."

"Marilyn Sow-roe. She'll be the blond in the white dress." At least he hoped she'd be in the white dress. Dwight's part of the bargain better have included helping him wrestle the beast into its costume.

"Good luck. I hope Marilyn does well."

Charlie's well wishes didn't align with her body language. Obviously she didn't think he could do it. That only made him want it more. He'd prove he could hang with the locals. Even if the closest he'd ever come to a pig before was eating a ham and swiss from that deli on East Forty-third.

"Thanks. See you in a bit."

She turned back to her clipboard, and he ventured outside. Vendors had set up around the beer garden in back, offering everything from pickled pig's feet to pork chops on a stick to pig-themed pottery. Employees scurried around taking care of last-minute details. A stage had been rigged at one end of the fenced-in area. The sound of squeals, snorts, and snuffling told Beck that's where he'd most likely find his pig. As he rounded the stage, Dwight waved to him, beckoning him over to the back end of a truck.

"Dude, you owe me big time for this." He held a handful of rope in one hand. Beck's gaze followed the line to where an enormous black-and-white-spotted pig lounged in the bed of the truck.

"Wow." He blew out a breath. "Thanks, man. So what do we do with it now?"

"Contest doesn't start until five. Do you have somewhere to keep it till then?"

Beck looked around. All the other pigs seemed to be contained in wire crates or cages. "No. You said all I needed was a costume and a gimmicky name."

"Well, I'm not gonna sit around here all day and hold your pig for you."

"I've got to help Charlie. Can you take it back to where you got it and bring it back closer to the start time?"

Dwight kicked at the tire with the toe of his boot. "You have any idea how crowded it gets around here? I got a good spot. If I leave and come back, I'll have to park half a mile away. Your pig, your problem." He handed the end of the rope to Beck and shoved his hands in his front pockets like he was afraid Beck would pass it back.

"But how do I get a dress on it?" His stomach dropped to his knees when he realized Dwight was going to leave him alone to fend for himself. Three shots of espresso and another one of those giant gourmet breakfasts hadn't been such a good idea this morning. The liquid rolled around in his gut like a giant tsunami wave gathering momentum.

Dwight backed away, putting one boot behind the other in a slow retreat. "Bribe it with treats." He yanked a small, crinkly bag out of his pocket and tossed it at Beck. It landed five feet away.

"Are those dog treats?" Beck reached for the bag but realized he'd have to let go of the rope. He glanced back at the pig, whose side rose and fell with each slobbery breath. Looked safe enough. He dropped the rope and stepped forward.

As soon as the end of the rope hit the dirt, the pig rolled to its feet and scrambled out of the truck. Beck dove for the rope and managed to get his hand wrapped around the tail end. The pig broke right to veer around a parked car, and the rope burned through Beck's hand.

"Dammit!" He looked up from where he'd landed facedown in the dirt. Dwight stood over him, one hand wrapped around the rope, Marilyn squealing in disappointment on the other end. "What happened?"

"Don't let go of the rope." Dwight waited for him to brush the dust off his jeans and then handed the rope back. "Smart sucker knows when to run. Now I suggest you find a place to pen it before you lose your winning ticket."

"Yeah." Beck led the suddenly compliant pig to where the treats sat in the dirt. "We need to get something straight here, Marilyn. I'm not going to take any more crap from you."

The pig seemed to evaluate him with its beady little eyes. Then lifted its tail and deposited the biggest, smelliest pile of poop he'd ever seen right smack-dab in front of his boots. Beck shook his head and shot a glance around. No one seemed to be paying a bit of attention to them. At least one thing in his favor. He wrapped both hands around the rope and began to drag the pig toward the fence line. Pen the pig. That was a great idea. And he knew just the place.

~ ~ ~

Charlie rounded the corner of the building and smacked into a solid wall. Weird. That hadn't been there before. She backed away, dazed, hand over her cheek. She could already feel it swelling under her fingers.

"Charlie. Oh hell. Are you okay?"

Strong arms circled her as she squinted up into the bright midday sun. "Beck?" The wall could talk, and it sounded a lot like Beck. She shook her head, trying to clear it.

"I didn't see you coming."

"Feels like I caught a horseshoe to the head."

"I'm sorry. It was an elbow. You need some ice?"

Her fingers tapped around the lump on her cheek. "I don't have time. I've got to get Baby Back dressed before the contest starts. Where are you going in such a hurry?"

"Just to clean up. I hope you don't mind, I put my pig in the pen with Baby Back. I didn't know I needed to bring a crate or anything."

"What do you mean you put your pig in with her?" Charlie jerked back to stare at him. "You can't put two strange pigs together who haven't been introduced!"

"Why not?"

"Because they might not like each other. What if they get in a fight and Baby Back gets hurt? What if one of them bites the other? What if they start to get rough and knock through the fence? Don't you know anything?" She pushed past him and stomped across the grass to the edge of the pigpen. "What's this?"

Baby Back stood motionless, dwarfed by the giant boar who'd mounted her and appeared to be doing his best to poke her in the backside. He grunted, squealed, and snorted, his rear end bucking up and down.

"Get away from her!" Charlie climbed on the bottom rail of the fence and waved her arms in the air. The boar continued to thrust. Charlie cleared the fence and landed with a splash in a puddle of mud. Unbelievable.

Beck raced around the fence to the gate.

"Help me!"

"How?" He opened the gate and took two small steps forward, stopping just inside the pen.

"Close the gate. Then help me get him off. She must be in heat. Dammit."

"Looks like he's getting off fine on his own." Beck shut the gate and stood stock-still while Charlie trudged through the dirt and mud.

"This isn't the time to joke." Charlie put her palms on the giant boar and pushed. Nothing happened. "Help me, he's too big, he's too…too—"

"Too into it?" Beck bit back a smile. "Yeah, I don't want to get in the middle of a budding romance."

"You think this is funny?" She blew a strand of hair out of her face. "Your pig is supposed to be a female. You do know what a female is, don't you?"

He picked his way through the mud puddles, moving toward her. "I do believe I'm familiar with the anatomy of the fairer sex." He lifted a brow.

Her stomach flipped at the reference to how familiar

she knew he was. He would pay for that last remark. "Get over here and help me."

"Think of it, Charlie." He continued to move closer. "It's like we're matchmakers."

"We are not matchmakers." She clamped her hands on her hips and glanced at the fence line, where a small crowd had begun to gather. "Your boar is deflowering my prize-winning pig...in public!"

Beck lifted his head, sweeping his gaze along the fence. "All right. What do we do?"

The pig continued to grunt and snort.

"Something. Anything," she muttered under her breath. "This is a *family* festival."

Beck took in a deep breath. After what seemed like forever, he set his hands on the boar's bristly back end and shoved it to the side. The boar squealed but didn't dislodge. Beck pushed again. Nothing happened.

The ridiculousness of the entire situation hit her full blast. "This is crazy."

He nodded. "That's the most logical thing you've said so far."

"We're going to have to do this together." She wheeled around and set her palms on the big boar's back.

"All right. I'm in." Beck stepped next to her, prepared to give it his all.

"Come on. On the count of three, let's give them a good push at the same time." Charlie counted, and they both pushed, finally breaking the pigs apart. Half the crowd cheered, and the other half booed. Baby Back scampered toward the covered part of her pen. The boar wheeled on them, an angry glint in his eye.

"Watch out. He's not happy." Charlie took a few steps toward the fence. The boar snorted, watching her every move.

"Here, pig." Beck waved his arms, distracting the boar. His head swung around, focusing his beady eyes on Beck. "Um, Charlie?"

"Yeah?"

Beck kept one eye on the boar while he backed toward the gate. "He's watching me, isn't he?"

"Appears to be. You're doing great though. Move slow. No sudden movements."

Beck's chest rose and fell as he made slow progress to the edge of the pen. "Let's settle this one fellow to another. I know you're disappointed, buddy. But you and Baby Back aren't meant to be."

Charlie couldn't help but smile as Beck tried to reason with the angry boar. In her experience, talk therapy rarely, if ever, worked with animals. She could tell him.

But…it might be more fun to let him figure that out for himself.

"She's too good for you, y'know. People come from miles around to—"

"Hundreds of miles, even," Charlie interjected.

"Hundreds, really?" Beck looked up at her.

"We even had a family from Alaska last summer. They heard about the pageant and brought their prize-winning swine all the way to Texas."

"What was her stage name?"

"She was Frost-Sty the Snow Pig. They padded her up in white cotton batting. She came in third."

"Huh." Beck took his eyes off the boar for a fraction of a heartbeat. But a fraction was all it took.

"Watch out!" Reacting on instinct, Charlie flung herself at his chest before he could be run down.

He gave a surprised shout as he caught her against him and they fell back together, out of the path of the bitter boar. Her elbow ended up jabbing into the hard muscles of his stomach. "What the hell, Charlie?" Beck said, sounding winded.

"You're welcome." She rolled off him, trying to figure out where the pig had gone.

"You're welcome?" Beck flung a sleeve over his face, wiping away the worst of the mud. At least she could see his eyes. Angry eyes. Eyes that didn't look at all thrilled to be saved from the path of a charging boar.

"Yeah. You're welcome for knocking you out of the way. He almost got you."

The boar must have used up all his energy on Baby Back followed by his final charge. He gave a dismissive snort and trotted toward the bucket of slop.

"I don't think that was necessary." Beck staggered to his feet. "Marilyn and I were working things out. We had an understanding."

"Marilyn was about to knock you on your ass and stomp you into the ground."

"Is that so?" He continued to fling mud from his hands. "Thanks to you, now I'm covered from head to toe in pig slop. Again."

"Not quite." She still owed him for that crack he'd made about how well he knew the fairer sex. Reaching into a particularly rich puddle, she gathered a handful of mud and flung it at the one patch of paisley yet to be stained by mud.

The mud ball splatted against his arm. "What the hell was that?"

"Now you're covered from head to toe."

"I probably deserved that." He smiled and dropped to his knees.

"What are you doing?" she asked, as his hand dipped to the ground.

"Payback." He grabbed a fistful of mud and lobbed it in her direction. The glob of mud smacked into her chest, splattering her face.

"You didn't." She glanced down at her shirt.

His eyes sparkled with humor. "Oh yes, I did."

Beck scooped up another glob and launched it at her. This one grazed her head, and she reached up to find a blob of mud running down her hair. Once she might be able to forgive. But twice? Hell no. It was on, and she didn't care who was watching.

She retaliated, scooping up handfuls of mud and flinging them in his general direction.

"Oh, no you don't!" He lunged for her, grabbing her around the waist.

She twisted away from him, then kicked her foot out to trip him. He stumbled, almost got back up again, and then fell to the ground, pulling her down on top of him.

Trapped against his chest, she took in a deep breath. Mud dripped from her hair, plopping down to splatter his shirt. Their gazes met. The smile spread across his lips reflected in his eyes. He was right—this was ridiculous.

"You about done flinging mud?" she asked, watching his lips as his mouth began to move.

"You about done wanting to fight?"

She sighed. "Yes. I don't want to fight anymore."

His smile widened. "So let's kiss and make up."

His suggestion hung between them.

"It's not that easy."

"It sure could be that easy if you let it."

She wanted it to be that easy, wanted nothing more than to put her faith in Beck and let him help shoulder her burdens. As she hovered on the edge of giving in, the small crowd erupted into spontaneous applause. Charlie glanced up—the sanctity of their private interlude had been breached. She wiped a palm over her cheek and winced at the tender spot under her eye.

"You okay?" Beck scrambled out from under her and offered a hand to help her up.

She stood, noticing the onlookers who ringed the pen. The fight and the bottled-up desire drained right out of her, and she raised her gaze to Beck.

He looked like he'd gone scuba diving in a pool of chocolate pudding. She lifted the hem of her T-shirt and wiped at her eyes with a clean spot. No longer pinned in place by the randy boar, Baby Back nudged Charlie's hand with her nose and she scratched the pig behind an ear.

"Can you do me a favor and get that boar out of here? Didn't you read the contest rules? Sows only. That means females."

He took on a sheepish grin and almost looked sorry. Almost. "I didn't know."

"Of course you didn't," she sighed. "Because you probably didn't read them." She sloshed toward the gate, then ducked through, leaving Beck standing in the middle of the pen. She'd gone and done it again—made a fool out of herself in public. At this rate, the loose lips in Holiday would have enough to talk about all the way through Christmas. Maybe even into next year if she didn't get a handle on herself.

"Now that's what I call mud wrestling." Darby caught up to her as she stomped toward the small barn. "Was that part of the scheduled entertainment?"

Charlie glared at her friend. "What do you think?"

"I think you like him."

"What?" She stopped in her tracks and threw her arms out wide. "I get attacked in a pigpen…a freaking pigpen… trying to save our mascot from being violated, and you somehow think that means I like Beck?"

"You're right." Darby clucked her tongue. "I don't think it. I know it."

Charlie growled and reached out with two muddy hands to grab her friend's shoulders. Maybe she could shake some sense into her. "What is wrong with you? Has everyone around here lost their ever-lovin' minds?"

Darby sidestepped to avoid her grasp. "Honey, I think it's you who's lost her mind. That man is driving you crazy. Get it over with. Put yourself out of your misery. Even Baby Back is getting some."

"You think that's my problem? That I need to get naked with Beck?"

"No. You already pretty much got naked with the man. I think you need to make some bacon. Even I'm overdosing on the sexual attraction between you two. I'm just suggesting you have a little fun. Let nature run its course and get him out of your system."

"Darby, have you noticed what I look like? I'm covered in mud and pig poop. You are certifiably insane if you think I've got sex on my mind right now." And she didn't have sex on her mind. Not at that particular moment in time. Five minutes before, when she'd been straddling her personal kryptonite, maybe the thought had passed through. But she'd never admit it. Not to Darby and definitely not to Beck.

"Have it your way, toots. But you keep this up, and you're going to self-destruct." Darby skipped backward and whirled around to head back to the party. "My way's more fun."

Ha, *more*. Charlie groaned. That's the only thing the future held with Beck—*more trouble*.

# THIRTEEN

"I'M SORRY, MR. HOLIDAY. RULES ARE RULES." MR. HILL looked anything but apologetic as he glanced over at Marilyn, a pig-shaped pink Popsicle in one hand.

"Can't we make an exception just this once?" Beck adjusted the strap of Marilyn Sow-roe's gown. Freshly bathed, coarse hair oiled to a sheen, the pig looked better than he did.

Mr. Hill sighed and shook his head. "Wouldn't look right for us to offer you special treatment, now would it? You're welcome to come up with another entrant. A *female* entrant, that is."

"And where am I supposed to come up with another pig on such short notice? Took me long enough to find this one."

"Maybe one of the other contestants has a backup." Mr. Hill shrugged and licked the sticky syrup off his stubby fingers.

"Forget about it." Beck huffed out a breath and wheeled around, trying to locate Dwight in the crowd.

In the ten minutes he'd been arguing with the attorney about letting him enter the contest, the grassy area designated as spectator seating had filled up. He tried to estimate the attendance. Had to be at least fifteen hundred. Maybe even two thousand. And if each one of the attendees had paid for a ticket and spent money on food, beverages, and souvenirs…Charlie was right. There was money to be made in performing pork.

He led his pig back to Dwight's truck and tied him to the edge of the bed. Let Dwight worry about dealing with the troublemaker. If he hadn't mounted Charlie's precious Baby Back, the gig never would have been blown.

Free from further obligations, he snagged a deep-fried delicacy from one of the many food trucks parked around the edge of the lot and found a spot at the end of a bench just in time to watch the show.

Presley walked to the center of the stage and grabbed the mic. "Welcome, everyone, to the Rambling Rose's annual Sweetest Swine competition. The contestants and their handlers have been working all year: creating their costumes, perfecting their prances, and tweaking their talents."

A smattering of applause rippled through the crowd. Talent? Charlie hadn't mentioned anything about having a talent prepared. He really should start to read the fine print. It might be a blessing in disguise that Marilyn had been disqualified.

"Before we get started"—Presley walked toward the front edge of the stage—"how about a little ham humor? Can anyone tell me what you get if you play tug-of-war with a pig?"

A little girl in the front row raised her hand.

"Ah, my niece Kenzie. What do you get, sweetie?"

She stepped to the edge of the riser where Presley held the microphone down to her level. "You told me this one before, Uncle Presley. Pulled pork."

Some people laughed. Some groaned. Some shook their heads and rolled their eyes, Beck included.

"Did you hear that? Pulled pork, people. Good one, huh? Shameless plug here. If you're in the mood for pulled pork, step inside and one of the staff will fix ya up with a heaping helping. Now, before y'all start squealin' for the show to start, let me bring out the first contestant. All the way from the beaches of Southern California, put your hands together for Miss Spamela Anderson."

The sparkly backdrop Charlie had rigged at the back of the riser shook. A guy in red board shorts, a lifeguard buoy slung over his chest, stepped through. With much coaxing and bribing, an enormous pink pig followed. Some sort of red fabric wrapped around her middle and between her legs. People laughed and pointed as the theme from *Baywatch* blared through the speakers.

Spamela snorted, made a quick circle around the stage, and darted through the curtain.

"Aw, I think she's feeling shy tonight. Or maybe she had an ocean rescue emergency. Let's hear it again for Spamela Anderson."

Before Presley could read his next index card, the curtain separated and a woman with another entrant strutted onto the stage. Beck barely recognized the bedazzled duo. Brittany and her blinding pig sparkled in the late afternoon sun.

"Next up, uh, Sweet Caro-Swine. And she'll be playing the drums. The drums? Really, Brittany?" Presley dropped the mic to his side while a kid ran out with a huge, flat drum and set it down in the center of the stage.

Neil Diamond's voice boomed through the speakers, and the crowd clapped along while he sang about hands touching, reaching out, and then there it was…the *bamp bamp bamp*. When the moment arrived, Sweet Caro-Swine pounced on the drum in time to the beat. Impressive. Even Presley cracked a grin and gave his cousin a sly wink.

The song ended, and Brittany and Sweet Caro-Swine bowed, apparently in no hurry to head backstage.

"Hey, girls, don't hog the stage. Get it, folks, hog? Seriously, I crack myself up." Presley slapped his thigh and pulled out the next index card. "We're going back in time for this next competitor. All the way back to the 1950s. Please welcome Piggy Sue to the stage."

Beck closed his eyes and shook his head. He had to be seeing things. But then he opened them again and…nope. The crazy pig had on roller skates. He didn't recognize the guy dressed up like Buddy Holly. He'd only met a handful of the local people, so that didn't surprise him much. What did surprise him was the poodle skirt, beehive wig, and, oh yeah, *freaking roller skates.*

Piggy Sue let her handler lead her around the stage on her skates. Beck wouldn't have described her moves as smooth, especially on the final turn when her legs splayed underneath her and her handler had to grab someone from the back to help him carry her off the stage. But…roller skates. So far Piggy Sue had his vote.

He sat through dozens of pigs, some more impressive than others. Oinkrah Winfrey had potential, but Mary Louise Porker lay down and wouldn't get up. Presley had to ask for a few volunteers to come up from the audience to physically remove the poor pig.

Finally, only one contestant remained.

Presley cleared his throat and moved to center stage. "We're down to the last entrant. I'm sure y'all remember her from last year as Riblet McEntire. This year she's stepped up her game. Ladies and gentlemen, I give you... Lady Hog-Ga."

The sun had set enough that the strobe lights had their intended effect. They bounced of the sparkly silver backdrop, and Beck had to shade his eyes from the dazzling display. Charlie and Baby Back spun onto the stage. The piles of material and bling he'd seen Charlie hard at work on earlier had looked nothing like the spectacle on stage. Huge three-foot wings spread out from a harness on the pig's back. A studded mask covered her face with slits cut out for her eyes, and her socks had been decorated to look like spiked heels. The speakers played a medley of Lady Gaga's current tunes while Baby Back and Charlie performed a well-executed, synchronized dance routine across the stage.

The crowd erupted into whistles, applause, and shouts of encouragement. Beck joined in. That performance deserved a standing ovation. And Charlie looked damn good in her blingy, hot-pink ensemble. All traces of mud and slop had been washed away, and her low-cut spandex leotard left little to the imagination.

After several minutes, Presley regained control. He announced the top three and brought them out on the stage.

"In third place, for those almost-perfect pirouettes... way to go, Piggy Sue."

That left Charlie and Brittany and their respective pigs. Beck wanted Charlie to win, but he also kind of wanted her to lose. If it weren't for Baby Back's appealing backside, his Marilyn Sow-roe might have been a contender.

How could he be harboring serious regrets about missing out on a pig beauty pageant? If only his dad could see him now...

Presley tapped on the microphone then lifted it to his lips. "In second place, for the fourth year in a row—"

"Again?" Brittany stomped to the front of the stage, grabbed the sash out of Presley's hand, and barreled down the steps, poor Sweet Caro-Swine struggling to keep up.

"That means your reigning Sweetest Swine keeps her title! Congratulations, Baby Back—ahem, I mean, Lady Hog-Ga."

Charlie and Baby Back dropped into a curtsey. The crowd clapped and whistled. Some threw pink roses. Others threw...pork rinds? That's what it looked like anyway. Charlie met his gaze. Beck gave her a solid thumbs-up. She deserved the win. He'd never seen anything like this in his life, and God willing, he never would again.

She blushed and looked away. But not before some sort of reluctant smile graced her lips.

⚜

Beck tapped on the closed office door. He and Charlie hadn't crossed paths most of the day, but it was time to make nice and apologize.

"Come in."

He cracked the door and poked his head through.

"Oh, it's you." She barely looked up.

"You expecting somebody else?" The bar had stopped serving about a half hour before. Though at two o'clock in the morning, maybe she *had* been waiting for someone.

The sigh that whooshed out of her gave him all the answer he needed. "Just going over tonight's numbers."

"Look, I'm sorry about the pig. I was only trying to fit in."

"Sit down."

He lowered himself into the chair in front of the desk before she could change her mind. "I didn't mean to cause so much trouble."

Charlie reached into the bottom drawer and pulled out a half-empty bottle of whiskey. She filled two tumblers with about an inch of the dark-amber liquid and passed one to Beck.

"Cheers." She clinked her glass with his and tossed her head back to down the shot.

He leaned back, relaxing into the well-worn chair. This wasn't what he'd expected. Quite the opposite of the ass-chewing he deserved.

"Charlie, I—"

"Drink your shot, Beck."

He swirled it around, then lifted the glass to his lips and drained it.

"Thanks. Sully and I used to toast together after a big night, and this one's going down in the record books. We cleared more than last year, and I don't even have all of the numbers yet."

"I'm the one who should be thanking you. I know I've only been here a few days, but it's clear my grandfather knew what he was doing when he hired you."

A half laugh escaped through her lips before she bit down and cut it off.

Beck leaned forward, putting his elbows on the desk. "I'm serious. You're the driving force behind this place."

"If you think I'm a force, you should have met Sully. I was scared half to death of him for the longest time."

"What happened?"

She tilted her head and focused her gaze on something over his left shoulder. "He saved me."

"You mean like a church thing?"

"What?"

"Like he laid hands on you or something?"

"Gosh no. Never mind. Forget I said anything. It was a long time ago." She lifted the bottle and nodded toward his glass. "Want more?"

"Just a little."

She poured another half inch into his glass, then put the bottle back in the desk drawer. "So where did you get the pig?"

"You mean Marilyn Sow-roe? Guess I need to rethink the name, huh?"

"Was it one of my guys? Shep? Presley?"

Beck shook his head. He could tell what she was getting at, but he wouldn't give up Dwight. "Nah. Just an honest mistake. I'll pay more attention next time."

The edge of her mouth quirked up before she could stop it. "Doing a balls check wouldn't hurt either."

She'd made a joke. A good sign. "I tried to tell the judges that Marilyn identified more with her inner diva. They didn't go for it."

"And thank goodness. That white dress was amazing. If you'd hadn't been disqualified, I don't think Baby Back would have won."

He smiled at the memory of Baby Back dressed up as Lady Hog-Ga. "There's always next year."

"You think you'll be around that long?"

He waited a beat before answering. He wanted to tell her he'd already made up his mind. That his dad would work something out with her so he could manage the Rose long distance and Beck could get back to his real life in New York. But the look on her face made him think she didn't want the confirmation. So instead, he shrugged his shoulders and emptied his glass.

"Stranger things have happened, right?"

"Mmm. Around here, strange seems to be the norm." He couldn't agree more. She shuffled the papers in front of her into a stack, making sure they lined up before she slid them into a file folder.

"Well, for what it's worth, I am sorry."

"I know." Her eyes met his. She chewed on her lower lip, like she was thinking about saying something.

"What?"

"A few of us are going down the Guadalupe tomorrow. I know you're probably busy getting settled and don't have time. I mean, it was just a thought and not even a good one. Forget it, I'm sure you've got better things to do, and—"

"I'd love to go."

Her chin lifted, and her gaze snapped to his. "You would?"

"You'll be there, right?"

"Yeah."

"Then consider it a date." He leaned over to set his glass on the desk.

"Oh, no, it's not a date." She stood up so fast she sent

the ergonomic desk chair into the makeshift credenza behind her.

He grinned at her reaction. "Are we going to do this again? I didn't mean a *date* date. Just that I'd see you tomorrow."

Her gaze danced around the room, not staying in one spot for more than a second. "Oh, yeah... I know."

The awkward silence that bubbled up between them made him want to laugh. Made him want to hightail it to the safety of his rental SUV. Made him want to do something stupid, like yank the hot-pink T-shirt over her head and finish what they'd started a few days before.

He stood. "So I'll see you tomorrow. What time do you want me to meet you?"

She stepped around him to open the office door. "It's easier if we pick you up on the way out of town. Say eleven?"

He nodded. "See you then."

The office door clicked shut behind him, and he wanted to pat himself on the back for his self-restraint. Another part of him wanted to barge back in and take her right there on the desk. Labor Day weekend suddenly felt very far away. But at least he'd see her again tomorrow. His gut clenched, a tightness radiating out from his core.

Floating on a river probably meant swimsuits. That created a couple of problems. First of all, he'd have to see Charlie half-naked all day. Based on what he'd seen of her so far, that would do nothing to help him maintain his self-control. Second, he didn't have a swimsuit with him. He'd either have to cut off a pair of his new jeans or find somewhere to buy a halfway decent swimsuit before eleven in the morning.

He ran a hand down the leg of his jeans. Damn, he'd just been getting used to them.

CHARLIE HOPPED OUT OF THE BACK SEAT OF PRESLEY'S Jeep and bounced up the sidewalk to Holiday's only bed-and-breakfast. She didn't bother to knock on the front door. Instead, she walked around to the back and let herself in through the mudroom. Darby's parents had only opened the place about ten years ago, but she'd still spent so much time there that it felt like a second home.

"Good morning, sunshine." Darby's dad sat at the small kitchen table, cup of coffee in one hand, the thin Sunday paper in the other.

Charlie hugged him from behind. "Morning, Mr. Knotts." Even though she'd known the Knotts family since birth, she still felt funny calling Darby's parents by their given names. They'd stopped urging her to.

"I hear you're taking our guest tubing today?" He folded the paper in half and set it down next to his mug.

She plucked a piece of bacon off the platter in the center of the table. "That's right. Thought it would be nice to give him a taste of the local scene."

"He seems like a nice guy, kiddo. How are you holding up with all the changes?" He tilted his head, like he was trying to get a read on her. Darby's parents had been a huge source of support when Charlie went through what she liked to think of as her "black period." Mr. Knotts had the sometimes-annoying gift of being able to tune in to peoples' moods.

"So far so good. It's not like I have much of a choice, is it?"

"Maybe it'll be good for you."

"Maybe what will be good for her?" Mrs. Knotts entered the kitchen through a swinging wood door that separated the heart of their home from the dining room. She held a carafe of coffee in one hand and a basket of homemade cinnamon-streusel muffins in the other. "You want some coffee, Charlie? I made a whole pot, and Beck won't drink it. Had some fancy-schmancy coffee maker sent in."

Mr. Knotts held up his cup, signaling a request for more coffee. "I was about to tell Charlie it might be good for her that someone else is coming in to take over the Rose. Maybe she'll take the opportunity to look for a job up in Austin or even Dallas."

Charlie's hand froze, inches away from grabbing one of the still-warm muffins from the basket.

"You're not suggesting she move away?" Darby's mom stopped refilling his coffee and set the basket down on the table. "Holiday wouldn't be the same without our Charlie."

"And Charlie wouldn't be the same without Holiday." Mr. Knotts pushed his glasses back up on his nose. "It might be just what she needs to get a fresh start though. Don't you think you've been hiding around here long enough?"

Darby's parents turned their gazes on her. She was about to speak, to defend herself against the accusation that she'd been avoiding living her life. Mrs. Knotts raised her eyebrows in encouragement. Mr. Knotts folded his hands together and set them on the table in front of him. The grandfather clock in the formal living room played through its hourly routine and began to chime.

"Gosh, look at that. Eleven o'clock right on the nose. Presley's in the Jeep out front. Do you mind if I grab Beck and we head out?"

Mr. Knotts shook his head and picked up his paper. Darby's mom set the basket on the table, then, one hand still wrapped around the carafe of coffee, slipped her other arm behind Charlie. "He said he needed to run upstairs and grab his things. If you want to wait for him in the front room, you can."

Charlie pressed a kiss to her other mama's cheek and pushed through the doorway into the dining room, where Beck's dirty breakfast dishes sat alone on the long dining room table. He must have been the only guest. The Bluebonnet Bed & Breakfast usually did a brisk business, especially on the weekends. Maybe Beck had scared the rest of the guests off. Still, it would be pretty lonely to eat breakfast alone every morning.

She almost felt sorry for him. But then he clambered down the steps, a day pack slung over one shoulder, a pair of cutoff jeans clinging to his hips.

"Hey, have you been waiting long?"

"Nope." *Just long enough to regret ever asking you to come along.* From the moment the invitation had escaped through her lips, she'd wished she could have taken it back. It's not that she hated Beck or didn't want him around. She just had to hold herself in constant check around him, and it would have been nice to take a day off and relax around her family and friends. "Ready?"

He walked ahead of her and held the front door open in response. She slid her sunglasses back in place to fend off the blazing light of day. Knowing she'd be bobbing up and down the river all day, she hadn't bothered to shower or put on makeup. She'd been doing good to roll out of bed and get her hair up in an elastic. Beck followed her out to the Jeep, where Presley and his latest girl of the month sat smacking lips across the stick shift.

Charlie grabbed on to the rollover bar and climbed into the back seat, knocking her brother's hat off in the process. "Cut it out, Pres. Save it for the river."

Presley wiped a thumb over his bottom lip, smearing Shana's cotton-candy-pink lip gloss onto his hand. He must have noticed his pink fingers because he wiped them off on his muscle tank before sticking his hand out to Beck. "Hey, bro. Glad you could make it."

Beck settled in next to Charlie, wedging his body into the tiny back seat. His hip pressed so hard against hers she wouldn't have been able to slip even a piece of paper between them. "Thanks for inviting me." Then he turned to Shana, who studied her mouth in the reflection of the rearview mirror. "Hey, I'm Beck."

Shana turned around in her seat and tossed a sparkly pink smile his way. "Shana. Presley told me all about how you're the new owner of the Rose. Nice to meet you."

The gears groaned as Presley shifted into reverse. "Y'all ready to have some fun today?"

Shana's hand squeezed Presley's leg, much closer in proximity to his crotch than his knee. Charlie chewed on her bottom lip, hoping she wouldn't regret this. At least not more than she already did.

As they cruised along the two-lane road into New Braunfels, the wind whipped through the Jeep, scattering her worries as wide as the green acres of grazing pasture that stretched as far as she could see. Between the roar of the wind and the blare of the country stations Presley kept flipping between, she and Beck weren't forced to make conversation. Lost in her own thoughts, she studied his profile in short side-glances. A few days' scruff made him look more casual and at home. Almost like a local. Except behind the designer shades, she figured he was probably counting the days until he could hightail it back north.

Even though he had months to go, the idea of him leaving sent a weird, prickly chill through her. Of course he'd leave. Why in the world would he want to stay? A guy like him, a successful entrepreneur in what most people considered the most important city in the world… Why on earth would someone like Beck ever even consider spending the rest of his days in a quiet town like Holiday?

Mr. Knotts's comments from earlier played through her head. What would she do when it was time to move on from the Rose? Would she have the guts to pick up and leave everything she'd ever known—everything she'd ever loved—for a chance to stop living in the past and start building a future? The thought terrified her in every possible way. She was meant to be where she was. Things would work out. They had to.

The Jeep came to a stop in the parking lot, and Presley hopped out and checked his phone. "Well, hell."

"What's wrong, babe?" Shana leaned her head against his chest and studied the screen.

"Tippy, Cash, and the rest of the crew are gonna be late."

"Wait, Cash is coming?" Charlie couldn't believe

it. He was the most serious of her brothers, and as a single dad, he rarely joined in on any fun and games.

"Yeah, I thought he was kidding at first. But Kenzie went to Dallas with Mom and Dad for the weekend, so I figured he could use a distraction."

That made sense. Cash wouldn't know what to do with himself without his five-year-old daughter around. "Well, how long are they going to be? Should we wait?"

"Nah, Tippy says to go ahead. Looks like it's the four of us this afternoon. Beck, give me a hand with the cooler?"

Charlie's throat constricted, and a wave of dizziness washed over her. The four of them? So the "date" was turning into a *date* date after all.

"You okay, Charlie?" Shana stood in front of her, wrapping her long brown hair into an elastic on top of her head.

"Yeah, um, fine."

"Will you lotion my back?" Shana whipped her tank over her head, revealing a skimpy string bikini top.

Presley yelled from behind the Jeep. "Don't you dare take my job, Char."

Shana smiled. "Never mind. Guess I don't need help after all." She took the sunscreen and walked toward Presley.

Charlie groaned.

"What's wrong? You really want to apply sunscreen to someone, I'll let you do me." Beck offered her a tube of sunscreen.

"Ha. No thanks."

"Have they been together long?" Beck asked.

"Long for Presley. Which means probably about a month." Spending the afternoon with Presley and Shana wasn't what she'd had in mind when she'd invited Beck to hang out with a big group of their friends. Now it looked like it would be the two of them floating down the river while trying not to watch Presley and Shana hook up for the next three or four hours.

"Y'all ready?" Presley hefted the cooler onto his shoulder.

"You sure you don't want to wait for the others?" Charlie asked. "I thought you told Shep and Brittany to come, too."

"I did. Shep has tickets to some concert in Austin, and Brittany's out in Amarillo. I can call Dwight if you want." His mouth quirked up, showing off the dimple in his cheek. Her mom always said Presley was a wolf in sheep's clothes. He knew how Charlie felt about Dwight and never missed out on a chance to give her a hard time about it.

"Okay, then, just us." Presley and Shana and Beck. She could do this. It would be…fun. She needed a day off from her worry and work at that bar. No matter what, she vowed she'd enjoy herself. "I'll get the tickets. Beck, can you and Shana grab the tubes?"

Ten minutes later, Charlie'd shed her cover-up and stood poised on the last concrete step, ready to plop into the river. She held the tube by the handles and nestled her bootie in the center. Shana and Presley had already launched, and she waited for the group of college-age kids in front of her to get a move on and get in the water. As they joked and jostled each other around, a pang of envy pinched her gut. Is that what she would have been like if she'd stuck it out at UT and had the typical college experience? Instead, she'd come home for spring break her freshman year to bury her fiancé and had never gone back.

"You okay?" Beck's voice nudged her out of her often-visited past.

"What? Oh yeah, I'm fine."

"You looked like you were somewhere else for a minute."

She gave him a smile, one she didn't actually feel. It was the same smile she'd pasted on all those years ago when people kept asking her if she was all right. The kind that let the person asking feel good about themselves for making an effort but didn't take away the ache in her chest or knit her broken heart back together.

"We're up." She turned and attempted to ease into the water with a tiny bit of grace. Her foot slipped on a moss-covered rock, and she splashed into the river, the water dousing her in cool drops.

Beck entered the river behind her and paddled to catch up. He lifted his leg and caught the edge of her tube with the heel of his foot. "Mind if we stick together?"

Charlie's gaze swept over the groups floating on the river. Presley and Shana were nowhere in sight. At least they'd left the cooler. It bobbed behind Beck in a small tube of its own. "Looks like we don't have much of a choice. The rapids aren't crazy, but you do need to pay attention if you want to stay in your tube. You ever done anything like this before?"

"I've been white-water rafting in Colorado a couple times. Also took an amazing trip with some guys in college. We kayaked down the Futaleufú River in Chile."

Of course he had. Because that's what guys like Beck were used to...bopping around the world on one adventure after another.

"How about you?" He clasped his hands behind his head and leaned back in his inner tube. She ripped her gaze away from his seriously cut chest and tried distracting herself with conversation.

"The Guadalupe is about as exciting as it gets for me. Although I haven't been out here in a couple of years."

"So can I ask you something?"

"If you hand me a beer." Today seemed like at least a two-beer kind of day. Maybe more, depending on whether she and Beck ended up spending the whole day alone.

He spun around in his tube so he could reach the cooler and passed her an ice-cold can, then took one for himself.

"All right, what's up?" She couldn't wait to find out what he might be wondering about. More questions about the Rose? Why her brother was such a douche? How many days left on his sentence?

"Who's Jackson?"

Her heart skittered to a stop as the noise of a Sunday afternoon on the river became muffled by the blood whooshing through her ears. Who'd told him about Jackson? Not that it was a secret. It just wasn't something she usually brought up to strangers. But Beck wasn't exactly a stranger. He was more of a… *Dammit.*

Her heart squeezed into a knot and then banged into motion. What was Beck to her? An employer. An irritant that festered like a sliver she couldn't work out from under her skin. An amazing kisser and the first man she'd felt any sort of attraction for since Jackson left her. Her cheeks warmed at the memory of their time in the truck.

"Charlie?" He adjusted his foot on her tube, rotating her so their heads moved closer together. "You don't have to answer. It's just Dwight said something about you dating a guy named Jackson."

"No, it's okay." What did she have to lose by sharing her story with Beck? "Jackson is…" No, that wasn't right. "Jackson *was*…my boyfriend." Somehow the simple term *boyfriend* didn't begin to do justice to what Jackson had been to her. Her past, her future, her life. "We dated forever—well, ever since my dad let me officially date. He enlisted in the marines right out of high school. Got killed during his first tour of duty in Iraq."

"Oh shit. I'm sorry. I'm going to strangle Dwight next time I see him."

"Yeah, he likes to stir up trouble. Sully always said he was lower than a snake's belly in a wagon's rut."

"Well, I haven't heard that one before, but based on what I know about him, I can see how someone might say that. I'm really sorry. I didn't mean to make you talk about something painful."

She took in a deep breath of the stifling summer air. "It's okay. It was a long time ago."

Beck trailed a finger in the still water. At this point on the river, the water barely flowed, meaning they could sit here for hours if the current didn't pick up. "Still, I've never lost anyone close to me like that. It must have been hard."

"Yeah. It was. My whole world turned inside out and upside down." She could still remember walking around like she was in a bubble, insulated from everyone else. How could they all go on like everything was okay? Her classmates had still complained about the food in the dining hall; her family had still talked about whether to breed more quarter horses or take on more cattle. She'd wanted to scream, shake everyone until their heads popped off, and blot out the sun with the storm clouds that surrounded her heart.

Instead, she'd had what the docs chalked up to a nervous breakdown and spent two weeks in Austin under medical supervision. Sully had visited her and offered her the job at the Rose during that time. She couldn't imagine what good he thought she'd be able to do, drugged up and bogged down by so much emotional baggage. But he'd had faith in her, and bit by bit, her smile had returned.

How could she tell Beck how sorry she was that he'd never had a chance to know his grandfather when Sully had been the one who saved her from herself?

She readjusted her position in her tube so she could lay her head down and soak up the sun's rays. A group of about twenty tubers clumped together floated nearby. The music from their speakers drifted across the water, and Charlie's feet bobbed up and down in time to the beat. Beck looked lost in his own thoughts, which suited her just fine. She closed her eyes and enjoyed the feel of floating on the water. Maybe they'd catch up to Presley, maybe they wouldn't. She didn't have anywhere else to be on a Sunday afternoon, and while the next couple of months stretched before her unknown, she'd give herself a chance to appreciate the here and now.

*HH*

Open mouth, insert foot. *Way to go, dumbass.* He'd not only strangle Dwight the next time he saw him, he'd also call in his tab and make him settle up before anyone else served him at the bar. No wonder Charlie seemed so guarded.

As much as she intrigued him and drove him to more cold showers than he'd taken since junior high, he refused to be the asshole who'd break her heart again. In the short time he'd known her and despite their near-hookup in the parking lot, one thing had become clear—Charlie didn't seem like the kind of woman who did things casually.

He'd have to rein it in and keep things on a purely professional level. Didn't matter that he'd tried and failed at that a few days before. Now that he knew more about her, he'd be more careful. Satisfied with himself for taking the high road, he relaxed into his tube. The peaceful float down the river provided a much different experience than battling the rapids in Colorado or fighting to stay upright in a kayak.

His adventures were usually fueled by adrenaline, the crazier the better. His dad always told him one of these days he'd end up dead or seriously injured. But so far, Beck had gone skydiving, bungee jumping, parasailing, BASE jumping, and cliff diving with only a broken leg to show for it. Living life in a high-rise surrounded by concrete got to him after a while, and he had to get out of the city and get his blood pumping. Maybe he had a little more of his grandfather's genes than he'd thought.

He mused on that for a bit until the current picked up.

Charlie nudged him with her foot. "Rapids up ahead. Hold on to your tube, and make sure we don't lose the cooler. Presley would kill you."

"Got it." Beck sat up straighter in his tube and watched the group in front of them bounce over the long stretch of rapids. One guy bumped into a big rock sticking out of the water and tumbled out of his tube. Amateur. He lifted his butt up to avoid hitting it on any of the rocks under the surface and reached over to grab Charlie's tube.

It spun out of his grasp, and she went down the rapids first. She nudged a rock and changed direction like a bumper car in a crowded arcade, getting caught up in the group ahead of them. Beck's tube followed. But with the cluster of tubes blocking the route in front of him, his tube spiraled toward the big rock he'd seen earlier. He tried to paddle away from it with one hand but got nowhere. A surge of water behind him sent his tube crashing into the rock. The cooler went sideways, and he scrambled to set it upright before Presley's entire cache of beer fell into the river. Back in control, he pushed off the rock with his foot. Pain sliced through the ball of his foot.

"Oh crap." A sharp part of the rock had left a cut along the bottom of his foot.

"You okay?" Charlie had grabbed on to a clump of long grass sticking up from an outcropping of rocks and waited for him along the riverbank.

"Cut my foot. It's not bad—it'll be fine."

"That's why they recommend water shoes." She lifted her legs and wiggled her feet, which were encased in ugly hot-pink rubber.

"Yeah, I should have thought to bring my stash of water footwear when I packed my bags. I usually strut along Fifth Avenue in them." She stuck her tongue out at him. "Or wear them jogging in Central Park. I love the squishy feel as my feet hit the pavement."

"Okay, Manhattan. I get it. You were ill prepared for

our little adventure today. We should have loaned you a pair of swim trunks and some Velcro sandals. Shame on me."

"That's right, it's all your fault."

"So is it my fault you're losing your tube, too?" She nodded toward his inner tube, which appeared to be losing some of its buoyancy.

He'd been more concerned about his bloody foot and hadn't noticed his butt had sunk a little deeper into the water. "Huh. What do we do about that?"

"Well, I guess you could climb up the bank and try to catch a ride back to the office."

Beck glanced up the steep riverbank. "Not sure I want to do that with a fresh cut on the bottom of my foot. Is there an option number two?"

She lifted her hips and slid over to one side of her tube. "We share." Her cheeks resembled the hot pink of her water shoes.

Share. With Charlie. In a bikini. The vow he'd made to take the high road and keep their interactions purely professional plopped into the water and silently drowned as he climbed into the tube beside her.

"You sure you don't mind?"

"I don't think you'd fit in with the cooler."

Beck glanced toward the miniature tube, more suited to a toddler than a guy his size.

"All right then. Here goes nothing." There wasn't enough space for both of them to sit side by side. He settled into the middle, and she rolled onto his lap, putting them hip to hip and skin to skin. The water droplets on her chest were close enough he could have licked them off if he'd wanted to. And God, he wanted to.

"I don't have anywhere to put my arm." She moved her

arm behind him, then back in front again like she was trying to get comfortable.

"Here." He slid his arm around her shoulders, giving her a place to lean.

"Thanks."

Her body was rigid next to him. With almost every part of them touching from head to toe, a certain part of him began to go rigid as well.

"Should we tackle the rest of these rapids?" Beck asked. His tube had lost air halfway down the bubbly section of river. With any luck, they'd make it the rest of the way without another screwup.

"Let's do it." Charlie seemed to look for a place to grab on. He almost laughed at the awkward look on her face.

"Just hang on to me, okay?"

She slung an arm over his torso and held tight as they kicked back into the flow and the tube drifted over another section of rapids. They lifted their hips in unison as they bumped, spun, and bounced over the rocks underneath them. Charlie's body hummed along his as she shifted, trying to anticipate which way the river would send them.

Finally in calmer water, her half-naked body nestled into his side, he tried to think of something to say to ease the tension between them. "How about another beer?"

"Yeah, that would be great." She seemed as eager as he was to have something else to focus her attention on.

Together, they wrestled the cooler close enough to grab another can for each of them.

"Cheers." Beck tapped his can against hers.

"What are we toasting?"

"Um, how about to surviving the white-water rapids of the great Guadalupe?"

Her lips screwed into a doubtful smirk. "White-water? Don't you think you're stretching it a bit?"

"Hey, I never popped a raft in Colorado. So far the difficulty level here seems to be on par."

"I bet Colorado is amazing."

"You've never been?"

"No."

"So where have you been? Where's your favorite place to go?" Her sitting half on top of him made for an awkward angle for conversation. But not nearly as awkward as having her ass rub against his crotch. *Professional, keep it professional.*

Charlie shifted against him and lifted her face toward his. "I haven't been anywhere. At least not anywhere outside Texas."

Her comment distracted him from trying to squelch his growing desire. "You're kidding. You've never left Texas?"

She shook her head. "Nope. I used to want to travel a lot, but not so much anymore."

"Why not? You afraid to fly?"

"I don't know. I've never been on a plane. Unless you count the tiny two-seater my dad uses to check on his cattle from time to time."

"Well, we're going to have to get you out of Texas sometime. Maybe come visit me in New York. You'd love it there." As he said the words, he wondered if they could possibly be true. What would be so special about New York for a gal who wrestled pigs and broke up bar fights between cranky cowboys? "The Statue of Liberty…

the Empire State Building…Times Square…it's like nowhere else on earth."

Charlie nodded, her cheek brushing against his chest. His skin prickled under her touch, every part of him aware of the way she molded herself against him. "Yeah, maybe someday."

"Is it your family? You have to stay close to manage the ranch?"

"No. My folks love to travel. They took a cruise in Alaska last year and have plans to do a tour of Ireland and Scotland next spring." She went quiet, and he figured he'd be better off not pressing the subject.

But then again, he was a slow learner. "So what's the deal then?"

"It's just me, okay?" Her cheeks flushed, and she pushed off his chest to raise herself up as much as she could. "When Jackson died, I was on spring break down in South Padre. I should have been at home."

"Charlie, you couldn't have done anything to stop that. Whether you were on a beach in Texas or a mountaintop in Brazil, there's nothing you could have done." Crap, what had he said? *Couldn't leave well enough alone, huh? Had to go and push her.* A tear slid down the side of her nose from under her sunglasses. He shouldn't have come today. Should have done what he'd planned and headed to Sully's place to start making it livable.

"He tried to call me." The words came out so softly he almost missed the fact that she'd spoken at all.

"What?"

"When he knew he wasn't going to make it. He tried to call me."

What was he supposed to say to that? He opened his mouth to speak, hoping somehow the right words would tumble out.

But Charlie kept going. "His Humvee hit an IED. The truck blew up. They got him back to base, but he'd lost too much blood. I didn't have my phone with me. Left it behind at the hotel while we sat on the beach. I was too worried about having fun with my friends." The tears free-fell down her cheeks. He wanted to say something, ease her pain, tell her it wasn't her fault. "He left me a message. I still have it. After all these years, I still listen to it every once in a while." She wiped at her cheeks, and a sharp bark of laughter rose from her chest. "Go on, tell me how ridiculous that is. How I need to stop living in the past, start looking toward the future."

He reached up and slid her sunglasses from her face. She looked up at him with watery eyes, hurt, wounded, raw.

"I'm not going to tell you that, Charlie."

She blinked, and a crease appeared between her brows. "Why not? Everyone else does."

"Well, then screw everyone else. When they've lived through losing someone close to them like that, then they can give advice on how you should handle yourself and how long you can be sad." It pissed him off to think that people would rush her through such a devastating part of her past. He didn't have personal experience with grief, but he had watched a buddy of his lose both his parents to a helicopter crash during college. As far as he was concerned, no one had a right to tell someone else how to feel.

She studied him for a long moment, then sniffled and ran her hand over her cheek again. "I never told anyone that before. About the message."

"I'm honored you trusted me enough to share. You okay?" He ran a hand over her shoulder, brushing back a stray chunk of hair that had escaped her elastic.

"Yeah." Her chest rose and fell as she inhaled and exhaled a long breath. "So anyway, that's why I don't want to move to Austin or San Antonio or Dallas. And that's why I've never traveled much from home."

"But he's gone now."

"I can't stand to be very far from the people I love. In case they need me. I let Jackson down, and I don't want that to ever happen again. I don't know, you probably think I'm crazy."

"I don't think you're crazy."

"You don't?"

"Nah. I think you're pretty incredible." As he said the words, he realized how much he meant them. He'd never met someone who wore her heart on her sleeve like she did. It was refreshing to not have to guess at what she might or might not be thinking or feeling. Not like everyone else in his life. With his heart unexpectedly full, he pulled her even closer to him and kissed the top of her head.

She pushed against his chest. For a moment he assumed she was rejecting the gesture. But then she lifted her head to kiss his cheek. "Thanks, Beck."

He wanted to move his head, to meet her lips with his. Sitting this close to her, their skin warmed by the heat of the afternoon sun, the river flowing underneath them, he wanted to cement this moment in time. Before he had a chance to react with anything more than a shake of his head, droplets of water doused them both.

"There y'all are. Didn't take you long to put the moves on my little sister now, did it?" Presley paddled closer, towing Shana's tube behind him. "Been looking for y'all for an hour now. I'm dying of thirst. Toss me a beer?"

Just like that, the mood lifted. Shana gave up her tube and climbed in with Presley so Beck could have his own again. He missed the way Charlie felt nestled against him, but the distance kept him from doing things he had no business doing. As the day wore on and the sun moved from straight overhead to hover at the edge of the horizon, Beck decided he was glad he had come. Even though by the time they made it to the end of the float trip, he was pruned, sunburned, and hungry. He and Charlie had reached a new level in their relationship. More like friends. Even if he would be taking nothing but cold showers during his stay, it would be nice to have a real friend in Holiday.

"Thanks for the ride. Y'all have a good night." Charlie stood on the front porch of the cottage she lived in on the edge of the family ranch. Presley and Shana had been so anxious to get rid of her and Beck that they dropped them off at Charlie's place so she could drive him back to the B and B instead of going into town. The Jeep circled around the dusty patch of gravel, then retreated down the drive.

"Thanks for inviting me to go with you today. I had a good time." Beck had his pack slung over one shoulder, and his button-down shirt hung open in front. She'd had her hands all over him that afternoon, and still she wanted more. It was kind of funny how she thought talking about Jackson with him would make her more upset when it actually made her feel like a little bit of weight had been pried off her chest. She'd had a good time too and wasn't quite ready to see the day come to an end.

"You in a rush to get back, or do you want to stay for a quick bite?" She pushed her sunglasses on top of her head and studied his profile.

"Depends. What are you making?"

"Depends? Really? You have a better offer down at the VFW or something?"

A teasing smirk slid across his face. "Maybe."

"Fish fry was on Friday. That's the only thing they make there that I'd be up for eating. I was thinking of throwing a steak on the grill. Maybe a salad and some bread."

Beck made circles on his chiseled abs with his palm. "You had me at steak."

"Come on in then." She walked across the porch and opened the front door.

"Don't people around here ever lock anything?"

The look of concern on his face made her laugh out loud. "Somebody would have to find my place before they could break in. I don't think I've ever slept behind a locked door in my life."

Beck shook his head. "I don't get it."

"You don't have to get it, Manhattan. Hey, will you check the fridge for me? There should be a rib eye on the top shelf. I wasn't expecting company, but I think it'll be big enough to share."

He made it to the kitchen and stuck his head inside the refrigerator.

"I'm gonna jump in the shower right quick and rinse the river water off. If you want to set the steak on a plate on the counter, that'd be great."

She pointed to the cabinet holding her dishes, then ducked into the bathroom. This was a bad idea. Right? It had to be. Her and Beck, alone at her place after they'd been literally stuck side by side all day. She'd almost died when his tube deflated. Being that close to him for so long, sharing her heart about Jackson, having body parts touch that shouldn't necessarily be touching…it had all caught up to her. A shower would be just the thing. She'd freshen up, cool down, and make the man dinner. Where was the harm in that?

Fifteen minutes later, showered, shampooed, and safely ensconced in her most unsexy yoga pants and three-quarter-sleeve Cowboys T-shirt, Charlie exited the bathroom. She'd wrapped her damp hair into a knot on top of her head and hadn't bothered with makeup. Beck stood in the family room, studying the wall filled with floor-to-ceiling pictures. Framed photographs of her ancestors, her and her brothers as kids, her folks, and dozens of friends and family members crowded the wall.

"Are you related to all of these people?" Beck asked.

"Most of them. The ones I'm not related to by blood I'm pretty much still stuck with for life anyway."

He let out a huff of breath. "I can't imagine."

"You don't have any brothers or sisters, do you?" She'd never heard Sully talk about any other grandkids, but he hadn't exactly kept in touch, so he might not know if Beck had siblings.

"Steps." Huh? He must have seen the blank look on her face, so he clarified. "Technically I have a stepsister from my second stepmom and a half brother on my mom's side. But no one I keep in touch with."

Nobody he kept in touch with? Poor guy. She couldn't imagine how lonely life would be without her brothers, even though sometimes she wished there weren't so many of them.

"Must be weird for you then, to think about me having so many relations. I have twenty-seven first cousins on my dad's side alone. Another nineteen on my mom's. Our family reunion kind of takes over the Rambling Rose. Sully let us use it every other summer to get everyone together."

"They all from around here?"

"Mostly."

"You're lucky. Probably doesn't always feel like it, but you've got people who have your back." Beck tucked his chin to his chest and spoke really quietly. "I wish I'd had the chance to know my grandfather."

Charlie resisted the urge to wrap him in a hug. That had only gotten her in trouble the last time she'd tried to offer comfort. But he looked so sad, she had to say something to break up the moment.

"He would have liked you."

Beck's eyes sparkled. "You think so?"

"I know so. Although he probably would have tanned your hide for tossing Senator Duncan's son in the mud."

"Not one of my finer moments," Beck agreed.

"Hey"—Charlie gestured toward the bathroom—"do you want to hop in the shower while I get dinner started?"

"What, in there?"

"Unless you want me to turn the hose on you out back."

"Oh, um, yeah. I guess I could take a quick shower."

"Good. Put some of that aloe gel in the medicine cabinet on your back and shoulders when you get out. It'll help with your sunburn." Could he tell she was nervous as all get-out, having him shower in her bathroom? She'd never entertained a man at her place. The few dates she'd been on, she'd met up somewhere with the guy. The couple of times there'd been a connection, they'd always ended up at the guy's place. Not that she'd stayed. Usually within about ten to fifteen minutes, she'd made up some excuse and escaped.

Beck grabbed his bag and took slow, unsure steps toward the bathroom. She wanted to laugh at the nervous uncertainty his body language showed. Instead, she unwrapped the steak and seasoned it the way her mom had shown her when she was a girl. She might not have mad skills when interacting with the opposite sex, but she'd never doubted her expertise in the kitchen.

While Beck took his time in the bathroom, she prepped the steak, heated up her cast-iron grill pan, and tossed a salad. She'd just pulled out a bottle of local cabernet when he opened the door and the steam escaped into the family room. He'd changed into fresh clothes—a pair of shorts and a Yankees T-shirt. His bare feet padded over her wood-plank floors as he crossed the family room and entered the kitchen.

"Here, let me do that for you." He took the bottle of wine and opener from her hands and easily slid the cork out. "Where do you keep the glasses?"

She pointed to a cabinet over the sink, and he reached around her for two long-stemmed wine glasses. He poured the wine and handed her a glass, then leaned up against the counter next to her while she chopped tomatoes to add to the salad.

"Thanks." She paused to take a sip.

"Need me to throw the steak on the grill?" he asked.

"Absolutely not. Around here we know how to cook 'em right." He cocked his head, tilting upward and revealing the copper-and-gold highlights in the scruff on his chin. "Best way to cook a steak is in a grill pan. Hand me the butter from the fridge?"

He navigated the cozy space like he'd been fetching butter and glasses in her kitchen for years. She took the butter and plopped a pat into the pan. It spattered and melted right away, then she dropped the steak in next to sear it.

"So I've been doing it wrong all these years?" Beck leaned over her, watching the steak sizzle in the pan.

"Don't take it personally. I think most people ruin their steaks that way."

"Will you teach me?"

She'd moved on to buttering the garlic bread before popping it into the oven. "Teach you what?"

"How to properly cook a steak?"

"You're serious?"

"Yeah."

"Okay, cowboy. Belly on up to the burner."

He stepped in front of the stove. Charlie moved next to him. "So right now we're searing it. Just a minute or two on each side."

"Okay. Should I flip it?"

"Go ahead."

He slid his hand into an oven mitt and grabbed the handle of the skillet, then carefully flipped the steak with the tongs Charlie handed him.

Charlie took a sip of her wine, trying to distract herself from the incredible nearness of Beck. He smelled amazing, and she wanted to reach up and run her fingers through his still-damp hair.

"What next?"

She nudged him with her hip. "Now we put it in the oven."

He slid the pan into the preheated oven and turned to her with a giant smile. "That was easy enough. Now what?"

Why did he have to look so darn kissable? "Now we wait."

"Okay." His fingers wrapped around the stem of his

glass. Her gaze followed it from the counter as he lifted it to his lips. A blaze of heat swelled from her gut, up her chest, and across her face, igniting everything in its path.

"What?" He held the glass away from his mouth and leaned against the counter.

Her heart pounded. Her chest heaved. This was it. She needed to either take a chance and make a move or put the man out of her mind once and for all. Her fingers moved up to touch his hair.

"What are you doing, Charlie?" His voice held an undertone—something soft, simmering, seductive.

"Nothing." Her hand lingered on his cheek, finally feeling the scruff she'd wanted to touch all day.

"It doesn't feel like nothing," Beck warned.

"No?" She stepped between his outstretched legs, sliding her feet between his. "I keep telling myself there's nothing between us."

"Nothing?" He set his glass down, then took hers and placed it next to his.

"Yep. Nothing."

His hand caressed her cheek. "So this is nothing?"

No, it was definitely something. Something big. Something terrifying. Something that set her so on edge she couldn't keep herself from diving headfirst into it.

She nodded into his chest, annihilating her vow to keep things professional. She'd never let herself even think of being with another man besides Jackson until now. But now she couldn't think of anything else.

"I feel like we're flirting with that line again here." Beck's mouth nestled against her ear. Goose bumps rippled along her skin. Her heart sounded like a bass drum in her ears. "I've tried to keep my distance. Tell me to go away. Tell me to stop. Tell me you don't want me as much as I want you."

She opened her mouth to speak, and nothing came out. Not even a squeak. She did want him. In the worst way. In a way that had nothing to do with keeping her distance. In a way that would obliterate the employee–employer line. In a way that would probably break her.

"I can't."

"I know. It's okay. I understand." He pulled back, his lids heavy with the same desire that simmered through her veins.

She caught his shoulders, preventing him from moving too far away. "No, you don't. I can't tell you that because it's not true."

"What are you saying?"

"I'm saying you're talking way too much, Manhattan." Comprehension graced his face. His eyes lit in appreciative surprise. Before she could change her mind, Charlie wrapped her arms around his neck and smashed her lips to his.

His arms clenched around her, and he nudged into her, deepening the kiss. Their lips meshed, parted, connected again. She lost track of time, of everything but the way his body felt next to hers. Closing her eyes, she allowed herself to feel him, really feel him, at every point their bodies connected. His mouth made contact with her neck. She took slow, measured breaths, faltering every time his lips landed on the sensitive skin behind her ear.

He spun them both around, then pressed her against the counter with his hips, showing her with his body how much he wanted her. Her heart did a happy dance in her chest, sending an "all systems go" signal through her central nervous system.

He cradled her against his chest and whispered in her ear. "I'm sorry. I know we shouldn't be doing this."

"Hey, I started it." She nestled her cheek into his chest. "But I need to tell you, it's been a long time for me."

His finger traced her the line of her cheek, stopping at her chin and tilting her face up toward his. "I know."

Her gaze met his. His eyes conveyed a gentleness she wouldn't have thought possible. It was time. The right time to take things further, to go all the way. Her stomach swirled around like that ride at Six Flags, the one that spun around faster and faster until the floor dropped out. He leaned closer, his lips grazing hers, and that was all the encouragement her body needed. She took the kiss deeper, trying to hold herself back, to slow down. His hands cupped her ass, lifting her onto the counter. She opened her legs to him, and he filled the space, pushing against her. She locked her ankles around his waist, drawing him closer, needing to feel him there, right there.

Her body craved more. More kissing, more touching, more skin. His hands twisted and tangled in her hair. All she could feel was in this moment. Time stopped, suspending her between never wanting it to end and needing to get over it as soon as possible. She'd waited eight years for someone to make her want to move on from Jackson. Eight years of emptiness, of trying to fill the hole in her heart and soul with work, with family, with friends. Now Beck was poised to fill that void. To lead her back to that place inside she'd disconnected from all those years ago.

She was ready.

Her body molded into his. Helpless to stop it, she let go with all the abandon of eight years of pent-up lust. Ravaging his mouth with hers, she tasted, sucked, nibbled at his lips. He lifted her off the counter, and they careened through the kitchen, bouncing off the table and sending a chair clattering to the floor.

"Bedroom?" he mumbled against her mouth.

"No time." She unhooked her legs from his waist and yanked him down to the couch.

They collapsed, him on top of her, scrambling to free themselves of shirts, shorts, and all the other annoying pieces of clothing that prevented full skin-on-skin contact. The leather couch creaked and squeaked underneath them, sticking to her backside as she raised her hips to slide her pants and panties down her legs. Finally, after the frantic removal of clothing, Charlie fell back onto the couch. This was really happening.

Beck traced a finger down her collarbone and between her breasts. "You're beautiful, Charlie."

She tugged under his arms, pulling him up so she could reach his mouth with hers. "I think all that fresh country air has about scrambled your brain."

He leaned down and took a nipple in his mouth. A moan wrenched through her. His hand went under her ass as his lips worked their way down her body, kissing a path from her breasts to her navel. She sucked in her breath as he circled her belly button with his tongue, then moved lower. Lower. Trailing kisses down her pelvis, her inner thigh... She urged him on, trying to position herself exactly where she needed him to go.

"You like this?"

"Mmm."

He slid a finger close to the epicenter of her need. "How about this?"

"Mm-hmm." Why was he talking? She tried to grab a handful of the leather couch cushion but couldn't get a grip.

"I know we shouldn't be doing this. It's probably going to make things awkward between us. Maybe we should stop."

Seriously? His face was inches from her skin, moments away from what she hoped would be some amazing tongue action, and he picked that moment to have second thoughts? She raised up on her elbows and blew a chunk of hair out her eyes.

"Are you kidding me?"

A smug, satisfied smile spread across his lips, like he knew some secret she had yet to figure out. "Yeah. I just wanted to be able to see your face when I did this."

He lowered his head, and his tongue took over. Her head rolled back, and her entire body went rigid as his mouth and lips took her to a place she'd only dreamed about for the past eight years.

"I want to make you feel so good." His words muffled against her thigh.

*Stop it with the talking already.*

"That's it, just like that."

She couldn't take it anymore. Her legs clenched around his neck, and with a move she'd perfected in years of backyard wrestling, she twisted her whole body and rolled him off the couch and onto the floor.

He landed with a thud on the giant sisal rug, and she followed. Her body draped over his, she straddled him and leaned down, nose to nose.

"No. More. Talking." To drive her point home, she attacked his mouth with hers. If he wasn't going to finish what he started, she'd take charge. He pulled back and opened his mouth like he was about to say something.

"Uh-uh. I said no talking." She put a finger over his lips. He grabbed it and slid it into his mouth, working it over with his tongue.

"I was just going to tell you I have a condom in my wallet. Back pocket of my shorts if you want to grab it. Seeing as how you've got me penned and all."

Charlie scrambled to her feet and found the shorts, the wallet, the condom. She ripped it open with her teeth and, since he was standing at the ready, slid it on.

"Not much for foreplay, are you, country girl?" Beck teased.

She straddled him, one knee on either side of his hips.

"Eight years," she growled out as she slid down onto him. There'd be time for foreplay and tenderness next time. Right now, she had a deep ache that demanded resolution. The pain didn't last long. She moved against it, through it, and slowed the frantic pace as she found herself on the other side. Beck matched her rhythm, seeming to finally understand that this wasn't a quick roll on the couch. This was primal. Her need came from deep inside—a place she didn't even think existed anymore.

She took what she needed, grinding into him, letting the momentum build within her until it couldn't be contained. Her knees scraped on the rough rug, her butt cheek cramped, and still she fought for her release.

And then it happened. Her body clenched, suspended in time and space.

"Let it go, Charlie," he murmured. "I've got you."

She met his gaze a heartbeat before her body took over. He watched her, the tenderness in his eyes intensifying the sensations racing through her veins.

Let it go she did. She let everything go. The heartache, the guilt, the need. She let go completely, and he took it all, whispering to her, urging her, guiding her to that place she needed more than anything.

Spent, she collapsed onto Beck's chest, feeling like she'd spent a day stacking hay bales, not three minutes putting an end to her dry spell.

His fingertips grazed her ribs. "You okay?"

Her cheeks hurt from smiling. "I'm better than okay." She put her palms on either side of his head and rolled her hips. "Seems like you could be a little better though."

"Oh yeah?"

She lifted up and eased back down on him. He hissed out a breath. "Better yet?"

"You keep that up, and I'll be better in a New York minute," he ground out.

Teasing him, she continued to slide up and down, varying the pace and enjoying the look of sheer restraint he wore on his gorgeous, scruffy face.

"I can't take it anymore. You're making me crazy." He thrust once more, his fingers digging deep into her hips, holding her tight in place as he followed her to his own release. "Damn. Charlie. You feel so fucking good."

Good didn't describe it. Awesome, magnificent, incredible...none of those words seemed to do justice to the way Beck made her feel.

"Oh my gosh. That was..." She struggled for words.

"Nothing, right?" Beck winked at her from his sprawled-out spot underneath her.

"We need to do nothing together more often." As she slowly floated down from the out-of-body experience she'd just had, a buzzing filled her ears.

"Beck?"

He groaned underneath her, still coming down from his own high.

"Do you smell that?"

"Smells like something's burning."

"And the buzzing. Do you hear the buzzing?" She climbed off and staggered to her feet while he took care of the condom. "The steak!" How long had the smoke detector been going off? She rounded the corner to the kitchen, Beck on her heels. Smoke filled the space, billowing up from the closed oven door. She pulled it open and grabbed for the handle of the pan, the hot pad sliding from her hand. Pain immediately seared her palm.

"Dammit!" She turned on the faucet and shoved her burned hand under the cold water.

"You okay?" Beck stood beside her. "Tell me what to do, Charlie."

The sound of his voice jarred her. *Think, come on, think.*

"Grab the hot pad and take that pan out back, okay?"

Beck nodded, snagged the hot pad off the floor, and whisked the pan through the living room and onto the back patio.

Her hand felt like a giant flame had swallowed it up. She needed to look, to see how bad it was. What was it her mama said to use on a burn? She couldn't remember. Beck returned to the kitchen, naked as the day he was born except for the ridiculous oven mitt on his hand.

"Can you grab the bread, too?"

He pulled it out of the oven and tossed the entire cookie sheet into the sink. Rising hysteria threatened to take over, but she wasn't sure if she'd end up laughing at how crazy Beck looked or crying from the angry stinging of her palm.

Before she had a chance to find out, someone knocked at the front door. "Charlie? Everything okay?" a worried voice called.

"Oh my God, it's Cash. Get your clothes on. He can't find you here like that."

Beck scrambled into the family room and scooped his underwear off the floor. "Where are my shorts? I can't find my shorts."

"Hold on a second," Charlie yelled from the kitchen.

The front door opened. Charlie yanked her hand from under the cold stream of water and dove behind the counter.

"What the hell's going on in here?" Cash's voice carried over the buzz of the smoke alarm.

A chair scraped across the floor. The buzzing stopped. Thank God. She let out the breath she'd been holding and peeked around the corner of the cabinet. Beck and Cash stood on opposite sides of the living room like an old-fashioned standoff. Beck had thrown his boxer briefs on backward. If she hadn't been so terrified, she would have giggled at the sight of him standing there, one hand on his hip, the other trying to adjust the saggy front of his backward briefs.

"Where's my sister?" Cash swiveled his head around, probably noticing her discarded clothes on the back of the couch and the floor. She cringed at the sight of her Victoria's Secret low-rise cotton briefs draped over the lamp on the end table.

To Beck's credit, he rocked back on his heels like he was trying to make himself appear even taller. "She's, uh, taking care of something." His gaze shot to the kitchen and found her hiding spot.

*Crap.* Cash wouldn't let it go. He'd be all over her like flies on shit in about ten seconds. That left her with one choice. She reached for the linen drawer.

*HH*

What in the world did she have on? Beck sized up Cash, trying to determine how to best defuse the situation when Charlie stepped out of the kitchen with a star-spangled tablecloth clutched around her slender frame, a bag of frozen peas in her hand. Her knees sported matching raw spots from rug burn, and two stars on the tablecloth lined up perfectly on top of her breasts.

"It's not what you think." She directed the words to her brother.

"Oh no?" Cash cocked his head. "Looks like exactly what I think. Unless you want to try to convince me your boyfriend always wears his underwear ass-backward and you like to hang out naked in Nana's handmade cross-stitched tablecloth while you pass the time?"

"What are you doing here anyway?" she asked. Beck liked the way she went on the offense, not seeming to care about her unusual patriotic display.

"I was at the house to pick up Kenzie. Dad saw the notification your smoke alarm was going off and asked me to come check it out. Things must have been pretty darn hot between the two of you to start a fire." He cracked a grin, a nice break from his usually somber expression.

"I knew there'd be drawbacks to having everything wired to the big house."

"It's smart, Char. Say your place catches fire sometime while you're"—he cast a glance at Beck—"out entertaining visiting royalty or something."

She snorted. "Visiting royalty? Come on, even you can do better than that."

"I can, and I will. Right after you go get some clothes on. You tryin' to scar me for life or something? As it is, I won't be able to unsee this." He waved his arms around, gesturing between Beck's shirtless chest and Charlie's all-American attire.

She stomped across the living room, grabbing her clothes along the way, then slammed the bedroom door behind her.

Beck and Cash didn't move, just stood in the awkward silence for a few beats. Then they both spoke at the same time.

"I'm—" Beck started.

"Hey, I—"

"Go ahead." Beck dipped his head toward Cash, signaling he should go first. What would Charlie's older brother think? If he even had an opinion.

Who was he kidding? One thing he'd learned about the folks in Holiday: everyone had an opinion about everything. And so far none of them had been shy about sharing it.

Cash cleared his throat and spoke low, so low that Beck had to lean toward him to make out his words. "You hurt her, and I'll have your balls for breakfast."

Beck gulped. He'd been threatened before, both physically and verbally. Sometimes he'd even deserved it. But not once had he felt the threat so intimately. Cash meant every word.

"Jesus." He shifted his weight to his other foot. "I don't think that will be necessary. We're all adults here."

Cash tucked his thumbs into his belt loops, leveling Beck with a smoldering gaze. "She's been hurt. Bad. And I don't want to have to pick up the pieces when you breeze on outta here in a couple months."

"I don't have any intention of hurting her." Beck put his hands out, palms facing Cash in a gesture of reassurance. The man carried a gun. He had no desire to piss him off.

"Well, good. That'll make Mom and Dad and the rest of the family real happy. We'll be expecting an announcement of the engagement real soon. Think a fall wedding will fit into your schedule?"

Before he had a chance to respond, Charlie burst back into the room, fully clothed and fully pissed, still clutching the bag of peas in her burned hand.

"Happy now?" She pointed toward the front door. "As you can see, the place isn't burning down. We had a little oversight in the kitchen. You can tell Dad everything's fine."

Cash raised an eyebrow, giving him that brooding, distant cowboy look that Beck had seen in Ralph Lauren ads. "Yeah, what exactly do you want me to tell Dad, kiddo?"

Her skin pinkened from the scoop neck of her shirt to the roots of her hair. "Cash Warren Walker, you are impossible. You tell him I was smoking out a gopher hole. That a snake crawled into my oven again and burned up when I turned it on to preheat. That I was messing around with the solder gun."

"Or I could tell him how I found you and the Holiday kid naked, rolling around on the floor of your living room while you burned one of his best rib eyes. That would get his heart thumping."

"Don't you dare. Now get on outta here." She moved behind her brother and pushed with one hand. A full head taller than her and twice as broad, he held his ground.

"I was just leaving." He tipped his hat toward Beck, mouthing the word *balls* before moving toward the door.

Beck shook his head. "Always good to see you, Cash."

Charlie finally got him to the front door, and Beck caught the affectionate hug that passed between them. Then Cash wrapped his arm around her neck, trapping her head under his armpit and rubbed his knuckles over her hair. "Noogie!"

She managed to escape by knocking him in the back of his knee. Cash gave her a half hug before she pushed him out the door, then slammed it behind him. Her free hand went to her hair, trying to smooth down the mess Cash had made. Beck wasn't sure whether to offer some comfort or pretend like nothing had happened.

"See what you're missing by not having any siblings?" She padded into the kitchen, and he followed. "I'm sorry for the intrusion. Dad has everyone's place wired to a central switchboard in the big house."

"That sounds…convenient?"

She tossed the peas back in the freezer, then stuck her head into the refrigerator and rummaged around. "Sure, if you need someone checking up on you all the time. Which I don't."

No, she didn't. But it seemed like her brother had different ideas. He couldn't be serious about expecting a proposal and a wedding. Some things in Holiday appeared to be outdated, but surely social norms and dating expectations weren't the same as fifty years ago. "Look, Charlie—"

Handing him a carton of eggs and a block of cheese, she withdrew from the fridge. "Steak's ruined. Looks like an omelet?"

"An omelet would be great. Can we talk about this?"

"About what? My annoying brother?" She pulled a grater out of the drawer. "Why don't you get your pants on and see if you can shred some cheddar?"

He went back into the other room, found his shorts under the couch, and tugged them on. "Cash isn't serious about a wedding, is he?"

"Well, of course." She cracked an egg against a bowl, then reached for another. "It's another Holiday tradition." Her face gave nothing away. She had to be joking.

"Really?"

"Sure. Just wait for the honeymoon. The whole family rents a giant RV. We even bring Baby Back along. Hike through the canyons out at Big Bend Park. Fry up a rattler or two." She winked. Thank God.

"All right. Now I know you're pulling my leg."

"And I promise I'll pull on a hell of a lot more after dinner if you get over here and grate that cheese."

He stepped to the counter, his heart not quite as tight as it had been a couple of minutes before. "So what are we doing here?"

She picked up the cheese and rubbed it along the grater. "See here, this kitchen gadget gives you nice, even shredded cheese when you rub this big chunk of cheddar along it."

He covered her hand with his. "That's not what I meant. Us. What are we doing here?"

The hint of humor left her eyes. "I don't know. This is new for me. Maybe we just take it one day at a time."

His lungs slowly released the breath he'd been holding. "And when I leave at the end of the summer?"

She set the cheese and grater on the counter and turned to face him. "That's a long ways away."

He gathered her into his arms, and she leaned against him. He'd come to Texas to find out about his family, not start a fling. Could Charlie even do casual? Could he? He had his doubts, but September *was* a long time away. And he'd have a hell of a lot more fun if he had someone to spend those sweltering summer nights with. "You're right. One day at a time sounds good."

She reached up and kissed him, making him want to forego cheese omelets and get started on the one day at a time right away.

<br />

chapter

# SIXTEEN

CHARLIE STUDIED THE FOAMY BREW IN THE MASON JAR mug in front of her. "And it was like this when you got here this morning?"

Shep nodded. "Yep. Dwight was the first to notice. Said his Lone Star was skunked or something. Look at the head on that pour. And it looks more like an unfiltered wheat."

She held the mug to her nose and inhaled. Definitely not Lone Star. Either they'd got a bad keg, or someone was playing a joke on them. As she considered which was the more likely option, Beck strolled in.

"Hey, you like the new brew?" He nodded toward the mug in her hand.

She set it on the bar, not hard enough to break but hard enough to splash some up and over the edge of the mug.

His lips corkscrewed into a frown. "Not a fan, huh?"

"What did you do?" She rounded the bar, hands on her hips.

"I heard you say something a while back about trying a new seasonal brew, so I talked to the rep and asked for some recommendations. This one's an unfiltered wheat with a hint of lemon. Perfect for an afternoon out at the lake or a picnic at the park. Crisp and refreshing on a hot summer day. And we've got plenty of those around here." He nodded, smug, satisfied, and oh so proud of himself.

"And where's your seasonal beer made? Austin? Waco? Amarillo?"

"Brooklyn. I thought I'd bring a little bit of New York to Texas."

"Brooklyn?"

"Just try it."

"Fine." She nodded toward Shep, who filled a clean mug with a couple of inches of foamy brew and set it in front of her. Taking a sip, she let the liquid roll over her tongue before she forced it down.

"Well?" Beck asked.

"It's awful. Shep, can I get a water? Quick?" She guzzled half the glass of water he filled. "You try it."

Beck sniffed the beer left in her mug, then downed a mouthful. "No, this isn't what it's supposed to taste like. They sent me the wrong stuff." He reached for her water.

She pressed a palm against the front of his tacky button-down. He'd gone all in with embracing the local culture, and today's shirt practically blinded her with the mishmash of pink, purple, lime green, and yellow paisley. Looked like a unicorn had pooped a rainbow all over his shirt and then danced in it. "You replaced our Lone Star—the official unofficial beer of Texas—with some skunked beer someone thought up in *Brooklyn*?"

"Hey, it came highly recommended. Besides, alcohol content is thirty-percent higher. Customers ought to be happy about that."

She let go of his shirt and shook her head. "That might pacify them a bit if it were drinkable. Shep, get the rep on the phone. He's got to come fix this."

"Sure thing, Charlie."

She leaned toward Beck. "Can I talk to you in private?" She didn't want to hash things out with an audience. It was bad enough people had been whispering about them behind their backs. Dixie even mentioned she'd heard someone taking bets on whether they'd "sealed the deal" already.

"What did I do?" Beck followed her to the office.

She waited for him to come in behind her, then closed the door. "You cannot, under any circumstances, open the Rose tonight without Lone Star on tap."

"It's just a beer."

"It's not just a beer. It's a way of life, it's a…" She struggled for the right word that would illustrate the severity of the moment.

"Tradition," he muttered.

"Yes. It's a tradition." She wrapped her arms around his, sliding her hands down his forearms until she held both of his hands in hers.

"Don't y'all ever buck tradition around here?"

Her jaw dropped.

"What? Is it so crazy to think they might appreciate a change once in a while?"

Charlie poked him in the chest. "You said 'y'all.'"

He scoffed. "Did not."

"You sure did. I'll make a cowboy out of you yet."

He pulled her close, nestling her into his chest. "I promise that beer is good. Real good. Something must have happened to it in shipping."

"Mm-hmm. We'll fix it."

"What would I do without you?" His chin rested on her head.

"You'd get your ass kicked for serving skunked beer, that's what you'd do."

Beck's hand smoothed over her hair. "Well, then thank goodness you're on my side."

"Always." She rose to her tiptoes and pressed a kiss to his lips.

He didn't need encouragement. Wrapping his arms around her midsection, he cupped her butt and lifted her onto the edge of the desk. Mouth to mouth, heart to heart, she ran her fingers through his hair. He'd let it grow, and she loved the way the ends curled over her fingers. He nudged between her legs, pushing her thighs apart with his hips.

"We don't have time," she mumbled into his mouth.

"Two minutes. Then I'll go take care of the beer."

Two minutes would turn into two hours if she let it. Time had a funny way of passing too quickly when she immersed herself in Beck.

He worked his hands under her shirt while his mouth connected with her neck. She moaned. What was two minutes in the grand scheme of things?

"Charlie?" The office door creaked open.

She hopped off the desk, right into Beck. One hand yanked her shirt down, the other went to his chest, pushing him back to create a little space between them.

Dwight's head poked through the crack in the door. "I'm not interrupting anything, am I?" The narrowed eyes and tight-lipped grimace showed he knew exactly what they'd been up to.

"No, I, uh, was just heading out front to talk to Shep about that beer." Beck stumbled backward.

"And I have to head out on some errands. We were just—"

"Talking," Beck said, at the same time she said, "Going over some financials."

Dwight squinted at them, obviously not buying the story they were selling. "I see. Dixie's out front collecting canned goods for some charity."

"I'll be right there." Charlie nodded, eager for Dwight to disappear.

"I'll tell her." He didn't retreat, just glared at Beck.

"You can go now," Charlie said.

He left but didn't pull the door closed behind him.

"I don't think Dwight likes me anymore." Beck hugged her to him.

"I wouldn't worry about Dwight." She snuggled against him for another long moment, then regretfully pulled away. "I've got to go. I have a ton of errands to run and then the vet's coming over to take a look at Baby Back. She's been acting funny for the past couple of days."

"You want me to come with you?"

"Nah. You take care of the beer situation. I'll take care of the pig."

Beck released her, but not before stealing another kiss.

She paused at the door. "Oh, and don't forget, my family is coming for dinner tonight."

"That's right. I'll be on my best behavior."

He'd better be. They'd been sneaking around and trying to keep things quiet, but everyone seemed to know what was going on anyway. And what they didn't know, they'd made up. Shep even told her one of the regulars said he'd seen the two of them skinny-dipping in the creek a couple days before. She'd decided she better clue in her family before her dad heard something through the grapevine and decided to test out his new bull castration equipment on her boyfriend.

Tonight would be the night. She'd invited the whole family to an early dinner at the Rambling Rose. Come tomorrow, she'd be either breathing easier or disowned. Based on the reconnaissance Darby had been running, it didn't sound like her brothers would be too rough on Beck. But there was one thing about the Walker boys she could count on—they were predictably unpredictable.

A few hours later, Charlie knelt down next to Baby Back and ran a hand over the sow's belly. "You sure about that, Doc?"

"Time will tell. But based on my experience, you've got yourself a pregnant pig here." He removed his glasses to wipe them on the edge of his shirt. "When did you say the incident occurred?"

Charlie counted backward in her head. "Been a couple of weeks."

"Then I'd expect she ought to deliver her litter right around Labor Day." He let out a slight chuckle. "Seems fitting, eh? Laboring on Labor Day?"

Fitting? No. Nothing about this situation seemed fitting. What was she supposed to do with a pregnant mascot? They'd never had a knocked-up sow on staff before. She thanked the vet for taking a look and sat with Baby Back while he packed up his things and made for the parking lot.

"What am I going to do with you?" Charlie muttered.

Baby Back snorted while she nudged her head under Charlie's hand, begging for another scratch.

Charlie couldn't wait to fill Beck in on the news. Technically, this was his problem. But he wouldn't know what to do with a pregnant pig any more than she did. They could figure it out together. They'd been doing a lot together lately. She blushed as she thought about how "together" they'd been.

She gave Baby Back the last apricot from her pocket and stood. Best get inside and share the news with Beck. They still had a few minutes before her family would arrive. She couldn't wait to see the look on his face when she told him he'd have grand-piggies.

Ten minutes later, she wasn't disappointed.

"You sure about that?" he asked. His brow furrowed, shoulders hunched.

"Um, not absolutely. It's not like we did an ultrasound and saw the little buggers swimming around inside."

"Well, then how does he know?"

"Doc Martin has been a large animal vet for thirty-five years." Charlie put her palms down on the desk and leaned toward him. "I want to know what Marilyn is going to offer in piglet support."

He cracked a grin. "Let's assume Marilyn is out of the picture. Baby Back is going to have to do this on her own. She'll have us, of course."

"Us?" Charlie raised her brows.

Beck stood, walked around the desk, and wrapped her in a hug. "Absolutely. I'm here for you. I had equal part in this and am going to make sure you don't have to handle this on your own. When's the due date?"

"Due date? What due date?" Brittany poked her head

into the office, an apron in one hand and her order tablet in the other.

"Nothing." Charlie broke the embrace. "It's, um, Baby Back. She's having piglets."

Brittany squinted, looking back and forth between Charlie and Beck. "The pig is pregnant?"

"Yeah. The pig. Crazy, huh?" Beck funneled his hands through his hair.

"Yeah, crazy." Brittany nodded like she wasn't convinced, then disappeared down the hall.

"Well, crap on a cracker." Charlie batted at his chest.

"What?"

Seriously, the man had no clue. "You'd better get on out there. I'm sure Brittany's telling everyone I'm knocked up now."

"The pig. We told her *Baby Back* is pregnant."

"Yeah, and you sounded so convincing. You're going to have to talk fast."

"Me?" His eyes went round.

"Yep." Charlie put her hands on his shoulders and whirled him around to face the door. "Right now my dad's probably headed out to his truck to grab his shotgun."

She wanted to laugh at the expression on Beck's face. He looked like he couldn't tell if she was pulling his leg or telling the truth.

"I'm not joking, cowboy."

He groaned. "I guess I'd better mosey on out there then."

"Beck?" He looked up. The low burn hit her gut as he met her gaze. Every single time. "If I were you, I'd run."

Beck laced his fingers with Charlie's and pulled her through the door and down the hall. It was still somewhat early, so only a few tables had filled up. He made his way to the one in the center of the room. The one where Tom, Cash, Statler, and Waylon had pushed back from their chairs and stood arguing with each other.

"Hey, what's going on?" Beck cleared his throat, trying to interject into the conversation, which appeared to be really more of a shouting match. He caught bits and pieces.

"...skin him alive..."

"...go get the justice of the peace right now..."

"...send him back to New York less a few body parts..."

"Hey!" He let go of Charlie's hand and tapped Tom on the shoulder.

The older man turned toward him, his face the color of the ripe tomatoes Beck had tossed into the eggs he'd made that morning. A vein bulged at Tom's temple. "You!"

Chairs scraped on the wood floor, boots clacked, and suddenly Beck found himself surrounded by an angry mob of Walker males. All of them except Presley. Presley had his feet kicked up on the edge of the table while he leaned back in his chair. He was the only one smiling.

Cash jabbed Beck on the shoulder. "Didn't believe me, huh?"

"I can explain." Beck put his palms out in surrender.

Waylon poked a finger into his chest. "You better be ready to do the right thing, city boy. How dare you take advantage of my baby sister—"

"If anyone is going to deck him, it's going to be me." Tom made a fist.

Beck's head buzzed with the threats and overwhelming anger circling him. He opened his mouth to say something, but a piercing whistle cut through the chatter.

Everyone stopped. Charlie stood on the bar, her fingers still wedged into her mouth, and let out another whistle. "Will y'all listen for a second?" Satisfied she had the entire bar's attention, she held a hand out and motioned to Beck.

His cheeks burned as everyone in the place rested the weight of their gaze on him. Shaking his head, he joined her on top of the bar.

She smiled encouragement as he took his place by her side. They were doing this. Didn't have much of a choice now. It's not that he didn't want to go public with their fling. But he'd figured news would make its way around naturally. Slowly. Privately. He hadn't been prepared to make an official announcement, especially not with four pairs of glaring Walker eyes tearing him apart from across the room.

"Go ahead, Beck. Tell 'em." Charlie tucked her arm through his.

"Me? Tell 'em what?"

"Tell 'em I'm not pregnant," she mumbled.

He cleared his throat. "So Charlie and I have some news we'd like to share."

Chaos erupted. Waylon and Tom headed their way. Even the people he didn't recognize started to talk among themselves, making it more than a little difficult to speak out over the din.

"Oh, for crying out loud." Charlie whistled again. The noise ceased. In an apparent effort to get her point across before all hell broke loose, she yelled, "I am *not* pregnant. Baby Back is. Due in September. Okay?"

She nodded, then scrambled down from the bar, leaving Beck standing there alone.

"But what about you and him?" Waylon shouted.

"Yeah? Are you violating my baby sister?" Statler joined in.

Beck glanced down at Charlie. She smiled up at him and held out a hand. He didn't have to take a stand—he knew that. But if he wanted to hold his own, to get her brothers off his back once and for all, and to prove himself to Charlie, he'd better step up and handle this. He put his hands up to hush the crowd. Charlie frowned.

"Not that it's any of anyone's business"—he began—"but Charlie and I are together. So all of you can stop whispering and talking about us behind our backs. No, she's not pregnant. No, we're not talking marriage, Cash." He sought out her brother, who shook his head. "But I'm falling for this amazing woman, so you'd better get used to seeing me around."

He hopped off the bar to stand next to Charlie. Wrapping an arm around her, he met her gaze.

Her eyes widened in shock. "That was, um—"

"Amazeballs," Darby interjected. "Now kiss her, quick, and let's get this dinner going. Ryder's about to have a meltdown, and I need to get some chicken nuggets in him, stat."

"Well, you heard the woman," Charlie said.

Beck cradled her face between his hands. He hadn't meant to declare his feelings in front of the entire bar. But he'd meant what he'd said.

With the applause of her family, the staff, and the customers who'd enjoyed the little display ringing in his ears, he pulled her to him and kissed her. Kissed her like he meant it. Kissed her like she deserved. Kissed her like he'd never be able to get enough.

## chapter
# EIGHTEEN

"WHAT DO YOU CALL THESE AGAIN?" BECK LIFTED THE deep-fried bite to his nose and sniffed.

"It's a jalapeno popper." Charlie tossed one into her mouth and chewed. "Just a cheese-stuffed jalapeno. Try one."

"No, thanks." He dropped it back into the red-and-white-checked wrapper, leaving it for her to enjoy.

If he'd been at home, he would most likely be joining his dad and Marion for dinner at his father's club. A low-key Father's Day where he'd give his dad another Hermès tie, or maybe a case of his favorite wine, imported directly from France. They might even take his dad's yacht out for a spin in the harbor and dine al fresco with uniformed staff waiting on them hand and foot.

Whatever he'd have been doing in New York, he could pretty much guarantee it wouldn't be anything like the Father's Day Fiesta that was going down on Main Street. Tables and tents lined the thoroughfare. The smell of sizzling onions permeated the entire downtown area. He'd seen everything from the standard chicken and steak fajitas to more exotic options like alligator and rattlesnake. So far he hadn't indulged in anything he didn't recognize, which meant his stomach had been grumbling and gurgling since he and Charlie had arrived.

Charlie bebopped down the street from stand to stand,

hugging friends, introducing him to the few residents in Holiday he hadn't had a chance to meet yet, and sampling a little bit of everything. Since Father's Day always fell on a Sunday, they both had the night off. Stepping out with Charlie at his side felt like they were making a statement. They weren't spending time together as coworkers tonight or sneaking off to his or her place to be alone for an hour or two. It was the first time they'd officially gone out in public since they'd officially decided to start dating.

The funny thing about it was that no one seemed surprised. For the first time in a very long time, Beck didn't feel a nagging sense of urgency to be anywhere else. He planned to enjoy putting in his time in Texas.

"Hey, Charlie, you seen Dad yet?" Cash came up behind them, his daughter by his side.

"Hey, Kenzie." Charlie bent down and gave the pigtailed girl a big hug. "You having fun?"

Kenzie held out a goldfish in a bag. "Daddy won this for me at the BB gun game."

Charlie's eyebrows lifted. "Wow. Just what y'all need, another pet, huh?"

"I was going for the giant stuffed cow, okay? They jack with the sights on those guns."

"Don't you shoot a gun on a regular basis?" Charlie bit down on her lip like she was trying to stifle a smile.

"Forget it. Have you seen Dad or what? Kenzie made him a card at the craft tent and wanted to give it to him before it gets messed up."

"Saw him a little while ago over by the beer tent." She nodded down the road toward the giant red-and-white tent at the end of the street, by far the busiest vendor at the festival. "Mom wants us to meet over in front of Whitey's at seven. We can give Dad his gift then and get the annual family picture."

Beck rocked back on his heels, enjoying the exchange. He'd never had a relationship like the one Charlie shared with her brothers. They'd tease back and forth, but the warm undercurrent was always there. Almost made him wish he'd had a brother or sister growing up.

"Wanna see my picture?" Kenzie poked him in the thigh.

"Sure." Beck leaned down toward the girl.

"Will you hold my fish?" She thrust the puffy, clear bag at him. He took it, holding it up to get a good look at the orange fish swimming round and round.

She held out the card and pointed to the stick figures. "It's our whole family. Daddy, Auntie Charlie, Grampa, Gramma, Uncle Waylon, Auntie Darby..." She rattled off the names of her uncles and cousins until she reached the end. Then she stood there, an adorable crease between her little eyebrows.

"What's wrong, sweetie?" Charlie bent down. "Your drawing is perfect. Grampa's going to love it."

"What about him?" Her lower lip stuck out in a pout. "I didn't put Uncle Beck in my picture."

Uncle Beck? Whoa. Beck took two steps backward before he even realized he'd moved. "Um, I, uh—"

"Oh, honey. Beck isn't an uncle. He's a—" Charlie shot a silent cry for help toward her brother.

Cash hooked his thumbs through his belt loop and began to whistle. Didn't look like Charlie would be getting any help from that direction.

"I'm just a friend." Beck held the fish out to Kenzie and

met Charlie's gaze. Her eyes held a hint of amusement with a little bit of… Oh hell, was that disappointment mixed in? "A very good friend." Still no smile. "Like the best kind of friend she could have."

"I thought Aunt Darby was Aunt Charlie's best friend?" Kenzie's lips puckered.

He couldn't explain his relationship with Charlie to another grown-up, much less a kid who barely reached his waist.

"I think what Beck is trying to say is that he wishes he was your uncle, but for now, he's a very good friend of your aunt Charlie's." Cash finally stepped in.

"Do they have sleepovers? Like I get to have with Allie sometimes?" Kenzie still hadn't taken the fish. She clamped her tiny fists to her waist, reminding him of Charlie when she was pissed off and confused.

"I think I see Grampa over there." Charlie pointed toward the striped tent. "Why don't you go give him your card, honey?"

Distracted, Kenzie skipped off toward her grandpa.

Cash snagged the baggie from Beck's hand. "Nice, Charlie. Real nice."

"What did you want me to say? You sure weren't any help." Charlie took the same stance as Kenzie from a few minutes ago. Fists on her hips, lips pursed. The family resemblance couldn't have been more obvious.

"She's not the only one who wants to know." Cash narrowed his eyes and nodded. "You know how it is around here. People are talkin', baby girl."

"Talking about what? I'm not pregnant; we admitted we're dating. What else can they possibly be talking about?"

"Give 'em an inch, and they want a mile. Everyone's saying the next logical move is for him to put a ring on it."

"Would you stop it already?"

"Hey"—Cash put his hands out in surrender—"you asked." Then he spun on his heel to follow his daughter.

Charlie turned to face Beck. "Well, that was fun. You okay? You seem a little, uh, shell-shocked."

Shell-shocked didn't begin to describe it. He and Charlie had barely started exploring the undeniable attraction that pulled them together. He wasn't sure if he was ready for the kids to start calling him Uncle Beck and inserting him into family pictures.

"You weren't kidding when you said everyone's in your business around here, were you?"

"Nope." She gave him a friendly jab in the stomach. "And it's only going to get worse."

"Worse, huh?" The initial panic edged away. This was Charlie he was talking about. He already couldn't get enough of the woman. And it wasn't like they were making plans to settle down and start a herd of their own. They'd decided to enjoy the summer, keep things casual, and have a bit of fun. No way could things get worse. They could only get better.

Charlie slipped her arm around Beck's waist and tucked her hand into his back pocket. He'd handled the exchange with Cash and Kenzie all right. At least he hadn't run off as fast as his broken-in boots could carry him.

Things had been good between them. Sure, they still bickered over how to handle things at the Rose a bit. Especially when he botched the paint job and had the

Rambling Rose covered in a coat of matte white instead of the trademark pink. The locals had nearly torn the clapboard siding off when they saw it. He swore to her he'd ordered pink but they must have gotten the order wrong. He'd looked so terrified when she'd confronted him, she had to believe him. And now, for the first time since Jackson died, she'd started looking forward to the future instead of slogging through the days, each of them the same as the one before. She'd found something—no, make that someone—who gave her hope. She'd found her smile again.

Beck leaned down, his breath tickling her ear. "Can I ask you something?"

"Is it about the family picture? I promise, I won't make you stand in for that. Mom has a rule that you have to be engaged before you get to be in the family photo."

He shook his head, his mouth flirting with the sensitive spot behind her ear. "No. It's about the sleepovers. I think Kenzie's right. Good friends have sleepovers, right?"

Her lungs squeezed, and whatever air they'd held became trapped. She nodded.

"So how does this work? Do I have to wait for an invitation, or can I invite myself over?" His nose nudged against her neck. Tiny sparks danced along her skin.

Beck at her place. Overnight. Sharing a bed. The thought sent a warm rush through her limbs. "Either way."

"Okay then." He pulled away, tightened his grip around her shoulder, and continued to lead her down the street.

"So…" she prodded. That couldn't be it.

"Just curious." He grinned, the crinkles at the corners of his eyes teasing her, making it into a game.

"Huh." If he thought she would ask him, he'd have a long wait coming. It would serve him right for being so sure of himself.

They meandered down the street toward Whitey's. Might as well get the big family picture over with. Her mother insisted on it every year. As much as everyone complained, sometimes it was the only time everyone stood still long enough to catch them in the same photo. Charlie enjoyed seeing how the family had grown and changed over the years. Once, she couldn't wait to have Jackson stand beside her. After he died, she'd been convinced she'd always stand alone. A single in the sea of mini-families that made up the tight-knit Walker clan.

But now, since Kenzie'd brought it up, she thought about what it would feel like to have someone stand next to her. Their commitment captured by Dixie's expensive camera, displayed on the walls of her mom and dad's place for everyone to see.

She fought not to let herself imagine what it would be like if that person were Beck.

They reached Whitey's. Her mom loved to line the family up on the wood steps. The built-in risers made sure everyone could be seen. She sat on the top step, pulling Beck down next to her.

"Everyone ought to be here in a few. You don't have to wait for us. If you want to wander while we do the picture thing, I can catch up to you after."

"And miss out on more kids calling me Uncle Beck? No chance."

She could tell he was teasing from the half smile that played over his lips. "I promise not to let anyone call you Uncle Beck."

"Really? It was starting to grow on me." He squeezed her shoulder and kissed the top of her head.

"You're joking, right?" He had to be joking. It was too soon. Way too much too soon.

"Yeah. Sounds too much like Uncle Buck. You ever see that movie?"

"Of course. John Candy. A classic." One of her favorites. She loved all the John Hughes movies from the '80s. She and Darby used to watch them all the time when they were in high school.

"Not sure I want to be that kind of uncle."

No. Beck wouldn't be anything like John Candy's character. Although she could picture him teasing and embarrassing her nieces and nephews if she tried.

He cleared his throat, pulling her out of the movie playing through her head. "But I do want to know one thing."

"What's that?"

"What do you want for breakfast?"

"Does that mean what I think it means?" Tingles raced along her spine. An overnight would be a big step. So far they'd only managed an hour here and there.

"You do like breakfast, don't you?"

She nestled into his side. "I love breakfast. It's my favorite meal of the day."

"Then you're in luck. It's the only thing I know how to cook."

Beck was right about one thing—she was in luck. Lucky they'd found each other, even if whatever fun they were having would only last for the summer.

As her family made their way toward them, down the main street of town, Charlie tilted her head up and kissed his cheek. "I'm kind of hungry for breakfast already."

BECK STOOD AT THE STOVE, A SPATULA IN ONE HAND, the last letter from Sully in the other. This one had no postmark on the envelope, just Beck's name scrawled on the front. Based on the date at the top, Sully had written it the day before he'd passed.

As he read the last line, Beck swallowed the lump of unexpected emotion that rose in his throat. His grandfather was nothing like he'd expected, nothing like his father had led him to believe. At least not if the words filling the dozens of letters were true.

It was all there, laid out in the black scrawl of his grandfather's hand, and over the past week, Beck had read every line. The early letters talked about how sorry he was about what had happened between him and Holiday. From what Beck gathered, Sully hadn't thrown his dad out on his butt. Instead, it seemed like Holiday had ratcheted out of control to the point where Sully didn't have a choice but to try some tough love to snap some sense into him.

The biggest revelation by far had been the fact that Holiday had stolen money from his own father's safety deposit box right before he left town. As the years passed, the pleas in the letters stayed the same. Sully offered forgiveness and a fresh start. But it appeared all of his letters went unopened and unanswered.

Beck tucked the last letter back into the envelope. How could his grandfather paint such a different picture of history than the one his own dad had shared? Sully was long gone and couldn't fill in the gaps. Every time Beck tried to ask someone around town about it, they talked in circles and finally told him it wasn't their story to share.

He didn't have a choice. He'd need to force his dad to face the past if he wanted to get answers and fill in the blanks. And he had to do that before he'd feel comfortable signing that paperwork Holiday needed. Beck would insist they add some sort of clause that would ensure everyone would keep their jobs. Especially Charlie. More than once he'd wanted to tell her about the deal he'd made. But he wouldn't break his word to his dad. He couldn't agree to terms unless Holiday gave him the go-ahead to be up front with her. She deserved to know.

"Good morning." Charlie padded out of the bedroom.

He turned toward her and wrapped an arm around her shoulders. "Sleep well?"

"No. When are you going to start making this place your own?"

He hadn't made any changes to Sully's place yet—hadn't even fully unpacked. He'd been living out of his suitcase and bought a queen-size air mattress rather than sleep in either Sully's or his dad's old beds.

"I'm working on it, okay?" He focused his attention on the scrambled eggs in the pan.

Charlie rubbed her hand over his back. The tension melted away under her touch. "You need some help?"

"Just finishing up the eggs." He reached around her to

grab two plates from the cabinet. "I've been reading those letters. The things he talks about, the stuff he says, it's nothing like what my dad led me to believe."

"I'm sorry. This has to be hard for you." Her arm went around his waist.

Just feeling the warmth of her against him made everything better. "I need to talk to my dad about it."

"You want to call him?"

"No." He glanced down, hoping his smile conveyed an acceptable apology under the scruff covering his lips. "Sorry, it's not you. I need to talk to him in person. That way I can get a read on him. He'd be too evasive on the phone."

Charlie nodded. "Okay. Whatever you need to do."

"Now how about some eggs? I promised you breakfast, right?" Beck scraped the spatula along the bottom of the pan.

She leaned against the counter. "That's right. What's that white stuff on top?"

"Feta cheese. I made them Greek style. Tomatoes, a little bit of cheese."

"Pretty fancy, Manhattan."

"Nothing but the best for you." He flipped the eggs onto a plate.

Charlie took it from him and sat down at the small table. He joined her, so close that their knees bumped together underneath.

"What do you think?"

She slid a forkful into her mouth, her expression not giving anything away. "Hmm. Interesting."

"Interesting good or interesting bad?"

Grinning, she scooped up another bite. "Let's

just say you could give Angelo a run for his money in the kitchen during brunch."

"Really?"

She nodded, her mouth too full to speak.

He didn't know why the fact she liked how he'd made her eggs made him smile so hard his cheeks hurt. But he did know that everything in Holiday had been better since he and Charlie had gotten together. In fact, everything in general had been better with her by his side.

"So, I've been thinking," he began, not sure how to best to broach the topic he wanted to bring up.

"Uh-oh. What happened, did it make your head hurt?" She set down her fork long enough to take a sip of coffee.

"Can you be serious for a second?" He loved the way she could fire back at him, and usually he enjoyed the banter. But this morning called for a serious conversation.

Her brow crinkled. "What's wrong?"

"Nothing. I just wondered if you'd be able to do something for me. A favor."

"Of course." The wrinkle between her eyebrows deepened. "Is everything okay?"

He swallowed. Here goes nothing. "Yeah. I told you I need to talk to my dad about Sully."

"Right." She put her hand on his arm. "I think that's a great idea. You need answers, and he's the only one left who can give them to you. What do you need from me? Want me to take care of things while you're gone?"

"No."

"Then what?"

"I want you to go with me." Charlie's hand fell from his arm. She stared at her plate, the sympathetic smile gone from her eyes. He edged his chair closer to hers. "I know it's asking a lot, but it would be so much easier if I had someone with me who had my back. Someone I can trust."

She gave a slight shake of the head. "New York. You want me to go to New York with you?"

"Just for a couple of days. I'll talk to my dad; you can see the Statue of Liberty. We'll do the whole tourist thing."

"You know how I feel about leaving Holiday." She played with her fork, turning it over and over in her fingers.

He wanted to erase the sadness and doubt in her eyes. "I'll be with you the whole time. It'll give us a chance to be together, alone, away from everything and everyone. A chance to focus on us for a few days."

"Us."

"Yes"—he put a finger under her chin, nudging it up so he could read her eyes—"*us.*"

"I do like the sound of *us.*" The edges of her lips lifted just a bit.

"So you'll go?"

"You really need me?"

Sensing a breach in her resistance, he pushed. "Yes. I do. I really, really do."

"Let me think about it," she whispered, barely loudly enough for him to hear.

At least she hadn't said no. "Come here." He pulled her onto his lap. "It'll be a great time. A weekend you won't ever forget."

With Charlie by his side, he'd have the support he needed to confront his dad once and for all. She'd get to know him on his turf, and he could introduce her to the things he loved like that Korean barbecue joint and that Brooklyn beer he'd tried to bring to Texas.

"I've always wanted to see the Empire State Building."

"We could go next month. I'm supposed to accept an award for my dad at a picnic in the Hamptons while he's on that cruise. We could fly in right before he leaves so I can talk to him, then we'd have the whole town to ourselves for the weekend."

Charlie nodded, considering his offer. "Maybe."

"Probably?" He dipped her back to kiss along her jaw.

"Don't rush me, Manhattan."

He'd take what he could get for now. He had a few weeks yet to convince her. "I'm not planning on doing any kind of rushing. But if you hurry up and gobble down those eggs, I figure we've got a good thirty minutes before we have to leave for the Rose."

"Well, I suppose it's okay to rush some things."

He dipped a finger under the neckline of the T-shirt she'd slept in, hopefully erasing any doubt about what he hoped to do with that extra half hour.

She scarfed down the last couple bites of eggs, then hopped off his lap and held out her hand. "Coming?"

"Give me five minutes and hopefully we both will."

She squealed as he grabbed for her waist. Missing by a fraction of an inch, he stood, ready to chase her down and do his best to turn that *maybe* to a *probably* and finally a *yes*.

## chapter

# TWENTY

THE DAYS TUMBLED INTO EACH OTHER, FROM ONE TO the next. Before he knew it, Beck found himself up to his boots in Walker get-togethers, including Tom's favorite. The Fourth of July Chuckwagon Extravaganza had surpassed his expectations in every way. Of course, he'd never been on a trail ride or eaten an authentic chuckwagon dinner around a bonfire before. First time for everything. The bonfire crackled, sending red and orange sparks into the night sky. Beck closed his eyes, lulled into a lazy, half-asleep limbo. A cowboy strummed his guitar strings while a chorus of crickets and those crazy-loud bugs Charlie called katydids played backup.

He shifted his butt around, trying to get comfortable. Sitting in a saddle for the two-hour ride to their dinner location had left him feeling sore and slightly chafed. No wonder the cowboys he'd seen on TV always looked bowlegged. Charlie told him this was a family-only Fourth of July celebration. By the time they'd all gathered at the Walker ranch and saddled up, they looked more like a band of pioneers moving out across the Mormon Trail than an extended family get-together.

He'd also learned one thing about the Walkers. When any of them said "family," it usually meant the entire town of Holiday. About a dozen wagons circled the fire, some of them in better shape than others. His stomach gurgled, probably struggling to digest the three helpings of barbecue chicken, cowboy beans, cheesy potatoes, and homemade biscuits he'd forced down.

Charlie stood from where she'd been sitting next to him, grabbed his hand, and pulled him to his feet. "Come on."

"Where are we going?" he whispered.

She stopped by the old-fashioned covered wagon her dad had driven to pick up a blanket. "Don't you want to see the fireworks?"

"Sure, but can't we see them from where we were sitting by the fire?"

"Not if we want to make out while we're watching."

Beck smiled. With the promise of getting his hands on Charlie, his body roused from the edge of sleepiness. They'd been working such long hours at the Rose over the past couple weeks they hadn't been able to spend much time alone. Seemed like someone was always knocking on the office door or pulling her away to settle some argument or problem. Now that he'd finally decided to stop fighting the laws of attraction and give in to them, ironically, they'd seen each other less than they did when they were bickering all the time.

Charlie finally stopped at the door of a dilapidated old barn they'd passed on their ride in.

"Here?"

"No. Up in the hay loft." She pointed the flashlight she'd brought at a ladder along the far wall.

"You sure this is safe?" He glanced up. Half of the roof had either rotted or blown away, leaving them exposed to a night sky full of stars.

"Safer than getting caught by my dad or brothers."

"Good point."

Beck held the ladder while she climbed up ahead of him. When he reached the top, she spread out the blanket.

"You naughty, naughty girl." He sank to a squat, waiting for her to finish. "What would your daddy say if he knew you led me away to try to take advantage of me?"

"What he doesn't know won't hurt him. Now, are you gonna kiss me or what?"

"What if I want to do more than kiss you?" He leaned into her, nudging her onto her back.

"I'd be disappointed if you didn't." She wrapped her arms around his neck and pulled him down on top of her.

He wanted to stop time and freeze that moment— with thousands of stars twinkling overhead, soft music drifting all the way over from the fire, and the woman he'd spent a lifetime waiting for in his arms.

"What are you thinking about?" She propped her head on her elbow and slid her hand under his shirt.

How could he think about anything with her this close? With her hands on his skin? With the taste of her on his lips?

"You."

She pushed on his abs. "Liar."

"Always you, Charlie."

He'd never before experienced the kind of feelings he had for Charlie. She infiltrated his thoughts every waking moment of every day. He even dreamed about her at night. At least the nights when she'd let him sleep. The sex wasn't just great, it was fucking fantastic. Deep down, a part of him knew they couldn't go on like this forever. At some point, he'd have to tell her he wouldn't be able to stay. But not yet. This thing between them was too fragile, and he needed to see where it might lead. He could always come back and check in on things. His dad would need someone to keep tabs on the Rose, and maybe he could split his time between New York and Holiday. There was still a chance they could find a way to make this work.

He leaned over and showed her with his mouth what he couldn't yet put into words. She responded, her kisses landing like sparks from the bonfire on his skin. He couldn't see a thing but recognized the sound of her lowering her zipper. He'd been hard since she took his hand by the fire. Didn't take much to get him turned on since he'd moved to Holiday. He struggled out of his jeans and tossed them to the side.

Charlie's fingers skimmed his abs, trailing lower to wrap around him. He almost bucked off the blanket when she took him in her mouth. She straddled his thighs and bent over him. He could barely make out her silhouette as she moved her head up and down, taking him deeper into her mouth each time. He could come right now if he wanted. She barely had to touch him, and he could free-fall into a release.

But he preferred to watch her when they made love. That little O of surprise always hit her right before she came undone. He felt around for his jeans and slid the condom from his pocket. Since he'd started spending time around Charlie, he'd learned to always be prepared. She'd caught him off guard more than once.

She shifted, taking the condom and unrolling it onto

him with practiced hands. He flipped her onto her back and pushed inside. She was always ready for him. Slick and hot and tight. So fucking tight he almost lost it.

"Now, Beck. Now."

The sky exploded above them. With every boom overhead, he and Charlie let loose their own noises of pleasure. Her nails dug into his back, urging him faster, deeper, harder. He thrust, giving her his all, everything he had, everything she needed. Her mouth formed into the little O, and her hips stilled. He pulled out slow, just the way she liked it, then eased in again, building momentum. She buried her mouth in his chest, muffling her gasps, letting herself tumble over the edge. He waited for her to come down from her high. Then she opened her eyes and watched him climax. The fireworks reflected in her eyes. Purples, yellows, blues, and reds burst into the sky, then faded away, growing dimmer and dimmer until it was just her and him and…oh God, something crawling over his butt cheek.

$\mathscr{H}$

"I still don't understand how Beck got stung by a scorpion on the butt. What were y'all doin' again?" Presley tilted his head, playing dumber than everyone already thought he was, and winked at Charlie across the kitchen island of their parents' house.

"We must have stumbled across a nest or something. It was dark. I don't know." Her face burned like she'd been the one to suffer from the sting instead of poor Beck. Her family didn't need to know what they'd been doing. Or that she'd started to fall so hard for him she didn't know how she'd survive when he'd inevitably leave at the end of the summer.

She tossed a glance toward Beck. "How are you feeling?"

The poor man leaned on his elbows on the counter, his jeans pulled down to expose a swollen, red knot on his left butt cheek. "I guess I'm doing as well as can be expected seeing as how my girlfriend's mother has her hands all over my rear."

"Oh, hush. One butt is like the next. With five boys, I guarantee you, this is nothing new." Her mama spread a paste of meat tenderizer and water onto the bite, then blew on it to get it to set.

Charlie bit her lip to keep from laughing.

Beck growled. "Don't you laugh, Charlie. This isn't funny. Have you ever been stung by a scorpion?"

Mama clucked her tongue. "Stop your wigglin' unless you want this stuff smeared all over your pants too."

"Yes, I have been stung by a scorpion before. And bit by a snake. So there. Suck it up, Manhattan." She rounded the island and covered his hand with hers.

"Hell, that snake was a tiny garter snake. Barely took a nip at you." Presley snapped a picture with his phone. "This is gonna look great online."

"Would you give me that?" Beck reached for the phone, but Presley skittered away.

"Presley, you stop that nonsense right now. And, Beck, if you move on me again, I'll take you over my knee and turn your other cheek just as red as this one. Presley, hand me that damn phone."

"Sorry, Mama." Presley turned over the phone with a bashful grin.

"Charlie, delete that picture, then you can take over. It's one o'clock in the morning, and I need my beauty sleep."

"Yes, ma'am." She took the phone and opened up the camera app. With the press of a button, the image disappeared and was replaced by a photo of Presley with two half-naked redheads draped over him. She tossed the phone on the island like she'd been burned. "Presley, you're going to hell."

"What's he done now?" Beck craned his neck to see.

"Nothin' I ain't done before. Y'all have a good night now." He blew a kiss to each of them and disappeared through the kitchen door.

"If that boy hasn't been the death of me yet, I suppose there's still hope." Mama wrapped Charlie in a hug and pressed a kiss to her cheek. "You keep an eye on that bite. He hasn't had a reaction yet, so I'm sure he's in the clear. But if his tongue starts to swell or he has trouble breathing, get him to the hospital right away."

"What do you mean my tongue might swell? Can I die from this?"

Mama placed a hand on Beck's arm. "You're going to be fine. Stay away from scorpions, okay?"

He nodded and rested his head in his hands. "Can we go now? I think I passed my limit for embarrassing situations about an hour ago when your grandma pinched my ass."

"You gotta admit that was funny. Poor Nana hasn't seen a fine cut of prime rump roast since Pawpaw died in '96."

Beck groaned. "I'm so glad I could accommodate her. Can we go?"

"Sure." Charlie helped him to the truck, where he sprawled out on his stomach over the back bench seat. Nothing like seeing her family examine her boyfriend's bare butt to put a damper on the evening. They'd been having a good time. No, a great time. Despite a few rough starts, Beck fit in like he'd been in Holiday his whole life. Every once in a while his city roots shone through. Like how stiff he sat in the saddle. But for the most part, he'd managed to charm the locals and even earn back their respect after that unfortunate mishap with the beer.

"You taking me back to your place?" His voice drifted over the seat.

"Yeah. My mom said I better keep an eye on you. How are you feeling?"

"Like I've been bit on the ass by a prehistoric insect. Do you think anyone bought the whole 'maybe we stumbled across a nest' story?"

"They might have been more inclined if you hadn't run around the bonfire with your jeans around your ankles."

There had been some wild stories coming out of the Chuckwagon Extravaganza over the years, but Charlie was fairly certain they'd be talking about this one for decades. After Beck had jumped up and raced away, she'd pulled on her pants, grabbed their stuff, and caught up to him at the bonfire. Her mom had shone a flashlight app on his bare ass, and they'd tossed him on a horse and hightailed it back to the ranch. She might not ever get him on the back of a horse again.

He let out another groan. "Can we pretend tonight never happened?"

"I don't think my nana will let you." She looked over

her shoulder and caught a glimpse of him hiding his head under his arm.

"Would you agree I suffered from complete mortification this evening?"

"Um, yes. No doubt about that."

"And you want to make me feel better?"

Where was he going with this? Leave it to Beck to twist any situation into a favorable outcome for him. "Sure."

"You're coming to New York with me then, right? I want you all to myself, even if it's only for a weekend. What do you say?"

He hadn't brought up the trip since the night he'd asked. She'd sometimes wondered if she'd dreamed the offer. She didn't know why, couldn't seem to put words to the nagging feeling of apprehension about leaving town. It was probably nothing. Now that she and Beck had grown closer and spent so much time together, there was no logical reason for her to say no. And it would be an amazing opportunity to get a taste of his life, what he was like on his home turf.

She took in a deep breath and answered on an exhale. "Okay."

"You will?" He shot to a seated position and kissed her cheek from behind. "We're going to have a great time, I promise."

He settled back on the seat, cussing under his breath as he tried to get comfortable again. Charlie took in a wobbly breath. There. No more flip-flopping or queasy stomachaches. She'd made up her mind. She and Beck were going to New York, taking the next step in their relationship. How could it possibly be a bad decision?

# TWENTY-ONE

"I DON'T KNOW. MAYBE I SHOULD TELL HIM I CHANGED my mind." Charlie moved around the bar, her morning chores such an ingrained routine she didn't even have to think about her next move.

Darby shifted June in her arms and wiped a line of drool from the baby's chin. "Honey, you've got to go. How can you say no to a free trip to New York?"

"It's easy. One word. No." Charlie slapped her palms on the bar, startling baby June, who let out a shriek and began to wail. "Oh my gosh, I'm so sorry, sweetheart." She rounded the bar and took the baby in her arms. "Let me take her."

"Yes, go see Auntie Charlie," Darby said, handing the baby over. "See if you can talk some sense into her."

Charlie glared at her sister-in-law while bouncing June on her hip. "Don't listen to Mommy. She doesn't know what she's talking about it."

"Yeah, Mommy's the crazy one." Darby leaned down and grabbed a striped stuffed pig from the diaper bag. "Auntie Charlie doesn't know a good thing when she sees it. She thinks she can bide her time and guys like Uncle Beck will just keep dropping at her feet."

"Don't call him Uncle Beck." Charlie grabbed the toy from Darby and wiggled it in front of June's face. "Mommy doesn't get it. She married the first guy who tried to kiss her. Things get complicated when you have to date as a grown-up."

"Oh my God, Charlie. You're the one who's making it complicated. You're a girl. He's a guy. There's chemistry. A lot of chemistry. What's so wrong about seeing where it goes?"

Baby June turned her head toward her mama's voice, a tiny wrinkle between her cute little eyebrows. "You're upsetting my niece. Besides, who would handle things here if I left? Just drop it." Charlie made kissing noises and pressed the pig against her niece's chubby cheeks.

"I won't. Between Shep, Angelo, and the guys, we can handle the Rose. You know that." Darby lowered her voice like she always did when she was about to say something Charlie didn't like. "Look, honey, it sucks that Jackson died. You should be married with your own baby on your hip right now. It's not fair that your life hasn't worked out the way you thought it would, the way we planned. But you've got a second chance. Beck's the first guy you've shown even a tiny bit of interest in. It's been more than eight years."

Warmth rushed from Charlie's gut to her cheeks. Her heart stuttered, and all of a sudden, June seemed to weigh a thousand pounds. "Leave Jackson out of this. That's low, Darby, even for you." She kissed June on top of her fuzzy, dark curls and passed her back to her mother.

"I want you to be happy. Life is stingy with second chances. I don't want to see you pass yours up. You know I love you, sweetie. Waylon and I—"

Charlie's eyes went wide. "Do *not* tell me you've been discussing my love life with my brother." Darby's silence provided the answer. "Who else has been figuring out my future behind my back?"

Darby bent down and rummaged through the diaper bag. "Darbs?"

"We're all worried about you."

"*All?*" Charlie pressed.

"Waylon talked to Cash and Statler…" Darby lifted the diaper bag and took a few steps toward the nearest table. "Your mama even said your dad was asking about when you and Beck are going to take the next step."

Charlie clenched her fists and took in a deep inhale in an attempt to keep from punching her ex-bestie. "Maybe the better question is who *hasn't* been discussing my love life?"

"Whose love life?" Presley stomped through the front room and into the bar area.

"No one. Darby and June were just leaving." Charlie's glare dared her friend to argue with her.

Darby searched through her bag and pulled out her car keys. "Yeah. I've got to get to the store. You're still coming for dinner next weekend, right?"

"Yeah. Can I bring someone?" Presley scooted behind the bar.

"Sure, Shana can come." Darby slung the strap of the diaper bag over her shoulder.

"Oh, Shana and I ain't together anymore. I'll bring somebody else. You got any cherries back here, Sis?"

"What happened to Shana? I thought you two were serious." Charlie opened the refrigerator and handed him a small jar of maraschino cherries.

Presley shrugged. "Didn't work out. Don't you have any with stems?"

"Why do you need ones with stems?" Charlie stuck her head in the fridge and pulled out a half-full jar of stemmed cherries, then paused. "Wait. Do I even want to know?"

"Stem-tying contest. I'll see which gals can tie a knot with their tongue. Gotta narrow the playing field somehow, y'know."

Charlie shook her head. Sooner or later, karma would catch up to her brother. He grabbed the jar from her hand, kissed her on the cheek, and took giant strides across the room.

"Oh, hey, Charlie?" He paused before leaving the room.

"Yeah?"

"Have fun in New York." The door clattered shut behind him.

"Even Presley knows about this?" She turned on her friend.

Darby smiled. "You could learn a thing or two from your brother, you know."

"Sure, like how to catch an STD."

"I was thinking more like how to let loose, have a good time, take a chance. I bet he'd go to New York in a heartbeat."

"I'm not sure Presley has a heart." Charlie bit her lip and turned toward Darby. "I know you're only trying to help."

"Hey, if you decide not to go to New York, you can always stick around here for that big ol' family dinner I'm hosting next weekend."

"Fine. That settles it. I'd rather risk death by jumbo jet than subject myself to the family right now."

Darby clapped her hands together. "Yay! You're going to have such a good time."

"Bye, baby June." Charlie dropped one last kiss on her niece's head. "Tell your mama if this goes south, it's all on her."

June smiled and reached for Charlie's hair.

"Oh, stuff it." Darby grabbed her and pulled her into a hug. "You're going to have the time of your life. Probably won't even want to come back once you get a taste of city life."

Charlie clung to her friend. This would be a big step. A giant, earth-shattering step. But Darby was right...again. How did that keep happening? It was time to move on. Beck would be right next to her. There was nothing to be afraid of. At least nothing she could admit to her friend. Darby would never understand if she tried to explain that having a good time was exactly what had her the most terrified.

⁓⁓⁓

Beck grasped Cash's hand and shook it hard. "Thanks, man. I really appreciate it."

"Feels weird saying it, seeing as how I'm enabling you to seduce my baby sister, but you're welcome."

"Maybe think about it more like you're encouraging your sister to take a giant first step in getting over her fear of leaving Holiday." He'd already gotten a weird vibe from Charlie's brothers, at least the ones he'd met. He didn't need any of them to flip into protective, kick-his-ass mode if they doubted his intentions.

"Yeah, I can live with that." Cash downed the rest of his

beer. "Gotta go. I'll make sure she gets to the airport, but I can't force her to get on the plane. And if she actually makes it to New York, it's all on you."

"I'm up for it. She'll have a great time, I promise."

Cash narrowed his eyes, not cracking a smile.

Beck grinned. "Relax. She'll have a great time seeing the city. Statue of Liberty, Empire State Building. That kind of stuff."

"Yeah. Can't wait to hear all about it." He stood, setting his empty beer bottle on the bar. "Just remember what I said before, and things will be fine."

His boots clomped across the wood floor, and Beck waited until Cash passed through the doorway before he got up off the stool and tossed the empty bottles in the recycle bin. Surely Cash would never make good on his threat of castration. But from what he'd seen during his brief visits to the ranch, depriving an animal of its balls seemed to be a regular occurrence around the Walker family. He'd have to make sure he didn't do anything stupid and that Charlie had the time of her life in New York.

He'd get the confrontation with his dad over with first and then be able to focus on the fun. It was too bad he'd promised to accept that award for Holiday Enterprises, but they'd still have plenty of time to sightsee and hopefully more than enough time to spend alone.

Something hard and cold inside Charlie had loosened and thawed over these past couple weeks. It would be great to get her away from the Rose, her family, and the constant pressure she seemed to be under. In talking with Cash and Darby, it sounded like Charlie hadn't had a real vacation in years.

After Holiday signed the revised agreement, Beck would be free to talk to Charlie about the plans for the Rose. He'd bring up the possibility of a future and what that might look like between them. Two more days.

But first, he had to make sure everything would be in good shape while they'd be gone. He made his way to the back room to grab a case of beer. The cooler sure wouldn't stock itself.

# TWENTY-TWO

CHARLIE WHIPPED THE LACY TANK TOP OVER HER head and tossed it on the bed to join the remaining contents of her closet. What in the heck did one wear to New York City? She half wished Darby had been available to help her pack. Or even Beck. But he'd left yesterday to attend some meetings before his dad left town on some cruise. So she was on her own. She'd almost canceled when she'd found out he wouldn't be there to hold her hand on the airplane. But staying in Holiday and dealing with the aftermath of chickening out would be worse than whatever fate awaited her in New York. And Beck had promised to be there when she got off the plane. So all she had to do was get on the nonstop flight.

She checked the clock on her nightstand. Cash would be picking her up in fifteen minutes, and so far she'd only thrown a pair of flip-flops and a nightgown in her suitcase. If only she'd had time to go shopping for some new clothes. Or thought to borrow something from Brittany. Well, screw it. If Beck didn't like her for who she was, then she didn't want to have anything to do with him anyway.

A horn blared from the driveway. Leave it to Cash to show up early. She scooped up half the items on her bed and tossed them in the suitcase, then zipped it up. The lacy tank top went back over her head, and she threw a lightweight plaid button-down on over it in case she got cold on the plane. She half pulled, half dragged the wheeled carry-on behind her down the hall and shoved her feet into her cute new boots as Cash flung open the front door.

"Ready, Sis?"

Her intestines seemed to hitch into a bowline knot at the sight of her brother. "Can you come back next Tuesday?"

He reached for the handle of her bag. "There's no gettin' out of this. I promised Beck I'd deliver you to the airport, and that's what I'm gonna do."

Charlie grabbed for the handle. "Maybe this is a mistake. We've got that concert at the Rose tomorrow night, and I don't feel so well. I think maybe that chili Angelo made yesterday didn't agree with—"

Cash put his hands on her shoulders, his eyes going all serious and intense. "Char, you're going to New York this weekend. The guys and me can handle the concert. And if Angelo heard you bad-mouthing his chili, he'd take that spit master job that joint in Dallas keeps offering him."

She studied the tips of her boots, the edge of the rug, anything to keep from having to make eye contact. "What if…I mean—"

"What? What's bothering you, baby girl?"

Charlie couldn't fight the grin that broke through her fears at the nickname. Sometimes she hated being the baby of the family. Especially with five older brothers. But when they weren't teasing her, trapping her in a headlock for a noogie, or running out on their chores and leaving her to clean up after them, they could be super sweet, and she loved them with her whole heart.

She hadn't told anyone but Beck about her irrational

fear of something bad happening while she was gone, and she wasn't about to voice it to Cash now. "Nothing. I'm just nervous about flying."

"Aw, that's easy." Cash pulled a couple of bills out of his wallet. "Drinks are on me. Buy yourself a shot once you get through security and then a couple of whiskeys once you get in the air."

"That's your solution? It's not even nine in the morning."

He pressed the cash into her palm. "New York's an hour later. By the time you get to the airport, they'll be having happy hour at the rate you're going. Now let's get outta here. I still have to stop for gas before we hit the highway."

Charlie let him take her bag out to the truck. She grabbed her purse and took one last look at her living room. The knot in her gut tightened, and she pressed her palms to her abdomen. *I can do this.* The horn blared from the driveway, making her jump. Before she let herself back out, she yanked the front door open and slid her shades over her eyes. *I've got this. Right?*

*—Ht—*

Ten minutes later, Dwight had her second-, third-, and fourth-guessing herself. Cash had stopped at the gas station in town. Why hadn't they gone a few miles up the road to the truck stop? While she waited for the ancient pump to dribble enough gas to fill up the tank, she tried to tune out Dwight's words.

"I don't see why you want to go someplace as big and dirty as New York City. You know they have rats there the size of a barn cat?" He flipped the toothpick around his mouth from one corner to the other as he leaned in the open passenger window. "And I hear folks up there have to have bars on the windows and five or six dead bolts the crime rate's so damn high. You'll probably have your handbag snatched right out from under you the second you get off the plane."

Cash shook his head and bumped a hip against the side of the truck. "What do you know about New York? Farthest north you've ever been is Oklahoma City. Don't listen to him, Char."

"You serious about that Yankee?" Dwight peered down at her, his baseball cap shading his beady eyes.

"That's none of your business, Dwight." Charlie crossed her arms over her waist and shifted against the seat belt. "We almost done here, Cash?"

"Yeah." The dial clicked to a stop, and Cash put the handle back on the pump. "Put it on my tab, okay?"

Dwight nodded and leaned away from the window, leaving his hands on the edge. "Don't know why that guy had to come mess everything up. It's about time Holiday didn't have a Holiday around. Better off without 'em."

Cash put a hand on Dwight's shoulder, pulling him away. "Don't worry, Char. Dwight here's gonna do his part while you're gone. We'll make sure the place is still standing when you get back."

Charlie glanced over at Dwight. "Thanks for helping out while I'm away."

He took his hat off his head and held it over his heart. "My pleasure. You let me know if he don't treat you right, okay?"

"Okay." She'd ignored Dwight's misplaced affections for the past few years. Poor guy hadn't been the same since he came back from the army. But now it seemed like time to finally put an end to it once and for all. Add that to the list of things to do when she got back.

For now she had plenty of other thoughts filling her mind. What if Beck was different once she got to New York? What if his family hated her? She'd be able to overcome just about anything except the one thing that worried her most.

What if fate punished her for putting her own needs first, like it had when she'd lost Jackson? It seemed like the only other time she'd reached for happiness, she'd been knocked down so hard she'd barely managed to get back up again. This time, there would be no Sully to rescue her. This time, the only person who could save her was herself.

# chapter
# TWENTY-THREE

CHARLIE FOLLOWED THE CROWD OF PASSENGERS OFF
the plane and into the airport while battling the surge of
light-headedness that threatened to consume her. She could
do this. She was a twenty-seven-year-old woman, for crying
out loud. She handled country-western singers with egos
the size of Texas. Surely she could find her way to the well-
marked baggage claim. Beck had said he'd meet her there.
Once she set her sights on him, everything would be fine.

She didn't want to admit to herself how much she'd
missed him over the past couple of days. She'd grown
used to seeing his scruffy smile every morning, even the
ones where he didn't wake up in her bed. She even missed
the whirring and spitting of his fancy-schmancy coffee
machine. He'd exposed her to what good coffee could taste
like, and she'd come to depend on his skinny vanilla lattes
to start her days.

After what seemed like a five-mile tour of the airport,
she finally reached the luggage carousel. She'd been so
focused on reuniting with her suitcase that she hadn't let
herself take a good look at her surroundings. While she
waited for the conveyor belt to start turning, she let herself
soak in the atmosphere of the big city.

The baggage claim area held an overflowing melting
pot of humanity—every kind of person she could imagine

and even some she'd never be able to come up with on her own. Groups of foreign businessmen mingled with flustered moms toting strollers and holding the tiny hands of toddlers. Some women looked like they'd stepped off a runway; others looked like they'd stepped off a street corner. Teens with low-slung jeans bopped by, giant headphones covering their ears. The man next to her lifted the lid off a cardboard container and dug into some sort of garlic, gingery noodle dish with a plastic fork.

Charlie's stomach growled in response. She'd been too nervous to eat breakfast and only gotten a packet of pretzels on the plane. Cash didn't dispense advice very often, so she'd taken his recommendation to heart and downed two little bottles of whiskey en route to New York. The drinks had made the time pass faster and also aided in keeping her blood pressure within normal range. But the little buzz she'd acquired had worn off, and the only thing that would settle her nerves now would be wrapping her arms around her own personal comfort item: Beck Holiday. Where was he anyway? The carousel began to turn, and the passengers surged toward the first few bags moving down the belt.

Roller bag trailing behind her, Charlie stepped through automatic sliding glass doors into the humid haze of a steamy early August afternoon. Maybe she'd misunderstood and Beck had meant he'd meet her at the curb. The suffocating scent of exhaust assaulted her nose, and she squinted against the glare of the sun reflecting off so much metal. She reached the curb and dug through her purse for her phone. Oh gosh, she'd never turned it back on when the plane had landed. What if he'd been trying to call all along?

While she waited for her phone to boot up, she propped her sunglasses on her nose and popped a piece of gum in her mouth. Groups of travelers swarmed around her, jumping into cabs, limos, and town cars. She'd never felt more alone in her entire life. The phone rang in her hand, and Beck's number flashed across the screen. Thank God. As she slid her thumb across the screen to answer, someone bumped her from behind. The phone flew from her hand and landed facedown in the street a few feet in front of her. She scrambled after it and immediately soared into the air and back onto the curb.

"You trying to get yourself killed, lady?"

She struggled to stand and faced the person who'd manhandled her to safety. "My phone."

A yellow cab screeched to a halt in front of her at the curb. On top of her phone.

"No, no, no." Charlie couldn't do a thing while a businessman loaded his carry-on and briefcase into the trunk of the cab. The second it sped away, she stepped off the curb and evaluated her phone. Or what was left of it. Her hot-pink case lay in pieces across a three-foot patch of concrete. Her screen had split into a gazillion pieces, and the button she'd used to turn it on and off had disappeared.

Her heart dropped into her boots. Jackson—a copy of her message from Jackson had been on that phone. Sure, she still had a copy saved to her hard drive at home. But this was the one she carried with her, her day-to-day connection with her past.

On the verge of losing her grip on control, she took in a few deep breaths. As hard as it was to face the truth, she couldn't bring her phone back to life any more than she could bring back Jackson. Even though it hurt like hell, she knew deep down inside it was time to let him go. She couldn't walk toward a future with Beck, whatever that might look like, if she still had both feet firmly planted in the past.

A horn blared, and an angry driver thrust a middle finger her way. What a welcome. She had half a mind to get right back on a plane and head home. The other half of her mind wanted nothing more than to burrow into Beck's side. Where could he be?

<hr>

Beck hurried through the baggage claim area. No Charlie in sight. She couldn't have up and left. Where would she go? She had to be terrified. For him, jumping from city to city had been a way of life. For Charlie, just getting her to agree to leave Texas had been a major accomplishment. It had been crazy to push this trip on her in the first place. They'd finally reached some neutral ground where they weren't fighting over everything all the time. She'd loosened the reins on the Rose, and they seemed to be growing closer together rather than further apart.

And now…this.

He ducked through the sliding glass doors to see if she'd stepped outside. His heart kicked into high gear at the sight of her. Shoulders hunched, boots tapping on the pavement while she hugged her purse to her chest, she perched on the edge of a bench near the taxi stand.

"Charlie."

Her head lifted at the sound of his voice. Relief flooded her face, and as she launched herself at him, he caught her in his arms.

Between kisses she half-heartedly ripped him a new one. "You're"—*smack*—"late!"—*smack*—"I"—*smack*—"thought you"—*smack*—"weren't coming."

"Hey." He pulled back, meeting her gaze. "I promised you I'd be here. I tried to call, but you didn't answer."

Her arms wrapped around his neck, and she settled her cheek against his chest. "I dropped my phone. A cab ran over it. Everything's gone. My pictures, my contacts, my message from Jackson."

"Oh, Charlie. I'm so sorry."

"When you weren't here, I thought maybe you'd changed your mind about me coming."

"I would never change my mind about having you here, okay?"

She nodded, finally letting her grip loosen. "Okay."

"We'll get you a new phone. I can't replace the message for you."

"I haven't even listened to it in months. Just having it with me made me feel...I don't know, like he was still with me in some way."

"He'll always be with you."

"I know. Sitting here, waiting for you, I realized I don't need to have that message with me all the time. He would have wanted me to move on."

"Sounds like Jackson was a smart man."

She smiled up at him. "He was."

He pulled her against him, pressing a kiss to her forehead. "Let's get you into the city. My dad wants to meet you before he leaves on his cruise tomorrow. Are you up for that?" He grabbed the handle of her bag with one hand and wrapped his other arm around her shoulders. "If you'd rather chill tonight, we can head back to my place."

"No, I'm fine." She offered a smile that appeared to require a bit of effort. "I'd love to meet your dad. Have you talked to him about Sully yet?"

"I haven't had the chance. But I will before he leaves tomorrow." He kissed the top of her head as he led her back through the baggage claim area toward short-term parking.

She tucked her arm around his waist, hooking her finger through one of his belt loops. "You're wearing your Levi's."

"Wanted you to feel at home."

The smile on her face was worth the look of disgust his dad had given him as he careened out of the office in boots and jeans. He cared about her more than anyone he'd been with in the past. But he still didn't know what came next.

Once he rode in the Founder's Day parade, he'd have the title of the Rambling Rose free and clear. He'd pass it on to his dad, get the go-ahead for the park in the Bronx, and come back to New York. But where would that leave him and Charlie?

He pushed the nagging thought out of his mind. Better to enjoy the here and now than spend a bunch of time and energy worrying about a decision that was still months away. No, not months. The months had shrunk into weeks. Time had a way of doing that recently, passing by faster than he wanted it to.

The taillights on his Porsche blinked and the horn beeped as he pressed the button on his key fob.

Charlie stopped, tilting a wide-eyed gaze his direction. "That's your car?"

"Yeah. Let me toss your bag in the back, and I'll get the door for you."

She stood by the trunk while he stowed her suitcase. "You sure you fit in this roller skate?" Her gaze swept up and down his frame, from his head to his toes, making him wish he hadn't agreed to dinner with his dad so they could head back to his place.

"Plenty of room, I promise." He held the door open for her so she could slide inside.

By the time he walked around to the driver's side door, she'd buckled her seat belt and had one hand wrapped around the handle above her head.

"You okay?"

She nodded. "I'll be fine. I've just never ridden in a vehicle shorter than me. Trucks, SUVs, and whatnot. I feel like a semi could drive right over us in this tiny tin can."

Beck unsuccessfully tried to stifle a grin. "Who's the fish out of water now, sweetheart?"

"I know, turnabout's fair play. You're not going to feed me anything weird, are you?"

"What, like cow balls?"

"I'm so sorry. I didn't know you then. Not like I know you now. I figured you were some hot-shot real estate tycoon sniffin' around to make a quick buck. I'd have fed you bull balls and pig's feet or whatever it would have taken to knock you down a notch or two."

"Well, thank God you stopped at bull balls. If you'd have fed me pig's feet, it would have been all over before it even started."

She twisted to face him, probably trying to get a read on whether he was joking.

"How do you feel about sushi?"

"Isn't that raw fish?" A furrow appeared between her eyebrows.

He backed the car out of the parking space and navigated through the narrow aisles of the lot. "You're going to love it."

"I don't know, Beck. Didn't you say you had some sort of barbecue place near your apartment?"

The car revved as he pulled into traffic, heading back into the city. He shifted into fourth and covered her hand with his. "You're on my turf now, little lady. And what was that you said a few minutes ago? Something about turnabout's fair play? Well, get ready to go for a spin then because I'm going to take you on the ride of your life."

# TWENTY-FOUR

CHARLIE SWIVELED HER HEAD FROM SIDE TO SIDE, TRYING to catch sight of everything as it raced by. Beck had been chattering nonstop since they'd left the airport, pointing out landmarks, passing along tidbits of local lore. She'd never seen him so animated, almost like he was more nervous than she was. He'd asked her if she minded a detour on the ride back into the city. Didn't matter to her. She was on his time now.

The idea that she wasn't responsible for anything or anyone else was too hard to embrace. She'd put everyone and everything else first for so long—so afraid that if she didn't she'd end up losing something important to her—that she hadn't been able to wrap her head around just having a good time.

She turned to look at Beck. He smiled, catching her hand up in his. "I'm so glad you're here."

"Me, too," she admitted. Although all the concrete, glass, and skyscrapers scared the crap out of her. She'd never felt so confined, so fenced in. How could so many people live in such a small, condensed space?

"Here's what I wanted to show you." Beck slowed to a stop next to the curb. A dilapidated old building crumbled away beyond a chain-link fence.

"Please tell me this isn't your apartment building," she joked.

"No. It's the lot I want to buy."

"Why?" Graffiti dotted the sides of the building, at least the sides that were left. Broken glass and trash littered the lot. What could Beck possibly see in a place like this?

"A promise to an old friend. I told you my nanny was German, right?"

Charlie nodded. He'd mentioned it once or twice.

"She used to bring me home with her on the weekends sometimes, when my dad was out of town. I never thought of her as having a place of her own. I guess I used to think she appeared and disappeared when I needed her. But as I got older I got to know more about her and the neighborhood kids she considered family."

"And she lived here?" Charlie couldn't make a connection yet. What did his nanny have to do with a lot in what appeared to be a questionable part of town?

"She lived on the next block over. We used to play kickball on a vacant lot. Up until recently, the kids still did." His eyes held a far-off, dreamy look like he'd stepped into the past. "But then my dad bought it to build some luxury apartments."

"I don't get it. What does this building have to do with your nanny?"

Beck turned the full strength of his baby blues on her. "Nonni made me promise that when I grew up, I'd make sure the kids in the neighborhood had a safe place to play. She knew I'd follow in my dad's footsteps, that I'd be in real estate someday." He shrugged. "Didn't seem like too much to promise the only mother figure I'd ever known."

Charlie squeezed his hand. "Where is she now?"

"She died a few years ago. I didn't even find out she was sick until after she passed. Dad and I were entertaining some investors on a golf trip to Scotland when I got the news." He looked at the steering wheel. "Now's my chance to make good on my promise."

"I'm sure she'd be proud of you." It seemed like the right thing to say, although it didn't do justice to the overwhelming feeling inside her. This was the kind of thing Sully would have done. How could he have known his grandson would turn out to be just like him?

Beck shifted into gear. "I wanted to show it to you. Next time you see it, hopefully there will be a park here."

Charlie brought her thoughts to her lips. "Sully would have liked this, too."

He rewarded her with a grin, making her glad she'd said something. Back when he'd first arrived in Holiday, any comparison to Sully had made his hackles rise. Now he seemed almost proud of the fact that he was like his grandfather.

Beck took in a breath and gave her hand a squeeze. "I wish we could put it off, but tonight's our only chance. Are you ready to meet my old man?"

An icy knot tightened in Charlie's gut. This was the one part of the weekend she hadn't been looking forward to—meeting Beck's dad. How could she keep her tongue in check when facing the man who'd broken Sully's heart?

"As ready as I'll ever be." She took in a deep breath. For Beck. She'd do it for Beck.

Charlie rubbed Sully's lucky coin between her fingers while Beck passed his keys to the valet. Throngs of well-dressed couples waited on padded velvet benches near the entrance. Her gaze darted from one super-model look-alike to the next. She and Beck stuck out like two trees on the open prairie with him in his jeans and her in her boots. The hostess greeted Beck by name and immediately led them back. Mr. Holiday must have been waiting.

He stood as they approached the table. A look of thinly veiled disgust floated across his face. Charlie let her gaze travel over his paunchy frame that had been well disguised by an expertly tailored suit. A smile that her mama would have called a "snake-oil sales-man's calling card" slid over his lips.

Beck didn't seem to notice. "Dad, this is my girlfriend, Charlie Walker."

"Charlie?" His eyebrows quirked as he offered a hand.

"Charlotte's my given name. But everyone calls me Charlie." She slipped her hand into his. He held it for a few beats too long.

"You're Tom's daughter."

"Yes."

"How is old Tom doing nowadays?"

Charlie gave a little tug to pull her hand away from his. Beck held out her chair, and she slid onto the seat. "Dad's doing fine, thanks for asking, Mr. Holiday."

"Oh, call me Holiday." He sank into the chair next to her. "Wine?"

The hostess immediately signaled the waiter, who'd been standing by on alert.

"No, just some water for me." Charlie smiled at the waiter. His gaze hit the floor.

"Let's get some sparkling." Holiday gestured to their glasses. "Can we get some sparkling water over here?"

"Right away, sir." The waiter disappeared for a moment, then returned with a large bottle of sparkling water.

By that time, Beck had pulled on a jacket the hostess had given him and taken his seat on Charlie's right.

"I see you didn't bother to dress for dinner," his dad observed.

Charlie's cheeks burned. "I'm so sorry. I didn't realize we'd be going somewhere so fancy."

"It's okay, Charlotte. Beck should have warned you." Ice clinked against a glass, and Charlie looked up, casting a watchful eye over Mr. Holiday, who sat across the table with a tumbler of amber liquid between his hands.

He made her nervous. Something about him was off—that was the only way she could explain it. Not that he'd been rude or said anything specific to make her uncomfortable. He simply put her on edge. Made her apprehensive. He seemed to be biding his time, waiting for something. It was just a sense she got. Like the way she could always tell a storm was coming even though the sky might still be a bright, brilliant blue.

Beck's dad cleared his throat and smiled. Like a cat who hadn't quite eaten the canary. Like a cat who wanted to bat the poor canary around a bit before taking the first bite. "So, Charlie, tell me more about this little bar you run."

She swallowed a gulp of her water. The bubbles hit the back of her throat, making her cough.

"You okay?" Beck's hand rested on her shoulder.

Nodding, she cleared her throat. "I'd hardly describe

the Rose as a 'little bar.' We've got about seven thousand square feet."

"That's right. Plus that swanky outside area. Do you still serve beer by the pigpen?"

"I'm sorry?"

Beck clasped her hand under the table. "Charlie single-handedly manages the entire operation. She books the talent, takes care of the staff—"

Mr. Holiday interrupted. "I'm sure your folks told you they knew me way back when."

Piercing blue eyes caught her mid-sip. She held the glass inches from her mouth, and it hit her. He and Beck shared the same eyes. But while Beck's could sometimes reflect the same coldness as his dad's, she'd also seen compassion, affection, and plenty of heat there. And not the kind of heat she imagined his dad had a flair for. Beck's eyes held the kind of heat that made her want to run away from him and bury herself in him at the same time. She doubted the older Holiday had the ability to channel that kind of passion.

"They mentioned it once or twice." What did Holiday want from her? Obviously he was trying to get a rise.

He downed the remainder of his drink. Had to be scotch or whiskey. She'd bet the Rose it was scotch. Some single-malt, expensive variety. "I doubt they shared many kind words about me over the years."

Charlie shrugged, not willing to play whatever part he'd cast her in. Putting on her big-girl britches and braving the plane and airport had taken its toll. At that moment, she wanted nothing more than to snuggle into Beck and feel his fingers trail down her

arm, over her back, under the hem of her tank. Goose
bumps raced down her limbs, and she shivered.

"You cold?" Beck removed the borrowed jacket to
drape it over her shoulders. Holiday signaled to the waiter
who showed up in less than a minute with another blazer.

Even though she'd only spent a half hour with the man,
she couldn't stand the way Beck's dad treated him. Like he
was a toddler who needed to be tolerated, not one of the
most confident, capable men she'd ever known.

Thankfully, the food arrived, relieving her of any
obligation to respond. As the waiter set the platters down
in front of them, Beck explained each dish. Spicy salmon
rolls, fresh sashimi, seaweed salad. Nothing looked familiar. And with fresh flowers decorating the plates, nothing
even looked edible.

The men confidently used their chopsticks to lift
chunks of fish and rice to their plates and then into their
mouths. Charlie struggled with hers for another minute
before stabbing a piece of pink fish and letting it drop onto
the plate in front of her.

Holiday motioned to the waiter, who always seemed to be
standing by. He slipped a fork next to her plate. Charlie set
the chopsticks down and tried to cut the piece of fish in two.

"Do you need a steak knife, Charlie?" Holiday asked.

She wouldn't give him the satisfaction. Beck gulped,
washing down a chunk of salmon. Charlie smiled, then
slipped the oversized bit into her mouth. She preferred her
fish blackened or panfried, but this wasn't exactly horrible.
Her tongue tried to make sense of the saltiness of the soy
sauce and the firm, sweet texture of the fish.

"They still probably don't serve much besides barbecue
in Holiday, is that right?" Mr. Holiday gave her a smug

grin, as if he were mocking her for her inability to use giant toothpicks as utensils.

"Mmm." With a mouth full of food, all she could do was nod.

"I sure am glad I managed to escape."

"Yeah, I wanted to ask you about that." Beck set his chopsticks down on his plate. "What happened to make you leave?"

Holiday tapped his napkin against his lips. "I don't think now is the time to discuss that, Son."

Charlie's gaze bounced back and forth between them.

Beck continued to push. "But I want to know. Mr. Hill said you and Sully had a falling-out."

"A falling-out. That's one way to put it."

"What do you mean?" Beck took a sip of his water. He appeared to be casually interested in a response, but Charlie knew better. She could have sliced the tension between him and his father with that steak knife Mr. Holiday had offered.

"My father never wanted me involved in the business. The more I tried to be a part of that dumb bar, the more I tried to help him out with new ideas, fresh marketing concepts, the more he pushed me away. Things between us were never like the way they are between you and me, Son. I want you to take an active role. You'll hold the reins of Holiday Enterprises someday." He leaned back from the table. "My old man couldn't stand the thought of us working together."

Beck's shoulders dropped. He reached across the table to cover his dad's hand with his. "I didn't mean to bring up a painful topic."

Couldn't he see how his dad manipulated him? She wanted to give Holiday a good kick to the shin, or an even more sensitive body part, under the table. But Beck needed to see his father for what he was on his own. Hopefully, he'd catch a good, long glimpse before it was too late.

Holiday brushed Beck's hand away and signaled to the waiter for another drink. "That's okay. No harm done. Now, Charlie, tell me, how's your family? Still trying to get by with that little ranching operation?"

Beck managed to change the subject and get her out of the hot seat when he asked his dad about the itinerary for his cruise. She spent the next twenty minutes pushing food around on her plate while listening to his dad go on and on about the ports he and his wife would visit. Athens, Barcelona, Santorini...the names were familiar yet foreign to her way of life. Making it to New York City felt like a major accomplishment. Another vivid reminder of how insignificant her little corner of Texas seemed compared to Beck's experience as a lifelong world traveler.

Finally, blessedly, dinner came to an end. Beck took care of the bill while his dad took care of finishing his third drink.

"Did you want to come back to the house for dessert? I know Marion was upset she didn't get a chance to meet you." Mr. Holiday stood and swayed slightly as the waiter returned.

"I'm sure Charlie wants to settle in. It's been a long day"— Beck brushed his hand down her back—"for both of us."

His father's eyes narrowed; he didn't seem the sort to miss a thing. "Of course. Charlie, I hope you enjoy your weekend."

"I'm sure I will."

"You want to wait here a sec while I give the valet my

ticket?" Beck squeezed her hand. "Dad, you'll keep her company for me for a minute or two?"

"My pleasure." Holiday sat down again and nodded toward the door. "Take your time. It will give us a chance to chat."

Beck gave her a reassuring grin and took off toward the door. Left alone with his father, she wrapped her arms across her midsection, feeling the need to protect herself from his steely gaze.

"My son tells me you're a whiz at managing that little bar."

"I enjoyed working with Sully. It's not the same now that he's gone, but the town needs the Rose."

He nodded. "That hellhole won't be much without it."

Something about his tone made Charlie bristle. He meant *wouldn't*, not *won't*. "But Holiday won't have to be without it. Beck's doing a great job."

"I'm sure he's enjoying his little vacation down in Texas. But he's going to take over Holiday Enterprises someday, and he'll be worth a hell of a lot more than... *Sully*. You probably can't even wrap your gorgeous little head around numbers with that many zeros after them." He brushed an invisible speck of lint off his sleeve.

Charlie's head spun, trying to make sense of Mr. Holiday's verbal assault.

"Ready to go?" Beck rejoined them, reaching for Charlie's hand.

She and Mr. Holiday stood at the same time. He made a move to embrace her with all the stiffness and grace of a scarecrow with a two-by-four stretched across its arms. "Enjoy your time in the city, Charlie."

She let him air-kiss her cheeks, then nestled back into Beck's side. The good manners her mama had trained into her won out over her urge to stomp on the man's shiny, tasseled loafers. She pasted on a neutral smile. "I enjoyed meeting you."

Mr. Holiday turned his attention to his son. "Beck, we'll touch base in the morning. I need you to send over that contract before my flight leaves." It was an order, not a request.

Beck nodded and pulled Charlie closer. When his father finally turned away and made his way to the front of the restaurant, he let out an audible sigh, and she felt his chest deflate like he'd been holding his breath through the entire encounter.

"Well, he's got all the charm of a cow patty in a china bowl."

Beck's eyes crinkled at the corners. "What?"

"Sorry. Just something Sully used to say." Her last interaction with Beck's dad had thrown her. Thank goodness they wouldn't have to spend any more time together during her stay. "Did you get what you wanted out of the conversation?"

"Not quite. But at least it's a start. You okay?"

"Your dad didn't seem to be a big fan of Holiday. Or me." What if Beck thought the same now that he saw how out of place she was in his neck of the woods?

The smile he gave her sent any lingering doubts scuttling away. "Well, darlin', you've already got a number one fan."

She couldn't help but smile at his brazen response. "Now are you going to take me to your place before I get tired of waiting and hop the next plane home?"

"Ms. Walker, I thought you'd never ask." He let go of her long enough to hold the door open for her. "Shall we?"

"Yes. And I hate to ask because I'm sure this is a fantastic restaurant, but—"

"What?"

Her stomach growled. She squinted up at him, not wanting to offend.

Beck let out a laugh. "Not a fan of the raw fish, huh?"

She shook her head. "Any chance I can grab a slice of pizza from one of those places I saw on the street?"

"I'll get you a whole pie."

She linked her arm through his, eager to get the fun part of the weekend under way. She'd been apprehensive about taking time away, but now that she was here, she wanted to make the most of the trip. The tension and stress of getting there and the uncomfortable aftermath of her conversation with his dad eased away under Beck's touch. With another seventy-two hours of having him all to herself spread out in front of her, she couldn't wait to get started.

# TWENTY-FIVE

BECK TRIED TO SEE HIS PLACE THROUGH CHARLIE'S eyes. She hadn't said a word since they'd gotten off the elevator and he'd unlocked the door. His apartment was nothing to be ashamed of, but he couldn't quite swing the payments on a penthouse suite like his dad. She'd really flip if she ever stepped foot in that monstrosity. Beck preferred his cozy two-bedroom in Chelsea to his dad's two floors of gaudy nouveau riche decor.

"Are you going to say something?" He wheeled her bag next to his black-leather sofa and put a hand on her back.

Charlie whirled around from where she'd stopped in front of the floor-to-ceiling windows. "Something. Your place is really something."

"You hate it, don't you?"

He hadn't turned on the overhead light, so the only light coming in filtered through the windows. Her expression was difficult to read in the semidarkness.

"I don't hate it at all. It's just…different from what I'm used to."

Different…that was the understatement of the century. Midtown Manhattan and Holiday, Texas, were about as polar opposite as two places could be. "How about some wine?"

"Sure." Her boots tapped on the hardwood floor as she took a self-guided tour.

Beck set two glasses of wine on the glass dining table and returned to the kitchen for the pizza. He put a slice on a plate for each of them, then folded his slice and took a bite. He'd been enjoying the barbecue and Tex-Mex that Holiday had to offer, but there was nothing like authentic New York pizza. He missed the ability to walk out the door and have every kind of cuisine at his disposal. There was always something going on in the city. Nightlife in Holiday consisted of whatever happened to be going on at the Rose.

"I can't believe you're eating pizza after devouring all that sushi." She came to a stop at the edge of the table and sat down next to him.

"And I can't believe you're here." He wiped sauce off his chin and smiled at her. Alone at last. Even when they were at her place or when she came over to Sully's, it never felt like they were truly alone. Someone seemed to notice every little thing they did. Whether his SUV was parked overnight in front of her cottage or the two of them disappeared into the office at the same time. There was always someone watching.

"I can't believe it either. Do you think everything is going to go okay this weekend? Maybe I should call Shep to check in." Her lips pursed.

"I already sent him a text. Let him know you got here and that your phone bit the dust so he should call me if he needs anything."

"Wow. I'm impressed. Think we can pick up a new phone tomorrow? I'd feel better if I had my own."

Beck slid his chair from the table and stood. "My

assistant is taking care of it. Should be delivered first thing in the morning."

Her eyes narrowed, and the corner of her mouth quirked up. "What's going on?"

He stood behind her, massaging her shoulders and neck muscles. "Just making sure things are taken care of."

"About that. Your dad said something tonight."

Beck leaned down to move her hair away from her neck and kiss a trail from her shoulder to her ear. "Oh yeah?"

Charlie leaned into him. "About the town not being much without the Rose."

"He's right. The Rose is what puts Holiday on the map."

"Yeah, but he almost made it sound like the Rose wouldn't be around much longer."

Beck stilled. That was one of the things he needed to address with his dad in the morning. He'd added a few clauses to their agreement, including the right for him to tell Charlie about the plans for the Rose. Holiday had been adamant that no one else know about their deal. But Beck couldn't keep the information from her, not with where they were headed in their relationship. He needed to be able to tell her that his dad was taking over and that she'd continue on as manager.

So he told her the truth, buying himself some time until he and Holiday had a signed agreement on both ends. "I have no idea what he meant by that remark, but I'll be sure to ask him. Now, relax. I want you to have a good time this weekend. It's our chance to focus on us. The Rose is in good hands. Your phone is in good hands."

"And now I'm in your good hands?"

"Mmm. Something like that." He backed away so she could slide out from the table.

She wrapped her arms around his neck and touched her lips to his. "All right, Mr. Manhattan. Show me what those good hands can do."

He was more than up for the challenge. It had only been a few days since he'd last lost himself inside her, and he wanted more, needed more. He'd never been like this with a woman. Sure, he enjoyed getting naked on a regular basis, but he'd always been able to keep his flings separate from his day-to-day life. Sex was more of a recreational sport, an outlet for pent-up energy, kind of like a great workout. He could schedule it in his calendar, then move on to the next task.

But with Charlie, it was different. When he wasn't with her, he thought about being with her. When he was with her, all he could think about was being inside her. When he was inside her, he couldn't think about anything else at all.

Consumed with need, he nudged her shirt off her shoulders and kissed along her collarbone. Her hands worked to untuck his shirt while their mouths met, parted, and met again. The woman generated a heat inside him that burned through his veins. He drew her into the living room without breaking lip contact. She fumbled with the buttons on his starched, white shirt. Too many clothes separated them. That needed to be rectified, stat.

He lifted her shirt up and over her head, leaving her standing before him in that sexy lace tank. He couldn't wait to get his hands on her, find out what she had on under that long skirt. She shouldn't wear things like that; it covered up too much skin.

On fire with an urgency he couldn't control, he

tangled his hands in her hair. He should slow it down. They didn't need to rush. They had all night, all weekend. His brain tried to put on the brakes, but his body demanded release. He reached under her tank and undid her bra, then slid the whole thing over her head, shirt and bra together.

"You're so beautiful." He paused long enough to tease her nipples into hard peaks with his tongue.

"All that sushi must have blurred your vision."

Why did she always downplay his compliments? "I mean it. You are, without a doubt, the most gorgeous, capable, brave, competent woman I've ever met in my entire life." He put a hand on either side of her face, forcing her to meet his eyes.

Reluctantly, she did. He wanted to kiss her uncertainty away.

"Do you have any idea how head over heels I am for you?"

Her hands reached up to cover his. She held his gaze. "If it's anywhere near what I feel for you, then we're both tumbling ass over teakettle together."

His breath stalled. Something between them had shifted, deepened. She had to feel it, too. The words hovered on the tip of his tongue. Three little words he'd never uttered to a lover before. "Charlie, I—"

She covered his mouth with hers, forcing his jeans down his hips. He stepped out of them, leaving his shoes and boxer briefs in a puddle on the floor.

Backed against the glass, Charlie spread her hands out behind her. "The window—"

"Tinted." He captured her mouth with his again and sandwiched her between the skyline of Manhattan and his body. "Did you get to check out the view?"

"What?"

"Like this." He spun her around so her palms pressed flat on the window. His hands reached under her skirt, relieving her of her panties.

"Oh." She tried to turn around, but he put a hand on hers, urging her to stay in place.

Her skirt floated to the ground. He nudged her legs apart, and she leaned forward, lifting her backside toward him. With the lights of the city spread out in front of them, his hips rolled forward as he guided himself inside her. She arched into him, the hunt for her own pleasure taking precedence over fears of window washers or nosy neighbors.

He wanted to pause the moment in time. Stamp his brain with the image of her leaning forward against his floor-to-ceiling windows in nothing but a pair of red cowboy boots. But he couldn't stop the momentum if he'd wanted to. She'd set something loose inside him that he couldn't control.

As she came apart around him, her body molded into his. "Beck, I'm close."

"I've got you, angel." He focused on her pleasure, and she took what he gave her, riding out the long wave of her release.

Before she came down, he let himself go, wrapping his arm around her waist and showing her with his body what he still hadn't been able to say out loud.

Satiated, he pressed a kiss against the fluttery pulse at the base of her neck.

"Welcome to New York, baby."

Charlie woke to the soft daylight filtering through the window. It took her a moment to remember where she was. Beck's. A brief recap of the night before played through her mind. Sex by the window. Sex on the couch. She'd even spread herself over the glass dining room table, and he'd taken her there as her ass made butt prints where his cereal bowl should have been. No wonder she was sore. It felt like she'd gone out for a daylong trail ride after not sitting in the saddle for months. She almost snorted at her bad joke. She had saddle sores from riding Beck. *Get a grip, Charlie.*

In the fuzzy light of early morning, she let herself take the look around she'd missed out on the night before. Beck's place was so…not Beck. At least not the Beck she'd come to know down in Holiday. Plain white walls served as a backdrop for all of the black, gray, and silver. Black-leather headboard, gray duvet. Black flat-screen on top of a dark-gray dresser. Not a drop of color except for her discarded clothing she could see through the open doorway to the living room.

She stretched her arms overhead and practically purred at the ache of satisfaction rolling through her exhausted limbs. Beck's voice drifted in from the other room. Probably on that phone call with his dad. She rolled out of bed and located a T-shirt in one of his dresser drawers. Her bag hadn't quite made it into the bedroom, and she didn't want to eat her breakfast in the buff.

Beck sat at a desk in the corner of the room in a pair of shorts and a polo. He held his phone in one hand and gestured her over with the other.

"I'm sending it over now. Take a look and let me know if you have any changes. Once you sign, I'll send a signed copy back, and we'll both be in good shape." He put his hand over the mic on his phone and nodded toward the table they'd desecrated the night before. "Got you a latte."

Seeing him here, on his home turf, made her heart hurt with the ache she knew would come. They hadn't discussed the future much beyond him asking her if she'd stay on to manage the Rose. She still held out hope that he'd fall in love with the Rose and with Holiday. That he'd leave his life in New York behind and make a commitment to the town. That she'd be able to honor Sully's wishes and secure the fate of the Rose. That maybe, just maybe, he'd fall for her.

She took a sip of her latte and drifted toward the window. Manhattan spread out before her. Her gaze flickered from one building to the next, to the strip of water she could see in the distance, to people the size of ants scurrying around on the street below.

Beck slipped behind her and ran his hands up her sides under the shirt. Her heart skittered at his touch, and her knees wobbled.

"You get everything squared away with your dad?" she asked.

"Almost. Just waiting on a piece of paper." He kissed the sensitive spot behind her ear. "How did you sleep?"

She turned around in his arms and nestled her head against his chest. "Good. When you finally let me drift off."

"I missed you."

A warm knot formed in her chest, radiating heat out from the center. She'd missed him, too, more than she wanted to admit.

"What are you up for today?" he asked.

She palmed the front of his jeans. "Obviously I know what you're up for."

"What can I say? I like the way you look in my shirt."

"Aren't you going to show me around the city? Or did you trick me into coming to New York so you could keep me locked up in your bedroom as your personal sex toy?"

"There it is. You found me out." He nibbled at her earlobe. "Now, about tomorrow. I took the liberty of making an appointment for you at the spa in my building in the morning. Do we need to pick up something for you to wear? You know when they say picnic it's really more of a fancy happy hour."

"A spa appointment? You afraid I'll embarrass you?"

"Of course not. I just want to spoil you."

"That might be nice. I brought a sundress and some sandals. Do you think I need to shop for something more formal? I don't want to stick out like a fly in the fruit punch."

"Where do you come up with this stuff?"

"What?"

"Fly in the fruit punch?"

"Just something my mama says."

Beck shook his head. "You'd look like dynamite if you tossed a burlap feed sack over your shoulders."

"You're not afraid I'm too country for your friends?" Her eyes sparked with a glint of fire.

"Absolutely not. I think you should wear your boots, a hat, and a guitar, like that guy we saw in Times Square last night, and pass yourself off as the Naked Cowgirl."

She swatted his side. "I don't want to scare everyone away before they announce your dad's award."

Her fingers ran through his hair. He must have had it

cut when he got home. She liked how it had been in Holiday, longer and a little shaggy on the sides. A little less polished and a lot more "go with the flow." She stood there for a long while, avoiding the temptation of dragging him back to bed. She wanted to brand this moment in time, stamp it on her heart, and emblazon it on her brain.

This man.

Without even knowing it, he'd given her so much already. He made her braver, willing to step outside her comfort zone. He made her feel. She'd been numb for so long. Because of Beck, she felt everything now—the good along with the bad. He'd jump-started her heart, like on those medical shows where the ER doctor yells "clear" and they shock the person right back to life. She'd owe him for that for the rest of her life.

Those Holiday men had a knack for pulling her out of her darkest moments. First Sully, now Beck. No matter what happened between them, no matter what the future held, no matter what he decided to do about the Rose, she'd always be grateful to him for bringing her heart back to life. For piecing it back together and allowing her to feel again. Even if he was probably going to end up breaking it in the long run.

# chapter
# TWENTY-SIX

CHARLIE TOSSED HER NEW PHONE INTO HER BAG, then took the hand Beck offered and climbed out of the town car he'd hired to drive them to the picnic. She smoothed her hair, which had been highlighted, trimmed, and swept into a twist. The shade of red the manicurist had painted her nails perfectly matched her lacy red sundress. She batted her eyes against the sun, feeling like she had some little insects stuck to her eyelids with those fake eyelashes on. Seeing Beck's reaction to her makeover had been worth the three hours she'd spent at the salon.

She hated the idea of flying home tomorrow. They hadn't had enough time together.

"You ready for this?" He squeezed her hand.

"I suppose. It'll be nice to go home and check on Baby Back, but I'm not ready to leave you yet."

"We've still got tonight."

"Yeah, but I don't get you all to myself."

"We have to stay long enough for me to accept the award. Then we can head back to my place, and you can have your way with me again." He rolled his eyes. "You're a hard woman to please, Ms. Walker."

"Oh, stop it. Just promise me you'll stay by my side the whole time." She was nervous enough about trying to fit in; she didn't want to navigate the upper echelon of New York society on her own all night.

"I promise."

If only she'd packed those heeled sandals she thought she'd thrown in her bag. Instead, her feet were comfortably encased in her cute boots. She wouldn't hesitate to wear boots with a dress at home. But how many of these chic fashionistas would be sporting Tony Lama's?

As they passed through the waterfront estate of one of Mr. Holiday's business associates, she scanned the guests on the lawn. White, beige, light blue, muted pastels. It was like entering some sort of high-class Easter party with the colors muted by a dim filter. She bit her lip and held her straw bag closer to her side. Beck squeezed her hand, probably trying to send a jolt of silent encouragement through his fingers.

Before she could fake some sort of illness and make a break for the car, an older couple approached.

"Beck, so glad you could make it." The man wore white dress pants with a light-blue blazer and a pin-striped oxford.

"Mr. Samuels, thanks for having us. My dad sends his regrets."

"We tried to change the date when we found out he'd be out of town, but you know how it is trying to get the party planner and caterer rebooked. Not to mention the florist." The woman gestured behind her, where tables with tall bouquets of flowers dotted the gigantic paver patio. She took Beck's hands and air-kissed both of his cheeks. "We're glad you could be here to accept the award on his behalf."

"It's my pleasure. Mr. and Mrs. Samuels, I'd like you to meet Charlotte Walker." Beck put his hand on the small of her back, propelling her forward.

"Charlotte, how lovely you could join us." Mrs. Samuels took Charlie's hand in hers and glanced toward the boots. "Can we assume you're from Texas? I hear that's where Beck has been hiding out this summer."

"Nice to meet you, and thanks for having me. Yes, I'm from Holiday."

Mr. Samuels let out a deep laugh. "We got such a kick out of that. Finding out your dad had a whole town named after him down in Texas. Welcome, Charlotte." Mr. Samuels took her hand in a firm grip. "Can't say we have any barbecue or cowboy fare. But you should try the lobster rolls. They're my favorite." He let go of her hand and patted his nonexistent belly. Seemed like everyone at the party could have posed for a fitness magazine. She didn't see a roll of skin, a wrinkle, or a flabby tricep on any of the partygoers.

"We don't want to monopolize the guest of honor. Why don't the two of you go mingle? Make sure you get one of the rhubarb martinis. The caterer said they're all the rage this summer. Rhubarb? Can you imagine? I've never made anything from rhubarb before." Mrs. Samuels twittered and waved a jeweled wrist in the air, like she'd just made a hysterical joke.

Charlie could imagine. Sully had taught her how to grow the tart plant as an annual in the shade of a giant pecan tree, and she'd perfected her own strawberry-rhubarb pie. But she hadn't had a rhubarb martini before. And by the looks of things, she was going to need at least a couple of them to get through the afternoon.

"I can't wait to try it." Charlie looped her arm through Beck's, hoping the physical contact would bolster her courage. This wasn't exactly the kind of place she'd imagined spending a summer afternoon. She stuck out like a platter of sizzling steak fajitas on a buffet full of paper-thin cucumber sandwiches and petit fours.

"If you'll excuse us, I need to go check in with the caterer." Mrs. Samuels touched Charlie's arm. "I do hope you enjoy yourself this afternoon."

Charlie nodded and smiled, doing her best to blend in to the five-foot floral display behind her.

Mr. and Mrs. Samuels turned away, leaving Beck and Charlie standing on the stairs leading down to the patio, where dozens of pastel-clad clones mingled among the flowers, white-linen-draped tables, and waitstaff holding trays of bite-sized savories.

"Do you see the bar?" Beck asked, scanning the large expanse of lawn.

"Is it that tent over there?" Charlie nodded toward an arbor draped in white linens and strung with flowers. She'd seen weddings that didn't match the level of decor of this "picnic."

Beck took her hand and led her to the tent on the far side of the patio. Along the way, he had to stop to shake hands, make a quick intro, and give a few nods and waves. By the time they reached the tall, portable counter, they'd been bumped through the crowd like those inner tubes on the Guadalupe.

"Did you want to try one of those rhubarb drinks?" he asked.

"Sure."

"We'll take a rhubarb martini and a club soda, please."

"You don't want something to drink?"

Beck grabbed a couple cocktail napkins. "Not until after I make the acceptance speech."

"Oh my gosh, are you nervous?"

"Nah, it's…" A muscle along his jawline pulsed.

She bumped her hip into his thigh. "You *are* nervous. Wow, finally."

The bartender handed them their drinks, and Beck took a sip of his water. "Finally what?"

"I finally get to see what you look like when you're nervous. How bad is it? Butterflies in the stomach? Feeling light-headed? You're not going to puke, are you?"

He took her elbow and steered her toward a cocktail table at the edge of the patio. "I'm not nervous."

"Mm-hmm, if you say so."

"Just a little, uh, tense. Want to make sure I don't blow it, you know?" His fingers fiddled with the paper napkin.

"Yeah, that's what the general population calls nervous. Don't you do stuff like this all the time?"

Beck lifted one shoulder in a half shrug. "Doesn't mean I enjoy it."

"What *do* you enjoy about your work?" She'd gotten to know the Holiday, Texas, version of Beck. Seeing him here, in his element, gave her a much more rounded picture of the man. It was difficult to reconcile the Hamptons-garden-party Beck with the Levi's-wearing version she'd gone head-to-head with in the pigpen. Not to mention hip-to-hip with in the truck and on her couch and so many other places. Her face warmed even thinking about it.

"I like the challenge. The idea of building something

from nothing. Or revamping a failing property into something successful."

"Like Sully."

"Excuse me?"

"The Rambling Rose wasn't doing so well when Sully took it over from his father. Of course, that was years ago, so it's not like I was there. But I've heard the story so many times I may as well have been." She took a sip of her drink. The tartness of the rhubarb mixed nicely with the squirt of lime. Maybe she could come up with some sort of rhubarb-spiked punch they could serve at the party after the Founder's Day parade. Heaven knew she had enough rhubarb in the freezer she could make gallons of it.

"What story?"

"Don't tell me you're interested in learning more about your down-home roots?" She batted her eyelashes at him, overplaying her flirting card in an attempt to both get his mind off his speech and distract herself from how out of place she felt.

"I've been looking through the scrapbooks at my grandfather's place. He had boxes of them. I even found a couple photos of you I snagged out of a shoebox."

Charlie's jaw dropped. "Me?"

Beck pulled out his wallet and handed her a small, washed-out photo of her and Sully on the front porch of the Rambling Rose. Her heart did a little two-step in her chest, her hand shook, and her eyes welled with tears. She hadn't seen this particular picture before. Someone must have snapped a candid around the time Sully brought her on board. Could Beck be developing a sentimental side? Maybe the importance of the town and the Rose was finally starting to sink in.

Before she could form her thoughts into words, a shadow darkened the tablecloth, and a man's voice cut through her visit to the past. "Hey, Beck. Who's this?"

Beck turned and caught the tall, dark-haired stranger in a grip that seemed to be half hug, half handshake. "J.T., I didn't think you were going to make it."

"Yeah, I wasn't sure myself. But Bella's plans changed, so here we are." He stepped aside, and the waifish woman behind him leaned in to give Beck the standard air-kisses on both cheeks.

"Hi, Beck. Who's your friend?" Her gaze raked over Charlie—a stark contrast to the friendly smile she offered.

"J.T., Bella, this is Charlotte Walker. She's the manager of the Rambling Rose. It's that place I've been telling you—"

"Charlotte. At last. You're like a Texas wildflower among all these boring white lilies." J.T. took her hand and lifted it to his lips.

Bella's eyes narrowed. "How long are you in town?"

Charlie looked back and forth between them. "Until tomorrow. And I feel more like a weed than a flower this afternoon." She gestured to her dress. "Beck wasn't exactly clear on the dress code."

"That's a man for you. Well, I think you look gorgeous. Red certainly is your color." Bella looped her arm through Charlie's and began to lead her away. "You don't mind if I steal you for a little bit? There are so many people I want you to meet, and I'm sure the boys have business to discuss."

Charlie cast a helpless glance over the top of Bella's head, but J.T. had already stepped in front of Beck and started yapping about something. Beck shot her a reassuring smile and turned his attention to J.T.

So much for sticking together. Before Bella pulled her into the crowd, she snagged her drink off the table. It was becoming more and more obvious she'd need all the help she could get to make it through the rest of the day.

*HH*

Beck half listened to J.T. while he tracked Bella and Charlie's progress through the crowd. He probably shouldn't have let Bella drag her away.

"So, did you get everything sorted out with your dad?" J.T. asked.

"Huh?" Beck's hands clenched as a colleague from another firm shook Charlie's hand across the patio.

"Dude. Where are you right now?"

Beck shook the twinges of jealousy away and let out a breath. "I'm here. What were you asking about?"

"Your dad. He give you the all-clear on the Morris Park project?"

J.T. didn't need to know that Beck had been having second thoughts. And third. And fourth. He had been on board with handing over his dad's birthright, but something Charlie said had him second-guessing things. It would only be fair for his dad to have a chance to make things right in Holiday, just like he'd be able to set things right and fulfill a dream by putting together the Morris Park property. But that meant his ties to the Rose, to Holiday, to Charlie would be severed. Even though he'd never planned to stick around, he'd been experiencing a slight change of heart.

"So far so good, although—"

"Although what?" J.T.'s eyebrows wrinkled. "What's holding you back? I thought we were going to try taking the company in a new, more philanthropic direction and start making a name for ourselves. Are you still in this?"

Beck ran a hand over his freshly shaved chin. He kind of missed the scruff he'd grown used to in Texas. "Yeah, I just need to figure out the best way to proceed. I want to make sure my dad's plans for the Rose align with what the town needs. He hasn't been there in so long. I think he's lost touch with what might be best."

"And how long am I supposed to sit around on my ass while you figure this out?"

"I'm sorry. I know you're in a tight spot. It's—"

"A tight spot? Bro, you know your dad keeps my balls in a vise. This is our chance to take on a bigger role. He won't give us a second chance. You've got one week to figure out how you want to spin this, or I'm walking."

"Look, I'm working on it, okay?"

J.T. leaned in close. Close enough that Beck caught a whiff of scotch on his breath. "I know exactly what or should I say *who* you're working on, and she doesn't fit into our plans. You keep thinking with your dick, and we're both going to get screwed, and I don't mean the kind that ends with your cowgirl wet dream screaming out your name."

Beck gritted his teeth together and wrapped his hand into a fist. Wouldn't be a good idea to lay out his coworker with an uppercut to the chin in the middle of the Samuelses' patio. "You leave Charlie out of this. I said I'll figure it out and I will."

"I know you will." J.T. backed off and clapped a hand

on Beck's shoulder. "Let's make sure it's sooner rather than later, eh?"

Before Beck could fire back a smart-ass response, Mr. Samuels tapped on a microphone that had been set up on the stairs.

"If everyone can find their seats, we'll get started with the ceremony." He took his wife's hand and escorted her to a table in front then motioned to Beck to join him there.

"Better go get your award." J.T. clucked his tongue. "If we get things going on our own, it could be you or me accepting that thing for ourselves in a few years. Not you standing in for your old man."

The award. The whole reason behind the stupid party. His dad would join leagues of powerful businessmen before him as the Fiscal Friends of NYC's Contributor of the Year. It was mainly a reason to get together, write off a weekend in the Hamptons, and make a bunch of business owners feel good about themselves for doing a good deed or two. Beck was proud of some of the projects Holiday Enterprises had sponsored. The company had donated land and a building for an after-school club for kids in the Bronx. And his dad had paid for an entire elementary school to attend a Yankees game.

Of course, Beck later found out they'd had to unload the property and building as soon as possible to avoid some major tax implications and rezoning issues. And his dad made sure a news crew documented the Yankees game in the hopes it would balance out some bad publicity he'd earned for forcing out a homeless shelter when he razed an entire block. Yeah, the elder Holiday didn't usually do a good deed unless there was something in it for him.

Beck brushed past J.T. to search out Charlie in the crowd. She wiggled her fingers at him in a wave, and the cage squeezing his heart eased a bit. They moved toward each other, meeting in the middle of a sea of tables.

"I think we're supposed to sit at the table up in front." He put his arm around her and steered her toward their seats.

"I feel like everyone's looking at me." Charlie peeked from side to side as they made their way past the other guests.

"If they are, they're just thinking how beautiful you look in that dress."

She smiled and shook her head, downplaying the compliment. He wanted her to feel at ease. If he could manage to work out a win on both fronts, he and Charlie would be spending a lot of time around his colleagues in places like the Hamptons. No doubt Charlie could manage to hold her own no matter where she went. If she had the desire, she could even get involved in some of his business deals. The idea of Charlie working some poor real estate exec over in her sweet Texas drawl made him break into a grin right there.

"What are you thinking about?" she asked as he held out her chair for her.

"You." She sat down, and he kissed her forehead before taking the seat next to her.

Her eyes sparked with that glint of heat and humor he'd come to appreciate. He'd have to figure out a way to have it all. Losing Charlie wasn't an option.

Charlie strolled across the porch of the giant seaside estate. Beck had gone to follow up with Mr. Samuels on a business lead while they waited for their driver to return. She wanted to take a few minutes to get her fill of the salty air and wrap herself up in the feelings spending the whole weekend with Beck had brought up. She settled into a white wicker chair and closed her eyes, letting the breeze kiss her skin and the warm glow spread throughout her limbs.

"Did you see the boots?" The woman's voice came from the lawn below. Charlie's eyes snapped open, but a large flowering bush prevented her from seeing who stood on the grass below.

"Oh my God, yes. And that dress. Who wears red to a garden party in the Hamptons?" Another female voice joined the first, and they both giggled.

Warmth flooded Charlie's face, and a coldness squeezed her heart. They were talking about her. Her boots. Her red dress.

"She stuck out like a whore in church with all that red. The nails, the lipstick. Was she wearing fake eyelashes? And that accent. It had to be fake. Who talks like that?" The first woman laughed so hard she snorted.

Charlie moved to the railing, trying to peer through the greenery to get a glimpse.

A bag unzipped, then the second woman spoke. "Here, have a tissue. I don't want you to mess up your makeup. What do you think Beck sees in her? She doesn't seem his type."

A mixture of rage and embarrassment coursed through her limbs, and she leaned over the rail. Who would talk about her like that?

"Probably killing time. I heard he has to spend three whole months in that dive before he gets his inheritance. Can you imagine? Snakes and cockroaches the size of rats. God knows what else."

"That makes sense."

The first woman shifted. Charlie caught a glimpse of auburn hair and a light-pink top. Bella? Could it be J.T.'s girlfriend, who'd been so polite to her?

"Yeah, J.T. and Beck are finally getting a project of their own to manage. Beck has to stay in Texas until some crazy parade to get that bar."

"So he's moving to Texas?"

"No, silly. J.T. said he's going to turn it over to his dad so he can come home for good."

"I can't believe Holiday Enterprises would waste time on a bar in some backwoods town in Texas."

"Oh, they'll probably do what they do with most of the businesses they buy—take it apart and sell off the pieces."

Charlie covered her gasp with a hand. Beck had told her early on he'd make sure she could stay on at the Rose, but was he really going to pawn her off on his dad? Couldn't be. That was before they'd started...what? Dating? Sleeping together? Could she have misread him? He'd been talking about booking events for next year. Had he changed his mind?

Would he really let his father destroy everything?

"You think they'll stay together?" the second woman asked.

"Who? Beck and the boot-scootin' harlot?"

How could Bella be so friendly to her face and then be so mean behind her back? Reminded her of junior high and the way one of the cheerleaders had mocked her for choosing 4-H over the pep squad. But that was nothing compared to the sense of betrayal she felt from Beck. She'd shared things with that man, pieces of herself, pieces of her heart and soul—and he'd been playing her the whole time.

The second woman giggled. "Yeah, I guess not. Well, good. I wanted to ask him to the Met's fundraiser next month."

"Aw, Naomi, you should. He'd be crazy not to go with you. But make sure you know what you're getting yourself into with Beck."

"What do you mean?"

"I hear he's a wild man in bed, but he'll never—"

"Excuse me, ladies?" Charlie used the term loosely. Enough was enough. She couldn't stand by while they rocked her world with rumors about the Rose, trashed her reputation, and talked about her and her…her what? After everything that had happened between them, what could Beck be to her now?

The women moved out from under the bushes and squinted up at Charlie on the deck. Bella had the decency to blush, her neck and cheeks taking on a deeper shade than her twinset. The second woman— Naomi, as she'd been called—gaped like a wide-mouth bass that'd been caught hook, line, and sinker.

Charlie gave them one of the smiles she saved for assholes at the bar, the ones from out of town who'd grab her butt, then try to play it off. "I couldn't help but overhear."

"Charlotte, oh heavens, we didn't know you were up there." Bella's hand fluttered toward her chest.

"Well, that's a relief. I'd hate to think what you might say if you knew I could hear you."

Bella and Naomi shared a glance between them

like they were trying to figure out how to make light of the situation.

Naomi shaded her eyes. "We were, uh—"

"You were talkin' about things you don't know nothin' about." Charlie didn't give them a chance to come up with some flimsy excuse. "Oh, and as for Beck?"

The two women looked back and forth from Charlie to each other.

"Y'all can have him." Before her knees turned the consistency of Mrs. Martinez's homemade salsa, Charlie sashayed to the end of the porch, swishing her lacy, red skirt with extra malice. She took the steps on shaky legs, only letting go of the pristine white railing when the driver of the town car took her hand and helped her into the back seat.

"Are we waiting on the gentleman?" He paused before closing the back door.

"No. Can you take me to the airport? LaGuardia?"

The driver nodded and secured the door, putting a solid barrier between her and the noise from the party, the smell of the sea, and the possibility of a future with Beck. As the car pulled away from the circle drive, she glanced back to see him rushing down the steps.

He belonged here. This was his world, not hers. For a brief moment, she'd let herself get swept away in the possibility that he might stay in Holiday. How stupid she'd been to think he'd settle down with her.

For years, her daddy had said, "You can take the cowboy out of Texas, but you can't take Texas out of the cowboy" or something to that effect. Why should Beck be any different? New York, these people, they were his crowd. He'd made that perfectly clear by choosing to follow in his dad's footsteps. He was turning his back on her, on Holiday, and on the Rose. And just when she thought Sully's words had finally reached him.

She'd never fit in here, and he'd never fit in at home. They went together about as well as caviar and collard greens.

She peeled the eyelashes off, letting them fall to the floor. Her lipstick came off on a tissue that she'd shoved into her bag. He'd gussied her up, trying to get her to fit in. But she didn't belong in his world. If this weekend had taught her one thing, it was she didn't want any part of it.

# chapter

# TWENTY-SEVEN

"Hey, Boss. Welcome back." Angelo tipped the brim of his baseball cap her way when Charlie entered the Rose on Monday morning. "Didn't think you were coming in until later on tonight."

"Plans changed." Truer words had never been spoken. After paying a change fee of more than what she made in a weekend of good tips to get herself on the last flight of the day from LaGuardia to Austin, Charlie had spent the three-plus-hour flight making plans. Or at least the last half of the flight. The first half she'd spent wiping her eyes with the two-ply paper napkins the flight attendant handed her and running through every exchange she and Beck had had over the weekend.

He'd been right. Taking the trip to New York had been good for her. It reminded her that she was as tough as he'd been giving her credit for all along. But he'd also been wrong.

There was no way they could figure out a way to make things work long term. He'd lied to her. How stupid did he think she'd have to be to overlook that little fact? They were from two completely different worlds. His was filled with doing whatever he had to do to get ahead. Hers had revolved around treating others like she wanted to be treated herself. Now she needed to channel the hardness

Beck had brought out in her, strap on some spurs, and kick her own life into gear.

"How was New York?" Angelo moved around the spotless kitchen like he owned it. Charlie vowed to do everything in her power to keep him there. Him and everyone else who depended on her and the Rose for their job, their way of life, their family.

"Bigger than I thought." She didn't add that it was smaller than she'd expected, too. Smaller in that she'd been made to feel about three inches tall at that picnic.

Angelo nodded. "Did you go to the top of the Empire State Building?"

"Yeah." Her stomach flipped at the memory of Beck wrapping her in his arms, pulling her against his solid chest, and pointing out all the landmarks from the observation deck. She shoved it down. "Everything go okay here this weekend?"

"Yeah. But we got a couple odd visitors this morning."

"What kind of visitors?" Probably a few more tourists wanting a picture with Baby Back.

"Shep's talking to them up front. Wanted to take some measurements and stuff."

Charlie didn't wait for him to finish. She stomped into the main dining room, where Shep sat at a table with two men in dark suits and a good ol' boy in a pair of jeans and some boots. Looked more like a Secret Service detail than appraisers.

"What's going on here?" She stopped at the edge of the table.

Shep gestured toward the man in jeans. "Hi,

Charlie. This here's Mr. Akers. He's over from Austin to take some measurements and photos."

"Like hell he is. What's going on?" Charlie's chest thudded like someone was doing a line dance on it.

"Ms. Walker, I'm an appraiser from Austin. Mr. Holiday made arrangements for me to handle the property here in his absence. He's got a need for an appraisal and—"

"We'll see about that." Her hand shook as she snagged the half-full coffee cups off the table from in front of them. "Gentlemen, I suggest you leave the premises."

"Ms. Walker—"

Charlie set her jaw and slowly turned to face him. "If you're not off my property in the next thirty seconds, I'm calling the sheriff's office. My brother works there and will be more than happy to escort you out of town."

"You can't keep us away forever. Mr. Holiday's given us permission to do what we need to do here."

"Then I suggest you get *him* to come on down and give you a formal tour. In the meantime, get the hell off my land."

"We'll be back."

"Nineteen, eighteen…"

Akers shook his head and stood. "Come on, gentlemen." The two brutes in dark suits pushed back from the table and followed him out.

"Nice job, Boss." Shep put a hand on Charlie's shoulder. "You okay?"

Her whole body shook like she'd been electrocuted by a live wire. Her thoughts scrambled. Her tongue took up too much room in her mouth for her to speak. Her heart sputtered, stuttered, and skipped inside her rib cage.

She took a deep breath. "I'll be fine." At least she would be once she made it through a confrontation with Beck.

He had no right to sell out her future or the memory of Sully's pride and joy—not even to his father. She couldn't wait to set him straight and send him scurrying back to New York with his fancy loafers and monstrous coffee machine, preferably with one or both of those items shoved up his fine, tight ass.

*※*

Beck pressed the End button on his cell phone. Charlie couldn't avoid him forever. She'd gotten spooked, he'd give her that. Inviting her to the picnic had been a bad idea. After she'd taken off in the town car, he'd caught Bella and Naomi whispering about her and grilled them both on what had caused Charlie to run off like that. Bella had apologized for not knowing how sensitive Charlie would be and clammed up when he pressed for more. In the end, whatever they'd said to her didn't matter. What mattered was that she'd left just when she'd finally started to let loose and have a little fun.

So he'd returned to Holiday to try to talk some sense into her. Sitting in the parking lot, he gazed at the front porch of the Rose through the dusty windshield. Live music drifted out the open windows. Someone must have been playing an afternoon set today. That was one thing he loved about the honky-tonk—he never knew what to expect from one day to the next. If someone walked through the front door with a guitar case, Charlie would usually talk them into playing a set or two.

Charlie.

He'd had two days to try to come up with what

he wanted to say to her. Yet, moments away from seeing her again, he still had nothing. Hoping some divine intervention would fill the void in his brain with the right words, he made his way around the building and onto the porch. Each thump of his boots on the wood steps felt like walking to a set of gallows instead of confronting the woman he'd hoped to build some sort of future with.

He pushed through the screen door and into the front room. The once-foreign, now-familiar smell of mesquite chips from the barbecue pit greeted him. Music played through the speakers, glasses clanked together, and the comforting hustle and bustle of the Rose on a weekday afternoon soothed his nerves.

"Hey, Beck." Shep nodded at him from behind the bar.

"Hi. You seen Charlie around?" he asked.

Shep tilted his head toward the office. "Back that way. Be careful though."

"How mad is she?"

"Dude, she's spoutin' off four-letter words I've never even heard."

Beck's stomach twisted, wringing itself out like the bar rag Shep held in his hand. "That bad, huh?"

"Who's your next of kin? If she finishes you off, can I have your coffeepot?"

"You bet." He'd love to shoot the bull with Shep, maybe even grab a cold one from the bar, but avoiding the inevitable wouldn't do any good. Time for him to take responsibility for his screwup and figure out if there was a chance to salvage anything with Charlie.

He tapped on the door of the office, half hoping she'd left for the day.

"Come on in." Her voice ricocheted around his internal

organs, sliced through his gut, and thudded like a cannonball into his chest.

"Hey." He pushed the door open a bit at a time and stepped into the room.

"Oh, it's you." She didn't smile. In fact, the look she gave him couldn't have been more chilling if she'd been shooting icicles out of her eyes. "Didn't expect to see you around here anytime soon."

He stopped at the edge of the desk. A few stacks of cash sat in front of her. She'd been counting up the till. "You left me on the steps. What happened, Charlie? You won't take my calls or answer my texts."

"It's over, Beck. I should have known better in the first place."

"Over? We were having such a good time." He put his palms on the desk and leaned her way, trying to get her to meet his gaze.

She let out a sharp laugh. "A good time? I suppose that's all this was to you—a fun little fling."

"That's not fair."

"Fair?" She jumped out of her chair and slapped her palms on the desk. "You want to talk to me about fair? Try working your ass off for eight years, pouring your heart and soul into something, and then having it ripped away from you on the whim of a self-serving jackass who's not even in it for the right reasons."

Stunned, he backed away from the desk and leaned against a chair. Is that what she thought of him? "What are you talking about?"

"You're selling us out so you can get your big chance to prove yourself to your dad, aren't you? He said something that night at dinner. While you went to get the car. Then Bella confirmed it. Took me a little while to put it all together, you know, being a hick without a college degree and all."

"Charlie, it's not what you think." He reached for her hand, but she snatched it away before they touched. "Yes, I agreed to pass the Rose on to my dad. But he said he wasn't going to change things. It'll stay the same, you'll see."

Her eyes swelled with unshed tears. "No, it won't. He doesn't get it. Never has. Sully knew it. The Rose needs you. And Holiday needs the Rose. It's the only thing that draws people in. Gives them a place to gather, to celebrate, commiserate, and escape the drudgery of the daily routine around here."

Beck shook his head. "I never said I wanted to save a whole town. I said I'd stick it out until the three months were up. I'm doing what I think is best. My dad will take over, and things will stay the same. Sully should have left it to him in the first place. It's his birthright, and I'm trying to do the right thing. You'll keep your job. The Rose will go on just like always."

She buried her face in her hands and took in a ragged breath. "You really believe him, don't you?"

"He promised." Beck even had the paperwork to prove it. His dad had sent back the revised agreement stating that he wouldn't make changes to the management of the Rose. All Beck had to do was sign on the line and make the deal official.

"I can't believe you trust him. Sully knew better. He wanted the Rose to go to you. If he'd wanted your dad to get his grubby hands on it, he would have left it to him. Everyone around here can see what kind of a man your father is. Why are you so blind when it comes to him?"

"Charlie…" He wanted to comfort her but didn't know how.

"I thought maybe you'd want to stay for another reason. I thought maybe, just maybe, you'd want to stay for us. For me."

And there it was. She'd tossed it out there, and he'd have to acknowledge it. He couldn't avoid or ignore the Texas-longhorn-sized truth in the room anymore.

"Oh, Charlie." He rounded the desk and gathered her in his arms. Every part of him wanted to tell her she was being ridiculous. Of course he'd stay. He'd never met anyone like her before, and he'd be a freaking dumb-ass to even consider walking away.

Her body stiffened. "Don't 'Oh, Charlie' me."

"What?"

"I'm done. I didn't want to do this to you. I was hoping we'd be able to make plans together. Build a future right here. But we don't belong together. You've made it clear you won't."

"I can't."

"No, Beck. 'Can't' implies there's something stopping you. It's not that you *can't* stay in Holiday. You won't."

"I've got a life in New York, but I still want to see each other."

"No."

"What do you mean 'no'?"

She maneuvered out of his embrace and pushed her palms against his chest. "I mean, I've spent the past eight years waiting for someone like you. Someone to turn my world upside down, inside out, and topsy-turvy. And now that I've found you, I can't imagine losing any of that. I've had a taste of having it all. And I loved it. So weekends aren't going to cut it for me. I want all of you."

"Relationships are a compromise. Fifty-fifty. Give-and-take."

She shook her head. "Relationships are one hundred-one hundred. That's how my folks have stayed together so long. Not by settling for half-ass holidays and seeing each other once a month."

"That's different though. Obviously we're not your parents. They're—"

"I'd rather be my parents than yours. Didn't you say your dad traveled all the time when you were a kid? I bet they barely spent any time together. No wonder your dad's on his fifth wife."

"Fourth."

"Oh, excuse me. Somehow I can't keep them all straight."

Truth was, neither could he. He wanted what Charlie wanted. He just wanted what he wanted, too. And the way he saw things, it would be impossible to get both. "So you want to just throw it all away?"

She shrugged her shoulders. "You're the one who's throwing things away."

"How? I'm the one who wants to try to work things out. Explain to me how I'm the quitter here?"

"Giving the Rambling Rose to your dad is like throwing it away. I don't know what he promised you, but I'm not going to stick around to see Sully's pride and joy ruined."

A vein at his temple began to twitch. He was going to have one hell of a headache later; he could feel it coming on. "Hey, if you don't want to help me anymore, then don't."

"Fine. I quit." The sparks flying from her eyes could have set the place on fire.

She couldn't mean it. Charlie *was* the Rambling Rose. But she'd pushed him too far to back down now. "When's your last day?" With only a few weeks left on his "sentence," he wasn't sure he'd be able to handle seeing her around.

"Figured I'd give you two weeks. I mean, I know I don't have corporate"—she made air quotes around "corporate" like it was a curse word—"experience, but I hear that's standard."

"Don't worry about the notice. I can take it from here."

"Suit yourself." She stood frozen in place for a moment. Long enough for his throat to constrict, for his lungs to seize, for his heart to shrink to the size of a golf ball. Then, leveling him with a final look, one that bottled up all her hurt and disappointment and pain, she was gone.

Beck staggered to the chair and slumped into it. He should be grateful. She'd handed him an easy way out. But instead of relief, he felt broken. Like pieces of him were lying all over the ancient, well-worn floor.

# chapter
# TWENTY-EIGHT

"CHARLIE?" DARBY'S VOICE CAME THROUGH THE DOOR, muffled but loud enough to disrupt the daytime talk show playing on TV. "Oh, Charlie. I know you're in there. I'm not going away. Open up."

Charlie pulled a pillow over her head, trying to drown out her friend's cheerful threat. Why wouldn't she leave her alone? By the time she'd gotten home from the Rose last night, Darby had already heard about her falling-out with Beck and filled her phone with texts. Unable to stomach the humiliation of dealing with her then, Charlie had downed a tad too much cheap whiskey and passed out on the couch.

Unfortunately her situation appeared just as bleak during the bright light of day. And now, in addition to being so pissed at Beck she couldn't think, breathe, or see straight, she'd also given herself one heck of a hangover. She should get up and find some ibuprofen. But that would require movement. And movement was still a few hours away.

The knocking stopped. Good. Darby never could wait her out. Satisfied she'd earned a couple more hours of peace, Charlie snuggled the pillow against her chest and tried to mute the chainsaw buzzing through her head by wishing it away.

"There you are." Darby exploded through the patio door, a triumphant look on her face, a large takeout cup of coffee in her hand.

"Go away." Pillow back over her face, Charlie tried to disappear under a cushion.

"I told you. I'm not leaving." The cushion sagged as Darby perched on the edge of the couch.

"Leave me alone."

"I brought drugs."

Charlie peeked out from under the pillow at Darby's outstretched hand. Two orange pills sat in her palm. Charlie's pulse quickened. Ibuprofen, inches away. Relief might not be out of reach.

"Coffee too." Darby held the pills and cup out in front of her—a bribe.

"I hate you." Charlie struggled to sit up, grabbed the coffee, and downed the pills.

"You love me, and we both know it. Now get up. We've got a transfer of title to stop and a hot city boy to run out of town."

Charlie slumped back against the cushions. "Forget it. It's done. He's already made arrangements with his dad. The Rose is as good as gone."

"Not yet. Didn't you say he has to ride on the Rose's Founder's Day float to meet the requirement of the will?" Darby's smile could have powered half the island of Manhattan.

"Yeah."

"So all we have to do is keep him from the parade and he won't get the title, right?"

"Right."

"So, who does?"

"I do. If Beck doesn't ride on the float, everything goes to me." She winced. "Damn. I wasn't supposed to tell anyone that."

Darby wiggled her eyebrows.

"Why don't you look surprised? That was a secret. Nobody was supposed to know."

"Well, your buddy Dwight happened to take Mr. Hill out fishing yesterday. They got to talking and drinking, and before anyone knew it, Hill let it slip that you're next in line. Of course, Dwight can't keep a secret—everyone knows that. So if your New Yorker got delayed somehow—"

"Darby, you're a genius." Charlie jerked upright. Her head seemed to split open like the watermelon her dad had chopped in half with an axe at the Chuckwagon Extravaganza.

"That's what I've been telling you for years. But no…Charlie's the brains, Darby's the sidekick." She examined her perfectly manicured nails. "It's so hard to be underestimated."

"All we have to do is keep Beck from getting on that float."

"Yep. And I've already started working on a plan. Let's put our heads together and figure out the details."

Charlie put her hands over her eyes. "I can't even think straight."

"Come on, you lush." Darby swatted her thigh. "A warm shower's just what you need. I'll whip up a batch of my Grandma Hudson's hangover cure while you're hosing off."

If Darby was talking about Grandma Hudson, she must really be concerned. She only pulled out those concoctions as a last resort. Charlie struggled against the gravity pinning her to the couch. First, shower. Second,

Grandma Hudson's homemade cure. Third, if she was still standing by that point, they'd come up with a diabolical plan.

"Fine. But go easy on the beet juice this time." She made it to a standing position and swayed, grabbing on to the edge of the couch to keep from falling over.

"You did a real number on yourself this time, girl." Darby took her arm and propped her upright. "You should know better than to waste valuable calories on a man like that. You want to blow a diet, let's spend an afternoon at the winery or try out one of the Pioneer Woman's new dessert recipes. That French silk pie recipe of hers is better than sex and lasts a hell of a lot longer."

Charlie snorted. "I love you." Darby was right. This would be the last time she'd drown her sorrows over a man. It had been so long since she'd had to, she'd forgotten it didn't work anyway. Once the floor stopped tilting from side to side, she made it across the room to the bathroom. "Thanks. I don't deserve you."

"Aw, honey, yes you do. You deserve it all…the man, white horse, and whatever else your tough little heart desires."

"No, no man." She'd let Beck distract her from what was really important and learned her lesson. No man would ever come before her own success again.

*⸻*

The door of his office opened without a sound. Didn't anyone knock anymore? Beck looked up from his desk as his father entered the room. Tan from the cruise, his tailored power suit in place, the epitome of the successful businessman back from two weeks of well-deserved respite. In contrast, Beck had already loosened his tie, hadn't shaved in two days, and could almost feel his skin turning the color of silly putty from the lack of vitamin D.

"Hey, Son. Managed to keep the business going while I was gone?" The elder Holiday crossed the plush carpeting to the desk and picked up a stack of papers.

"Yeah. How was your trip? Looks like you got some sun."

"We had a great time. You look like shit though. Are those country folks getting to you? You trying to grow a beard?"

"No, I've been swamped." Typical. No "thanks for taking care of things while I was gone" or "you did a great job." Truth was, he did probably look like hell. Flying back and forth to try to keep the Rose afloat and take care of Holiday Enterprises over the past few weeks had him working fourteen- to sixteen-hour days. Not that he'd been able to relax in what little downtime he'd had. Images of Charlie had tripped through his head. Her showing him how to two-step, covered in mud in Baby Back's pen, wrapped in that damn star-spangled tablecloth.

"I met some potential investors on the ship. I'm having Joyce set up a meeting next week, and I want you to join in. You've got one more trip to Texas, right? When do you get back?"

"I'm headed down tomorrow. Back on Sunday."

"Good. And you've got that paperwork, right?"

Beck held up the contract he'd signed that morning.

His dad grinned, a smug, satisfied smile. "Make sure I get a copy of that before you leave today. We can put that place to rest by the end of next week at the latest. It's time you focused your attention on the family business, not my old man's pipe dream. Are you with me on this?" Holiday toyed with a Texas-shaped crystal paperweight Charlie had given Beck a few weeks into their relationship. She'd wanted to make sure he'd think of her when he flew back to New York from time to time to take care of things.

"When you say 'put that place to rest'...what do you mean exactly?" An icy coldness seeped into his chest. Ever since Charlie had walked out on him, insisting his dad had an ulterior motive, Beck had held out hope she was wrong.

Holiday tossed the paperweight from one hand to the other. "I've got no interest in running a bar halfway across the country. I'll shut it down and take it as a loss. Maybe sell it for the land. The broker knows someone handling a few other parcels down there and said some crazy Californian with ties to the area might be interested."

"But we made a deal." Dammit. He'd seen his dad put aside friendships and cut people out of his life for the sake of the company. But his own father's legacy? How could he sink that low?

"Yeah, I told you I wouldn't make any changes to the management. I never said anything about not closing the whole operation."

"Dad, the town relies on the Rose. You can't shut it down."

"I can do whatever I want. It's just a bar. A backwater bar in a backwater town." The paperweight slid from his hand and crashed onto the desk. A chunk of the panhandle smashed into sparkly shards.

Beck clenched his jaw and nodded, finally

accepting the truth. Of course Holiday would think of it as just a bar. But as Charlie had been saying all along, it was so much more.

He couldn't let that happen. Charlie may have cut him out her life, but he couldn't let hers get ripped out from under her. When he'd made the deal with his dad, he'd been assured things would stay the same. He couldn't stand to be the cause of all those people he'd come to know losing their jobs. Angelo. Shep. Dixie. All the waitstaff and event helpers. They depended on the place. The whole town relied on the Rose for the tourists it brought in, a regular hangout to hear some good music and catch up with family and friends. That place had become a home for them—for *him*.

And his father was ready to ruin it all.

Holiday cleared his throat. "Got time for lunch today? I'd like to touch base on that project up in Morris Park. I know you had some childish fixation with it, but I think it's about time we found a better use for your talents."

The blood drained from Beck's face, and a heaviness pressed down on his skull. This was his moment. Either the next thirty seconds would establish him as his father's right-hand man, the son who would always remain under the scrutiny and control of an unrelenting dictator, or he'd turn his back on everything he'd ever wanted. The job, the success, the power, the money.

And for what?

A girl, a bar, and a couple hundred strangers who lived in a town bearing his last name?

Beck took a deep breath and ripped the contract in two. He waited for the shock and disappointment to settle on his father's face.

Instead, Holiday laughed. "I'm two steps ahead of you, Son. Making a deal with you would have been the cheaper option. But I'll get my hands on the Rambling Rose one way or another."

"How? If I'm not planning on giving it to you, how exactly do you plan to do that?"

Holiday smirked. "Anyone bother to tell you what happens if you're not on that float?"

"Mr. Hill said a third party will inherit everything."

"That third party is your girlfriend. My crazy old man wrote her into his will. She'd get it all: the cash, the land, the bar."

*Charlie?* Did she know about that? If she did, why had she tried so hard to convince him to stay? "How do you know?"

"You can buy all kinds of information if you offer enough cash."

Beck shook his head. "Charlie would never sell it to you. She cares too much about Holiday."

"True." Holiday nodded. "But she won't have to sell it. Sully should have had someone from a real law school write his will. Stu's already found a loophole. When you don't show for the parade, she'll inherit the bar. Then I'll file so many lawsuits that her head won't stop spinning until long after her cash runs out."

Beck clenched his jaw together. How had he been so blind? There was only one thing to do now. "And what makes you so sure I won't show for the parade?"

"You really want to give all of this up?" Holiday motioned at the opulent furnishings surrounding them. "The corner office? Drinks with the mayor? You get on that float and you're done here."

Beck's heart battered the walls of his chest. He let his gaze rest on his father's smug grin for a long moment. Then he stepped around him, making a beeline for the door.

"Where do you think you're going?"

He had to make this right. Charlie needed to hear about this new turn of events, and she needed to hear it from him. His decision made, Beck didn't slow down. "I'm headed back to Holiday. Back where I belong."

"So you're clear on what we need you to do, right?" Charlie set a bottle of Coke on the bar in front of Dwight.

He took a long swig and wiped the corner of his mouth with the ragged hem of his shirt. "Crystal. Pick him up at the airport and bring him straight to you at the Rose."

"How hard can it be, Charlie? Even Dwight can handle this." Darby pulled her keys out of her purse. "Now come on, we've got to get down to the sheriff's office so we can finish up the float."

Charlie sighed. She'd had second thoughts about sending Dwight on an errand of this magnitude. But what other choice did she have? Beck's flight would land at the Austin airport in about two hours. He'd sent her a text telling her he needed to talk to her about something important. Wouldn't take a genius to figure out what that was about. He probably wanted to give her a heads-up so she could be the one to break the news to the town. He'd made a deal with the devil on the Rose, and as soon as the parade was over, Beckett Holiday Jr. would come in and change everything.

Beck was the one who'd be getting the surprise though. She and Darby were sending Dwight to fetch him, so they could get their hands on him first. If she couldn't talk some sense into him, she vowed she'd sit on him if she had to, just to keep him from getting on the parade float tomorrow. No parade meant no Rose for Beck. If Dwight would come through, they'd all end up smelling like roses.

She rested her hand on Dwight's arm. "Call me if anything goes wrong, okay?"

Darby smacked her gum. "Come on, now. We're already running behind."

"Thanks, Dwight. I really appreciate it." Charlie gave him an awkward half hug and called out to Shep. "We're heading out. See you in a bit."

"Don't worry about a thing. I'll take care of the sorry sack of shit." Dwight popped a toothpick in the corner of his mouth and lifted his eyebrows.

Charlie's stomach rolled over. Every part of her screamed that she'd regret putting her trust in Dwight. She hadn't had much of a choice. She couldn't bring one of her brothers in on her plan. They'd rat her out to her dad. Hopefully no one would find out until it was too late.

She followed Darby out the back door, past the shiny new paint job. Sully would have been so disappointed. She was glad he'd passed on to a better place. Where the Lone Star always flowed and the Rose would always be pink. And if she had something to do with it, that would be the way things would stay.

She just had to get through the next twenty-four hours. She'd made her bed and now had to lie in it. Even if that meant sleeping alone for the rest of her life.

⚡

The August heat hit him like walking straight into a barbecue pit. New York had its share of humidity, but this? This was an entirely new level of hell. Beck tapped his boot on the sidewalk, waiting for Dwight. He'd sent a text earlier saying he had to be in Austin for something and would pick him up for the ride back to Holiday. Beck could have politely declined but figured he could pump the guy for information on the ninety-mile drive.

Dwight's truck cut across two lanes of traffic and came to a stop next to him. Before he could toss his bag in the back, Dwight got out and walked around the truck.

"Howdy, pardner. Glad to have you back." Dwight clapped him on the back with one hand and reached for his suitcase with the other.

Beck yanked open the door and climbed up onto the bench seat.

Dwight hopped in and eased the truck away from the curb. "Thirsty? I brought you some water for the drive."

"No, thanks. Maybe in a little bit." He'd hydrated on the plane, and he didn't want to take the time to make any extra stops on the way. His top priority was getting to Charlie in time to fill her in on his plans.

Once he'd made up his mind, he couldn't wait to tell her. He'd almost caved and called her last night but wanted to talk to her in person. Being this close and still so far away was the worst kind of torture.

"Ya have a nice flight?"

"Yeah, sure. How have things been around here?" Making small talk with Dwight might literally make him lose his mind.

"Swell. Been a little weird with Charlie not working at the Rose. Business is down a bit. Folks around there don't like change, y'know."

Beck nodded. That little nugget of information

had become abundantly clear over the past few months. If he'd only listened to Charlie in the first place. She'd told him not to replace their Lone Star with an out-of-town craft brew. She'd practically drowned him in mud when he accidentally entered a boar into the pig beauty pageant and ended up leaving her with the first pregnant mascot the Rose had ever had.

Thank God she'd believed him when he'd told her the white paint had been a mistake. He'd heard enough about it from Shep. The locals were still staging sit-ins and distributing flyers all over town. Their tagline of "Don't Drink Till It's Pink" did have a bit of a ring to it. Once he made it through the festivities of the weekend, Charlie could paint the building whatever color she wanted. He'd even help. The thought sent a charge of anticipation through him. What would it take to get Dwight to drive faster?

"Gotta stop for gas. You sure you don't want anything?" The truck swerved off the highway, and Dwight slowed to a crawl.

Beck leaned over and checked the gas gauge. "You've got half a tank. That's more than enough."

"Gauge is broken. I was supposed to fix it this afternoon but had to run to Austin for a part instead."

*Great, just great.* At the rate they were going, it would be nighttime when they got there. The Founder's Day festivities would be in full swing, and he probably wouldn't get Charlie to himself until she was too tired to stand up straight.

Dwight stopped next to a pay-at-the-pump spot, climbed down, and disappeared inside the convenience store without starting the gas pump. Beck hopped out and swiped his credit card, then inserted the nozzle into the tank. By the time the truck had filled up, Dwight still hadn't come out of the store, so Beck headed inside. Dwight sat in a hard, laminated booth with a steaming cup of coffee in front of him, flipping through the pages of a magazine.

"Dwight. What are you doing?"

"I'm tired. Been helping out at the Rose, working overnights at the station. I needed some caffeine, y'know?" He wiped his hands over his eyes, emphasizing his words.

"Give me the keys. I'll drive." Beck held out a hand, fully expecting Dwight to toss him the keys.

Dwight bit his lip, then shot out of his seat and out the door. "Damn. Keys are in the truck."

Beck followed, catching up to him as he climbed down from the running board.

"Yep. Keys are locked in the truck. Crap, wonder how long that's going to take?" He rolled his eyes, and a flash of something crossed his face. Almost looked like smug relief.

But why would Dwight be relieved at the delay? Beck peered in through the window. The keys sprawled on the driver's side floor mat.

"That sucks, huh?" Dwight shook his head. "Probably be a couple hours before someone can run up here with the spare set."

"Did you just toss those in the cab?" He could have sworn they weren't there when he got out of the truck.

Dwight's eyebrows knit together. "What kind of crazy talk is that? Wanna grab something to eat at the diner?" He gestured toward the café attached to the truck stop.

What was he playing at? Was he trying to keep

him away from Charlie? "You go ahead. I'm going to see if I can get a locksmith or something."

"Want me to order you a bite?" Dwight licked his lips and hooked his thumbs through his belt loops. "Might be a while."

"Sure. You pick, okay?"

"You got it." Smiling, Dwight turned toward the café.

With the jackass out of the way, Beck surveyed the parking lot. In the sea of semis, pickups, and work trucks, there had to be someone who could jimmy the lock on an old truck. A giant custom RV rolled past, revealing the answer to his prayers—a late-model cargo van with J&B's Locksmith Service on the side. Beck crossed his fingers and started across the parking lot.

chapter

# THIRTY

CHARLIE CHECKED HER WATCH. BECK'S FLIGHT HAD BEEN scheduled to land more than an hour ago, and she hadn't heard a word from Dwight. She should have known better than to send a proxy.

"Hear anything?" Darby tucked a pink-tissue-paper rose into the chicken-wire framework of their parade float.

"No. Do you think I should call him?"

"Not unless you want to end up on the phone with Beck."

"No. I can't do it over the phone. I need to see him in person." She sighed. She'd have to wait it out. With any luck, Dwight would text soon and let her know when they'd be there. "You almost done with that side?"

She and Darby had spent the past three days working on the float. Technically, she'd quit on Beck, which meant she shouldn't need to help with the Founder's Day festivities. But she figured by the time the parade was over, Beck would either have agreed to let her buy in to the honky-tonk or she and Darby would implement plan B and she'd own it outright. Either way, she felt an obligation. With the final touches complete, all they'd need to do tomorrow was show up and climb aboard. It was kind of nice being able to just focus on the float this year. In years past, Charlie had pulled all-nighters trying to manage the Rose and still do justice to the long-standing tradition of having the biggest float in the Founder's Day parade.

"Give me ten more minutes." Darby stood and stretched. "What else do you have to do tonight?"

"Finish the decorations for the Founder's Day Fling. That's it. I'll probably even get to bed before midnight. That will be a first on the night before the parade." She tried to keep her voice light for Darby's sake. There was no way she'd be able to turn in before she had a chance to chat with Beck. He might have screwed her over professionally, but unlike him and the crowd he hung with, she had a heart and was willing to work toward some sort of compromise. Even though she was madder than a rattlesnake with its tail tied in a knot, some tiny, buried part of her still cared about him.

Once Dwight delivered him, she'd try to talk him out of transferring the title to his dad by offering to buy into the Rose herself. Granted, she didn't have that kind of money set aside, but she had good credit and Mr. Hill would vouch for her at the bank. She'd manage the Rose and Beck could go back to New York and be his daddy's yes-man. Her promise to Sully would be honored by keeping the Rose in the Holiday family, and Beck would get his park. But if he didn't agree, would she really be able to keep him away until the parade ended?

"You bringing anyone to the fling tomorrow night?" Darby gave her a side-eye glance. She knew better than anyone how much Beck had come to mean to Charlie.

"What do you think?"

"I think you need to call that nice cowboy you met on the plane on the way to New York."

"Never shoulda told you about that." Charlie had

mentioned it once. But with Darby, once was all it took. "I told you, I'm done with men."

"We'll see."

"See about what?" Cash came up behind them.

"Nothing. Darby was saying she thinks our float will win first place again this year." Charlie gave her friend a pointed look.

"No, I wasn't. I was telling your baby sis that she ought to invite someone to the fling tomorrow night." The smug grin on Darby's face smacked of self-righteousness.

Cash slung an arm around Charlie's shoulders. "I think that's a great idea. You need to get out there more."

Charlie shook her head and shrugged away from him. "Says the man who hasn't been on a date in five years."

"Hey, we're not talking about me." He shifted his weight from one foot to the other. "Can y'all lock up? I'm heading out."

"Sure. Thanks again for letting us build the float here." Charlie hugged her brother. Of all of her siblings, he was the one she worried about the most. He had such a good heart. He adored his daughter, but since Kenzie's mom had passed, Charlie wished he'd find someone new to share his life with.

"Good luck tomorrow. You think Beck's going to show? The whole town's been taking bets on whether he'll be there for the parade."

Darby sucked in a big breath, and Charlie gave her a silencing glare. "Don't know. Haven't talked to the jerk in more than two weeks."

"I sure hope he shows. We've got some unsettled business to attend to." Cash looked from one of them to the other.

"You're all talk." Charlie shook her head. "Beck told me about your threat. You go anywhere near him, and I'll tell Mama about that time you and Lori Lynne sneaked out and—"

"That's enough of that." He opened his mouth like he wanted to say something else but closed it again.

"I guess we'll find out soon enough." Darby linked her arm through her brother-in-law's and walked him to the door of the giant metal garage. "Have a good night, Cash."

"Yeah, bye, Cash. Give my niece a hug and a kiss. Tell her I saved her a spot on the float tomorrow."

"All right. Stay out of trouble, you two." He shook his head one more time then disappeared through the doorway.

Darby skipped across the concrete floor. "Think he suspects anything?"

"How could he suspect something? We haven't done anything yet."

"Yeah, but—"

Charlie's phone pinged. An incoming text. She glanced down. It was from Dwight.

"Dwight says Beck's connection in Philadelphia was delayed and he might not even get in until tomorrow morning." Charlie tilted her phone toward Darby to show her the text.

Darby squeezed her arm. "Well, crap. What does that do to your plan? Have you really thought this thing through? I know you think he's going to go for it, but what if he doesn't? What happens to the Rose then?"

Charlie's lungs deflated at the sight of the text. Short,

shallow breaths did nothing to battle the feeling of not being able to breathe. "Maybe I should call him and spill my guts over the phone. If he says no, then we can have Dwight execute plan B."

"I really like plan B. Can't we skip ahead to that?"

"I want to give him a chance to make things right on his own first. Deep down, he's not the puppet his dad makes him out to be. If I can talk to him, I know he'll come around." Or at least she hoped he would. Beck had changed during his time in Texas. Getting to learn about his grandfather had made a difference, she knew it. He was more like Sully than his calculating father. He had to be; otherwise she never would have fallen so hard so fast.

Darby whooped and spun around, pulling on Charlie's arms, trying to get her to join in her happy dance. "Either way, the Rose will be safe!" Finally, apparently noticing Charlie's lack of enthusiasm, Darby stopped. "What's wrong? You've got to be thrilled about this, right?"

"What if he gets here and I don't have time to talk to him? Or what if he says no? Can I really go through with this? Keeping him off the float will be like stealing. That would make me no better than them, it—"

"You're not stealing. You're saving the Rose. You're saving Holiday." Placing her hands on either side of Charlie's face, Darby went nose to nose. "It's not your fault his flight got screwed up, right? Maybe this is fate's way of handing the Rose over."

Charlie groaned, letting the desperation seep out of her on a whiny exhale. "I don't know. What would Sully want? I promised him I'd keep it in the family."

"Honey, you were more family to him than his own flesh and blood. It's your call. You know I'll back you up whatever you decide to do, but you've got to make this decision." Darby held her gaze.

Damn mind reader. She put her hands over Darby's and pulled them away from her cheeks, giving them a squeeze. "Balls to the wall. The way I see it, I don't have a choice. Not if I want to save the Rose."

"'Atta girl." Darby grabbed her shoulders and almost strangled her with a hug around the neck. "Let's wrap this up and get over to the Rose to finish things. We don't need to bring anything, do we?"

Charlie battled the burning apprehension rising in her chest. "Nope. I took everything over there yesterday." She tossed the remaining float-making supplies into a cardboard box and snapped off the lights in the large metal outbuilding. This was a dumb idea. It was going to backfire, and Beck would sue her for kidnapping and obstructing a real estate transaction.

Wait. Was that even a crime?

Screw it. It sounded enough like a crime to make her stomach cramp.

She'd pulled Darby and Dwight into her illicit activities, too. They'd all go down in a disappointing last-ditch effort of saving the Rose. Probably spend the rest of their lives under house arrest or worse.

But the alternative was harder to accept. If Beck did show up on that float tomorrow, the Rose would be gone. Who knew what his dad would do with it? She'd heard rumors of someone snatching up some land around Holiday, but no one knew who was buying or what their plans were. Charlie owed it to her employees, the residents of Holiday, and, most of all, Sully to keep things the way they'd always been.

"Let's hit it." She flipped the lock and pulled the door closed behind her. For better or for worse, it was too late to turn back now.

*⊬*

Even the way Dwight swallowed his tea had begun to annoy the heck out of Beck. It had taken forty-five minutes and a hundred bucks to get the keys out of the truck with no help from Dwight. By the time Beck took care of that snafu, he'd found Dwight lounging in a corner booth at the diner, two orders of chicken fried steak on the way.

"Can we get this to go?" Beck fidgeted with a packet of sugar, eager to hit the road again. Every minute he wasted was one more he could have been hurtling closer to Charlie.

"How am I gonna eat chicken fried steak in the truck?"

"I'll drive. You can eat on the way." Why was Dwight dragging his feet so much? It almost seemed like he was stalling on purpose. The idea took root in his head like one of those wood ticks he'd watched Charlie remove from behind Baby Back's ear. Just burrowed in and wouldn't let go.

"It'll be out in a quick sec. I'm starving. Charlie's had me runnin' errands all over town today, and I didn't get my lunch. Ten minutes, then we'll get going, okay?"

"Ten minutes. If you're not ready to go after that, I'll leave your ass here and you can find your own way back."

Dwight nodded and took another sip of his tall iced tea.

"I'll be back in a minute." May as well hit the bathroom while he waited for his dinner. It didn't look like Dwight would budge until he got his heart attack on a plate. As much as he wanted to get to Holiday, the anticipation of a chicken fried steak with homemade country gravy and a biscuit or two on the side sent his stomach into giddy somersaults.

He'd tried to find some greasy spoon in the city that reminded him of the down-home cooking he'd had in Holiday. With a restaurant every couple of feet, it hadn't seemed like such a hopeless cause. But no matter where he went, the food didn't come close to the kind of mouthwatering, butter-laden, calorie-ridden deliciousness he'd been served at the Walker family dinners.

When he returned to the table, their food had arrived—two giant platters overflowing with steaks almost the size of a manhole cover. Beck's gut grumbled as the appetizing scent of fresh buttermilk biscuits hit his nose.

"Dig in." Dwight spoke around the huge bite of steak and mashed potatoes he'd shoved in his mouth.

"Don't mind if I do." He tucked into his dinner like a man who hadn't eaten in weeks as opposed to a few hours ago. Experience had taught him he'd regret it later, but he couldn't help himself. Good home-style cooking reminded him of Charlie. And thinking of Charlie smoothed the anxious jitters away. How would she react to his offer? They'd been through a lot this summer, but hopefully she'd come to the same conclusion he had. That they belonged together.

Sure, they'd gotten off to a rocky start. And his time in Holiday was filled with more ups and downs than that roller coaster he'd ridden on Coney Island as a kid. But for the first time in his life, he'd learned what it meant to belong somewhere. To someone.

He'd probably always struggle a bit with the locals. They'd never truly forgive him for being born outside their great state of Texas. But he felt at home there, despite being an "outsider." So he was willing to make some sacrifices. Even if it meant he had to walk away from his lifetime dream to start a new one with Charlie.

Convinced he was doing the right thing—the only thing that mattered—he couldn't wait to fill her in. If he could toss back this steak and get Dwight on the road, he could be cradling Charlie in his arms before nightfall.

With each bite, cutting the huge steak into pieces, spearing it with his fork, and lifting it all the way to his mouth seemed to take more effort. His vision clouded at the edges, and Dwight's voice echoed from a few city blocks away. Then everything faded from gray to black.

# chapter
# THIRTY-ONE

THE LAST TRACES OF A DREAM EDGED AWAY, LEAVING him in a semiconscious state. He'd been dreaming about Charlie. They'd gone tubing, and she'd been wearing that sexy bikini. He reached out to touch her cheek before she faded away. His arm wouldn't budge. He became aware of an ache in his shoulder. What the hell?

His eyelids weighed about a hundred pounds each. His mouth felt like it had been stuffed with cotton. Water. He needed water. And the use of his arms.

He cracked his eyelids open, fighting against the gravity pulling them down. Peering out between the slits in his eyelids, he came face-to-face with an unshaven, foul-breathed Dwight.

"How ya feelin' this morning?" Dwight used his fingers to pry Beck's eyes open. "Anyone home in there?"

Beck struggled to sit up. A zip tie held his wrist to the rail of a metal bed. "What's going on? Where am I? Why are you here?"

"So many questions." Dwight unscrewed the cap from a bottle of water and held it out. "Want a drink?"

"Can you cut me loose so I can sit up first?"

"Nope. But I can help you up." Dwight grabbed him by an arm and levered him to a seated position. "Better?"

"Not much. Get this off me."

"Sit still and take some water." Dwight held the bottle out, and Beck grabbed it with his free hand to take a swallow.

"And what happens when I need to take a piss? You thought about that?" Ridiculous. He'd always figured Dwight was a Froot Loop short of a full bowl, but this stunt was a stretch, even for him.

"Hmm. I suppose I can help you drop trou, but you're on your own for the shake and dribble."

Beck yanked and twisted his wrist. An explosive tide of rage threatened to take over, but he swallowed it back. *What good will that do?* Maybe he could reason with Dwight. There had to be something he wanted or needed—some reason he was doing this.

"What's it going to take, Dwight?"

"For what?"

"For you to let me loose and pretend this never happened?"

Dwight pulled a canvas chair in front of the bunk and plopped down. "I'm not interested in negotiating. I'm working for the greater good."

"What's that supposed to mean? And where are we anyway?" His eyes struggled to adjust to the semidarkness. Looked like he was in some windowless cabin or something.

"Ironically enough, we're on your property. At least it's yours for the next couple of hours."

"What time is it?" He jerked hard at the restraints, realizing. "The *parade*. I've got to talk to Charlie." Panic rose, a shock of adrenaline to his already-thumping heart.

"Yeah, that's not gonna happen." Dwight propped

his feet on the edge of the bunk and crossed his ankles. "See, Charlie doesn't know you're even here. She wanted me to bring you to her so she could talk you out of turning over the Rose to your dad." Dwight tapped at his temple. "But I got to thinkin'. If you don't show up, she gets everything, don't she?"

"How do you know that?" He shouldn't be surprised that the confidential contents of the will had leaked their way out to the general population of Holiday.

"Took Hill fishing. Folks don't give me much credit for paying attention, so they don't feel the need to shut their traps when I'm around."

"What are you talking about?"

Dwight shrugged. "Charlie said your dad's gonna close the place. That means my friends would be out of a job and I'd be out of a place to hang out."

This was a whole new level of crazy. "What did you do? Slip something in my drink last night?"

Dwight jabbed his pointer finger at Beck's nose. "Bingo! You really are a hotshot, ain't ya?"

Beck struggled against the zip tie tethering his wrist to the bed rail. "Screw you, asshole. Get me out of here right now. There's been a misunderstanding. I need to talk to her."

"Yeah, and next you'll try to sell me an island off the coast of Kansas. I knew you'd be a fast talker." Dwight wiggled his eyebrows. "I'm onto you, and you ain't gonna talk me into anything. Now settle down. We've still got about"—he checked his watch—"three hours until I figure it's safe to let you loose."

"But I've got to get to Charlie and tell her she was right. The only way to keep my dad from getting the Rose is for me to get on that float."

"Nice try. That's a bunch of mumbo jumbo."

"I'm not lying. There's a loophole in the will. My dad will fight to the end to get control. Charlie would lose everything. Go ask Hill if you don't believe me."

Dwight leaned forward, resting his elbows on his knees. He stared at Beck for what felt like a long time. "You're not bullshittin' me?"

"I swear."

"Swear on something I can believe you about."

"Like what?"

"I dunno. Your mama's grave."

"She's alive."

"Then pick someone else. You got another relative who's passed?"

"Just my grandfather." The man he'd come to know and respect more than the father who'd raised him.

Dwight stood. "I don't know. You never even met him. This doesn't feel right to me."

"How about I swear on the Rose? My love for Charlie?"

"Nah. I'm still not so sure you're not trying to pull a fast one."

Beck tried to calm down enough to put himself in Dwight's boots for a split second. Any longer than that and he feared his head might explode. The guy loved beer, cars, and women. "I swear I'm telling the truth. If not, let my copy of this year's *Sports Illustrated* swimsuit issue get drowned by a leaky keg of Lone Star beer while my Porsche gets trampled by a stampede of longhorns."

Dwight ripped his hat off his head and held it

over his heart. "Dear Lord. I'm no fan of yours, but even I would never wish something like that on my worst enemy."

"So you believe me now?"

"Doesn't seem like I have much of a choice. You really have a Porsche?"

"Yes. Untie me?" Beck pulled his hand away from the bed rail so Dwight could cut him free.

"Will you let me drive it someday?"

"Sure. If I ever bring it to Texas, I'll let you drive it, okay?" Like that would ever happen. If Charlie didn't run him out of town, he'd have to trade in his Porsche for a truck. Or at least some big-ass SUV.

"Hmpf." Dwight flipped a knife out and sliced through the zip tie, and a few moments later, Beck rubbed his wrist. When the feeling finally returned, he stood up and grabbed Dwight by the scruff of his T-shirt. He pushed him against the wall, lifting him up so his feet dangled six inches off the floor.

"Hey, put me down! I let you go. You can't beat me up."

Beck gritted his teeth and drew back a fist, wanting nothing more than to slam it into Dwight's jaw. "You idiot. Do you have any idea what you've done? Where's my phone?"

Dwight shielded his face with his hands. "I tossed it in the trash can at the diner. I'm sorry. I was trying to help Charlie. You don't deserve a woman like her."

Dammit. He loosened his grip on Dwight's shirt, letting him slide down the wall until his feet hit concrete again. "That's one thing you're right about. She deserves a hell of a lot better than me. Where's your phone?"

Dwight handed him an ancient flip phone.

Beck messed with it, trying to get a signal. "Battery's low. Do you have a charger?"

"Nope. And I let the air out of the truck tires so if you got loose, you couldn't go very far. We can try hitching from the road."

"Not enough time. The parade's going to start soon." Beck took the stairs two at a time and emerged in the middle of a field of tall grass. "Where are we?"

"Sully's place. I guess he put this bomb shelter in back in the '50s. I thought it'd be a good place to hide you."

"Remind me later to kick your ass. Now, which way's the house, and how far away is it?"

Dwight shielded his eyes with his hand and scanned the field. Looked the same in every direction except for a path of beaten-down brush off to the right.

"That way. Follow me." The grass parted and swallowed Dwight as he moved off to the left. Not wanting to lose him, Beck jogged to catch up. If they could get to Sully's, maybe he could reach the parade in time. He just needed a little bit of luck.

"No, that way." Dwight swung ninety degrees to the left.

Make that a lot of luck.

Charlie eased her foot onto the brake. "There?"

Darby motioned her to back up another couple of inches. "Got it."

*Finally.* With the float firmly attached to the hitch on the back of Charlie's dually, all they had to do was drive into town and join the parade lineup. The Rose was almost safe.

Darby hopped into the passenger seat. "Who's that?"

A trio of shiny, black SUVs came to a synchronized stop, blocking their exit from the parking lot. A couple guys in suits emerged from the lead vehicle. The same men who'd come with the appraiser trying to take measurements and pictures.

"Oh no. They work for Beck's dad." All the air squeezed out of her lungs as a head of silver hair emerged from the back seat. "No, no, no." Charlie's hands shook as she slid her sunglasses over her eyes.

"Honey, who is that?"

"Beck's dad. Sully's son."

"What's he doing here?" Darby bounced on the seat next to her. "Do you think he's looking for Beck?"

Charlie forced herself to take in a breath. "I don't know. But whatever he wants, it can't be good."

"Do you want me to go talk to him?"

Charlie nodded toward Dickwad Number One. "Too late. I think he's heading this way."

At that moment, her phone rang. Dwight. Where was he? She hit the speaker button.

"Charlie?" Beck's voice exploded into the cab of the small truck.

"Beck, is that you?"

The man rapped on the driver's side window.

"I'm on...way. Don't...to anyone." Static crackled through the line.

"You're breaking up. I can't hear you." She glanced at the man at her window. He motioned for her to roll it down.

"You going to open it?" Darby leaned forward.

"Beck? You there?"

"We need to talk." Hell yeah they needed to talk. "Be there...as possible. Do not...my dad. Trust me..."

"What's he saying?" Hands shaking, Charlie tilted the phone toward Darby.

"I don't know. Sounds like he said don't do something about his dad. What are you going to do?"

"Beck?" Charlie tried again.

The mountain at her window made a move to grab the door handle. She slammed her elbow onto the lock, preventing him from opening it. His mouth morphed into a menacing frown, and he pointed at the window.

"Open the window," Darby said.

Charlie cranked the handle and lowered the window an inch. "Yes?"

"Ms. Walker?" The question came out in a burst, like machine-gun fire.

Darby practically climbed over Charlie's lap. "Who's askin'?"

"Mr. Holiday wants to have a word." He motioned Beck's father over.

"Charlie. Is my dad there?" Finally, Beck's voice came through.

She didn't respond. Beckett Sullivan Holiday Jr. approached the truck. Twenty feet. Fifteen. Ten.

Panic bubbled up from her gut to her throat like the foam from a bad keg. She tried to move her hands from the steering wheel, but they wouldn't budge.

Holiday reached the window. "Ms. Walker, it's a pleasure to see you again."

Her limbs turned to jelly. "Wish I could say the same, Mr. Holiday."

He chuckled, the noise grating against her nerves like a jackhammer on steroids. "You and I need to talk. Beck's decided he doesn't want to go through with our little deal. There's nothing worse than a son who turns his back on his father, wouldn't you agree?"

"What's he talking about, Charlie?" Darby nudged her in the side.

Charlie ignored her. "That's ironic, seeing as how you only want the Rose so you can turn your back on your own father and shut it down."

The shock that registered on Holiday's face was either authentic or Academy Award worthy. "Did he tell you that?"

"You hinted at it yourself, that night at dinner."

"Oh, Charlie. You must have misunderstood. We've got to keep Beck from getting on that float. If he does, he's going to sell the Rose out from under us. We'll both lose."

"Charlie?" Beck yelled through the phone. "He's lying. Get out of there. Trust me."

"I can't do this." Charlie's gaze flew from the phone to Darby to Holiday.

"That's right, Charlie. Don't give him what he wants." The smug smirk on Mr. Holiday's face sent a jolt of adrenaline through her. Her foot stomped on the gas, and her fingers came back to life. She gripped the steering wheel, swerving to avoid the trio of SUVs, and charged over a flower bed by the curb. The sheriff's prize rosebushes flattened under the tires, and the float bounced from side to side, sending wads of tissue paper scattering in their wake.

"Yeehaw!" Darby wrapped her fingers around the handle above her head. "You go, girl."

A glance in the rearview mirror showed Mr. Holiday racing back to the SUV. Based on what she knew about the man, the sleight wouldn't sit well with him. That meant she needed a plan C. It wouldn't take him long to set his posse in pursuit.

"Beck?" The phone had fallen to the floor during their escape.

Darby picked it up. "He's not there. Must have lost him. Who do you believe? Beck or his dad?"

"I can only handle one crisis at a time." *Think, Charlie, think.* "Where's Waylon this morning?"

"What?"

"My brother…your husband. Is he at home?"

"Yeah. He's getting the kids ready. They're going to meet us at the lineup."

Charlie's mind spun through possible delay tactics. "Call him, will you?"

"Sure. What are you thinking?" Darby punched in the number.

"Tell him to open the gate from the east pasture to the west. We'll drive by in ten minutes."

"You think that's going to work?"

"You got a better idea?"

Darby spoke into the phone and relayed Charlie's instructions. "Done."

Charlie reached a hand over and squeezed Darby's arm. "Thanks. Will you keep trying Dwight's number? I need to talk to Beck."

"You bet. What about the goons?"

"We need to lead 'em around some back roads until Waylon has a chance to set up."

"And here they come." Darby whipped her head around, and Charlie checked the rearview mirror.

Having the fourteen-foot float dangling off the back of her dually would make it easy for them to catch up. She increased her speed. Hopefully the damn thing would stay attached. It wouldn't go over very well if they showed up for the parade without a float.

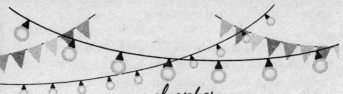

*chapter*

# THIRTY-TWO

BECK YANKED THE TARP OFF THE MONSTROSITY FILLING Sully's garage. Dust motes filled the air.

Dwight bent over coughing. "How long has this thing been sitting out here?"

"I don't know. Do you think it runs?" Beck examined the antique tractor with a skeptical eye. The body shone with a new paint job. But had Sully rebuilt the engine?

"Let's fire it up. See what we have to deal with." Dwight flipped his baseball cap around backward and bent over the engine.

Beck climbed onto the metal seat and turned the key. The engine sputtered and spun out.

"Again." Dwight adjusted something.

Back and forth they went, Beck twisting the key and Dwight shouting instructions. Ten minutes later, Dwight's hands were black from a mixture of oil and grease, and the tractor hummed, the engine running smoother than most of the cars Beck had been in over the past month.

"You did it." He stood and climbed down from the seat.

Dwight wiped his hands on a rag he'd found on Sully's workbench. "It's my superpower. Give me something with wheels and an engine, and I can make it do anything I want. Now if I only had that special touch with the women."

"No kidding. Me, too. You ready to take it out on the

open road?" Assuming Dwight's fix would hold, they still had to make it into town to get to Charlie.

"Yeah. Hey, I wanna come clean about something."

"Can it wait?" Now was the time for pushing the tractor to max speed, not heartfelt dude-to-dude confessions.

"Nah. I need to get it off my chest." Dwight scuffed the toe of his boot on the concrete floor.

"Go on. We need to get out of here."

"You know I had it bad for Charlie there for a while."

Was he kidding? "Okay, Captain Obvious. Let's go."

"Not yet." Dwight wrapped a greasy hand around Beck's arm, leaving a black handprint. "Oh, sorry, bro."

"Just hurry. So you like Charlie. I got it."

"I did like Charlie. She never felt the same way. I thought if I could run you out of town, I'd have a better chance with her."

"With Charlie?" Pulling the info out of him was like extracting an overdue payment from a bankrupt investor.

"Yeah. So I overloaded the circuit that time. When the power went out. You remember?"

"I forgive you. No harm done, okay?"

Dwight glanced to the side and tucked his thumbs in his pockets. "That's not all. The bad keg of beer? I did that, too. And switched the order for the paint from pink to white. Just wanted to scare you off."

An overwhelming renewed desire to kick Dwight's ass across Conroe County hit him. He suppressed the urge to grab the man in a headlock.

"I'm sorry. I wanted things to stay the same. For Charlie to be happy. I suppose if she can't be happy with me, then, well, I guess you're the next best thing."

Beck didn't want to dwell on the fact that Dwight

somehow thought Beck was the second-best choice. The man had balls, that was for sure. "No hard feelings, okay?"

Dwight caught him in a half hug. "Thanks, man. I'll make it up to you, I promise."

"I'm going to take you up on that right now."

"Huh?"

Beck scrambled onto the puttering tractor. "Get your ass in the driver's seat, and get me to Holiday. I have no idea how to drive this thing."

—*H*—

The truck careened around a hairpin turn.

"Did we lose the float?" Charlie gripped the wheel and aimed for the center of the road.

"Still back there." Darby spun around in her seat. "I see Waylon. Almost clear."

Charlie focused on Waylon. When they passed the gate, he'd swing it across the road. Hopefully the hinges hadn't rusted out. They hadn't had a need for it since they'd started grazing the herd on the other side of the property. But once upon a time, her dad had gated off this stretch of private dirt road that ran through their property to keep the cows contained. With some luck, it would come in handy today.

The truck blazed past, and Charlie caught a glimpse of Waylon pushing the gate into place.

"You did it." Darby clapped her hands together.

"We did it. What's he doing now?"

The three black SUVs had stopped at the gate, but Waylon ran behind them, holding something long in his hands.

"Oh my God. He's got those spike strips he took from Cash."

"Why in the world does he have spike strips?" Charlie didn't slow down to wait for the outcome. The more distance she put between her and Mr. Holiday, the better.

"Somebody at the high school was driving over the football field. Waylon borrowed them and set them out so they could catch the kids. I guess he still had them in the garage."

"Remind me to give my brother an open tab at the Rose. For life."

Charlie kept an eye on the rearview mirror all the way into town. Waylon's tactic must have worked. No black SUV rammed them from behind, and there was no sign of Beck's dad when they reached the start of the parade route. The flatbed trailer they'd built the float on had taken a bit of a beating, and they'd left a trail of pink tissue paper halfway across the county. But there were still a few minutes before the parade began, so they had plenty of time to make repairs.

Darby climbed out of the truck and got to work stuffing fresh pink-tissue-paper roses into the holes in the chicken wire. Charlie shielded her eyes from the sun and scanned the makeshift parking lot for Shep. She'd left him in charge of getting Baby Back to the parade. Charlie hadn't wanted to drag Holiday's Sweetest Swine along all day, not in her delicate condition, while they made final preparations.

A loud rumbling made her turn around. An antique pink tractor came chugging down the middle of the road. Sully's. He'd painted it pink and used it to pull the parade float. She hadn't been able to get it started earlier this summer and hadn't bothered to ask Dwight to take a look. It was easier to use her truck. Faster, too.

Dwight sat on the metal driver's seat with Beck standing behind him. They got closer, and Beck jumped down and ran the rest of the way.

"Charlie." He caught her in a hug, knocking her off-balance and pulling her against his chest.

This couldn't be happening. She put her palms against his chest and pushed. Even rumpled, without a shower or a chance to brush his teeth, he still sent her heart into a tailspin. But she couldn't let him get within ten feet of the Rose's float. She might have entertained thoughts of a future with him. Might have actually seen herself playing Mrs. Manhattan once upon a time. Might have even liked it.

But this was it. Him or Holiday. Her desire for saving her hometown trumped any leftover feelings she'd harbored for the traitor.

"Get away from me." She shoved with all the might her five-foot-two frame contained.

He didn't budge. "Hey, I need to talk to you."

"Well, I don't want to talk to you. Not now. Not later. Not ever."

"I'm going to change your mind about that, I promise. But first, my dad's here. You were right—he wants to shut down the Rose."

"I saw him. Waylon disabled their caravan of Escalades. I don't think we'll have to worry about that. As for you—"

"Charlie," Darby yelled from the back of the float. "He's here. I don't know how he did it, but you've got Mr. Holiday and the Dickwad Brigade incoming."

Beck took her face between his hands. "I should have fought harder for you. For the Rose."

She closed her eyes, letting herself relish the feel of his hands on her skin for what she was sure would be the very last time.

"What's going on?" Darby jogged over to where they stood.

"I've got to get on that float." Beck turned Charlie toward the truck and propelled her forward. "If his goons get here before we take off, they'll never let me get to the end of the route."

"But if you're on the float—"

"I'll get the Rose."

"And you'll turn it over to your dad or sell it yourself. I can't let that happen. I've—"

"My dad's trying to keep me from the float. There's a loophole in the will. If I don't inherit the Rose fair and square, he's going to use every resource at his disposal to make sure the Rambling Rose is ripped away from you." Beck glanced back. "You've got to trust me, Charlie."

Her heart squeezed. Tears welled up in her eyes, threatening to spill over.

"It's yours," he said. "Sully would have wanted you to have it. But I can't give it to you unless I get on that float." Beck leaned down, his eyes searching hers.

She wanted to believe him—desperately wanted to think he'd make good on his word. But her mind kept racing back to when she'd trusted him before. And he'd let her down. "Beck, I—"

His hands wrapped around her arms. "I love you, Charlotte Walker."

"What are we doing here, Charlie?" Darby had climbed behind the wheel. The floats in front of them had started to move.

Charlie hesitated. Long enough to see the caravan of black Escalades screech to a stop behind them. No time to think. No time for a new plan. No time for second-guessing herself. "Darby, put it in gear. I need you to bump us to the front of the line."

"You got it, Boss." Darby stuck a thumbs-up out the window.

Charlie pushed Beck toward the float as Shep jogged across the road with Baby Back on a rhinestone leash, her Sweetest Swine sash stretched around her growing belly. "I don't have time to explain. Can you get Baby Back on the float and hold on tight?"

"Yeah, sure." Shep didn't break his stride. He lifted Baby Back's front legs onto a set of low steps they'd cut into the side of the float, and she clambered up to take her place of honor.

"You're sure this is the only way?" She grabbed onto Beck's hand as they reached the steps of the float.

"I promise."

She held his gaze for a long moment. Long enough to recognize the love shining in his eyes. What did this mean? Would he stick around? There was no time to talk. He already held her heart in his hands. She'd have to trust him not to crush it to bits. She reached into her pocket and pulled out Sully's lucky coin, then rose to her tiptoes and pressed a kiss to Beck's cheek while she tucked the half-dollar into his front pocket.

"You need this more than I do right now. I trust you. Now go!"

Beck scrambled up the steps, then looked back and winked at her. That tiny signal spurred her into motion.

She raced to the driver's side window. "Go, Darby.

You've got to floor it and get to the end of the parade before it's too late."

"You got it, girl." The fire engine in front of her hadn't started moving yet, so Darby pulled around it. Past Whitey's giant pair of Styrofoam cowboy boots. Past Dixie and her dance partner doing a square-dance demo on the flatbed of the classic country AM station's float. Past the 4-H club members with their goats, cows, horses, and pigs trailing behind them on leads.

Charlie stood on the curb, watching the float careen down the road to finally bust into the lineup in front of the high school's marching band and behind the crazy clown cars of the Shriners.

Before she could let out a sigh of relief, she caught sight of a couple of Holiday's thugs. They must have abandoned their SUVs to canvas the crowd on foot. She stepped behind a vendor holding a big bunch of balloons, and they took off again. They'd never get through the crowds lining the parade route. Beck would get his ride.

# chapter
# THIRTY-THREE

BECK HELD ON TO THE FLOAT WITH ONE HAND AND Baby Back's leash with the other. The marching band played while the float crept through the small downtown. He let go every once in a while to wave, calling out to friends and acquaintances he'd made during his time in Holiday. This must be how his grandfather had felt when he'd ridden in the parade every year.

Fresh feelings of loss bubbled up, threatening to turn what should have been the sweet buzz of success into a bittersweet moment of nostalgia. How he wished he'd had the chance to meet Sully. It had taken him a while, but he'd come to see his grandfather in the legacy he'd left behind…in the Rose, in the people of Holiday, in himself. Finally, the float came to a stop at the end of the route, the newly renovated park on the edge of town.

Beck handed Baby Back's leash over to Shep. "Can you take care of this for me?"

"You got someplace to be?" Shep asked as he wrapped the lead around his hand.

"As a matter of fact, I do. I'll catch up with you later, okay?"

Darby leaned out the window of the truck. "Hey, where are you going?"

"I've got a few things to take care of. Tell Charlie I'll find her in a bit, okay?" He broke into a jog. The first step of his plan was complete, but he needed to see the rest through.

Darby shook her head. "You'd better not be running away."

He waved her off. No more tricks. No more lies. No more trying to be someone he didn't want to be. He couldn't wait to get started. But first, he needed to take care of something. Something that looked a lot like his dad arriving in a caravan of three ridiculously out-of-place, giant, black SUVs.

Beck walked toward his father as he exited the first vehicle. "You're too late, Dad."

His father tilted his sunglasses down and peered over the rims, an amused smirk on his lips. "Excuse me?"

"I said you're too late. It's done."

Holiday huffed on the lenses of his glasses and pulled a handkerchief from his front suit pocket. "I forgot how damn dirty this place gets. The dust alone will make you insane."

"There's nothing for you here. No reason for you to be here or get involved. Why don't you head back to New York?"

"I made you a good offer on that rattrap. It's not too late to change your mind. I can't believe you're going to turn me down and give up the chance to have a piece of the pie, Son."

"I don't want a piece of your pie." Hell, he didn't even want to sit at the same table as his father anymore. To think that once that had been the sum of his life's aspirations—to impress his dad and earn a spot on the management team.

"I don't think you mean that. What about your buddy J.T.? The two of you seemed to be in cahoots. Are you going to walk away from him? Turn your back on a friend?"

That stung. Beck was prepared to take responsibility for trashing his own career. But the thought of causing J.T.'s future to implode nagged at him. "This is all on me. J.T. shouldn't be punished for one of my decisions."

"I'm glad to hear you say that. The boy shows initiative. I think I'll put him in charge of that hotel project in the Village when I get back."

Three months ago, that project had been Beck's. The threat of his dad ripping it away would have had him begging for another chance. But not anymore. He'd seen the kind of corruption and inflated self-worth his dad's aspirations had caused.

"Good. He'll do a great job for you." For a split second, Beck considered how it might feel to spit at his dad's feet. He wanted to sully those sassy, shiny Italian loafers.

"What about you, Son? You've lost everything. Kind of screwed yourself over now, haven't you?"

He'd never get it. Wasn't worth the breath it would take to try to explain things to him. "Yep. That's me. Self-screwing. All fucked up. I think I'm going to hang out here for a bit. See if I can find a place to crash until I figure out what I want to do next."

Holiday slid his sunglasses back in place and pocketed the handkerchief. "I've got to say, I'm disappointed in you. You're just like him, you know."

"Who?"

"Your grandfather. He was a damn fool. Could have made something out of himself, but he wouldn't leave this hellhole. Enjoy his legacy. It's all you've got left."

Beck could have let his father go with that. Let

him have the final word like he always had. But this might be the last time he'd share air with the man. He had to know the truth.

"That's why you left, isn't it? You couldn't stand not being the most important Holiday in town. So you took the key to Sully's safety deposit box and cashed in all those savings bonds he had. You built your business on your father's back. The sad thing is, he would have forgiven you for that. But you couldn't let it go, could you? You've spent your whole life trying to prove to everyone that Beckett Sullivan Holiday Jr. isn't the piece of shit his father always knew he was."

Holiday spun around to face him. "You don't know what you're talking about."

"But I do, Dad. Sully sent both of us letters. Letters you marked 'Return to sender.' He begged you to come home. Said he'd forgive you for stealing the money. He wanted his family back. But you were too proud, weren't you?"

"He was never a father to me. He loved that damn bar more than he ever cared about his own son. You can't imagine what that feels like."

Beck wanted to laugh out loud at the irony of that statement. "I read the letters, Dad. You were jealous of the legacy he was building. The legacy he wanted to leave for *you*."

"We're through here. I've got better things to do than listen to you spout off about things you know nothing about."

"You ever want a real relationship with me, one not based on what I can add to your bottom line or how well I can kiss your ass, you'll know where to find me."

His dad didn't look back. He climbed into the waiting dust-covered SUV. Beck watched until the vehicle became a speck on the horizon, waiting for some sort of emotion to hit him. Nothing.

A few long seconds passed before Dwight shuffled over. "Wow. And I thought my old man was an asshole."

Beck shook his head and let out a defeated laugh. "Yeah. At least that's something my dad will always be best at."

"Hey, man to man, I'm sorry about earlier. I promise I was only doing what I thought would help Charlie. If you wanna kick the shit outta me—"

Beck clapped a hand on Dwight's shoulder and turned him toward the tractor. "Forget about it. That's what family does—look out for each other. Now…want to drive me over to the Rose? I've got a Texas-sized apology to make, and I'm going to need some help."

# chapter
# THIRTY-FOUR

CHARLIE PARKED AT THE EDGE OF THE LOT AND scrambled out of the truck. What a day. Over the past forty-eight hours, she'd grown to appreciate the term *bone-tired*. Everything ached. She wanted to fall into bed, pull the covers over her eyes, and sleep until Christmas. But it was only four o'clock. In three hours, all of Holiday would descend on the Rose for the annual Founder's Day Fling. And according to Beck, she'd be in charge. This time not only as manager but as owner and operator of the oldest honky-tonk in Texas. It hadn't sunk in yet.

She'd spent the past couple hours driving all over Holiday, looking for Beck. He wasn't downtown where he'd left her at the start of the parade. Wasn't at Sully's. Wasn't at the bomb shelter where Dwight admitted to hiding him overnight. God, she could strangle that idiot with her bare hands for what he'd put both of them through today.

Beck wasn't answering his phone or responding to any of her texts. There was so much she wanted to say to him. So much she needed to say. He couldn't avoid her forever. She'd make sure things were ready to go at the Rose and resume her search.

"Hey, Boss." Angelo called out from the barbecue pit. He'd been smoking brisket for the past two days. "How was the parade?"

She stepped over the long grass on the side of the building. Add that to the list: someone needed to mow the lawn. "Memorable. You ready for tonight?"

"I will be."

"Good. Should be a big crowd. Everyone setting up inside?"

"Yep."

Charlie nodded. Where would she be without the reliable help of folks like Angelo and Shep? She owed Darby and Waylon a year's worth of babysitting for what they'd done for her today. But that's what it was all about. Looking out for the people she loved and knowing she could count on them to have her back, too. She entered the building and headed toward her office. She expected to hear the sounds of pots clanging in the kitchen, servers setting up the tables in the dance hall, and Shep slinging bottles into the cooler. Instead, music drifted through the speakers. The band wouldn't set up until six.

As she moved toward the ballroom, the music got louder. She'd recognize Charlie Daniels's voice anywhere. What was going on?

She paused at the entrance to the room. Thousands of twinkle lights crisscrossed through the rafters. Vases of pink roses decorated every table. Where had everyone gone? She walked to the center of the dance floor and turned in a slow circle, peering into the dark corners of the room. Charlie Daniels sang on, the familiar lyrics like a balm to her soul.

Beck crossed the stage and hopped down onto the dance floor. The sight of him smacked into her like a bucking bronc's heels to the chest, and she didn't know whether to hug him or tackle him for all the stress and worry she'd suffered over the past several days.

"Where have you been? I've been looking all over town for you."

He met her in the middle of the dance floor and set down the pink paint cans he held in both hands. "I need to talk to you, Charlie."

"Where is everyone?"

"I sent them outside."

"Who did this?" She gestured to the lights and flowers. Darby had suspended some giant pink-tissue-paper balls from the beams crossing the ceiling, but this, the lights, it was breathtaking.

He raised a hand. "Guilty."

"When?"

"Just now. Dwight helped. I think he felt bad after he finally confessed about skunking my beer, changing the paint color, and kidnapping me overnight."

She placed a palm on his chest, preventing him from getting any closer. "He did that all on his own. I just wanted to talk to you."

He caught her hand. "I know. I should have listened."

"Where's your dad?"

"He left. I don't think you'll have to worry about him again. I met with Mr. Hill right after the parade and signed the paperwork." He handed her a fat envelope. "The Rose is yours now."

Her eyes welled, tears threatening to spill over. "You don't have to do that."

"Yes, I do." He tugged her close and started to sway to the music.

"But what about your park? Your promise to your nanny?"

"I'll sell my apartment and my car. With the money Sully left me, I can still afford to make the donation in my own name."

"Are you sure?"

His lips met her hairline, and a shiver raced through her. "Positive. It's the way it's meant to be."

She trembled, chilled by his admission. "But it's not fair."

"Yes, it is. Sully would have wanted you to have it." He stopped moving and pulled back to meet her gaze. "I'm so sorry. I agreed to hand the Rose over to my dad long before I got to know the people in Holiday. Before I really got to know you. At the time, I saw the Rose as my dad's due and my ticket to a guaranteed seat at the table of his company."

"And now?" Her breath hitched in her throat. His answer could break her. She braced herself, steeling her heart against his response.

"Now?"

She nodded.

"Now I know what matters. You've taught me so much in such a short time. How family doesn't necessarily mean the people who share your DNA. About putting other people first and not expecting anything in return." He tipped his head down, his voice so soft, speaking right against her lips. In time with the music, he sang the lyrics with Charlie Daniels: "How very much I love you."

"I love you, too." His mouth found hers, and the Rose faded away. Nothing existed except her and Beck, cocooned against the rest of the world in their own little bubble. The kiss moved from tentative to testing to torching in the space of seconds. She was toast. This was it for her. She had the Rose. She had Beck. She had it all, everything she'd ever hoped for and never thought she'd be able to hold.

The sound of applause burst her little bubble, and she backed away from Beck to see her family and staff filling the dance hall. Their hands clapped together, their smiles reflecting the happiness in her heart.

"Does this mean you're staying in Holiday?" She tucked her chin against her chest and gazed up at Beck. She'd never get tired of seeing that face, not if she lived to be as old as the Texas hills.

"I hope so. But it depends on you."

"On me?"

"Yeah. I quit my dad's company and gave up the Rose. Any chance you might be willing to give me a job?"

"A job, huh?" She tucked her hands in his back pockets and nuzzled into him. "Well, I do need someone to clean out Baby Back's pen."

"From Midtown Manhattan to slopping out pig stalls, huh? If it means I get to see you every day, the answer's yes."

"Good. Now, will you be my date to the fling tonight?"

"For as long as you'll have me."

Charlie closed her eyes and sent a silent prayer of thanks to Sully. He had to have had a hand in this. No other logical explanation would do. She only hoped that Beck meant what he'd said. Because a lifetime with him wouldn't be long enough, and she intended to hold on to him for the rest of hers.

# Epilogue

*One Year Later*

CHARLIE CLIMBED ONTO THE FOUNDER'S DAY FLOAT, a leash in her hand. Poor Baby Back had retired from public appearances, but they'd kept the runt of her litter from last summer—a three-hundred-pound beauty named Pork Chop. Beck joined her and gave Shep the thumbs-up, signaling they were ready to move out. The new flatbed Beck had built this year's float on provided a much smoother ride than last year's, and there was plenty of room for the whole family.

Charlie let her gaze linger on the gathering of Walkers. Her mom and dad stood at the back of the float, their kids and grandkids nestled around them. Waylon and Darby sat on a couple of bales of hay with their kids sandwiched between them. Cash and Kenzie waved to the crowd. Statler and Presley blew kisses to the women lining the parade route. As the truck began to inch down the road, Charlie turned to her Texas transplant.

He'd come to mean so much to her over the past year. His real estate background and marketing expertise had doubled their income. He'd completely revamped Sully's old place and had plans to add on and turn it into the kind of home where they could raise a family.

When Shep stopped the float in front of Whitey's so the Shiners could do their coordinated spins, she turned to Beck and gulped in a breath of hot, humid air.

"Beck?"

"Yeah, what's up?" He peered at her from under the brim of the new cowboy hat she'd bought him.

"Hold this?" She handed him Pork Chop's leash. "I need to ask you something."

"Now?" He glanced at her, raising his hand in a wave to Dwight and his brand-new girlfriend on the side of the road.

"Yes. Now."

Her tone must have caught his attention. He gave her a questioning look. "Everything all right?"

"God, I'm just going to say it, okay?"

"What's wrong, Charlie? You look like you're about to pass out."

"You okay, hon?" Darby handed June to Waylon and scrambled over a bale of hay.

"What's going on?" Presley twisted around and lifted a longneck. "Y'all need a drink?"

Cash clamped a hand to his hip. "You're not supposed to be drinking in public. It's illegal."

"Well, then, I guess I'd better finish it up right quick." Presley tipped the bottle up to drain it.

"Can everyone be quiet for a minute?" Charlie yelled.

Even the spectators stopped cheering. An awkward bubble of silence surrounded the Rambling Rose's float.

She took in a wobbly breath. Passing out might not be out of the realm of possibility.

Beck cupped her cheek, worry causing his eyes to crinkle at the edges. "What's wrong?"

"Okay, here goes. Will you marry me?" The words tumbled out, leaving her stunned and in shock. She'd intended on asking, just thought she'd be a little more romantic in her delivery.

The moment seemed to last forever. No one moved—not her parents, not her nieces and nephews, not even Pork Chop. Then, all of a sudden, everything seemed to move at warp speed.

Her family surrounded them. Darby and her mom wrapped her in a hug. Tom and her brothers clapped Beck on the back, and the kids danced around them singing a song about Aunt Charlie and Uncle Beck sitting in a tree.

A shriek cut through the chaos. Beck stepped onto a hay bale, his fingers stuck between his teeth like she'd taught him how to whistle. "Hey! Y'all might not have noticed, but I haven't exactly answered the question yet."

Charlie's heart sank into her boots. Where was he going with this? Had she managed to misread the entire relationship again?

Beck set the leash down on the hay bale and stepped on it with his boot to hold Pork Chop in place. A grin slowly stretched across his face. "Damn, girl, I've been waiting for months for you to bring that up."

Confusion shot holes through her thought process. "What do you mean months?"

Beck knelt down and pulled a small box out of his pocket. "I've been carrying this around with me for weeks now. Didn't feel right asking you to marry me first. I didn't want you to think that I was only after the Rose."

"After all this time? I wouldn't think that."

"I know. But others might. This ring belonged to my grandmother. I'm sure Sully would have wanted you to have it. I love you, Charlie Walker. More than I ever thought I could love anyone or anything. Marry me. Let's make it official."

Her eyes welled with tears. Happy tears this time. "Yes! I love you, too. Yes, yes, yes!"

He stood and slid the gorgeous oval-shaped engagement ring on her ring finger. The folks lining the parade route cheered. Her family surrounded them, offering congratulations and hugs. They were going to make it official, which meant she'd become a Holiday. And she'd finally be able to keep her word to Sully that the Rose would stay in the Holiday family after all.

"Can we go somewhere far away for the honeymoon? Maybe somewhere you've never even been?"

His eyebrows rose. "You sure about that?"

"Yep. This will always be home, but I want to see the world. It's time for me to stretch my wings a little bit."

"Hmm, Bali maybe. Or Thailand. We'll have to give this some thought."

Charlie laughed at the serious look on his face. "Surprise me, Manhattan."

She'd never have guessed this would be how it would work out. For her, it was a win-win-win. She'd gotten the Rose, she'd gotten the guy, and she'd kept her promise. They locked lips, putting on quite a show for the spectators lining the parade route.

Until a squeal and a shriek from somewhere in the crowd broke them apart.

Charlie looked down where Beck's foot rested on the hay bale, no leash in sight. "Where's Pork Chop?"

Beck glanced to the right. "She was here a second ago."

Like mother, like daughter. Charlie caught sight of the

pig's tail end disappearing behind the line of chairs on the curb. "We've got a runaway, and it's your turn."

Beck hopped off the float and went after the pig. Charlie cupped her hands around her mouth and yelled after him. "Better catch her before she finds Mrs. Martinez's garden."

The float began to move again, and she looked out over the main street in town. She had a business and a fiancé and was surrounded by friends, family, and more love than she knew what to do with. It didn't seem fair for one country girl to be blessed with so much. But she was going to hold on and enjoy it. Even if she did still need to train Beck on proper pig management.

They had time.

A lifetime.

# ABOUT THE AUTHOR

Dylann Crush writes contemporary romance with sizzle and sass. A romantic at heart, she loves her heroines spunky and her heroes super sexy. When she's not dreaming up steamy storylines, she can be found sipping a margarita and searching for the best Tex-Mex food in Minnesota. Although she grew up in Texas, she currently lives in a suburb of Minneapolis/St. Paul with her unflappable husband, three energetic kids, two chaotic canines, and a very chill cat. She loves to connect with readers, other authors, and fans of tequila. You can find her at dylanncrush.com.

# *TEXAS RODEO*

A groundbreaking contemporary Western romance series with real-life Texas rodeo action

## By bestselling author Kari Lynn Dell

### *Reckless in Texas*

Bullfighter Joe Cassidy is a hotshot in the ring...but falling in love with fierce single mom Violet Jacobs? That's a whole new rodeo.

### *Tangled in Texas*

Injured bronc rider Delon Sanchez thinks things can't get worse...until he learns his physical therapist is his oh-so-perfect ex, Tori Patterson.

### *Tougher in Texas*

When rodeo producer Cole Jacobs loses one of his cowboys and his cousin sends along a replacement, he expects a Texas good ol' boy. He gets longtime rival Shawnee Pickett.

### Fearless in Texas

Rodeo bullfighter Wyatt Darrington can never let Melanie Brookman know the truth: that he's been crazy in love with her for years.

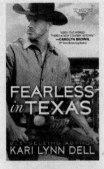

### Mistletoe in Texas

Hank Brookman is ready to return home for the holidays and make amends. Most of all, he hopes Grace McKenna will give him a second chance at love so they can celebrate Christmas—Texas Rodeo style.

---

"A fun, wild ride!
You need to pick up a Kari Lynn Dell."

**—B.J. Daniels, *New York Times* bestselling author**

For more Kari Lynn Dell, visit:

**sourcebooks.com**

# ROCKY MOUNTAIN COWBOY CHRISTMAS

Beloved author Katie Ruggle's new series brings pulse-pounding romantic suspense to a cowboy's Colorado Christmas

When single dad Steve Springfield moved his family to a Colorado Christmas tree ranch, he meant it to be a safe haven. He quickly finds himself fascinated by local folk artist Camille Brandt—it's too bad trouble is on her trail.

It's not long before Camille is falling for the enigmatic cowboy and his rambunctious children—he always seems to be coming to her rescue. As attraction blooms and danger intensifies, this Christmas romance may just prove itself to be worth fighting for.